Kate Grenville's bestselling novel *The Secret River* received the Commonwealth Writers' Prize, and was shortlisted for the Man Booker Prize and the Miles Franklin Literary Award. *The Idea of Perfection* won the Orange Prize. Grenville's other novels include *Sarah Thornhill*, *The Lieutenant*, *Lilian's Story*, *Dark Places* and *Joan Makes History*.

'An outstanding study of cultures in collision . . . a chilling, meticulous account of the sorrows and evils of colonialism . . . Kate Grenville is a sophisticated writer'
Guardian

'This is a novel everyone should read'
Irish Times

'This is a moving account of the brutal collision between two cultures; but it is the vivid evocation of the harshly beautiful landscape that is the novel's outstanding achievement'
Mail on Sunday

'A vivid and moving portrayal of poverty, struggle and the search for peace'
Independent

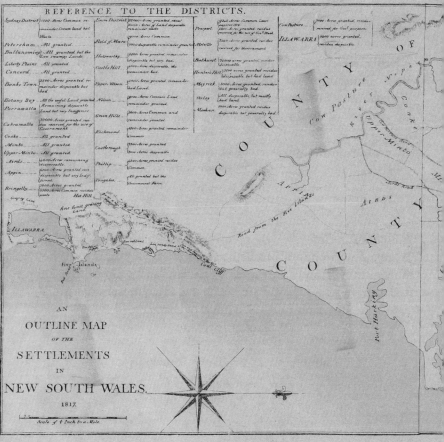

REFERENCE TO THE DISTRICTS.

AN
OUTLINE MAP
OF THE
SETTLEMENTS
IN
NEW SOUTH WALES.
1817.

Scale of ¼ Inch to a Mile.

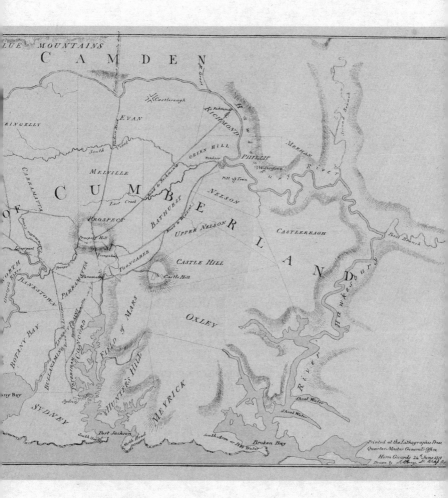

The
SECRET
RIVER

KATE
GRENVILLE

INTRODUCED BY DIANA ATHILL

CANONGATE

This Canons edition published in Great Britain in 2018 by Canongate Books

First published in Great Britain in 2006 by Canongate Books Ltd,
14 High Street, Edinburgh EH1 1TE

First published in Australia in 2005 by
The Text Publishing Company

canongate.co.uk

2

Grateful thanks to the Map Collection, State Library of Victoria, and the
New South Wales Public Office for permission to use 'An Outline Map of the
Settlement in New South Wales, 1817' by S.A. Perry

British Library Cataloguing-in-Publication Data
A catalogue record for this book is available on
request from the British Library

ISBN 978 1 78211 887 9

Typeset in Minion by Palimpsest Book Production Ltd,
Falkirk, Stirlingshire

Printed and bound in Great Britain by Clays Ltd, Elcograf S.p.A.

This novel is dedicated to the Aboriginal people of Australia:
past, present and future.

CONTENTS

INTRODUCTION

Grenville's great-great-great grandfather Solomon Wiseman was a Thames lighterman. Although he had risen from much humbler beginnings, he was still one of London's very poor, so stealing a few planks of timber from a load was not something shocking to him or his mates. But he was caught, and in 1805 was sentenced to be hanged. At the last moment he was reprieved and given the alternative sentence of transportation to Australia. His wife was sent with him as a free settler, not unusual at a time when there were few women in the colony, a problem to which sending out the wives of convicts was a cheap solution.

Convicts, once there, were put to work as slaves to people who had served their sentences and risen to be 'settlers'. A man whose wife was a free settler could be given to her as a slave, and that happened to Wiseman. Tough and sensible, he made use of his skill at working with boats, and did well, getting his ticket of leave (a sort of parole) in 1810 and his full pardon in 1812. He established his family on a piece of fertile land on the Hawkesbury River, where he eventually built a fortress-like house, and became a citizen of consequence.

As a child, Kate Grenville was taken by her mother to see that house. Her mother was unusual in being proud of her convict ancestor, and passed on to her daughter stories about him which the family had preserved. It was this, combined with a quick glimpse of what colonisation had really meant to Australia's original inhabitants, that caused Grenville to begin researching her family's history with a view to writing a non-fiction book about it. The more she learned, however, the less she felt she knew; until one day the novelist she truly is took over, and she decided to free herself from her ancestor by changing his name. The Hawkesbury River was still there, with the house Wiseman had built, but now it had been built and was inhabited by William Thornhill, and that inexplicable phenomenon, the novelist's imagination, set about creating something which her readers cannot fail to recognise as truth. Research gives this book its rock-solid framework; imagination brings it alive.

It is possible for an English reader to feel indifferent to *the idea* of a novel about Australia, particularly if it concerns the country's relationship with its Aboriginal population. We have enough guilts of our own, so we tend to package up other people's, label them as deplorable and put them out of mind. We want novels to tell us about things to which our nerves can respond, things we can see and smell, desire or flinch from, not just find interesting in a dutiful way. So it is important to know that this novel is not 'about Australia'. It is about a man called William Thornhill and his wife Sal, how they were plunged into an experience so bizarre as to be almost inconceivable, what it did to them and how they survived it. It would be an obtuse set of nerves that failed to respond to their story.

Never again will dazed and filthy people emerge, after nine months in the stinking darkness of a ship's hold, to see a rocky cove scattered with a few temporary-looking buildings, under a hammering sun, at the edge of endless miles of monotonously grey-green bush. Never again will a pair with two children, one a baby, be issued with a couple of blankets and a week's victuals, given a floorless wattle-and-daub hut and told to get on with it. This 'household' was to support itself, making no call on Government Stores: probably the most economical method of dealing with felons ever devised. The Thornhills, who knew nothing of the world beyond a small area of London slum and a few miles of a tidal river, might well have been undone by a situation demanding so much courage and resourcefulness. Some convicts survived by hook and some by crook (having the worst of one brought out by hardship can, and often did, result in survival), but the Thornhills were among those who were to discover an extraordinary amount of the best in themselves – an unspectacular and everyday best, but it has to be admired whatever subsequent actions they were driven into.

The central and most dramatic part of Grenville's story comes from the nature of those subsequent actions, against which admiration has to struggle. The boundless grey-green emptiness was not, of course, empty. Its inhabitants were good at fading into it when they needed to, but they were still there. In almost every respect their culture was the opposite of that of the colonists, and neither side knew the other's language – though even if they had been able to communicate freely, it was unlikely that they could have collaborated. It was not just that the Aboriginal people were black and went naked while the colonists were white and thought nakedness indecent. A much graver difference was that the existence of the colonists depended on recognising ownership, while to the Aboriginal people that concept was foreign.

After William Thornhill found that he could make a living ferrying goods between Sydney and the settlers who had established themselves as farmers on the banks of the Hawkesbury, he saw that he could make an even better living by becoming a farmer himself. A white man acquired land just by choosing a patch, planting a crop on it and saying 'Mine'. There was no visible indication that it was owned by anyone else, and indeed it was not so owned in any sense understood by the white man. But it might well be a place where, in their season, yam-daisies grew plentifully, so when that season came round a tribe of the Aboriginal people moved in to harvest them, being careful to leave pieces of root in the ground so the daisies would come back next year. They had been doing this for generation after generation, and if someone came along, saw the yam daisies as weeds and rooted them up, the tribe would go hungry next season. Unless, of course, they helped themselves to the corn growing where the daisies once were, which seemed to them the natural thing to do. Food was not yours or mine, it was for people, so people ate it. This was the kind of misunderstanding that made disaster inevitable.

The ways in which Grenville conveys the increasing tension between the two communities are uncannily effective. When the Thornhills had chosen their site they cleared a space and built a hut on it. The ground was stony, the trees for posts were unequal in size, the sheets of bark for roofing and walls were awkward to handle, so the hut was lopsided and frail. By day the constant activity necessary for survival claimed attention to the point at which anxiety was pushed aside, but when night fell and they huddled within their unreassuring shelter, listening to the breathing of the bush, its rustles and creaks . . . Grenville soon has her readers feeling almost as twitchy as the family. And even by day, the bush's shifting shadows could suddenly look like a half concealed figure – and sometimes *were* such a figure – which was extremely disturbing. And when a group of Aboriginal people did in fact materialise, and built its shelters and lit its fires only just out of sight, and began to move about its mysterious doings as though the Thornhills did not exist, the men carrying their efficient-looking spears, every nerve had to be strained in order to believe that they were not hostile.

Most of the few and scattered settlers failed to make that effort, and some acted on their certainty of being threatened with horrifying results. William Thornhill, essentially a decent man, was sickened when he saw things of which one of his neighbours boasted, but he said nothing about it to Sarah, so gradually he became complicit with the unspeakable, simply because – if he was to prevent his wife from panicking, which would mean abandoning his precious piece of land – unspeakable was exactly what it was. He didn't know it at first, but he was being edged into a furtive undeclared war.

Kate Grenville, as a child, asked her mother what had happened to the Aboriginal people when their ancestor started life as an Australian, and her mother said that by the time he got there they had all moved away into the country's interior. That, over the years, had become the comfortable thing to be sure of. But her research brought Grenville face to face with the truth, and it was not just awkward. It was hideous. There are times when it takes a strong stomach to be involved in it alongside William and Sarah. But Grenville also – and this is the great strength of her novel—calls up sympathy, because once men on the far side of the planet had decided to colonise this land and to start the process by dumping felons on its shores, which meant disregarding whoever happened to live there, the individuals being dumped became the situation's victims as much as those who were being dumped on.

What distinguishes a great story from one that is simply good is how much it continues to resonate in the reader's mind, how it makes one feel on closing a book that one is emerging from a real world. It is not easy to identify the quality of writing which brings this about, but in telling the story of the Thornhills' survival, and revealing the true nature of the vast stage against which it unfolded, Kate Grenville does undoubtedly command it.

– Diana Athill

The
SECRET
RIVER

STRANGERS

The *Alexander*, with its cargo of convicts, had bucked over the face of the ocean for the better part of a year. Now it had fetched up at the end of the earth. There was no lock on the door of the hut where William Thornhill, transported for the term of his natural life in the Year of Our Lord eighteen hundred and six, was passing his first night in His Majesty's penal colony of New South Wales. There was hardly a door, barely a wall: only a flap of bark, a screen of sticks and mud. There was no need of lock, of door, of wall: this was a prison whose bars were ten thousand miles of water.

Thornhill's wife was sleeping sweet and peaceful against him, her hand still entwined in his. The child and the baby were asleep too, curled up together. Only Thornhill could not bring himself to close his eyes on this foreign darkness. Through the doorway of the hut he could feel the night, huge and damp, flowing in and bringing with it the sounds of its own life: tickings and creakings, small private rustlings, and beyond that the soughing of the forest, mile after mile.

When he got up and stepped out through the doorway there was no cry, no guard: only the living night. The air moved around him, full of rich dank smells. Trees stood tall over him. A breeze shivered through the leaves, then died, and left only the vast fact of the forest.

He was nothing more than a flea on the side of some enormous quiet creature.

Down the hill the settlement was hidden by the darkness. A dog barked in a tired way and stopped. From the bay where the *Alexander* was anchored there was a sense of restless water shifting in its bed of land and swelling up against the shore.

Above him in the sky was a thin moon and a scatter of stars as meaningless as spilt rice. There was no Pole Star, a friend to guide him on the Thames, no Bear that he had known all his life: only this blaze, unreadable, indifferent.

All the many months in the *Alexander*, lying in the hammock which was all the territory he could claim in the world, listening to the sea slap against the side of the ship and trying to hear the voices of his own wife, his own children, in the noise from the women's quarters, he had been comforted by telling over the bends of his own Thames. The Isle of Dogs, the deep eddying pool of Rotherhithe, the sudden twist of the sky as the river swung around the corner to Lambeth: they were all as intimate to him as breathing. Daniel Ellison grunted in his hammock beside him, fighting even in his sleep, the women were silent beyond their bulkhead, and still in the eye of his mind he rounded bend after bend of that river.

Now, standing in the great sighing lung of this other place and feeling the dirt chill under his feet, he knew that life was gone. He might as well have swung at the end of the rope they had measured for him. This was a place, like death, from which men did not return. It was a sharp stab like a splinter under a nail: the pain of loss. He would die here under these alien stars, his bones rot in this cold earth.

He had not cried, not for thirty years, not since he was a

4

hungry child too young to know that crying did not fill your belly. But now his throat was thickening, a press of despair behind his eyes forcing warm tears down his cheeks.

There were things worse than dying: life had taught him that. Being here in New South Wales might be one of them.

It seemed at first to be the tears welling, the way the darkness moved in front of him. It took a moment to understand that the stirring was a human, as black as the air itself. His skin swallowed the light and made him not quite real, something only imagined. His eyes were set so deeply into the skull that they were invisible, each in its cave of bone. The rock of his face shaped itself around the big mouth, the imposing nose, the folds of his cheeks. Without surprise, as though he were dreaming, Thornhill saw the scars drawn on the man's chest, each a neat line raised and twisted, living against the skin.

He took a step towards Thornhill so that the parched starlight from the sky fell on his shoulders. He wore his nakedness like a cloak. Upright in his hand, the spear was part of him, an extension of his arm.

Clothed as he was, Thornhill felt skinless as a maggot. The spear was tall and serious. To have evaded death at the end of the rope, only to go like this, his skin punctured and blood spilled beneath these chilly stars! And behind him, hardly hidden by that flap of bark, were those soft parcels of flesh: his wife and children.

Anger, that old familiar friend, came to his side. *Damn your eyes be off*, he shouted. *Go to the devil!* After so long as a felon, hunched under the threat of the lash, he felt himself expanding back into his full size. His voice was rough, full of power, his anger a solid warmth inside him.

He took a threatening step forward. Could make out chips of sharp stone in the end of the spear. It would not go through a man neat as a needle. It would rip its way in. Pulling it out would rip all over again. The thought fanned his rage. *Be off!* Empty though it was, he raised his hand against the man.

The mouth of the black man began to move itself around sounds. As he spoke he gestured with the spear so it came and went in the darkness. They were close enough to touch.

In the fluid rush of speech Thornhill suddenly heard words. *Be off*, the man was shouting. *Be off!* It was his own tone exactly.

This was a kind of madness, as if a dog were to bark in English.

Be off, be off! He was close enough now that he could see the man's eyes catching the light under their heavy brows, and the straight angry line of his mouth. His own words had all dried up, but he stood his ground.

He had died once, in a manner of speaking. He could die again. He had been stripped of everything already: he had only the dirt under his bare feet, his small grip on this unknown place. He had nothing but that, and those helpless sleeping humans in the hut behind him. He was not about to surrender them to any naked black man.

In the silence between them the breeze rattled through the leaves. He glanced back at where his wife and infants lay, and when he looked again the man was gone. The darkness in front of him whispered and shifted, but there was only the forest. It could hide a hundred black men with spears, a thousand, a whole continent full of men with spears and that grim line to their mouths.

He went quickly into the hut, stumbling against the doorway so that clods of daubed mud fell away from the wall. The hut offered no safety, just the idea of it, but he dragged the flap of bark into place. He stretched himself out on the dirt alongside his family, forcing himself to lie still. But every muscle was tensed, anticipating the shock in his neck or his belly, his hand going to the place, the cold moment of finding that unforgiving thing in his flesh.

6

PART ONE

LONDON

In the rooms where William Thornhill grew up, in the last decades of the eighteenth century, no one could move an elbow without hitting the wall or the table or a sister or a brother. Light struggled in through small panes of cracked glass and the soot from the smoking fireplace veiled the walls.

Where they lived, down close to the river, the alleyways were no more than a stride across, and dimmed even on the brightest day by the buildings packed in hugger-mugger. On every side it was nothing but brick walls and chimneys, cobblestones and mouldering planks where old whitewash marked the grain. There were the terraces of low-browed houses hunched down on themselves, growing out of the very dirt they sat on, and after them the tanneries, the shambles, the glue factories, the maltings, filling the air with their miasmas.

Down beyond the tanneries, turnips and beets struggled in damp sour fields, and between the fields, enclosed behind their hedges and walls, were the boggy places too wet to plant in, with rushes and reeds where stagnant water glinted.

The Thornhills all stole turnips from time to time, running the risk of the dogs getting them, or the farmer hurling stones. Big brother Matty bore a scar on his forehead where a stone had made a turnip less tasty.

The highest things were the steeples. There was nowhere to go in all these mean and twisted streets, even out in the marshy low ground, where some steeple or other did not watch. As soon as one of them was hidden by the elbow of a lane there was another staring down from behind the chimneys.

And under the steeple, the House of God. William Thornhill's life had begun, as far as his own memory of it was concerned, with the grandest house that God had: Christ Church beside the river. The building was so big it made his eyes water. On the gateposts there were snarling stone lions that his mother lifted him up to look at, but they made him cry out in fear. The vertiginous lawn seemed to engulf him as he stood in its emptiness. The bushes stood guard in a line, and tiny insects of humans laboured up the vast steps of the entrance far away. He was dizzy, lost, hot with panic.

Inside the church he had never seen such a vault of ceiling and such light. God had so much space it could frighten a boy from Tanner's Lane. Up at the front were complicated carvings: screens, benches, a great construction that towered over the people sitting in the pews. It was a void into which his being expanded without finding a boundary, all in the merciless light that blasted down from the huge windows and left everything cold, with no kindly shadows anywhere. It was a place with no charity in its grey stones for a boy with the seat out of his britches.

He could not understand any of it, knew only that God was as foreign as a fish.

~

From the time he knew his own name, *William Thornhill*, it seemed that the world was crowded with other William Thornhills. For a start, there was always the ghost of the first William Thornhill, the brother who had died when only a week old. A year and a half later, in 1777, a year with a bit of a ring to it, he himself had come into the world, and they gave him the same name. The first William Thornhill was a handful of dust in the ground, and he was warm flesh and blood, and yet the dead William Thornhill seemed the first, the true, and himself no more than a shadow.

Over the river in Labour-in-Vain Court, there were some distant cousins, and more William Thornhills. There was Old Mr Thornhill, a shrivelled little head nodding on top of some dark clothes. Then there was his son, Young William, a man altogether hidden behind black beard. At St Mary Mounthaw there was a William Thornhill who was a big boy of twelve and pinched the latest William Thornhill whenever he got the chance.

Then when the wife of Uncle Matthew the sea captain had a new baby, it was William Thornhill too. They visited with the baby and said its name, and everyone turned to him, smiling, expecting him to smile too, and he tried. But his sharp sister Mary, the oldest, saw his face fall. Later she punched him on the arm. *Your name is common as dirt, William Thornhill*, she said, and the anger rose up in him. He punched her straight back and shouted, *William Thornhills will fill up the whole world*, and she had no comeback to that, smart and all as she was.

~

His sister Lizzie, too young to hem sheets but old enough to carry a baby on her hip, had the care of the little ones. As a six-year-old she carried baby William to keep him from the mud, so that the smell of Lizzie, the coarse texture of her unruly hair coming out from under the cap, was more motherly to him than his mother.

He was always hungry. That was a fact of life: the gnawing feeling in his belly, the flat taste in his mouth, the rage that there was never enough. When the food came it was a matter of cramming it into his mouth so his hands could reach for more. If he was quick enough, he could grab the bread his little brother James was lifting to his mouth, break a piece off and get it down his gullet. Once it was swallowed no one could get it back. But Matty was doing the same, ripping the bread out of William's hand, his eyes gone small and hard like an animal's.

And always cold. There was a kind of desperation to it, a fury to be warm. In the winter his feet were stones on the end of his legs. At night he and the others lay shivering on the mouldy straw, scratching at the fleas and the bedbugs, full of their blood, that nipped them through their rags.

He had eaten the bedbugs more than once.

There was one blanket for the two youngest Thornhills, and each other's smelly bodies the best warmth. James was older by two years and got the best of the blanket, but William, though smaller, was canny. He forced himself not to sleep, waiting for James's snores, so he could pull most of it over himself.

You were forever hungry, his mother told him when he asked about himself, but had to stop for her cough, an explosion that ripped through her body. It sometimes seemed as though her cough was the only strong thing left in her. *Greedy little bugger you was*, she whispered at last, and he went away ashamed, hearing his empty belly rumbling even then, and something in him going stony from the dislike in her voice.

Lizzie's story was the same, but different. *Greedy*, she cried, *my word you was, Will, and look at you now, great lumps of boys don't come out of thin air.*

Her voice did not say that being such a great lump of boy was a bad thing to be, and when she said, *Hollow legs, we called you*, she said it with a smile.

Lizzie was a good sister for a baby to have, good with a sugar rag, strong at carrying. But when William was not yet three, the mother grew big and fretful, and another baby replaced him as the youngest, the one that Lizzie carried around on her hip. William, already haunted by the dead William Thornhill he had replaced, was now haunted by this other brother, John. It seemed he would forever be squeezed tight before and after.

Below him was John, and on top of him were Lizzie and James, the biggest brother Matty, and Mary, oldest of them all, scary with her shouting voice always scolding. She sat with the mother, crowding in around the little window sewing the shrouds for Gilling's. Then there was Robert, older than William but younger too. Poor Robert never had more than half his wits, and less than that of his hearing, after he had the fever when he was five and nearly died. William had heard his mother scream one day, *Better if you had died and been done with it!* It made him go cold inside, for poor Rob was a kindly boy, and when his face lit up at some little gift, he could not wish him dead.

Pa worked at the cotton mill, the maltings, the tanneries, nowhere for very long. His cheeks were hollow with points of red on them as if he were angry, and he crept about half asleep, always weary. When he spoke or laughed, the words or the mirth became a long wet rattling cough. *Victualler* was how he had described himself at John's baptism, but victualler meant nothing grander than a few gloomy men from Mr Choubert's tannery, gathered together in one of the Thornhills' two rooms, drinking ale out of dirty wooden tankards and eating pies the mother had made: too much pastry, not enough filling. When the tan-pits froze over in the winter there were no customers and the room was bleak, smelling of old ale in the floorboards and the cold chalkiness of ash in the fireplace.

Then it was lean times for the Thornhills. At five, William was old enough to go with Pa round the streets at dawn with a stick and a sack, gathering the pure for the morocco works. Pa carried the sack, young William was the one with the stick. Pa walked ahead, spotting the dark curl of a dog turd from his greater height. If none could be found, then there was nothing but brown water from the river as a belly-filler. But when Pa saw one, it was the boy's job to push it into the sack with the stick, trying not to breathe in the stink. The worst was when the dogs chose the cobbles at Tyer's Gate with the wide gaps between, so the stuff dropped into the gaps and he had to gouge at it with the stick, or even with his fingernails while Pa stood coughing and pointing.

A full sack of pure was worth ninepence at the morocco yard. He had never asked what they used it for, only felt he would rather die than go on scraping the stuff off the cobbles of Southwark.

Except that the ache in his belly was even worse than the stink of the shit.

Ma was willing to risk less smelly ways to buy a loaf of bread. They watched her one day from behind a cart, William and Lizzie and James. Thornhill thought she looked obvious, lurking and slinking and tight-faced. Hold your head up, Ma, he wanted to call. And smile!

They saw her approach the trestle of books. The bookseller was inside her shop and it was hard to see if she was watching. William wanted to run across the road and lift the book himself, she was taking so long and looking so black about it, fingering the books and flipping their pages when she knew no more of her letters than the man in the moon. Then at last she slipped one into a fold of her apron, but looked at it as she did it, and used both hands so she nearly dropped the baby: it was clumsily done.

Suddenly the shop woman was there beside her, shouting,

Now give me that, if you please, Missus, and they heard Ma cry out, too shrill, *What! I have nothing of yours!* but clutching at the book in the folds of her apron so it gave her away. The shop woman, a stringy old boiler, jerked her arm so Ma fell down on her knees and the book fell and the baby too, rolling onto the cobbles and setting up an almighty roar.

The shop woman pounced on the book, and, while she was stooping for it, Ma from her knees gave her a clout across the back of the head. Old and all as she was, the woman was up in a trice and hit Ma on the shoulders with the book—they could hear the thwack of it from across the street—all the time hanging onto her and yelling, *Thief! Thief!* Ma was up now, the baby under her arm, and she began to kick out the legs of the trestle and claw all the books till they lay in the mud.

This was the signal for the children behind the cart to rush over and grab at the scattered books. William got one in each hand, right under the woman's feet, so she let go of Ma to grab them back, and when he stepped away, Ma ran and now the woman was spinning from one to the other in a dither. Two gentlemen stepped out of the Anchor to come to her assistance, but by then the Thornhills were gone like a lot of rats up the alley.

They got a book each. William's was the best, red leather with gold lettering, good for a shilling at Lyle's, no questions asked.

~

He grew up a fighter. By the time he was ten years old the other boys knew to leave him alone. The rage warmed him and filled him up. It was a kind of friend.

There were other friends, of course, a band of boys who roamed the streets and wharves together, snatching cockles off the fishmonger's stall at Borough Market, scrabbling in the mud at low tide for pennies tossed by laughing gentlemen.

There was his brother James, a whippy boy who could climb a drainpipe quicker than a roach, and poor simple Rob smiling at everything he saw. There was bony little William Warner, the runt of a litter on Halfpenny Lane, and Dan Oldfield whose father had drowned, being the passenger in a wherry trying to shoot London Bridge at low water, the boatman half-stupefied with liquor at the time. Dan was famous for his ability to steal roast chestnuts from the pedlar in Frying Pan Alley, enough to be able to share them, hot out of his pocket, with the other urchins. One frozen morning at Dan's suggestion he and William had pissed on their own feet: the moment's bliss was almost worth the grip of cold that came after. Then there was Collarbone from Ash Court with the red mark across half his face. Collarbone liked Lizzie. *She has skin like a nun*, he told Thornhill, wonderingly, and then, perhaps thinking of his own livid skin, blushed red to the roots of his hair.

They were all thieves, any time they got the chance. The dainty parson could shrill all he liked about sin, but there could be no sin in thieving if it meant a full belly.

Rob came to the other boys in their little rat-hole by Dirty Lane one day with a single boot that he had taken from where it hung outside a shop. He would have got the other too, he said, but the bootmaker saw him in a looking-glass. The man ran after him, and caught him, Rob said, but he was old, and the boy was able to get away. William hefted the boot in his hand and said, *But what is it worth to you, Rob, just the one?* And Rob thought long, his face creased with the effort, then through his loose rubbery lips, on a spray of spittle, cried out, *I will sell it to a man with one leg! It is worth ten shillings at least!* and it was as if he already had the money in his hand, his face fat with satisfaction at his scheme.

~

When Lizzie played mother to John, and then to baby Luke after that, Lizzie's friend Sal from Swan Lane became sister to William. Sal was the only fruit of her mother's womb. Had been a bonny baby, but she had cursed the womb as she left it, for every baby after her sickened and died within the month.

Her family was a notch up from the Thornhills, for Mr Middleton was a waterman, as his father had been, and his father's father before that. They had lived in the same street in the Borough for as long as anyone could remember, in a narrow house with a room upstairs, a fire of coals in the winter, glass in the windows, and always a loaf of bread in the cupboard.

But it was a sad house, filled with the tiny souls of those departed babies. With every promising son who had sickened and died, Mr Middleton became a sterner and more silent man. His trade was his consolation. He was out every morning, the first of the watermen to be waiting at the steps. He rowed all day and came home when darkness fell, never speaking, as if looking inward to his dead sons.

Sal's Ma and Da were gentle with their precious child. The mother would hold the girl against herself, putting a hand along the side of her face, calling her *poppet* and *sweet thing*. Within the means of the household, Sal was indulged with every delicacy she could desire: oranges and sweetbreads and soft white bread, and for her birthday a blue shawl of wool as fine as a cobweb. It was another way altogether of being a Ma and a Da, and William—whose birthday was not even remarked—looked on wondering.

Sal flowered under such care. She was no beauty, but had a smile that lit up everything around her. The only shadow in her life was the graveyard where her brothers and sisters were buried. They haunted her, and made her puzzle, the way they had no life while she, deserving it no more than they, had all the love that should have been shared out. That shadow made her soft in a way new to William. He knew no one else like her, who could not bear to watch the head cut off a hen, or a horse beaten in the street. She had run at a man whipping a little dog one day, shrilling at him, *Leave off! Leave off!* and the man had shrugged her away and might have turned the whip on her, except that William pulled her, gripping her arms tight until the man and the cringing dog had disappeared around the corner, when she turned her face into his chest and cried angry gusts of tears.

It was easy to wish to belong in this house, number 31, Swan Lane. Even the name of the street was sweet. He could imagine how he would grow into himself in the warmth of such a home. It was not just the generous slab of bread, spread with good tasty dripping: it was the feeling of having a place. Swan Lane and the rooms within it were part of Sal's very being, he could see, in a way no place had ever been part of his.

If he was haunted by the presence of so many brothers and sisters, Sal was haunted by so many absences, and the two of them found a comfortable common ground. They slipped off together, away from the mean smelly streets, striking out between the fields of turnips and cabbages, jumping over the ditches in which water lay all year, down to the patch of waste ground at Rotherhithe that they thought of as their own. There was a spot where bushes curved around in which they made a little hovel to shelter from the wind. Down there the big pale sky, the sheet of dun water, the sounds of waterbirds cawing, was a different place altogether from Tanner's Lane, and William felt himself become a different kind of boy. He loved that place, its emptiness and its clean windy feel. No houses, no alleyways, nobody watching, except now and then the gypsies passing through, but they were soon gone and the place was theirs again.

When it started to rain, softly, evenly, persistently, he and Sal would still linger, a bag over their heads, watching the grey river dimple under the rain, not looking at each other, but staring out side by side, the rain a reason not to disturb the arrangement, a reason to go on sitting wedged up close together, watching the white puffs of their breath mingling.

Something about her face made him want to keep watching it. There was no remarkable feature to it, except perhaps the mouth, a top lip that was full all the way along, not thinning thriftily towards the corners the way most people's did, so there was an impression of generous eagerness, as if at any moment she was about to smile and speak. He loved to watch that mouth, waiting for her to turn to him with a thought in her eyes that she would share with him, so they could laugh together.

With Sal there was no need to be a fighter or guard himself every moment. A boy could be a boy, and do foolish things, such as showing her how far he could spit. They watched the glittering gob fly through the air and land on the grass. When she tried, William watched her mouth as she pursed it up, gathering the spit, and shot it out. She could not spit as far as he could, but he let her think she could, so the pleasure of the moment would continue.

He loved the way she called him Will. His name had been used by so many others that it was stale with handling, but Will was his own alone.

At night, being kicked in the back by James, hearing Pa and Ma coughing in their sleep, Rob snoring and snorting beside him, the rats running through the rotting thatch, feeling the gooseflesh on his legs and his belly growling from having nothing but watery gruel in it all day, he thought of Sal. Those brown eyes, the way they looked at him.

Thinking of her, he was warmed from the inside.

~

During his mother's last illness, the year William turned thirteen, the lions on the gateposts at Christ Church haunted her. She re-lived, over and over again, a memory from her childhood of climbing up onto the fence and reaching out to pat them. He could see how her body felt it, again and again, being snatched away as her father whipped her off the railings, and the pain of the cuff around the ear he gave her. *I were just reaching out,* she said, and smiled with her death-pale lips, remembering. *I were as near as near. Then—whoops!—down I go.* Her skinny arm, roped with sinews, the skin papery, stretched out towards the dirty whitewashed wall, her gnarled hand opening, and her face lit by the sweet yearning smile of that long-ago girl.

She died soon after. There was no money for the parson to say a prayer over her—she went into the common hole. By way of remembrance, the next day William took a clot of muck under his coat wrapped in a bit of rag, and went down to the church. The lions stood there still, that haughty look on their faces just the same as when his mother had smiled and reached out for them. He got the muck out from under his coat and hurled it at the nearest one, a thick black gobbet smack in the middle of that smug snout. Wipe the smirk off your face, that did, he thought, and was heartened by the memory on the long walk home. He never saw the lion again without a glow of satisfaction, because all the rain in the world had never got out the mud from one of its nostrils.

~

Soon after that, Pa died too, coughing his way into another hole in the damp ground of Bermondsey. That left the family without a head. Big brother Matty had gone for a sailor-man on the *Osprey*, had been away now for four years. They got word he was in Rio de Janeiro, then a year later that he had been shipwrecked off the Guinea coast and was on the *Salamander*, bound for Newfoundland, and hoped to work his way back to them, but nothing had been heard from him for two years.

James had gone over the river one day when he was four-teen and not come back. Sometimes they heard things: how he had got away with a silver candlestick out of an open window, or climbed down a chimney to relieve a gentleman of his watch while he slept. It was on the shoulders of William that the survival of the others seemed to depend.

For a while he took his father's place at Mr Pott's Manufactory, but the cotton dust, the din and the pounding of the machines was unbearable, and, on the day he saw a little shrimp of a child stamped to bits by the engine when he was sent crawling underneath to clear a jam, he left and did not return. He worked then at White's tan-yard, humping the reeking skins on his back in a stench of blood gone bad, from the carts over to the vats where the stained men sourly eyed him. It was his greatest fear to have to become one of them, plunging up to his waist in the pits, hardly human.

When there was no more work there, he worked with a shovel at the maltings, scooping up the waste malt that the goodness had been soaked out of, so that what was left was a vile-smelling mass of fibrous stuff the colour of a baby's shit.

For a while he was at Nettlefold & Mosers, his job being to sweep up the swarfings from underneath the lathes, shovel them into sacks, and lump them up into the wagons. He was all day up and down the ramp with a hundredweight of swarfings on his back, hanging onto the ears of the bag over his shoulder with all his strength, keeping himself focused so as not to fall. He felt that his back would break, but at least swarfings did not stink. In bed at night afterwards the muscles of his legs would twitch, still labouring.

The best work, when he could get it, was being a lumper down on the wharves. Down there the wind came in fresh off the river, and the ships tied up three and four deep at the wharves told him there was a world beyond Bermondsey. There was a man down there on Sloane's Dock, a beggar who had once been a sailor-man, with a green parrot that travelled on his shoulder so there was a long streak of white down his back. The thing stepped from claw to claw, nibbled at his ear, screamed when anyone came too close. It was a bird out of a dream. Yet here it was, its colours gaudy on the man's shoulder.

He loved the docks for their excess. So many casks of brandy, sacks of coffee, boxes of tea, hogsheads of sugar, bales of hemp.

With such a quantity, how could a little be missed?

William came across a group of men one day in a corner of the warehouse, up on the third floor, irons in their hands. It was the work of a moment to lever the lid off the nearest hogshead. The wood came up with a splintering noise that seemed to fill the whole place, except one of the men had a coughing fit to cover the noise, and there inside was the dull brown sparkle of the sugar. The sheer mass of it made it seem another substance from the way he had only ever known sugar before, as a precious twist in a bit of paper. Looking at it, the spit rushed into his mouth.

Well, one of the men said, *what a shame, the cask is broke*, and another spoke up with the straight face of a parson: *Waste is an abomination, saith the Lord*. William thrust his hand in with the rest of them, laughing to feel sugar in fistfuls, and crammed his mouth full of it, the sweetness starting up a savage craving so he could not stop. The others meanwhile filled up little bags they had dangling inside their coats, and were gone while William was still licking the sugar off his palms.

Overhead he could hear the rumble of the barrows over the floor, the squeal of the pulley as loads were drawn up the side of the building and manhandled in, and closer at hand there were footsteps. He glanced around, but the pile of casks and packages hemmed him in.

He had no little bags hanging inside his coat, only his greasy old felt hat, so he whipped it off and began to fill it, shovelling the sugar with both hands, and when the hat was full he tried to get some into his pockets, but the stuff stuck to everything it touched, would not pour, only clung and clogged.

And now there were footsteps just on the other side of the bales of hemp, coming closer. He put the hat under his arm and started to make for the back corner where he could hide it somewhere until the end of the day, but even as he turned, even as he tucked the hat under his arm, he was right up against the striped chest of Mr Crocker the gangsman. *This is a pretty trick, Thornhill*, he shouted. *A feed for the nits, eh?* and struck the hat away from under his arm so the sugar scattered across the floor. *Make a monkey of me, would you, Thornhill?*

But William Thornhill had his story ready. *It was broke open, sir, when I come across it*, he said. *As Jesus is my saviour.* The words felt no lie. He could see it all in his mind's eye: himself, coming around the corner of the hemp parcels, seeing the hogshead there, the splintered top, the sugar lying scattered. *There was a deal of the sugar between the hogsheads and the wall, sir*, he said. *There were a man there bid me take it, it seemed no wrong, sir, as God is my witness.* He could hear his voice rich with conviction.

But Crocker did not listen to the story, did not even bother to hear him out. Crocker's was a plain world in which a boy

23

found with a hat full of sugar, in the vicinity of a hogshead of sugar broken open, was a thief.

All hands stopped work to watch as Thornhill was whipped a hundred yards along Red Lion Quay.

Crocker pulled Thornhill's shirt off and dragged his britches down to his knees, and shoved him in the back to start him off. The flail landed smack on the skin of his back so he could think of nothing but getting away from it, but the britches hobbled him and Crocker was there beside him for every step that he stumbled along.

The lesson, he learned, was do not get caught. Collarbone showed him how to tap a cask of brandy with a screw, nice and clean so the loss would not be noticed. He gently tapped one of the hoops towards the tapering end of a cask, and used his gimlet to bore two small holes through the wood where the hoop had been. Then he produced a tin pipe, made in two sections to fit neatly into his pocket, and drew off the brandy into a bladder he had hanging inside his coat. Thornhill breathed deep of the hot heady fumes of brandy. Just the smell was enough to warm a person from the inside. Collarbone offered it to him. *Bit of a waxer, Thornie?* Thornhill took a gulp, then Collarbone seized it back and took such a deep drink Thornhill could hear the fluid going down his throat.

When both of the bladders had been filled and hung back on the loops in the armpits of his coat, Collarbone got out a pair of splines he had already made, tapping them into the screw holes. Then he hammered the hoop back down over them. *What the eye don't see, Thornie,* he said with a wink. *Eh? Like it says in the Good Book.*

~

There was one morning every November when he woke to a quilted silence. The room was lit as from below, the split and

24

sagging timbers of the roof, the shingles black with years, painfully illuminated. Even with his head under the blanket he knew it was there waiting for him: snow. It smoothed over the piles of filth, stopped the stinking tanneries in their tracks, covered the smells under its whiteness. These were good things.

But the winter he turned fourteen, the river froze over, stone-solid for two weeks. Down on the ice there was a frost-fair, with Irish fiddlers and dancing bears, chestnut stalls and every man and woman loose-mouthed with gin. For those without the pennies to pay for the chestnuts and liquor, though, the fair was a time of being pinched hard. With the river froze over, there was no work on the ships, no work at the tan-yards.

In the little room off Mermaid Court, the Thornhills were starving. Mary was stitching away at shrouds as if her life depended on it, her fingers too cold to work properly, but the window that gave her light had no glass, so it let in the wind as well. Lizzie, taken with the quinsy, lay abed groaning and panting, John was out trying to lift potatoes from Tyrrell's stall with young Luke watching out, and there was Rob mooning about smiling, poor loon, when there was nothing to smile about.

It was Mr Middleton, that gloomy, though kindly man, who saved him. One more baby had died, yet another son who would not grow to learn his father's trade and inherit his father's business. Something had shifted in Mr Middleton, some hope finally died. *He is gone very stern, Will,* Sal told Thornhill. *Says there will be no more babies.* After a long silence she went on: *No sons. Only me.* He heard how she tried to keep her voice light, airy, saying words of no consequence, but he could hear the misery in it.

But then Mr Middleton told Thornhill that he would take him on as apprentice. *No thieving, mind,* he warned him. *Any thieving and you are out on your ear.* For the sisters, Mr Middleton knew a man who needed plain sewing done, which would keep the wolf from the door.

~

On the hardest freeze of the year, a day in January when the pearly clouds themselves seemed made of ice and the air was painful to breathe, Mr Middleton took Thornhill up St-Mary-at-Hill to the Watermen's Hall for his binding. A door led into a draughty passage flagged with worn stone, and here boys waited to be bound over. The bench they had to sit on was hard, and too narrow for a bottom, and the cold from the flagstones froze his feet in their wooden pattens, but he felt that on this day his life might lunge forward out of its rotten past. Mr Middleton sat puffing beside him from the steep climb up the hill and Thornhill felt breathless too, with the possibility of a future better than anything he could have hoped.

If he could get through the seven years of the apprenticeship he would be a freeman of the River Thames. Folk always needed to get from one side of the river to the other, and coal and wheat always had to be got to the docks from the ships that brought them. As long as he kept his health he would never outright starve. He swore to himself that he would be the best apprentice, the strongest, quickest, cleverest. That when freed in seven years he would be the most diligent waterman on the whole of the Thames.

With a trade behind him, he could marry Sal and keep her. By and by Mr Middleton would need a strong son-in-law to help him in his business and, in the natural course of things, inherit it. All the closed doors of his life might spring open from this day forward.

The stairway was out of a dream, curving upwards like a coil of orange peel around a slender rail, towards the radiance pouring down from the skylight. At the top he hung back, had to be almost pulled by Mr Middleton into the grand room and stand on the Turkey rug under the glitter of the chandelier, feeling the fire blazing away, staring at the dark solemn pictures on the walls.

He stayed in the lee of Mr Middleton, who looked sterner than ever, his shoulders held back like one of the guardsmen at the Palace, as he faced a vast mahogany table behind which sat half a dozen men in robes. One, weighed down with a great bronze chain over his shoulders, said, *Morning Richard, and how is Mrs Middleton?* And Mr Middleton spoke back in a wooden sort of voice, *Middling, Mr Piper, we can't complain.*

Thornhill had never heard anyone address Mr Middleton by his first name, or seen him like this, tight with anxiety and humility. He saw that these men sitting behind their mahogany table were as far above Mr Middleton as Mr Middleton was above him. He had a sudden dizzying understanding of the way men were ranged on top of each other, all the way from the Thornhills at the bottom up to the King, or God, at the top, each man higher than one, lower than another.

The man with the chain asked, *Who is this lad, Richard?* And Mr Middleton answered in the same stiff way, *This is William Thornhill, your lordship, and I am here to vouch for him.* Another of them asked, *Can he handle an oar?* And a little one on the end chimed in, *Has he got his river hands?*

Mr Middleton's voice was happier now, on solid ground as he answered, *Yes, Mr Piper, I had him row from Hay's Wharf to the Sufferance Dock and from Wapping Old Stairs to Fresh Wharf for this past week gone.* The man with the chain cried, *Good man!* in the sort of way he might have spoken to a boy, but Mr Middleton stood quiet, not seeming to think it cheek to be spoken to in such a way, which made Thornhill all the more apprehensive.

The flames were becoming uncomfortably hot on his behind. He had never been near such a roaring in a fireplace, had never known what it was to be too much heated, but he could feel the glow of it piercing his britches. His bottom was just about on fire, but he could not move forward without seeming impertinently close to the gentlemen in their robes. It all seemed part of the ordeal, something he must endure, along with the glances of these men who could reject him if they fancied.

Mr Piper was saying it again, *Good man*, but he was an old trembly sort of man, and it was clear that he had forgotten who was a good man, or why, patting his own arm as if congratulating himself.

Then a bald man said, straight to Thornhill, *Blisters healed yet, sonny?* And Thornhill did not know whether to say yes or no, or even whether he should speak at all. His palms were still puffed up from all the heavy rowing Mr Middleton had been making him do, but they were no longer bleeding. He held them out without speaking, and there was a general laugh.

The bald man said, *Good lad, they have the look of a waterman's hands already, eh gentlemen? License granted, I would say,* and it was done.

~

Mr Middleton was a good master. For the first time in his life, Thornhill was not always hungry, not always cold. He slept on the flags of the kitchen on a straw mattress, rising and sleeping with the tide.

The tide was a tyrant. It would not wait, and if a lighterman missed the flood to get a load of coal up the river, even strong William Thornhill could not row against it, and would have to wait twelve hours to the next.

His blisters never got a chance to heal. They grew till they burst, then they formed again, burst again, bled again. The oar-handles of the *Hope* were brown with his blood. Mr Middleton approved of that. *Only way to get your river hands, lad,* he said, and gave him a knob of fat to rub on them.

Seven years seemed a lifetime, but there was a lot to learn. The sets of the tide from Wapping over to Rotherhithe, where the tide swept onto Hay's Roads and the eddies would drag a man down in a second if he fell overboard. How at Chelsea Reach the currents pulled and pushed at the boats because, they said, a set of fiddlers had been drowned there years before, and the river had been dancing in that spot ever since. How an oar, four times as long as a man, could take charge of its owner. How to shift the oar from the rowing crutch in the bow, canting the blade with a turn of the wrist, then running along the narrow gunwale with the oar as far as the quarter and with a quick weigh-down on the handle flinging it against the stern post.

Sometimes he forgot that he'd ever had to learn all the things he knew.

He learned other things, too, about the gentry. How they would make a meal of every farthing of the fare before they got in, arguing with long sentences full of *my good man*, and beating him down if there was a crowd of boats at the steps, and fares in short supply. How in the end he might take a fare from Chelsea Steps to St Katherine-by-the-Tower for a couple of pennies, just so as not to go home with nothing for the day. The way the actors on their way to the theatres at Lambeth dallied at the steps, keeping the boatman waiting there in the water holding the boat steady for as long as they pleased, getting in with never a glance at him, and practising their lines the whole journey as if they were alone in the world, the boatman nothing more than part of the landscape.

He discovered that the gentry had as many tricks as a rat to dun a poor waterman. He took a fellow across the water, who told him to wait, for he would return shortly to be taken back over, and would pay him then for both trips together. Thornhill waited five hours, unwilling to lose the shilling he was owed, before he realised that the cheating shark must have cozened another waterman for his boathire back again.

Trusting gentry was not something he did twice.

But a waterman also needed to learn their whims and fancies: when they would arrive at Whitehall Stairs, wanting to be taken across to Vauxhall Gardens, and when they would want to come home again. To know when the whiting were running and they would want to go down to the Friend in Hand or the Captain, to sit out in the yard there beside the river and gorge themselves, and whether it was worth a waterman's while to wait there or to row back up to Cornish Stairs where there might be a gentleman wishing to be taken to his country house at Richmond.

As the best prentice on the river, Thornhill had a way with the gentlemen, a loud cheery thing that he did, that rode above the plaintive cries of the others. *This way!* he roared. *Step right down to the Hope, sir, finest vessel on the river!* He would whip off his old hat. His head of thick glossy hair was, he knew, better than any hat: with such vigorous hair, who could doubt the vitality of the rest of the system? He gestured grandly as he'd seen them do at the music hall, *Finest boat in Christendom, sir, not a boat on the river can come to her!* and pointed to the Doggett's badge on his sleeve, that showed he had won the apprentice's race. *Here to Gravesend in four minutes over the two hours, sir, I'll have you to Billingsgate before you can get your snuffbox out.*

The gentry seemed another species, more enigmatic than any Lascar, and it came upon him as a surprise that they might be driven by the same impulses as any other human animal. He was up to his thighs in the water one day, holding the boat up to the ramp, so his fares could get in without wetting their feet. He hardly glanced at them as they hailed him, being concerned only to get enough fares for the day and go back to Mr Middleton's warm kitchen. His legs were numbed, but the upper part of him was frozen, wet from the recent shower of rain, and whipped by the wind. He could smell his own hair, damp under his cap from the rain, a doggy sort of smell, and the wet old wool of his blue coat, and the red flannel waistcoat that had been a gift from Mr Middleton, whose frame could no longer be accommodated within it now that he had such a strong apprentice to do the work for him. The boat was bumping against his legs, driven in by the sharp wind that was whipping the surface into waves, and he was gripping the gunwale with both hands, busy steadying it, when he heard the plummy tones of the gentleman. *Be cautious, my love,* he said. *Don't expose your leg to the boatman!*

He was a white-faced, thin-chested fellow with a little pink rosebud mouth, his curls falling down his cheeks from under his hat, all care as he took his lady by the hand and around her back. His glance at Thornhill, standing in the mud and the water, his hands frozen in shape gripping the gunwale, was not so much one of scorn as of triumph. *Look at me, fellow, and what I have got!* It was a look that said that the white silk legs, and everything attached to them, were his property, in a way there was nothing in the world that was William Thornhill's property, excepting only his black cap, shrunk in so many rains, that sat on top of his head like a pimple on an elephant's behind.

The gentleman looked as though he would not know what to do with a female leg, and although he touched her, there was no pleasure in the touch: the woman, white stocking and silk slippers and all, was a thing he took pride of ownership in, but there was no love in that *my love.*

And there was the leg, level with the boatman's eyes as its owner got herself over the gunwale, close enough, had he wished, to reach out and touch its silk surface. The slipper on the end of the leg was a miracle of frivolity, down here at Horsleydown Old Stairs, on the muddy ramp. It seemed impossible that such a substantial person as this woman could be supported on two such tiny slips of poison-green silk. There was no back to the thing, but a little heel that gave her ankle a special fineness, and as she placed the slipper on the bow, the foot was turned outward so the curve of the ankle, the back of the foot, the daintiness of the heel, were all proffered for Thornhill's close inspection.

Up past the leg was her face, and the mouth in the face said that she thanked her husband kindly, *my love*, for his care, but the face said she did not expect much fun from him, only this namby-pamby gallantry.

She did not look at Thornhill, and yet her leg spoke to him, its exposure meant for him. Did she hope to provoke the blood-less husband, by showing leg to a mere boatman? Or was it for her own satisfaction, to remind herself that there were other kinds of men in the world, ones who knew what to do with a leg when they saw one?

In the next moment, the gentleman had pulled the skirt down, interposed himself between them: had somehow got them both into the boat, his bottom at one stage brushing Thornhill's face as he climbed in. Thornhill had his hands full holding the boat, so inept were his passengers, and when he got in himself, feeling his wet legs weak with cold, hardly under his instructions, his passengers were sitting in the stern and the white skirt was well down, the green slippers out of sight.

But the owner of the leg spoke: *Henry dear,* she said, *I am afraid my slipper is all but ruined.* She extended her leg out in front of her, and indeed the poison-green silk gleamed with river-water, and the little furbelow on the front hung sad and bedrag-gled. Her skirt was hiked up almost to the knee so that north of the slipper was the leg again, and beyond that the shadows where a man could guess at all her other charms.

My love, said the man more sharply, *you are exposing your leg!*

And now the woman definitely looked at Thornhill, and by God it was a sultry teasing look, though gone so quick no husband could find anything to blame. The glance that passed between them was the glance of two creatures, male and female of the same species, recognising each others' blood.

The dandy put his arm around his wife's shoulders now, although not to Thornhill's eye in a way that promised anything of an interesting nature when they got to the shrubbery of the Vauxhall Gardens.

In any race for survival with this Henry, Thornhill knew he would have been the victor, lad though he was—shipwrecked, for instance, the dandy would have pined and drooped and died, while he himself would have known how to prosper. And yet, in this particular desert isle of London, this jungle full of dangerous creatures in the year 1793, Thornhill was at the mercy of such mincing pansies, who looked at him as if he were of no more account than a bollard.

Not all the gentry were of that ilk, however, and he had his few regulars who spoke to him like another man the same as themselves: Captain Watson, for instance, who always asked for him at Chelsea Stairs, and with whom he had a steady arrangement of a Wednesday forenoon when he visited his ladyfriend over in Lambeth. He'd hold the boat up on the ramp for the captain, a stout sort of gentleman, to make it easy for him to step aboard, and never mind how hard it was to launch again off the ramp with his portly behind in the stern, because he was a good fellow and did not haggle with a poor man over a few pence.

A waterman's brain was exercised from the moment of waking, when even without rising from the bed he could guess the state of the river, the tides, the wind. These were his books: the colour of the sky at dawn, the cries of the birds over the river, the set of the waves at the turn of tide. From them he could tell where he would best find his fares.

After a time the mud-choked water and the ships it carried, thick on its back like fleas on a dog, became nothing more than a big room of which every corner was known. He came to love that wide pale light around him out on the river, the falling away of insignificant things in the face of the great radiance of the sky. He would rest on the oars at Hungerford Reach, where the tide could be relied on to sweep him around, and stare along the water at the way the light wrapped itself around every object.

~

Of a Sunday, Mr Middleton did not always require him to work, and he and Sal found time to be together. He loved to be with her, watching the thoughts dancing beneath the skin, and would not have tried to explain it to anyone else. He had the feeling he could say anything to her, any confession, any shameful truth. She would listen, and answer with some cheerful kindness.

That first winter she took it into her head to teach him his letters, as her mother had taught her. To please her he agreed, but he was not sure about it. Marks on paper seemed to sap the power of the mind. He had seen Sal write things down in order to remember them: a list for going to the draper or the grocer, where he himself would have simply carried such a thing in his head. Numbers, too. He had seen many a gentleman need to get out a pencil and scrap of paper from his pocket to work out the fare to Richmond and back, two passengers one way, one the other, plus a packet one way and the Sunday surcharge. He, ignorant waterman, had meanwhile done the sum in his head, added the ten per cent for goodwill and the sixpence for the Benevolent Fund, before the gentleman had even found a flat place to rest the paper.

They did it at the table, sitting squashed together on the same side, with a candle in its holder casting a sputtering light. He could smell the fruity femaleness of her, a thing like the memory of strawberries left in the wood of the punnet, that sweet flowery fragrance. She leaned in to him and said, *No ink to start with. Just hold it—see?—like this*, and held up her own small hand, showing.

When he tried, it was maddening, pernickety, unnatural. The way his hand worked with an oar made sense. His fist closed around it and his thumb kept it all in place. This holding of a feather was a contortionist's trick, pincering in with fingers and thumb, twisting the whole hand sideways, the quill rolling in his grip. Only his desire to please her made him persist.

When they added ink to the nib and he scraped the feather down the paper, the nib snagged and spattered. Black droplets and smears were bold on the modest white surface. Sal laughed and he nearly tipped the whole table over there and then and hurled out of the room, down to the river where he was master of himself. He could row to Richmond and back against the tide. He had won the Doggett's Coat and Badge, rowing against a foul wind, straining to keep a boat's length ahead of Lewis Blackwood the whole way. He had not let his mind go anywhere but into his arms and his hands. Pulling across the line ten yards ahead of Blackwood, he had felt that any feat of strength or endurance would be within his grasp.

Just not this squibby business squeezed in tight against a table.

Seeing his face, Sal seemed to understand that this was not a laughing business. She dried the ink off the table, the paper, the nib, his fingers, and dotted out a T on the page. *Just go over them dots, Will*, she said. *We will leave the W for now.* He approached the nib gingerly to the line of dots, controlling the runaway tip with all his power. The first time he overshot: a wavering horizontal line cut through the dots and beyond. He tried the second line, watching the trail of ink. A wobble in the middle, but there it was: two lines, a letter T.

He became aware that his tongue was far out of his mouth, helping the tip of the quill along. He pulled it back, licked his lips, laid down the pen, heard his voice rough as he said, *Enough for tonight.* Sal looked at the page with the marks. *Look, Will,* she said. *How good you are doing it now, against them you did at the start!*

He rubbed at his hand where it was cramped. To his eye the marks he had made were shameful, nothing more than foolish scratches. He wished to crush the page to pulp. But she was nudging him with that elbow of hers, that arm that liked to alight along his, and saying, *I promise you*—but lightly, it was a promise hardly necessary to make—*I promise you that by next Sunday you will write that W, fair as ever was.*

Winter wore away, and there it was at last, his whole name: *William Thornhill*, slow and steady. As long as no one was watching, no one would know how long it took, and how many times the tongue had to be drawn back in.

William Thornhill.

He was still only sixteen, and no one in his family had ever gone so far.

~

Love came upon him so gradually that it was not even given the name. As the years of his apprenticeship wore away he knew only that, out on the river where the wind cut keen through his old coat, he was warmed by the thought of her, sitting with her mother, threading the needle for her and stitching away at shirts or handkerchiefs. He marvelled at her efficient fingers, doing the edges of the white squares with tiny deft movements too quick to be seen. One moment there was the ravelling edge, the next it was rolled under, turned in, magicked into a tidy scroll of fabric in the time it took her mother to squint at a needle.

He did not know what it was that melted something in him, so he felt his face grow smooth with thinking of her, could even drift away into a dream of her that stayed with him all day, until he trudged up the steps at night hearing the water squelch in his shoes. Lying on his straw in the kitchen, waiting for sleep, the knowledge that she was above him in her room under the roof made something thicken in his throat. Sometimes, coming across her by surprise, he found he could not quite breathe for a moment, or find the words to answer her greeting. *Why Will!* she would always exclaim, quite as if it were a surprise to her that her father's big-shouldered apprentice was filling the doorway, stooping to save his head from the low beam. She was a one for touching, would take hold of him when she spoke, and he would feel it there long afterwards: her little hand on his arm, speaking to him through the stiff fabric of his coat.

Rotherhithe was being grown over now with tanneries and knackeries and rows of tenements where there had once been those marshy spots where two children could find a place of their own. Even the gypsies had been chased away. But they found that the yard of Christ Church at the Borough, where it backed onto the river, was a hospitable place in fine weather. Among the tombs two people could find a little privacy.

Dawdling in the pleasure of being together, whispering,

crouching behind one of the stone boxes, Sal read out the writing along the side, one slow word at a time. His job was to keep track of the words she had already read, so she could concentrate on the one at hand, because it was too hard to read and to remember all at once.

Sal's voice was especially sweet getting her tongue around the knots of words: *Susannah Wood Wife of Mr James Wood Mathematical Instrument Maker*, she said. *She was tapped nine times and had 161 gallons of water taken from her without ever lamenting her case or fearing the operation.* Thornhill blurted out, *Like a bladder of sack, sounds like*, and saw her trying not to laugh. *Oh Will*, she said, *think of the the poor soul, and us finding it a joke!* She took his hand so he felt how soft and small it was within the stiff claw of his own. Smiled, so he saw her dimple: just the one, her face itself winking at him.

He stared out at the river, where the tide was beginning to swirl the water upstream, trying to find the words to say what pressed up out of his heart. *There is something*, he started, and felt a fool, not being able to go on. He started again, heard himself loud and definite, *Soon's they make me a freeman, first thing I'll do is marry you*, then he thought she might laugh, a prentice from Tanner's Lane saying such a thing, but she did not.

Yes, Will, she said. *And I'll wait for you.* Her eyes searched his face, serious for once. He could see her looking separately at his eyes, his mouth, back to his eyes again, reading behind the words the truth that was written on his heart. He looked into her eyes, close enough to see the tiny copy of himself there.

He longed for the seven years to run their course. He had only to let time pass, and another life would be waiting for him.

~

38

They wed the very day of his freedom, just before he turned twenty-two. Mr Middleton let him have his second-best wherry by way of a wedding gift, and they took a room not far from Mermaid Row, where husband and wife could make free with each other in a way the place behind the tomb of Susannah Wood had never allowed.

It turned out that Sal was a saucy one in bed. That first night, she came up close against him. She was afraid, she said, of the dark. Took his arm, needing, she said, something by way of support. He felt the warmth of her, her noisy breath tickling his ear. They had to keep things quiet, for the walls were paper-thin. There was a man in the next room whose every cough was as clear as if he were in the bed with them.

What happened next was nothing loud or forceful. It hardly even seemed as decided as an action. It felt merely an unthought process of nature, a seed bursting out of the dirt or a flower unfurling from the bud.

The night became the best part of every day. Now they had a bed to themselves, she loved to curl around him, a candle guttering on the stool. Her breasts lolled out in a way that shocked and aroused him. She would peel a tangerine and feed him the segments slippery from her own warm mouth, and when they had done all the things with tangerines and mouths that could be done, and the candle had snuffed itself out in a pool of tallow, they lay together and told each other stories.

Sal liked to tell about Cobham Hall, where her mother had been in service before marrying Mr Middleton, and where she had gone with her mother for a month once when she was a girl. A few things stayed in her memory: the carriageway up to the entrance, a green tunnel of poplars. Starched damask on the tables, stiff as hide, even in the servants' quarters. And the proper ways of doing things. There had been a grapevine there, she said, and once or twice the treat of grapes in the servants' dining hall. The housekeeper had scolded her for taking a single grape from a bunch. *Eat what you like, the old thing told me,* she said. *But never spoil the bunch, get the grape-scissors and cut a sprig.* She turned to Thornhill and whispered, *Fancy, Will, scissors just for nothing but grapes!* The only grapes Thornhill had ever known were the few he had picked up from the ground, broken and muddy, when the market was finished.

Thornhill preferred the stories they told each other about their futures. They would have children, naturally, and her strong husband, that Freeman of the River Thames, would make a good thing of life as a waterman, and later on he would go into the business with her father.

Thornhill could hardly believe that life had given him this corner to turn. Only the calluses on his palms and the ache in his shoulders reassured him that it was real. This was no fairy-tale, but the reward for a man's labour. He lay in the dark, listening to Sal wonder aloud whether she would like a boy first or a girl, and rolled his thumb over the calluses as if they were so many sovereigns.

Seven years of ferrying the gentry from one side of the river to the other had sickened Thornhill for that work. Once he was a freeman he chose to work on the lighters, rowing loads of coal and timber. Not everyone had the strength to manage a fully laden boat in the treacherous eddies of the Thames, but he did. He had never been afraid of hard work, and it was cleaner than truckling to gentry for a few extra pence.

It meant also that he could employ his brother to give him a hand. Rob was not up to much in the brains department, but he was the strongest man on the river, and biddable. Rob's calves would bulge, his arms strain and the placket at the back of his britches would open below the button, threatening to burst, as he heaved up a sack of coal. But he could work all day for no more than what would keep body and soul together.

Together, the Thornhills made a good pair.

~

A year after they were wed, the child was born, a healthy boy. He lay crowing, crying, exclaiming, making prodigious amounts of fawn-coloured shit and great arcs of piss when unswaddled. They had him christened William, but he was always Willie. Another William Thornhill in the world was not too much, not when it was his own son.

The baby lay gesturing at Thornhill in a secret code, blinking slowly at the figure bending over him, pointing to his father's nose with a tiny finger as if to pronounce on it. The powerful little red mouth was never still, the lips pursing, puckering, spreading, pouting, the fists jerking at air, expressions flickering across his face as constantly as waves on the surface of the ocean.

He loved to pick his son up and feel the weight of him against his chest, his small arms around his neck, the innocent smell of his hair. Loved to watch Sal, sitting by the window smiling to herself as she stitched another tiny smock, or bent over the boy crooning. He heard her humming as she went about her tasks. She could not keep a tune, but for Thornhill that wavering melody became the sound of his new life. He went about smiling at nothing.

~

In the year of the boy's second birthday, winter came early and sharp. The winds and the clouds were such as Thornhill had never seen before. They were always enemies of the boatmen, and this year the hardness of the wind and the quality of the cold was all they talked about, up and down the river. It was going to be a bad winter.

When clouds scudded overhead and dropped a shower of rain, his coat, that could turn the water if it did not come down too heavy, was soaked through and the wind off the river sliced through the worn-out wool. It scoured his cheeks and made his whole face red, swollen, stone-like. He could bear it as well as the next man. He did not complain. It was as pointless to complain about the weather as it was to complain that he had been born in Tanner's Court in Bermondsey in a dank stuffy room rather than in St James Square with a silver spoon waiting to have his name engraved on it.

It was almost a relief when, in the small days of January, the pool above London Bridge grew a pearly skin like the cloud on old eyes. One morning it was no longer river but an expanse of rough grey ice, the boats stuck in it as fast as bones in fat. Then it was a matter of the three of them getting into the bed together to keep warm, stretch out the money they had put by for such a day, and wait for the thaw.

It was in that month of the freeze, with no money coming into any household by the river, that Thornhill's world cracked and broke.

First his sister Lizzie came down with the quinsy she had had as a girl, lying flushed and panting on the bed, crying with the pain in her throat. The physick cost a shilling a bottle, only a small bottle too, but it seemed to do little good, no matter how many shillings were spent on it.

Then Mrs Middleton slipped on a patch of ice outside the front door and fell hard against the step. Some part of her was broken, it seemed, and did not want to mend. She lay rigid and waxy-faced with the pain, her mouth stiff, her lips bloodless, refusing food. The surgeon was called several times, at three guineas a visit, but he was said to be the best man for that sort of thing.

Mr Middleton hovered by her bed, sweating in the room, kept as hot as an oven because that brought some relief to the poor woman. The new apprentice, who might have hoped for a rest while the river was frozen, was kept busy lugging coal up the stairs.

As the weeks passed, Mr Middleton grew gaunt, his eyes set in dark rings. A little nagging cough began to keep him company. When Thornhill and Sal went to visit they would hear the cough on their way up the stairs, and know him to be sitting by his wife's pillow, stroking her hair or patting her brow with a camphor cloth.

The only time his face cleared was when he thought of some delicacy that might tempt her to eat. Then he could not be still, setting off straight away and walking for miles to get brandied cherries in a jar, or figs in honey.

The Thornhills met him at the door one day, a day cold enough to crack the very cobblestones. He was setting off to walk to the apothecary at Spitalfields to get a concoction of oranges and cinnamon that someone had suggested. Sal tried to dissuade him, and Thornhill turned him around to point him back into the house, offering to go in his place. But there was a surprising depth of obstinacy in Mr Middleton, and he pushed his son-in-law's hand away. Sal and Thornhill exchanged a look in which they shared the thought that he probably could not bear to spend another afternoon dabbing at his wife's waxen face with the camphor cloth in her stifling room. To be striding along the frozen streets would give him a sense of doing something useful, at least until he returned with the oranges and saw his wife barely taste them before refusing more.

So they let him go. Thornhill watched him swing off down the lane, walking as fast as the hard frost would allow, his breath puffing out ahead of him. Nearly ran after him, he looked such a small figure against the snow heaped on the pavement, but did not.

It was dark when he came home, silent and white in the face. The mixture was safe in his pocket and he did not even take his coat off before going upstairs to try his wife with a mouthful of it. She smiled her strained smile, lifted her head to take a taste off the spoon, then lay back exhausted and would take no more.

Sal got him down to the kitchen, got him out of his coat and muffler at last. He sat passively under her hands, staring into the fire. When she knelt to take off his boots she exclaimed—they were wet through, his feet mottled with the chill of them. He had fallen in a drift of snow, he said, and while he had waited for the apothecary, the snow in them had melted, and stayed melted all the way home.

He started to sneeze after supper and next day woke up flushed and sweating, shivering under four blankets, tossing his head on the pillow. The surgeon came again, for the husband this time. He cupped him and gave him something thick and brown in a small square bottle that made him drift into a kind of sleep from which he called out hoarsely and struggled to escape the bedclothes. In spite of the medicine, the flame of the fever consumed him. His cheeks were scarlet, the skin dry and hot to the touch, his tongue furred and grey, his eyes sunk back into their sockets.

Within a week he was dead.

When they told Mrs Middleton she cried out once, a terrible hoarse sound. Then she turned her face to the wall and did not speak again. Sal sat with her all day and slept at the foot of her bed. The surgeon was called again and again, until the table by the bed bristled with bottles of potions and pills. But Mrs Middleton's slide towards death would not be stopped by anything the surgeon could do. With each day that passed she shrank further into the bedclothes, her eyes closed as if she could not bear to see the world any longer, slipping away behind her skin.

At last a grey dawn came when she was stiff under the blanket. They laid her in her box at Gilling's, beside Mr Middleton's, waiting for the ground to thaw so they could bury them.

It was only after the ice on the river broke up, the hole dug and the prayers said over the two coffins as they swayed down on the undertaker's ropes, that the Thornhills realised everything was gone.

Mr Middleton had done all that any man could do. He had lived thriftily and put cash aside. He had put money into well-made boats and kept them in repair, had made sure his apprentice was honest and worked hard. His business had been good, his life cautiously prosperous.

But as soon as he was gone it fell into pieces with amazing speed. In that frozen month his savings were devoured. The surgeon had come every day, and hardly a visit passed when he did not prescribe some new cure that cost a pound the bottle. The uneaten jars of brandied cherries and figs in honey sat on the pantry shelf. Even though there was no work for him to do, the apprentice had still to be fed, and with the river frozen, all that coal he had carried up the stairs had cost five pounds the sack.

Worst of all, the landlord's man had still come by for the rent every Monday. Whether the river was frozen or not, whether a man could work or not, did not matter to the landlord's man.

To Thornhill, the house on Swan Lane had always seemed a fortress against want. Surely no harm could come to a man who owned such a thing as a piece of ground with a dwelling on it. If a man had a roof over his head he could batten down, no matter how hard times were, and wait for them to get better.

He had taken a long time to understand that the house had

not been owned, only leased. When he did, it was as if some vital part of himself had dropped away, leaving a void. The house on Swan Lane, always so warm, so safe, was now as cheerless as any of the tenements of his childhood.

The rent was in arrears, and the furniture had to be sold to pay it. Sal and Thornhill watched even the bed Mrs Middleton had died in, which seemed scarcely cold, being carted off. When that was not enough, the bailiffs came after the wherries, first the *Hope* that the apprentice worked, so he had to go and find another master to serve out his time, and then the second-best one too, that Thornhill could not prove was a wedding gift. The river had barely melted, Thornhill had done just a week's work, when he watched them take his wherry in tow. His livelihood disappeared away under Blackfriars Bridge. From now on he would be a journeyman, rowing other men's boats and never knowing when he would be told there was no work for him.

He sat for a long time on the pier at Bull Wharf watching the red sails of the sailor-men bellying out as they tacked from reach to reach. The tide was pushing in from the sea. Across the surface of the river, pocked, pitted, rough, ran another kind of roughness, a buckle in the water crossing from one bank to the other. Behind it pushed water of a different character, barred and furrowed: the sea. He watched the tide, and thought of how the river would go on doing this dance of advance and fall back, long after William Thornhill and the griefs he carried in his heart were dead and forgotten.

What point could there be to hoping, when everything could be broken so easily?

~

Sal pushed back against it all. She sat with her father during his illness, rubbing at his feet which in spite of the fever were as cold

46

as a corpse. When he died her mouth went grim, as if there was someone she wanted to punish. When her mother went, she walked to Spitalfields and back—as her father had done—for some fine red velvet her mother had always admired, and stood over the man from Gilling's until the coffin was lined with it just the right way. Her mother's face was chalky against the velvet, but it gave Sal some satisfaction, and until her parents were in the ground she kept going, bustling from room to room moving objects into cupboards and out again, taking every cup down in the kitchen and washing it, every saucer and every spoon, getting down on her knees with a pail to scrub the floors. It was as if she thought she could work her parents back to life.

When the first coffin—her father's—hit the bottom of the hole with a hollow knocking sound, like a knuckle on a door, she broke down, as Thornhill had known she must. Her cries were not so much grief as a kind of indignation at this thing that was happening. She pushed the side of her hand into her mouth, as she had in the throes of childbirth, and Thornhill was once more afraid she would split the skin.

But the tears finished something and she accepted the coming of the bailiff's men better than he did. As her father's armchair was hoisted onto the cart, Thornhill had to look away, but she did not. She watched until it turned the corner and was gone. *Well*, she said, and looked at Thornhill. *Thank the Lord he ain't here to see, Will, he paid seven pound for that chair off a man in Cheapside, I remember the day he brung it home.*

It was Sal who saw, before Thornhill, that they would have to give up the attic as extravagant. She went out in the lanes and alleys, the baby on her hip, inquiring for a cheaper place. When that, too, became too dear for them, she went out again until she found another, even cheaper. When they were on the bottom rung of the ladder of accommodation, with only the street itself below them, she still kept looking for something cheaper but better, moving their few things while Thornhill was out on the river.

There was the basement room in Sparrick's Row, where the water came in from the yard and had to be kept out with a dam of rags; and a similar one around the corner in Cash's Grounds; from there across the river hard by St Mary Somerset, where the bells drove them mad; back across the river to Snows Fields, but they were robbed there so they went to Brunswick Lane near the maltings, in Butler's Buildings, where they came to rest. Third floor back, one broken window and a cupboard missing its door. Every Monday Sal counted out four shillings for him to take downstairs to Mr Butler, standing at the front door drumming on the floor with his stick to tell his tenants it was time to pay. It was robbery at that price, and the stench from the maltings nearly choked them. But it was dry, and the cesspit in the yard freshly emptied, and the chimney smoked only a little. *We will get used to the stink, Will,* she said.

He saw that he had married a terrier, and could only admire her, being himself in a trance of despair in which he blindly worked but could not find the will to care about a leaking roof or a stopped chimney.

We got each other, she reminded him on the pile of rags that was their bed in Butler's Buildings. He felt her shaking against him and thought she was crying, as she did sometimes, stormily, passionately, out of nowhere. But she was laughing. *Each other and all them fleas, that is,* she said. *We won't never be lonely here,* she went on. *Will we?* And was pushing up against him in the way she knew he could not resist, and finally calling out in triumph.

Butler's Buildings was what he had known through his childhood. Having once hoped for something better, and been within

48

reach of it, he could not face going back to it. Left to himself, he would have let himself slip under the surface of life like a man fallen into water that was too cold to fight.

She kept him going, even when hunger began to pinch. He had not forgotten how wearisome it was when the emptiness was always there. He was tired at the thought of it, would have turned his face to the wall, the way Mrs Middleton had, and given up. Had never thought that a Freeman of the River Thames could go hungrier than a prentice, could be as starving as ever he had been in Tanner's Lane. He tried to put a brave face on it, but he knew that hunger could last a lifetime.

Sal, perhaps from innocence, treated want as a temporary accident, something two people as quick as themselves could overcome. She took a couple of eggs off a stall one day, slipping them into the baby's shawl while everyone was watching a couple of dogs fighting. She made a good story of it to Thornhill that night: *I'd a got three, Will, only the bleeding dogs kissed and made up too soon.* She laughed, remembering, and he laughed with her, both of them warmed with the egg in their stomachs. *Started sniffing each other's arses, that weren't no good to me!*

It was her first theft and she was as proud of it as a child.

He told her what a clever thief she was, but his heart was heavy. His life was going backwards.

From the tiny window of their room they could see the fowls in Ingram's yard underneath them all day, scratching, bustling, flying at the crusts and peelings flung out the kitchen door by Ingram's cook. The Thornhills would have fought the fowls for those crusts, except that Mr Ingram's servant was always in the yard, and watched the Thornhills sourly, knowing what was in their minds.

It was Sal's idea. It was a matter of being Johnny-on-the-spot, she said, and keeping their wits about them. They waited until they saw the servant staggering towards the privy one afternoon, undone by liquor. Thornhill dashed down and seized the nearest hen and got it under his coat and up to their room again. They had it out and were just about to wring its neck when there were feet on the stairs, and shouts of *Thief!* But quick-witted Sal thrust the thing out the window, where it landed on the roof of the little outhouse below and stalked about there clucking while they tried to shoo it off, back down into the yard. The stupid thing stood there cackling, and they could hear the servant yelling out, *I seen a fowl come out the window!*

When Mr Ingram came in, red-faced, in search of his hen, there was nothing there, only a feather on the floor. When he looked out the window he saw the hen on the roof below. But Thornhill claimed he had just woke up, was about to go down to the port to begin work, and Sal swore blind, *He has not left the room in the last six hours, and the damned fowl must have got up on the roof itself, we know nothing of it whatsoever, as God is our witness.*

When Ingram had gone, grumbling, the Thornhills laughed together. For having to be suppressed, their laughing went on longer than it might otherwise, because what was really so funny? Then there was a long silence in the room. Sal picked up a fold of her old skirt, the only one she had now, stained and patched and ragged round the hem, and said, *We are just about so our stomachs are flapping on our backbones, Will,* and all the fun had gone out of her voice. *That is the fact of it.*

He worked, day after day, for whoever would employ a journeyman with no boat of his own. He carried the gentry to and fro and came to hate them warm in their furs, their hands deep in their pockets, their eyes almost hidden by their caps, feet snug in big warm boots, while his bare ones were freshly wet a hundred times a day and froze in between times while he waited for their pleasure.

When he could, he worked on the lighters owned by luckier men, and had only the wind and the tide to hate. With a load of coals or timber he pulled away at the oars, reduced to an animal, head down and mind blank. He felt like a man who had lost an arm, still waving the stump around. There was a great emptiness in him, which was the space where hope had been.

~

There were such things as honest watermen. The dour God-botherer James Mann at St-Katherine-by-the-Tower was one. He was steady, had his regulars who insisted on him, and did not waste money on a pipe of baccy or a mess of fried eel while he waited for fares, but cracked an abstemious walnut and made it last.

But a waterman with a wife and child could not live on what he could earn. Most watermen were thieves, although some went about it in a more businesslike way than others. Thomas Blackwood had a lighter, the *River Queen*, number 487, which looked the same as any other lighter until he raised the false bottom to reveal the compartment in which quantities of lifted objects could be spirited away.

In the general way of things only foolish men were caught—those too bold, working in daylight, or without having greased up the right men. But a man could be unlucky too. Collarbone was one of life's unlucky ones: to be born with that bright port-wine stain over half his face was already a cruel fate. But perhaps in his case some other man made a pound or two by informing. There was no shortage of men who would do that.

Collarbone had been a watchman on Smith's lighter at Customs House Quay, with thirty-three casks of best Spanish brandy in the hold. He went on his watch at six, and at midnight another man came to relieve him, but as Collarbone stepped onto the dock the officer of the watch stopped him and rubbed him down and discovered the bladders in his coat pocket. Collarbone wrenched away, leaving his coat in the officer's hands, and pelted up St Dunstan's Hill, but another officer was waiting for him there and he was caught. Being of a fine quality, the brandy was worth more than forty shillings, so there was no argument but that Collarbone must hang.

The day before, Thornhill went to see him in Newgate. They sat together at the long table which was one of the luxuries of those condemned to die, and Collarbone told him the whole story. *Then I pull out the gimblet and the tube and I says, I suppose this is what you is looking for?* And grinned at the memory, as if it was nothing but a story.

But Thornhill could imagine it, was familiar with the choking feeling of thievery and knew it to be no joke. No matter how often he did it, there was that feeling of the breath already stopped in his throat by the fear of it, even before they got him and hanged him.

Collarbone had laughed, but now he went a greasy pale. Hid his face in his hands. When he looked at Thornhill again his eyes were wide, not seeing the man in front of him. It was as if he was trying to stare his way right out of this room, all the way back to that day two months before, when he had got up and eaten a slice of bread for breakfast, standing by the window in his small clothes, and had not yet laid a hand to the cask of Spanish brandy that had brought him to this place.

Being turned off was a nasty death but if you were lucky it was over in a trice. The executioner, having weighed you the night before and done certain sums, calculated the distance you had to drop to break your neck clean. The next morning at eight o'clock, the trapdoor opened beneath the man with the rope around his neck and he fell a short distance as if jumping into the river off Lambeth Pier. If Mr Executioner had totted up the numbers right, he jerked up short, his head snapped sideways by the knot, his neck broken.

But such quick death was no spectacle. The crowd grew restive, threw peelings and bones at the body twirling on the end of the rope like a sack of coffee being hoisted up the side of Lamb's warehouse.

There, in the condemned cell, Collarbone begged Thornhill to buy him a quick death, and for old time's sake Thornhill did, doing the rounds of Warner and Blackwood and the rest, and putting half a crown in himself. He got the coins through the grille, into the outstretched hand attached to Mr Executioner's invisible body. It was all a man could do for a friend.

Sal had pawned the stool and their second blanket to provide the half-crown but would not go to witness the hanging. It seemed right, somehow, to keep Collarbone company on his last journey, so next morning Thornhill stood with Rob in Newgate Yard in the grey light of the dawn and watched his friend take the few awkward steps up to the scaffold. Mr Executioner stepped away and Collarbone fell.

But it seemed that Mr Executioner had done his sums wrong after all, or the coins slipped through the grille were not enough. The fall did not break Collarbone's neck, only tightened the thick rope around his windpipe. Thornhill could hear the gargling as he tried to breathe, saw how his feet kicked and kicked at the air, his shoulders writhed, his head in the canvas hood tossed desperately, twitching like a fish on a hook.

The crowd approved of Collarbone's death.

It was Rob's first hanging. He stared with his mouth open and when it was finished, poor Collarbone finally cut down, he turned and spewed onto a little dog pawing at its mistress's skirt, and the woman screeched as raw as a Billingsgate fishwife in spite of all her fine silks.

Clean as a whistle, pet, he told Sal. *Never felt a blessed thing.* She looked away quickly and did not meet his eye again, only went on darning the heel of her stocking, darning the darn over the darn. She sighed and turned the thing around in her hand so she could come at it with the needle from another angle, and he did not know whether she believed him or not.

~

Mr Lucas was a fat man with a striped waistcoat that made the most of his belly. He was the owner of several lighters and had a foreman, Yates, to employ such lightermen as he pleased. Yates was a fair man and spread the work around.

The word was, Lucas had his eye on being Lord Mayor of London. He was a pious sort of fellow, at least on a Sunday, because that was what got a man to be Lord Mayor of London, and he took a dim view of roguery on his boats. Other masters might turn a blind eye, letting the poor lightermen have a few perquisites, but not Matthias Prime Lucas. A man whose heart was set on being Lord Mayor of London needed every penny for the buying of grand dinners and the supplying of gifts, and it did not leave much for being generous to his workers.

John Whitehead had been foolish enough to be caught at Brown's Quay moving seventy pounds of hemp out of a lighter belonging to Mr Lucas. Whitehead had gone on his knees, it was said, and begged mercy of Mr Lucas, but Mr Lucas had spoken of making an example. Whitehead had swung.

In the beginning Thornhill was cautious, now and then helping himself to a bladder full of Portuguese sack, or a box of tea. He had one or two near misses, with the officers swooping down out of nowhere. By the time he had been three years in Lucas's employ, he had learned the value of a moonless night and the importance of having a skiff close at hand to make away in. Whitehead had been caught because he had not slipped the marine police enough. Thornhill kept them well oiled with bottles of French brandy. The only thing a man could not guard against was the gabbers, those men who for five or ten pounds would inform.

Thornhill had his web of useful men. One of these was Nugent at Messrs Buller & Co, Shipowners, a clerk who appreciated a few shillings extra. It was Nugent who let him know about the Brazil wood, worth nigh on ten pounds the piece, arrived on the *Rose Mary*.

So when Yates the foreman told him to go down to Horselydown, to the *Rose Mary* of Mr Buller's line, and bring a load of timber up the river to Three Cranes Wharf, he was ready. He made sure the moon would not rise that night until near dawn, and told Rob to stand ready to join him down at the *Rose Mary*.

The evening before, he took the empty lighter down with the tide to Horselydown, arriving there at midnight. He made the lighter fast to the side of the *Rose Mary* and lay down in it for a few hours' sleep before daylight, when he would load the timber and wait for the tide to take him up to Three Cranes Wharf.

So far, he was as innocent as the driven snow.

He enjoyed these nights on the river, the comforting sound of the water against the hull. The *Rose Mary* beside him was nothing more than another texture of blackness against the blackness of the sky, where the stars were blotted out by cloud.

A man with a clear conscience did not need to fear the dark.

He thought of Sal, tucked up in the bed with the child. She had come to him, that very morning, and told him that there was another on the way: another mouth to find food for. She had laughed at the way his eyes went straight to her belly. *It ain't showing yet, Will!* But had taken his hand and laid it on her pinny, over the place where his seed had planted itself, and smiled into his face.

She never asked too closely about where their money came from, was only pleased to have a loaf in the cupboard and clean milk for the child. She knew as well as he did that a lighterman who was too scrupulous was likely to starve. But he felt in her a turning-away from the truth of that, and he never shared with her those nights on the river when he fingered something or other that was not his own.

When day came there was no sign of Rob and he could not wait for him, so he had to hire a man called Barnes from the wharf, with hardly enough wit to know how to pick up the other end of a beam and lower it into the lighter. As he chivvied him, he grew angry with Rob, and with himself for thinking such a halfwit could remember his own name, let alone to meet him at the promised hour.

Mr Lucas came on board late in the morning to point and shout. By the time he got there, the bulk of the wood was already loaded onto the lighter, but Thornhill had not seen any Brazil timber, only deal, and was starting to think Nugent had been misinformed. He shouted up to Lucas, *We are just about full up, Mr Lucas, I take it there ain't no more to be got?* Lucas gave him a look, and held up his marking-hammer with a funny kind of smile. *Just a little more in the cabin,* he called down. *Six pieces of Brazil that I will put my mark on.*

Thornhill could feel an airiness in his body. It was the feeling he always had, no matter how many times he took the step outside of the law: a lightheaded mix of fear and need. But he made his face a rock so it showed nothing.

Lucas stood watching from above while Thornhill and Barnes

loaded the Brazil timber, four long planks and two shorter pieces. The lighter was already so full there was nowhere to put the Brazil other than on top of the rest. Even in its rough-dressed state, he could see how fine a timber it was, a rich red colour with a close-figured grain. As they put the shorter pieces in, Thornhill saw the marks Lucas had made on each piece: a little square hammered deep into each end.

For a moment he thought better of his plan. It was hardly an idea, just a trickle of cold water down the back of his collar. *He knows, do not do this.* His heart beat loose enough to shake his chest. He knew what this feeling was called: it was fear. But fear was not enough to stop anyone lifting objects from their owners. It was just part of a lighterman's life, like his wet feet. The problem was simple: fear did not pay the rent.

Lucas stood on the deck of the *Rose Mary* with his big hands on his big hips, watching each piece of timber onto the lighter. *I do not like that timber being uppermost, Thornhill,* he called down. *It is worth fifty pounds.* Thornhill stood in the lighter looking up at him. *Would you have us unload,* he said, *and lie it in the hold under the rest?* Lucas looked at him for a moment. *No,* he said. *But make sure no harm comes to it, man.* Thornhill squinted up into the brightness, where Lucas looked down at him. *Very good, Mr Lucas,* he called obligingly. *You can count on me.*

By three o'clock in the afternoon the lighter was loaded, but the tide was running out strongly so it was a matter of waiting. Thornhill had some food and sat on the load watching darkness fall. Around eleven o'clock he heard the change in the river's voice that meant slack water had arrived, the tide about to turn. He let go the lighter from the side of the ship and felt the flood tide carrying it upstream. He had only to guide with an oar.

He shot through the middle pier of London Bridge and

tended over towards the Middlesex bank. He could see nothing except a faint texture that showed him where the river was. By his speed under the bridge he judged the moment when he would come to Three Cranes Wharf, and swung the vessel around to where the shore must be, working her up into the tide until he was alongside the dock. The tide was running against the wooden dockside, but it was still too low to unload.

He could hear his skiff jerking on its painter at the end of the wharf where he had tied it up the day before. It was waiting to receive the Brazil wood. But until he set his hand to the timber, he was still an innocent man.

The watchman was in his little outhouse at the end of the wharf. Thornhill could see the tiny gleam of yellow light from the doorway. He would be tucked up tight in there with a drop of something to keep him warm.

Thornhill called softly as the lighter came alongside the wharf, *Rob, Rob are you there?* No one answered. He decided he must do it all himself, and was getting ready to leave the oars and spring forward to cast a line around the bollard, when there was Rob's voice in the darkness. *Will, here I am*, he whispered hoarsely. *Give us a cast on shore, man, for God's sake*, Thornhill called. He hurled the line up and by a miracle Rob got hold of it and fastened it, so the lighter rode the current quietly.

Thornhill climbed onto the wharf. *Damn your eyes, Rob,* he hissed. *Why ain't you come down to lend a hand with the lighter?* He could see it was his brother, but could not make him out and was spared the hangdog look on his silly face. *I come as soon as I could, Will,* he whined. *As God is my witness.* Trying not to shout in his exasperation Thornhill said, *Forget God, man, get yourself down and hand us up the stern sheet and be quick about it.*

He had just made the stern sheet fast to the bollard when he heard a sound beyond the lighter: a splash, the hollow wooden knocking of an oar against its pin. It crossed his mind, nothing more substantial than the shadow of a bird's wing out of the corner of his eye, that something was not right. He peered and strained into the rustling darkness but saw only its tantalising shifts and textures.

They had to unload the Brazil wood into the skiff almost by feel. They moved the timbers down as quietly as they could, scraping them over the gunwale of the lighter, feeling the skiff twist under the weight. He could sense Rob take the weight, then the hollow noise as he eased each piece down. The small sounds seemed thunderous.

They had moved the fourth piece when suddenly at the end of the lighter there was a commotion, a clattering and thumping, several pairs of feet in several pairs of boots, running along the lighter to where Thornhill and Rob stood holding the flitch of timber. *Thornhill!* Lucas's voice shouted. *Thornhill, you rogue!* In that moment all the dread he had been feeling rose up to swallow him. He should have listened! Should have listened to that cool little voice that had said, *This time they will get you.*

Lucas had something in his hand. Thornhill saw a glitter of metal and knew it to be the short hanger Mr Lucas carried with him everywhere. He heard it slice the air near him, the sound of the blade through the air filling him with panic. He retreated onto the skiff, stumbling on the timber, a helpless blind man. *For God's sake do not!* he heard himself call out, feeling his flesh cringe from the blade, but Lucas was shouting, *Come here you blackguard*, and Thornhill felt a hand clutching at his sleeve.

He jerked up his arm and freed it, felt hands fumbling at his collar, and stumbled along the skiff with Lucas following him, but he heard Lucas trip on the oars and crash full-length. He heard the grunt as the wind was knocked out of him, imagined that big striped belly squashed like a bladder. He got to the skiff, Rob already in it—slow, but quick enough when it came to saving his own skin—and undid the rope. As he pushed away from the lighter and began to row, he heard one of the pieces of timber slide off the gunwale into the water, sending the little boat rocking so they near capsized.

He was gasping with the fright of it, but also with a convulsion of the stomach that he recognised as having some relationship to laughing.

Rob seemed more aggrieved at the loss of his coat than the nearness of his escape, earnestly telling Thornhill, *My coat were there, my good thick coat!* And—each time remembering as if for the first time—*my wiper, how will I blow the snot, Will?* Then his phlegmy laugh came from out of the stern, his voice jumping. *My wiper, Will, think of that, Mr Lucas got my wiper for his very own.*

Rob's brain was a peculiar one, with pockets of sense in it like plums in a pudding.

He thought they were clean away, but there was Lucas's voice, roaring from the lighter, *Yates! Get them, man!* Turning around, Thornhill saw something moving on the shimmering blackness of the water: another skiff closing on them. He dug his oars in, so deep, so sudden, to turn the boat, that Rob was sent sprawling sideways.

As he had for the Doggett's race, Thornhill shrank his being down to nothing but his arms, his shoulders, his feet straining against the board. He rowed so hard he could feel his backside lifting off the thwart, and he thought he had left the skiff behind. A quick glance over his shoulder let him see the square bulk of the cathedral, and he made for Crawshay's Wharf just along from it, had got the oars shipped and was about to make fast when out of the splashing blackness another boat was upon him, and a big person scrambling from it into his own, making it rock and tilt, and there was Yates panting, *I have got you, I will shoot you if you attempt to escape.* Even in this moment, Thornhill wanted to laugh and say, *Coming the high horse sits odd with you, Yates.*

Rob let out a yell, the boat lurched, and there was an almighty splash. His brother had gone over the stern and no more was heard from him.

Thornhill could see the bulk of Yates, smell the pipe he always had about him. Yates was not a bad man, had been a lighterman himself. Over the years, plenty of things had stuck to his fingers. *For God's sake have mercy, Mr Yates,* Thornhill pleaded. *You know the consequence!* He saw the bulk hesitate and he tried again. *You known me ten years, Yates, would you have me swing?*

And while Yates stood, not advancing on him, saying nothing, Thornhill made a lunge aft, athwart of the boat, and sprang over the side. The tide was but half in, so the water was up to no more than his thighs, and there was Yates's skiff bobbing alongside. It was the work of an instant to feel his way to the knot, slip it free, and pull himself into the boat. As Thornhill pulled hard away there was no sound from Yates.

Yates might have been a merciful man, but Lucas was not. A man who knew himself destined to be Lord Mayor of London was not one to turn a blind eye to a work of thievery. There was a reward advertised, not for Rob whose body was found washed up at Mason's Stairs, but for himself, William Thornhill. Who was going to resist ten pounds?

So they came and found him where he was hiding out up the river at Acre Wharf, next to the flour mill.

~

In Newgate the people were packed tight in stone cells with hardly enough room on the dirty pallets to stretch out at night. The walls were blocks of fine-hewn stone, not a chink anywhere, of such a size they needed no mortar. Their mass alone was enough to lock them into place, and lock the people in behind them.

Sal had given up the room in Butler's Buildings and had joined Lizzie and Mary sewing shrouds. They all came to see him in the cell, pretending good cheer. Sal had brought Willie, holding fast to his little hand. He was four: old enough to be fright-ened at what he saw in Newgate, but young enough to be damaged by it. Thornhill loved to feel the child in his arms, against his chest, but told Sal not to bring him again, there was prison fever about.

They had brought such food as they could spare: a piece of bread and some splinters of dried herring. They watched while he took it. He could see the hunger in their eyes, and did his best to eat, to please them, but he could not seem to, his throat already closed up.

He tried not to think of their happy days. In Newgate that soft hopeful part of him was hardening over, becoming lifeless like stone or shell. It was a kind of mercy.

Sal took charge. She had worked it out. The thing that a man needed in Newgate, more than a loaf of bread and a blanket, was a story. There must always be a story, she insisted, no matter how red-handed a man was caught. And a man had to believe it himself, so that when he came to tell it, it felt like God's sworn truth.

He saw that she had gone to the heart of the matter. He had heard a boy in the yard saying over and over to himself, and to anyone who came near: *It is all a lie, it is all for the reward.* The boy tried it in different ways, with different emphasis, a child with broken front teeth who seemed little older than Willie. *It is all a damned lie, it is all for the damned reward.* He was like those actors Thornhill had rowed across the river. When the moment came, in the white glare of the limelight, the line would be there, having replaced all other thoughts by nothing more than repetition.

The story had to take on such conviction that bit by bit the fact of the event—in the boy's case, some business of stealing a piece of bacon from a shop—was replaced by another one, the way an oyster might grow over a rock. Then it became nothing so crude as a lie. A person could tell the new one, in all its vivid reality, with the wide eyes of someone who was speaking the truth.

A man had come up to you and given you the coat. You had found the piece of carpet on the road. A man had said he would give you a penny if you took the box to Gosport Street. As God was your witness, you were innocent.

Sal had already worked it out for him. He had made the lighter fast, but owing to the lowness of the tide he had left it, planning to come back at high water to unload. He had trusted the watchman further up the wharf to keep an eye on the timber, but while he was away some person unknown must have come up on the river side, without the watchman hearing, and removed it.

It was a sound story, with no gaps or leaks. He loved her for her wit in seeing it so clear, and giving it the words that made it the truth. *You will get out of this, Will*, she whispered, embracing him as she left. *They ain't going to get you, not if I got anything to do with it.*

Her love and her strength gave him heart, were a kind of wealth, he saw, that others did not have. When his wife and sisters had gone, he stood straighter, walked taller, looked the turnkeys in the eye. *I made the lighter fast, meaning to come back to her later.*

The next day word went round the yard that a man called William Biggs, accused of stealing two ducks, value twenty-five shillings, had that day told the court that he was as innocent of the crime as the child unborn, and had been acquitted. In Newgate Yard, with the murmured stories of injured innocence all around them, the idea caught on like cholera. *As innocent as the child unborn*, Thornhill heard the man next to him muttering. *I am a soldier, I had just come off duty, there was others in the house besides me, I am as innocent as the child unborn.*

He added it to his own story as he rehearsed it to himself. *I made the lighter fast meaning to come back later to unload, I am as innocent as the child unborn.*

~

The court of the Old Bailey was a bear-pit. Down in the well of the court there was a great curving table full of crow-like barristers in their black gowns and their grey periwigs, and standing humbly around them the mass of witnesses waiting to be called, and the ushers lounging against the panelling.

On the next layer up, the jury men sat along one wall, four by four, packed into dark-panelled pews, too far away to make out their faces in the dimness of this vast space. Opposite the judge, the witness was pinned into a little box with his back to the light coming in from the high windows.

Those tall white windows, full of light, were cousins to the ones at Christ Church. They showed, if Thornhill had doubted it, that the judge was gentry, the same way God was gentry.

Above the witnesses a mirror tipped the daylight from the window full onto their faces. By that cold dull light, that gave faces a metallic look, the judge and jury could peer into the soul of the person on the stand. Behind the witness there was another, smaller mirror, and a man in a periwig like the barristers' with an inkwell and a big ledger in front of him, in which he wrote down each word.

That was almost the worst of it, that anything anyone said, be it never so false or condemning, was there forever, with no margin of forgetfulness where human mercy might step in.

Way up near the ceiling were the public galleries, cut off from the court by a high wall of panelling and columns that held the restless public in behind them. He stared up, hoping to find Sal, but could only see a vague restless mass of people. Now and then an arm dropped down in front of the panelling or there was the flash of a shawl flung over a woman's shoulders. He saw a straw hat bent down over a head by means of a scarf tied under the chin. Sal had a hat she wore that way, and perhaps that tilt of the head was hers as she craned past others to see down into the court.

He heard a distant cry, a woman's voice. Was it calling, *Will! Will!* and was that her arm waving to him?

It was, he thought, and he loved her for it. As the prisoner at the bar he did not dare call back. That would be as bad as calling out in church. In any case, she was in the other world, the one he was leaving. She was dear to him, but down here he was on his own.

He stood up in the prisoner's dock, a high pedestal where he was on display as if naked to the whole court. His hands were tied hard behind his back, forcing him to bow his head. He kept trying to straighten up, to look his fate in the eye, but the pain in his neck forced him again to hunch. Up so high, he could feel the rising vapours of those below him in the court: all those bodies encased in their clothes, all those chests breathing in and out, and all those words, passing around through the air.

He was struck by the power of the words. There was nothing going on in the court but words, and the exact words, little puffs of air out of the mouth of a witness, would be the thing that saw him hanged or not.

It took him some time, when he was first pushed up onto his pedestal, to see the judge behind his carved bench: a tiny grey face, dwarfed by his full-bottomed wig, by the layers of his robes, by the lapping collar with the gold edging, until there was no trace of the human within.

~

Mr Knapp, the lawyer who had been assigned to speak for him, was a languid sort of a gent, and Thornhill held out no hope from that quarter, but Mr Knapp surprised him. Mr Lucas had said his piece, and then Knapp was speaking to him, in a weary sort of way, so that Thornhill did not at first realise he had found something of a chink: *I understand you, Mr Lucas, to have said it was a very dark night, and therefore the only opportunity that you had of knowing who was the man, was that it was the voice of Thornhill?*

But Mr Lucas saw where this was going and coughed into his fist before saying stiffly, *I knew him by his person, when I got to him*, and Mr Knapp still seemed to pay no attention, asking casually, *But you knew him only by his voice?*

A man with his sights set on the gold chain of office was not going to be confused by any half-asleep barrister and Lucas answered crisply, *I believed that the person I saw in motion was the prisoner, and when I got to him, I knew him to be the prisoner at the bar.*

Now Thornhill was fully listening, and for the darkness of the night he began to give the greatest thanks. Knapp set a little trap, saying, *That is, in other words, you knew Thornhill when you got up to him?* But Lucas coughed again, shifted, rubbed an eye, could see the problem advancing towards him. *I identified him by his voice repeatedly before*, he said impatiently. Mr Knapp shot back, giving him no time to think, *From that you were led to suppose it was Thornhill—you were not certain of it until you came up, and found that it was so?*

Lucas was too clever to be caught. He gripped the counter in front of him, sunlight falling across his shoulders and the eerie light of the mirror full on his face. When he spoke he seemed to be reading off the dust eddying in the shaft of sun. *I did not hear any voice at the time the wood was in motion. At that time, if I had been asked, I could not have sworn to the person of Thornhill.* He paused to pick his way between the words, then went on very steady and slow as if spelling something out for one of the Robs of this world: *I can now swear that one of the persons that I saw, when the wood was in motion, was Thornhill, that I could not then swear to. When I got near him, that person was Thornhill, and I never lost sight of him, because I saw the very person that was moving the wood was Thornhill.*

Even Mr Knapp could find no chink in that masonry of words.

When it was Yates's turn, Thornhill saw how unhappy he was. He kept glancing across the well of the court at him, squinting against the light from the mirror, his big white eyebrows moving up and down, his hands busy fiddling with the edge of the counter in front of him as if to fiddle away so much trouble.

Mr Knapp looked up at the far-off ceiling as he said, *You had no opportunity of observing the face of the man—it was much too black a night to observe countenances?* He was almost speaking to himself.

Yates began to smooth the counter as if stroking a dog. *It was, I allow,* he said. *I will speak by the voice, the shape and make of the man.*

And now Mr Knapp came to life, snapping out his words so Thornhill could see how Yates cringed. *What, speak to the shape and make of a man on a dark night?* Poor Yates began to bluster. *I do not say that I can,* he said, *unless I was particularly well acquainted with him.* His bushy eyebrows were a semaphore of

67

distress as he floundered on. *I do not mean to say directly I can, or cannot speak to the facts in this case.*

Down at the witness table in the well of the court, Mr Lucas stared up at him. Even from the prisoner's bar, Thornhill could see the beads of sweat appearing on Yates's domed forehead. Mr Knapp insisted, *It being a moonless night, you cannot make out that you knew him by shape and make?* Thornhill thought, are those little words, shape and make, going to be the difference between life and death?

Poor Yates, glancing from Lucas to Thornhill, began to mutter and stutter. *I should be sorry to say anything that is an untruth,* he said, but Mr Knapp had no mercy, and kept coming on. *That was a hasty speech, that you knew him by shape and make? You mean that you could not?* And now Yates was broken, uncertain of all his words, continually glancing at Mr Lucas. *I was in the act of closing with this man,* he mumbled. *It was impossible but I must know him from his speaking to me. I knew him by his voice.*

He glanced quickly at Thornhill. *I might have hastily spoke about his shape and make,* he said, and then stood stiff as a bit of wood with his hat squashed under his arm, the wan light from the mirror falling full on his face, furrowed with misery.

~

The moment where Thornhill was allowed to tell his story was upon him so abruptly that he found the words he had gone over with Sal had evaporated from his mind. He could only think of the start of them, saying *I tied up the lighter meaning to come back to her later,* and he knew there was more, but what was it?

He found himself staring at Mr Lucas as he blurted out, *Mr Lucas knows there is no lighter on the river can come to her,* but even as the words left his mouth he knew they had nothing to do with the case at hand, and he called out desperately, *I am as innocent as the child unborn*, but the words had no meaning after so much rehearsal.

In any case the judge, way up behind his bench, was not listening. He was shuffling papers together and leaning sideways while someone whispered in his ear. Lucas was not listening either, his hand feeling for the watch in his pocket. Thornhill saw the silver lid spring open, saw Lucas glance at the face of the watch, press it closed again, tweak a nostril with thumb and forefinger. His own words, which had sounded with such conviction in Newgate Yard, fell hollow and were swallowed up.

Now the judge was fiddling with the black cap, sitting it carelessly on the long grey wig so it hung over one ear. He began to speak, in a thin high voice that Thornhill could barely hear. Down in the body of the court one of the lounging ushers, a corpulent gent in a bulging dirty white waistcoat, caught sight of someone he knew across the room and made a mincing wave and a little smirk. A barrister fiddled with the grubby ruffles at his neck, another got out his snuff-box and offered it to his neighbour.

It seemed the court could scarcely be bothered to listen as William Thornhill, in the time between two heartbeats, was found guilty and sentenced to *be taken from this place and hanged by the neck until you are dead.*

He heard a cry, from the public gallery or from his own mouth he did not know. He wanted to call out, I beg your pardon, Your Worship, there has been some mistake, but now the turnkey was grabbing him by the upper arm, forcing him down the steps, and through the door into the tunnel that led back to Newgate. He turned his head towards the public gallery. Sal was up there somewhere, but invisible. Then he was back in the cell with the others, but without his story, stripped naked of his tale of injured innocence, stripped of everything but the knowledge that his moment of hope had been and gone, and left him now with nothing ahead but death.

~

Sal came to see him in the condemned cell. Even her footsteps on the bare wooden floor told him that she had not given up. Behind the carefree girl he had married there was another person, he saw now with some wonderment: no girl, but a woman. Her humour had not been extinguished, only darkened and thickened by this other thing that had always been there waiting to be needed: a stubborn intelligence as unyielding as a rock.

She had been making inquiries, she said. Had asked around, found out what a man did who was condemned to die. *It is letters, Will,* she told him. *You send letters up the line is how it works.* There was a chilly briskness to her, although he saw that she found it hard to meet his eye, as if afraid she would see something there to break her resolve. Despair, he was learning here, was as contagious as fever, and as deadly. *You got to get that creeping Jesus to write to Captain Watson,* she said. *No good me trying, I don't know them sorts of words.* She did not look into his face, but reached across the table and took his hand, squeezed it so hard he felt her bones. *Today, Will, not a minute later.*

He trusted her, and went to the man she meant, a man whose legs were twisted and wizened and who crept from cell to cell. If a person had any item of value about him that he was prepared to part with, this man would write any kind of begging letter he wished.

He gave the creeping cripple his thick woollen greatcoat. It was like cutting off an arm, for without it he would never live through a lighterman's winter again. But it was a good coat, worth a good letter. And he would never be a lighterman again, unless this man could write the letter that might get him out of this place.

70

When the cripple had done, he read it out to him.

It was as if written by Thornhill himself to Captain Watson, his regular from Chelsea Stairs, the only man of standing Thornhill knew. It told how sorry Thornhill was for what he had done, how it was the first offence, and how earnestly he prayed to God to be spared. It enumerated Thornhill's dependants, his idiot brother, his sisters all alone in the world, his helpless wife and babe, and another on the way in his wife's guiltless belly.

Thornhill held the paper in his hand, staring at the black loops and swirls of the cripple's clerkly hand, so different from Sal's careful letters. He could not make sense of any of them. To his eyes these were nothing more than marks such as a beetle might make, crawling through a puddle of porter spilt on a table. He despaired that his life depended on such flimsy things.

Miraculously, the letter spawned another. Captain Watson wrote his own letter up the line to a General Lockwood, who apparently had the ear of Mr Arthur Orr, who was by way of knowing Sir Erasmus Morton, who was second secretary to Lord Hawkesbury. Lord Hawkesbury was the end of the line. In his hands lay the power to reprieve, or not.

Good man that he was, Captain Watson had sent a copy of his letter to Sal. She tried, but could not decipher the fancy letters, so they got the cripple to read it out. He read fast, showing off how well he could do it: *Whereas William Thornhill convict bows and prays with humble submission depending on your Lordship's clemency and charity to spare his life, while he and his will ever pray that you and yours may ever flourish like the green bay tree that grows by the water, praying may the Sun of Joy shine round your head, and may the Pillow of Peace kiss your cheek and when the light of time makes you tired of earthly joys and curtains of death close the last sleep of human existence may the Angel of God attend you.*

And so on, so many flowery words Thornhill lost the thread of them. When the cripple had finished and crept away, they both sat in silence. Sal smoothed and smoothed at the edge of the thick paper, where it had got dog-eared. Thornhill thought she probably felt the same coldness at her heart that he did. It was impossible that the thick hempen rope could be unknotted by such persiflage as this. He feared that Captain Watson had not judged right. Why had he gone on about the Pillow of Peace when what was surely required was a speech of what an upstanding fine man he was, a reliable provider for his wife and child?

He and Sal nodded at each other and even found it in themselves to smile, but he could see she thought he was as good as dead. Her eyes slipped sideways as she spoke, as if he was becoming transparent, no longer a person in the world.

Sal was ailing, although she denied it. She had lost flesh and grown wan. Lizzie had got them a job of sheets to hem, two dozen, and Sal did them with Lizzie and Mary, but the price of thread had gone up and the price of hemming had gone down. There was a man wanted Willie for a sweep, needed a boy that size to send up the narrowest flues, but the boy cried with fear at the thought of those dark tubes. And now, Sal said, no more work was to be had. She had begged Mr Pritchard, but there were no sheets to be done, and Mr Pritchard had said there was no call for handkerchiefs neither.

There was a little silence between the two of them then, but then Sal cried out, *If no one is blowing their damn noses, are they snotting in the gutter then?* Her laugh sounded forced in the quiet room, but it broke the moment where they had both lain down under the burden of life. He made himself laugh too, and looked into her eyes. She took his hand again and did not look away.

She would have to go on the streets. They both knew that.

He looked at her with the eye of a customer and saw that she would have to brighten herself up, rouge her cheeks, curl her hair, set a brazen look on her face. For her sake, he forced the smile of a living man onto his mouth.

Sal had committed no crime, but she was sentenced, just as surely as he was.

~

One morning the turnkey came to the cell door and bawled out his name. Thornhill expected the worst and called out, *Not yet! Friday sennight they said!*

The turnkey looked at him, did not hurry to reply. *Do not piss yourself, Thornhill,* he said at last. *Listen, man.* He stood back for the clerk to come to the doorway and read from the piece of stiff paper in his hand, his voice barely audible: *Whereas William Thornhill was at a session holden in the Old Bailey in October last tried and convicted.*

He was gabbling as fast as he could, his duty only to read the words, not to make sure anyone could follow them. His scratchy voice could not penetrate the various noises of the room: the talking, the spitting, the coughing, the shuffle of wooden pattens on the flags. Thornhill pushed further forward and was in time to hear his crime, those familiar words that made him flinch inwardly every time he heard them: *Tried and convicted of stealing Brazil wood from a barge on the navigable River Thames and had sentence of death passed upon him for the same. We in consideration from favourable intercessions humbly represented unto us on his behalf are graciously pleased to extend our grace and mercy unto him.*

Not sure what he was hearing, Thornhill made himself go stony, one huge ear, to hear the next words: *And grant him our pardon for his said crime on condition of his being transported to* the Eastern Part of New South Wales for the term of his sentence, viz, for and during the term of his Natural Life.

There was more, but Thornhill had stopped listening. His hands and feet had gone very cold, his knees weak, but he had to make sure. *I am to live?* he asked, looking from one face to the other, and the turnkey shouted impatiently, *Yes mate, but if you would rather swing just say the word.* The clerk, shuffling out another piece of paper with a blob of sealing wax on it, said, *There is more,* and started to read again. *I am directed by Lord Hawkesbury to desire that you will permit…*He stopped and glanced at Thornhill quickly, then away, as if afraid that the glance of a condemned man might turn him to stone. *What is your wife's name?* he asked, but Thornhill felt that words, thoughts, knowledge of anything in the world except the fact that he was to live, had left him. What did his wife's name have to do with anything?

The turnkey was shouting now. *Your wife, man, what is your damn wife's name?* and Thornhill answered, feeling his stiff lips shaping the words, *Sal, Sarah Thornhill.* The clerk went on, *That you will permit Sarah Thornhill the wife of William Thornhill convict who is to be embarked on the Alexander transport, commander Captain Suckling, to have a passage with her husband in lieu of Mrs Henshall who has declined accepting that indulgence and also the infant of the said William and Sarah Thornhill.*

The turnkey snorted. *Meaning that your wife has the pleasure of a sea voyage along with you, Thornhill,* he shouted. *And may God have mercy on her soul!*

PART TWO

SYDNEY

It was a sad scrabbling place, this town of Sydney. The old hands called it The Camp, and in 1806 that was pretty much still what it was: a half-formed temporary sort of place.

Twenty years before it had been one of the hundreds of coves hidden within a great body of water as complicated as a many-fingered hand. One hot afternoon in the January of 1788, with big white birds screeching from the trees by the shore, a captain of the Royal Navy had sailed into that body of water and chosen a cove with a stream of fresh water and fingernail of beach. He had stepped out of the boat and caused the Union Jack to be hoisted on a spar leaning crookedly upright, and declared this place part of the extended territories of King George III, Sovereign of Great Britain, Defender of the Faith. Now it was called Sydney Cove, and it had only one purpose: to be a container for those condemned by His Majesty's courts.

On the September morning that the *Alexander* dropped its anchor in Sydney Cove, it took William Thornhill some time to see what was around him. The felons were brought up on deck but, after so long in the darkness of the hold, the light pouring out of the sky was like being struck in the face. Sharp points of brilliance winked up from water that glittered hard and bright. He squinted between his fingers, felt tears run hot down his face, blinked them away. For a moment he glimpsed things clear: the body of shining water on which the *Alexander* had come to rest, the folds of land all around, woolly with forest, blunt paws of it pushing out into the water. Near at hand a few blocky golden buildings lined the shore, their windows a glare of gold. They swam and blurred through the spears of light.

Shouting beat at his ears. A sun such as he had not imagined could exist was burning through the thin stuff of his slops. Now, on land, he was seasick again, feeling the ground swell under him, the sun hammering down on his skull, that wicked glinting off the water.

It was a relief to be sick, neatly, quietly, onto the planks of the wharf.

Out of this agony of light a woman appeared, calling his name and pushing through the crowd towards him. *Will!* she cried. *Over here, Will!* He turned to look. My wife, he thought. That is my wife Sal. But it was as if she was only a picture of his wife: after so many months he could not believe it was she, her very self.

He had time just to glimpse the boy beside her, pressed in against her leg, and the bundle of baby in the crook of her arm, when a man with a thick black beard was pushing her back with a stick. *Wait your turn you whore*, he shouted and clapped her with his open hand on the side of the head. Then she was swallowed up in the press of faces, their shouting mouth-holes black in the sun. *Thornhill! William Thornhill!* he heard through the muddle of noise. *I am Thornhill*, he called, hearing his voice cracked and small. The man with the beard grabbed at his arm and in the remorseless clarity of the light Thornhill saw how the beard around his mouth was full of breadcrumbs. From the list in his hand the man bawled, *William Thornhill to be assigned to Mrs Thornhill!* He was shouting so hard that crumbs fell out of his beard.

Sal stepped forward. *I am Mrs Thornhill*, she called above the din. Thornhill was stunned by the light and the noise, but he heard her voice clear through it all. *He is not assigned to me, he is my husband.* The man gave her a sardonic look. *He might be the husband but you are the master now, dearie,* he said. *Assigned, that is the same as bound over. Help yourself dearie, do what you fancy with him.*

The boy clutched a handful of Sal's skirt and stared up at his father, big-eyed with fear. This was Willie, five years old now, grown taller and skinnier. A nine-month voyage was a quarter of a lifetime for a lad so young. Thornhill could see that his child did not recognise the hunched stranger bending down to him.

The new baby had been born when the *Alexander* put in at Cape Town in July. Sal was lucky they were in port when the pains started. They let him see her afterwards, but only for a moment. *A boy, Will,* she whispered. *Richard? After my Da?* Then her white lips could manage no more words, only her hand pressing his had gone on speaking to him. A moment later they took him back to the men's quarters, and although he could sometimes hear the babies beyond the bulkhead, he had never known which might be his.

Now he did not need to strain to hear him. The baby's cries were sharp painful blows in his ear.

Will, she said, smiled, reached for his hand. *Will, it is us, remember?* He saw the crooked tooth he remembered, and the way her eyes changed shape around her smile. He tried out a smile in return. *Sal,* he started, but the word turned into a choked gasp like a sob.

~

His Majesty's Government issued Mrs Thornhill, master of the assigned convict William Thornhill, with a week's victuals, a blanket or two, and a hut up on the hillside behind the wharf. That was the extent of what His Majesty felt obliged to provide. The idea was, the servant William Thornhill would work for his master, in this case his wife, at whatever employment might be found. He was in all respects a slave, obliged to do his master's bidding. The felon would thus remain a prisoner, but the master would do the work of a guard. In the case of a family, it meant that the whole household would be able to support itself and come off the Government Stores.

His Majesty's mercy, saving so many from the noose, was made possible by this ingenious and thrifty scheme.

From that first afternoon, then, the Thornhills were on their own.

Steep and bony, bristling with slabs of rock, the hill where their hut had been pointed out to them was inhabited by humans as a cake might be by ants. A few lived in huts, but most had made dwellings beneath the overhanging rocks that stepped up the slope. Some had hung a bit of canvas up by way of wall, others had leaned a few boughs against the opening. The Thornhills' wattle-and-daub hut by contrast was grand, even though it provided no luxuries beyond the mud-caked walls and the floor of damp earth.

The three of them stood at the doorway looking in. None seemed in any hurry to enter. Little Willie had got his thumb into his mouth and stared glassily, avoiding Thornhill's glance. *Least it ain't a cave*, Sal said at last. He could hear the effort in her voice, a pitch too high. *Not a worry in the world*, he made himself say. The boy twisted his head to look up at him, then buried his face, thumb and all, into her skirts. *Snug as anything*. To him his words sounded as hollow as a man talking in a barrel.

The sun was slipping behind the ridge and damp air was beginning to shift down the hill. A man and a woman came along the hillside from another cave towards the Thornhill family. The man sported a huge matted beard but was otherwise quite bald, the woman had a sunk-in toothless mouth and a skirt that hung in shreds around her calves. Both their faces were dark with dirt and they staggered with drink. The man carried a smouldering stick, the woman a kettle. *Here*, the woman said. *We brung youse this, lovey, help youse out.*

Thornhill thought it was a joke, because the kettle had a wooden bottom. Laughed in the woman's face, but she did not laugh back. *Dig a hole*, she started. A hiccup that jerked her whole chest stopped her. *Light the fire. Round it.* She had to close her eyes from the force of the hiccups. *Good as gold*, she cried. Came right up to Thornhill to lay a hand along his arm, so he smelled her, rum and filth. *Good as fucking gold!*

The man was so drunk his eyeballs were swivelling around in his head. He shouted in a booming voice, as if the Thornhills were half a mile away, *Look out for the poxy savages, matey*, and laughed a gusty laugh full of rum. Then he grew serious and bent at the knees, staggering, to peer at Willie. *They's partial to a tasty bit of victuals like your boy there*. He bent to knead Willie's chubby cheek with his hard fingers, so the boy began to cry and the woman, still hiccupping, dragged the man away.

They cooked the rags of salt pork on sticks in the fire and laid them out on pieces of bark by way of plates. Having no pannikins, they drank the tea that the woman had given them straight out of the spout. The bread fell apart in their hands but they picked up the crumbs from the ground and ate them, feeling grains of dirt crunching between their teeth.

The baby, sucking noisily on Sal's tit, was the only Thornhill to finish the meal with a full belly.

They sat on the ground outside the hut in the dusk, looking down at the place they had come to. From up here on the hillside the settlement was laid out plain. It was a raw scraped little place. There were a few rutted streets, either side of the stream threading its way down to the beach, but beyond them the buildings were connected by rough tracks like animals' runs, as kinked among the rocks and trees as the trees themselves. Down by the water was the wharf, and a few grand structures of brick and stone pressed in along the shore. But away from the water the buildings unravelled into hovels of bark or daub, nothing more than sticks plastered together with mud, set in mean yards enclosed by brush-wood fences. Hogs rolled in the pale mud beside the stream. A child naked but for a clout of rag between its legs stood watching a pack of dogs snapping at a hen with its chicks. A man dug in a patch of ground behind a fence leaning all skewiff.

It all had an odd unattached look, the bits of ground cut up into squares in this big loose landscape, a broken-off chip of England resting on the surface of the place.

Beyond was mile after mile of the woolly forest. It was more grey than green, tucking itself around the ridges and valleys in every direction, uniform as fabric, holding the body of water among its folds.

Having never seen anywhere else, Thornhill had imagined that all the world was the same as London, give or take a few parrots and palm trees. How could air, water, dirt and rocks fashion themselves to become so outlandish? This place was like nothing he had ever seen.

For every one of the years of his life, this bay had been here, filling its shape in the land. He had laboured like a mole, head down, in the darkness and dirt of London, and all the time this tree shifting its leathery leaves above him had been quietly breathing, quietly growing. Seasons of sun and heat, seasons of wind and rain, had come and gone, all unknown to him. This place had been here long before him. It would go on sighing and breathing and being itself after he had gone, the land lapping on and on, watching, waiting, getting on with its own life.

Down below Thornhill could see the *Alexander*. With a sick lurch he remembered the hammock, the knot in the beam above his head, an always-open eye watching him while he woke or slept.

Night after night, lying there, he had thought of Sal until the memory of her had become stale. But that was her hip pressed in against him now. That was her thigh stretched out alongside his. If it were not for Willie, sitting with his knees drawn up to his chin, making himself small, he would be able to turn and see her eyes, her lips, feel her warmth against him as they embraced.

Up the hill behind them, a bird repeated a sad regretful cry, *Ah, ah, ah.* But it was the only sad thing in the whole world.

~

It was hard to leave the fire and go into the cheerless hut. Thornhill went in first with a burning stick to light the way, but it only flamed for a moment, then choked them with the smoke, so he threw it outside. They spread the blanket out by feel and laid the baby down on it. He gave a sigh as if the ground underneath him was a feather bed, and was asleep at once.

At first Willie could not be got to lie down beside the baby, although he was exhausted, close to tears, his voice gone high and querulous. Thornhill had hoped that he and Sal would be able to go back to the fire and talk, stitching up the nine-month's gap in their lives, but the only way Willie would go to sleep was with Sal beside him, so the three of them lay down side by side. Sal had the last edge of the blanket. Thornhill was on bare dirt, listening for Willie to become quiet.

At last he felt Sal shift against him. *He's gone off, Will,* she whispered. *Poor little bugger.*

83

They had not touched, other than that touch of leg against leg, up till now. He felt a kind of shyness: Sal had had her own voyage, invisible on the other side of the bulkhead, and who knows where she had arrived?

He thought she might be feeling the same. Her shoulder pressed against his and her leg was lining itself up alongside his, but diffidently, as if by accident. He could feel the warmth of her, her flesh and skin. He felt her hands moving over his chest and up to his face, working to remember the husband she knew.

Thank you Mrs Henshall for declining the indulgence, she cried, trying to whisper but blurting it out on a laugh, and in that moment she was with him again, that cheeky girl, his Sal, finding poor Susannah Wood funny. He laid a hand along her thigh, turned to her so he could dimly see her face, that he loved so well. He knew that she was smiling.

And Mrs Thornhill, he said. *I got to thank her too, pet.* Her fingers threaded themselves into his and squeezed hard. He heard that she was crying: but smiling too, crying and smiling both at once. *Will*, she whispered, and tried to say more, but the touch of their hands was all the words they needed.

~

The first morning, Thornhill wondered if the black man he had confronted in the darkness had been only a dream. By daylight, the memory of their conversation—*Be off! Be off!*—was hard to believe.

It was easier to turn to the familiar, this speck of England laid out within the forest. Sydney looked foreign, but in the ways that mattered to the Thornhills it was the Thames all over again. It had no means of surviving except for the thread that bound it to Home. The authorities hoped for crops and flocks eventually, but in the meantime the settlement turned inwards, towards the ships that brought the necessities of life. Between the wharf and these ships full of flour and pease, nails and bonnets, brandy and rum, the boats of the watermen plied backwards and forwards just as they had done on the Thames.

Thornhill seemed to have been pulling on an oar all his life. It made little difference whether the water on which he did it was called the Thames or Sydney Cove.

He worked for many masters but in particular for Mr King, who had built one of the stone storehouses that had floated in Thornhill's vision that first day. Alexander King was a tidy fellow with tiny ears flat against his head and a dimple in his chin big enough to lose a boot in. He was a cheerful sort of man who took satisfaction in amusing people, and Thornhill always obliged. His laughter was all the more sincere for knowing that the joke was on Mr King.

Mr King had a finger in many pies, but the one of immediate interest to Thornhill concerned certain casks, containing certain fluids precious in the colony, which Mr King had caused to be brought on ships from Madras, from Calcutta, from the Indies. Mr King would come down in the morning, stand on the wharf in the sun and, with a list in his hand, punctiliously count the casks on their way to the Customs men: so many of Jamaican rum, so many of French brandy, so much Ceylonese gin. Paid up without a murmur, smiling as he did it, because he knew that other casks, not appearing on his list, were being looked after by night. That was Thornhill's job: privily to convey those casks from the ships to a bay around the point from the settlement, where they were safe from the grasping hand of the Master of Customs.

You will get your share, Thornhill, King told him, smiling his calm smile, the smile of a flourishing man. *You will find it better than coin of the realm.* Thornhill had no concerns about not getting his share. *You may rely on me, Mr King*, he said, and they shook hands on it.

Mr King was a happy man, and did not grieve about the tiny splined holes under the hoops, and the gimlet in Thornhill's pocket. He did not grieve because he did not know, tucked up safe in his feather-bed while Thornhill was busy in the dark.

~

Morning and evening the Government chain gangs clanked and shuffled to and from the split-timber barracks where their hammocks were packed in so close together the convicts became part of each other's dreams.

Without Sal, Thornhill would have been assigned to one of those gangs. Failing that, to some settler who, in exchange for victuals and a suit of slops once a year, could do with him pretty much as he pleased. A man could be lucky, and be assigned to some master of kindly stamp who would feed and clothe his convicts properly and at the end of a year let them apply for a ticket of leave. But for plenty of masters the charm of having men obliged to work for nothing was irresistible. Those masters would make sure their servants were accused of some mis-demeanour or other before the year was out, so they would never get their ticket.

The ticket of leave was a peculiarity of New South Wales. Here, three-quarters of a year away from the fields of wheat and sheep in England, the working of the land to produce food was urgent. The authorities had realised that if the place was ever to sustain itself, it would be by free labour and not the reluctant time-serving of felons. The ticket was a way of making men free enough to benefit from their own sweat but not free enough to stop being prisoners.

As little as a twelvemonth after arriving, a convict could apply for his ticket, and with that safe in his pocket he could walk about as free as any Legitimate. He could sell his labour to anyone he chose, or take up a piece of land and work for no one but himself. The only limit to his freedom was that he could not leave the colony. For folk who had thought to die an ugly death, that seemed a light enough fetter.

But for the next twelve months, until he could apply for his ticket, Thornhill would have Sal as his master. It made a good joke between them. In the nights, on a pile of the fern the old hands called bungwall that was covered with a piece of canvas, he would turn to her. *I had best call you Mrs Thornhill, madam*, he said, and squeezed her body, that he had felt in his imagination for those months at sea, and never tired of having now under his hands. *Yes, Mrs Thornhill. No, Mrs Thornhill. At your service, Mrs Thornhill.* Many things in this place were bewildering, but the feel of her body was still the thing he knew best in all the world. Sal moved closer and the fern beneath the canvas shifted too, like a restless creature in the bed with them. *Why Thornhill*, she whispered. *My good man. Let me think now, how can you service me?*

~

The place ran on rum the way a horse ran on oats. Rum was the currency of all exchanges, there being little coin. As well, rum promised consolation for the fact that everyone in the colony might as well be on the moon.

A man could hardly take a step in the settlement without coming to one of the open-sided shelters, nothing more than a roof of bark held up with a few lopped saplings driven into the dirt and a counter of wattle-lathes, where rum could be got at any hour. Men sprawled on upturned barrels with their heads on the counter, far gone but still clutching a pannikin so tight

87

their knuckles were white, and behind the counter thin-faced fellows with sunken cheeks stared blankly at their world.

What with the rum Mr King knew about, and the rum he did not, the Thornhill household soon moved into another hut down by the stream. It was made mostly of mud, but bigger than the first, and it had the luxury of a stone fireplace and a sod-lined bark chimney. The rain tended to come in through the roof, also of bark, but they reminded each other of how superior it was to the room in Butler's Buildings, especially in respect of ventilation.

It was Sal's idea to make the hut into two rooms with a bit of canvas suspended from the rafters, and to set up a grog-stall in one of them. She proved canny at the inn-keeping game, using the charm of her smile to jolly the customers along while she poured another tot of Mr King's Jamaica. Willie ran about on the muddy track outside, and the baby Dick lay quietly in his cradle.

At the end of each week Sal would count up the takings, from Thornhill's work on the water and from her own selling liquor, and hide them away in a box under the bedding. Then they would get the children to sleep in their corner. Thornhill would fill his pipe and pour them a good tot of Mr King's best French brandy—the very same that the Governor enjoyed in his grand house on the hill—and they would take their ease on the bungwall, their feet resting on the lump made by the box of coins.

One of the pleasures of those murmured times was telling each other about their future. A person who was willing to work, and who did not piss it all up against the wall, could make good in no time: they saw that all around them. Captain Suckling, once commander of the *Alexander*, was one such. In London, Suckling was nothing but one more hard-faced sea captain with the toes sticking out of his boots, but he had got himself land here and swaggered around the place now in a silver-buttoned waistcoat. He had filled out, his face shiny with good living, clean-shaven to a purple gleam.

Even men who had started out as felons could work their way through the system—from assignment to ticket of leave to pardon—within a few years. He saw them standing on the wharfs, looking about them as if they owned the place: men no better than he was, who had got their freedom and made their pile, and now could look anyone in the eye.

By and by, the Thornhills told themselves, they would have enough put aside to go back to London. They would get a little neat house in the Borough, the twin of the one in Swan Lane except that they would be sure they owned the freehold. Out on the river, there would be a wherry sound as a pippin tied at the wharf, and a good strong prentice to row it. They would take their ease by the fire in a warm parlour, a stuffed armchair cushioning their bones and a girl to bring in the coals. *My word, Will*, Sal would whisper, curling herself in against him, *I can just about smell the butter on the toasted muffins she'll have fetched us!*

Two wherries, why not, and a couple of prentices.

One of them paisley shawls from India, Sal whispered. *And never do my own washing ever again.*

Thornhill could see himself taking his ease in the Anchor with a plate of whitebait and a tankard of best bitter, and the kind of look about him that came from having gold put away safe in the bank. Men in a smaller way would greet him as he strolled down to the river with his pipe after lunch. *Good-day Mr Thornhill! Fine day Mr Thornhill!* He knew he would make a good rich man, having had so much practice as a poor one.

A little luck, a deal of hard work: with those, nothing could stop them.

~

Out on Sydney Cove pulling an oar, Thornhill could imagine himself back on the Thames, but Sal could never for a moment stop seeing the differences between that place and this. She was astonished every time at the rain, no gentle drizzle that misted everything over soft and grey, but lightning and thunder loud as cannon-fire, and water hurling itself down hard out of the sky, trying to make holes in the ground. *By God, Will,* she would say, *have you ever seen anything like it?* and by the livid shocks of lightning he would see her eyes wide, as if at a circus where some trick was being performed.

Their hut swarmed with creatures they had never seen before: bold lizards that eyed them unblinkingly, sticky black flies, lines of ants that could reduce a lump of sugar to nothing in a night, mosquitoes that could sting through cloth, creatures along the lines of a bedbug that buried their heads in skin and swelled with human blood. Sal learned from their neighbours how to deal with them, setting the legs of the table in dishes of water against the ants, hanging switches of pungent leaves at the doorway to discourage the flies. Against the blood-suckers and the nits she cut the children's hair. Having no scissors, she used the knife so Willie's ears stuck cruelly out of his close-cropped head, the knife-hacked hair standing up in tufts. With his thatch of feathery hair gone, Dick's neck looked as fragile as a twig.

She was inclined to take it personally about the trees, wondering aloud that they did not know enough to be green, the way a tree should be, but a washed-out silvery grey so they always looked half dead. Nor were they a proper shape, oak shape or elm shape, but were tortured formless things, holding out sprays of leaves on the ends of bare spindly branches that gave no more protection from the sun than shifting veils of shadow.

Instead of dropping their leaves they cast off their bark so it dangled among the branches like dirty rags. In every direction that the eye travelled from the settlement all it could see were the immense bulges and distances of that grey-green forest. There was something about its tangle that seemed to make the eye blind, searching for pattern and finding none. It was exhausting to look at: different everywhere and yet everywhere the same.

When the hot weather came—confusingly, at Christmas—it was like no hot weather they had ever known. The sun rose up into a sky wan with heat and hung there pouring brassy light down on everything through the whole endless day, a burden on the shoulders, until it slipped behind the mountains to the west. There were no slow twilit evenings. Darkness came down sudden and absolute.

Everything they had owned in London had been pawned, or sold, or stolen during the voyage. Even his old leather hat, and Sal's good blue shawl that her father had given her—even those had gone. But there was one thing she had brought from London that became more dear to her than any of those other objects because it was the one that remained to her: a broken piece of clay roof-tile that she had found in the sand by Pickle Herring Stairs the morning of her last day in London. It was worn and rounded from the tides of years, but the bulge along the edge could still be seen where the clay had been pushed into a straight line, and the hole where it had been tied on to the batten. The hole was not quite round, and its inner edge retained the grooves where a stick had been jabbed through the damp clay.

I'll take it back to Pickle Herring Stairs by and by, she said, rubbing her thumb over its smoothness. *Right back where it come from.* The thing was like a promise, that London was still there, on the other side of the world, and she would be there too one day.

To everyone else, the grog-shop was nothing more than Thornhill's, but she gave it a name: the Sign of the Pickle Herring, just for the pleasure of hearing the words in her mouth.

Thornhill noticed that Sal never ventured beyond the few streets of the township, dusty and muddy by turns. He assured her that even the Governor's lady took the air down along the point, where the forest was not too thick, and sat on a rock there watching the sun go down, and that if she were to go with him along the track to the lighthouse at South Head, she would find it worth the walk to see the way the ocean flung itself against the great cliffs of blind stone. She went with him once or twice as far as the Governor's garden, leaning on his arm like a lady with her squire, but he knew that it was only to please him. On the top of that small rise she turned away from the wild forest and looked back down the hill at the settlement.

Where she liked best to be was down at Sydney Cove. He would see her sitting on the public wharf there, her legs hanging over the side, Willie running about on the strip of sand and Dick in her lap, staring at the ships moored out in the bay. He would row out to one of the ships, load up the lighter, and row back to the Customs Wharf, and she would still be there, the hair blowing across her face in the afternoon sea breeze.

The ships anchored in the port were the end of the long string that joined this place with the one they had left behind. What Sal saw as she stared out at the *Osprey* or the *Jupiter* was herself climbing on board and turning her back forever on Sydney Cove, getting the bit of roof-tile out of her pocket ready to put back on the sand at Pickle Herring Stairs.

~

The black natives of the place seemed to come in two sorts. The visible ones were those who lived in the settlement. There was a man who hung about the Thornhills' hut, so black his skin swallowed the sunlight. They called him Scabby Bill because his face had been mauled by the smallpox. More than once Thornhill went out of the hut at night on a call of nature and found him near the door: a piece of the darkness moving as if the night itself was standing up to take hold of him. In that moment he was not just Scabby Bill who whined all day for a bit of bread. Thornhill felt a quick pulse of fright, then the man turned away and was gone.

In the morning Scabby Bill could be found sleeping up against the back wall as if he owned it, collapsed into angles, one long skinny leg sticking out, his entire naked black body on full view except for the once-pink bonnet on his head, sitting on black hair frizzed as if singed, a tattered ribbon hanging down over one ear, one hand closed around a silk fan gone to shreds, his eyes nearly closed, singing and chuckling and frowning by turns. When he woke he coughed in long spasms the way Thornhill remembered his father having done before he died.

Yet he was still a fine figure. The sunlight fell on the crags and slopes of his face, the eyes cast into deep shadow beneath the ridge of brow. The creases beside his mouth could have been carved in stone. On his muscular shoulders and chest were rows of scars.

This was a town of scars. On board the *Alexander*, Thornhill had once seen Daniel Ellison flogged, after he had forgot himself so far as to raise his hand to a guard. All the male convicts had been brought on deck to witness his punishment. Later Thornhill watched over weeks as the wounds thickened into lumps, the skin slowly closing.

On a lag's back the point about the scars was the pain that had been inflicted, and the way they marked a man to his dying day. The scars on Scabby Bill's chest were different. It seemed that the point was not so much the pain as the scars themselves. Unlike the net of crisscross weals on Daniel Ellison's back, they were carefully drawn. Each scar lined up neat next to its neighbour, a language of skin. It was like the letters Sal had shown him, bold on the white face of the paper.

At times during the day Scabby Bill would appear in the doorway, a black silhouette against the sun, calling, *Missus, Missus*. The first time she saw him there, Sal blurted out a high embarrassed laugh, and turned away from his nakedness. Thornhill saw the colour flood into her face—he had never stood before her naked—and smiled to see that cheeky wife of his reduced to confusion by a shameless black man.

But like everything else that was peculiar here, Scabby Bill's nakedness soon became ordinary. She grew used to him calling at her, and would tear a bit off the loaf to give him.

He would take his crust and go and she would say, *Thank God, Scabby Bill has buggered off*. She did not seem to fear him: he was the same as the ants or the flies, a hazard of the place that had to be dealt with. Every time he left, she was confident that it was for good. *He's gone off to die, Will*, she would say. *Taken his bleeding cough and gone under a bush somewhere*.

He saw that she understood it as a transaction. In exchange for a crust of bread he would leave them be. But later they always found him back again, leaning up against the wall.

Scabby Bill accepted crusts, but what he preferred was a sup of rum. Liquor seemed to act on him with astonishing power. Thornhill envied him, the way it went to his head so quick, so entire. *If them others got legless so quick we'd be out of business*, Sal said. A white man might have to be coaxed along to empty his pockets before the world seemed a friendly place to him, but Scabby Bill needed hardly a mouthful.

It turned out that Scabby Bill was good for business, because for the promise of rum he could be got to dance. Everyone liked to watch him gather the sticks of his limbs together and get to his feet, stamping into the dirt, thudding so the dust flew up, staggering and calling out, pointing his ragged silk fan at his audience, droning through his teeth to himself. Men came from all the streets around, cheered to watch this black insect of a man capering before them, a person lower in the order of things even than they were.

~

The other sort of native was the kind that Thornhill had met on that first night, when they been on the very edge of civilisation. This sort of native was invisible to those like Sal who confined themselves to the township. They lived in the forest and in the bays where settlement had not yet reached, and melted away if any of the new arrivals tried to come close. Even in the few months Thornhill had seen the settlement grow, he had watched how those hidden ones retreated with each new patch of cleared land.

They wandered about, naked as worms, sheltering under an overhang of rock or a sheet of bark. Their dwellings were no more substantial than those of a butterfly resting on a leaf. They caught their feeds of fish, gathered a few oysters, killed a possum or two, then moved on. The most Thornhill ever saw was a silhouette stalking along a ridge, or bending over with a fishing spear poised to strike through the water. He might see the splinter of a canoe, fragile as a dead leaf against the dazzle of the sun on the water, with a figure sitting in it, knees drawn up to its shoulders, or a twist of blue smoke rising from some hidden place in the forest. But the canoe had always gone by the time he rowed over to it, and the smoke vanished when he looked at it too closely.

During the day, if a person kept to the settlement and did not look about himself too hard, he would see no one out there in the tangled landscape. He might even imagine that there was no one there at all. But at night, a man out in a boat on Port Jackson saw the campfires everywhere, winking among the trees. Sometimes the breeze brought the sound of their singing, a high hard dirge, and the rhythmic clapping of sticks.

There were no signs that the blacks felt the place belonged to them. They had no fences that said *this is mine*. No house that said, *this is our home*. There were no fields or flocks that said, *we have put the labour of our hands into this place*.

But sometimes men were speared. Word would go round the settlement: that so-and-so lay at this moment in the hospital with the spear still in him and the doctor shaking his head. That another had got one in the neck so the life had pumped out of him in a minute and left him as white as a piece of veal.

Thornhill never spoke of those spearings to Sal, but she heard of them from their neighbours, and he had found her more than once poring over the smudged pages of the *Sydney Gazette*, her finger under the words, mouthing them out to herself. *They got him just along the way here*, she said without looking at him. *Just around in the bay*.

But there was no point dwelling on the spears of the blacks. They were like the snakes or the spiders, not something that could be guarded against. He reminded her that even in London a man might be killed for the contents of his pocketbook. He meant it as a kind of reassurance, but Sal went silent. He came to dread seeing the *Gazette* spread out on the table.

Whatever he said to Sal, he was glad to spend his days out on the water. On land he was always within range of a spear.

~

Down in Sydney Cove, working for Mr King, Thornhill met more than one old friend from the Thames, among them Thomas Blackwood. The false bottom to Blackwood's *River Queen* had done him proud until the day someone had blabbed. He had been condemned to death, and then to life.

Blackwood was a big man, bigger even than Thornhill, with a lighterman's brawny calves and arms. He had a kind of rough dignity about him, a closed-in quality, like a bag drawn up tight around its contents. He ran deep and silent, his face always turned away, his eyes always elsewhere. His few words were broken by something like a stammer.

It was not polite, here in this township of men and women with histories, to inquire too closely, but he asked Thornhill straight out one day, what had brought him to New South Wales. And watched him narrowly as he told the tale of the Brazil wood. *Somebody blown the gab on you*, Blackwood said with finality. *Lucas don't go on the river at night for his health.* After a while he said, *A bugger blown the gab on me too. Had his eye on the reward.* He laughed a hard laugh with no mirth in it. *My word but the maggot is sorry now*, he said. *Feeding the fishes at Gravesend for his pains.*

Blackwood did not have the appearance of a man bowed down by his fate. On the contrary, he was doing well for himself. He had got his pardon and had a boat of his own now. It was another *Queen*, a sea-going sloop with no need of a false bottom, because the passage-trade between Sydney and Green Hills was enough to bring a man a legitimate living.

The Green Hills were a fertile stretch of country on a river fifty miles inland, the best place that anyone had got food to grow in this sandy land. A rough track ran there from Sydney, but absconders and blacks hid in the forest on either side, waiting for a man with a full cart. The better way to get crops to market was by the river, sailing down its length until it met the sea, and then beating down the coast the thirty miles to Port Jackson.

Thornhill had noticed that Blackwood enjoyed giving the river its name: the Oxborough, it sounded like. There was always a little wry twist to the word in his mouth, as if there was something funny in it. Then he heard it again: Hawkesbury, and got the joke. Blackwood also owed his life to Lord Hawkesbury, but did not love him any the more for that. *A fine deep river, plenty of water*, he said. He seemed to like the idea of Lord Hawkesbury in his own river, his eyes popping and the bubbles rising.

The other good joke about the river was that a lighterman might get rich there, and for once, a lighterman had a better chance at riches than gentry. Everyone in the colony knew that the Hawkesbury was the place to make your pile—either by farming its fertile land or by trading the grain of those who did— but not everyone had what it took. It needed a man with a strong boat to weather those thirty miles of ocean. It took a taste for adventure, too: the Hawkesbury was almost as remote from Sydney as Sydney was from London. If a man got into difficulties on its unmapped reaches, he was on his own. Most of all, making money out of the Hawkesbury took a man with a taste for danger, because it was there that the blacks were most numerous and most warlike. They gathered by the hundred, it was said, and descended on the lonely huts of the farmers. Tales came back of men speared, their huts robbed, their fields burned. The *Gazette* had a handy expression that covered all the things the blacks did, and suggested others: *outrages and depredations*. Not a month went by without some new outrage or depredation.

But Blackwood did not read, and when Thornhill mentioned the outrages, he said nothing. It seemed that Blackwood had arrived at some kind of accommodation with the river, but it was private, and he would not be drawn on it.

Thornhill watched the *Queen* sail away down Port Jackson with Blackwood at the tiller, his convict servant trimming the sail, and a month later they would be back again, with a hold full of wheat and pumpkins, and nothing to say about where they had been or what they had done.

~

At the end of a twelvemonth Thornhill applied for his ticket. It was a simple enough thing: the master vouched for his servant's good character, then the servant stood at the counter in the superintendent's hut and watched while the clerk turned to the page in the ledger in which his name was written. *Thornhill William Alexander transport*, the clerk said, scratching with his nib in one of the columns. *Ticket of leave, October the fourteenth, 1807.*

The ticket itself was just a slip of paper with words printed smudgily on it, but it was more precious than any coin. Sal wrapped it in a scrap of calico and put it away in the moneybox. *Off you go, Thornhill*, she said. *Your master set you free, why are you still here?* and even Willie, watching from the doorway, saw the joke of it.

No sooner had Dick started feeding himself than Sal got with child again. This new Thornhill, James, was born in the March of 1808. Perhaps it was the oppressive damp heat draining Sal's strength, but he was a sickly baby, pale and waxy, staring out of dark-rimmed eyes, with bony limbs and a tadpole-belly. In his heart Thornhill said goodbye to the lad, did not even think of him by name.

James—Bub, as they called him—wore Sal out with his fretting all night. Half asleep she rocked him in her arms until he slept and she lay down, but then the child would start up again with his jerky crying and wake Willie and Dick too. She stood rocking Bub, getting a dipper of water for Willie, singing a little song to soothe Dick, and in the morning her eyes were red as she got them their bread and tea. Thornhill saw that she was prepared to wear herself away to nothing for her children. He remembered a bitch in Frying Pan Alley that had done the same, letting her pups suck the life out of her until she lay down one day and could not get up again.

~

It was three years now since the Thornhills had arrived with nothing, and Thornhill was proud of the fact that his family could eat meat three times a week and always had a loaf in the cupboard. Working for Mr King had turned into a good thing.

Willie and Dick were growing into fine strong lads, and if Bub planned to die, it was not because his father failed to supply his wants. Christmas Night, 1808, Thornhill and Sal toasted each other with a bottle of Mr King's madeira that later had them groaning into each other's ears like newlyweds.

It was not too long before Thornhill more than once began to catch Mr King looking sideways at him. He had taken on another clerk, one who was more fastidious about his lists, and did not respond to hints about benefits that might come to people who knew how to turn a blind eye.

Thornhill had heard about a place to the south where felons were sent who committed offences in the colony, a place of punishment within punishment. It was called Van Diemen's Land, and the tales of what went on there made the blood run cold.

It seemed to Thornhill that it might be time to move on. He had not listened to the little voice that tried to warn him that night at Three Cranes Wharf. This time he would listen.

It surprised him that Sal was in agreement. *We best make sure them boys have got their father*, she said, holding Bub up to her shoulder to quiet his grizzling. *Thank you Mr King, you done us proud, but we best call it a day.*

Not long after, Thornhill saw the *Queen* sailing awkwardly up to the wharf with Blackwood alone in it. The story was that on the way back from Green Hills his convict servant had decided to anticipate Christmas cheer by a few weeks, and fallen overboard with a skinful of rum. In the treacherous currents of the Hawkesbury he had sunk without a cry. Blackwood was doing no one favours, but needed a man handy with a boat and willing to venture beyond the safety of the township.

Thornhill did not hesitate. Working for Blackwood might not keep a man in French brandy, but it would save him from Van Diemen's Land.

There was another thing. He was discovering in himself a passion to see this place, this Hawkesbury that everyone spoke about but few had seen.

~

Thornhill had gone west up Port Jackson on the *Rose Hill Packet* a few times, and in Mr King's boat he had explored many of its coves. But when Blackwood put the tiller over hard coming out of Sydney Cove and pointed the *Queen* due east, the familiar was soon left behind. They passed the island called Pinchgut, once a prison, and Garden Island, where they could see a man chipping away at rows of something leafy. After that there was no more sign of settlement, only pale loops of beaches and sombre forest.

As they neared the Heads, where the *Alexander* had sailed in three years before, the *Queen* began to tip in a heavy swell, and further out Thornhill could see the water black with wind. *Got a nice blow*, Blackwood called. *For your first time.* Thornhill glanced back at where Blackwood stood riding the movement of the boat, the tiller in his hand. He did not remember ever having seen Blackwood grin before.

Nothing had equipped Thornhill for what greeted him as

they passed between the headlands. Blasts of wind set the *Queen* bucking. He could feel them tugging at the roots of his hair, the noise bursting in his ears. It was January, high summer, but the wind came straight off the ice far to the south.

The glittering expanse of the ocean rose into stately swells that had taken half the globe to build their bulk. They rose up steeply, streaked with white foam, and shredded along the ridges into teeth of broken white water. The wind caught at the rags of foam and sent them flying straight out over the surface.

Riding those majestic swells, Thornhill could feel the boat being picked up, pushed forward and dropped. Spray from the bow reared up slowly, burst, fell back. It seemed leisurely, even playful, until it smashed down hard enough to kill. The wave passed underneath and moved on indifferently, its back a smooth gleaming bulge as it continued towards the land.

He tasted the salt on his lips, realised he was frightened.

After half a day of this, the wind swung round to the nor'-east so they had to beat against it, long zigzags out and back through the ocean. On each tack the boat heeled and Thornhill tensed himself for the moment it would tip over. Always off to the west was that rim of land, with threads of smoke rising here and there and crescents of golden beaches, one after the other, between sombre headlands.

Blackwood pointed and said, *In there*, but Thornhill only saw another arc of beach at the base of another length of dull green forest. Blackwood made himself plainer. *Where the river comes out*, he said. *Our Hawkesbury.*

Then he swung the tiller and let out the sail a little, so the boat curved round into an opening in the line of the coast and lurched in the following sea. A blunt headland, the shape of a hammer, rose up to port. To starboard a lion of rock reared up, baring its stone breast out to the sea and the unending winds.

As the *Queen* pointed towards the gap between the island and the headland, Thornhill saw that Blackwood was tight as a fiddle-string. Those great slow swells, steady enough when they had plenty of sea room, were being funnelled into a tight neck of water that broke them into an angry chop and surge. The wind split against the pieces of land, eddying, veering, buffeting in confusion. The *Queen* seemed absurdly tiny, tossed like a leaf.

Blackwood never took his eyes off the water, did not even seem to blink. His brown fist was closed around the tiller, his eyes half closed against the spray and wind, his cheeks wet as with tears. He leaned forward to keep his footing, his solid lighterman's legs braced against the planks.

The *Queen* was a tough little lump, shuddering up and crashing down into the waves, but Thornhill had heard of boats pounded to pieces in such seas, the planks springing out of the stem, water pouring in. His fear had gone beyond feeling now, to a numbness where he could only watch Blackwood and hope. He gripped the gunwale and would have prayed, if he had known any God to pray to.

Then they were through. The sea was still churning and seething beneath the boat, but the wind was muted by land on all sides. They had pushed through into another geography altogether.

They call this Broken Bay, Blackwood said. *River comes in yonder.* He pointed ahead, where Thornhill could see only confusing stretches of water and thickly forested headlands. *Best hidden river in the world,* Blackwood said with satisfaction. *Never find your way in nor you'd been shown like I'm showing you.*

Looking inland, where gusts of wind scraped at the water, Thornhill strained to find that secret river. In every direction, the reaches of Broken Bay seemed to end in yet another wall of rock and forest. A man could sail around for days and never find his way into the Hawkesbury.

Blackwood pointed the boat towards a solid wall of land, a heaped-up ridge that tumbled down into the water all cliffs and skinny trees that grew out of the very stones themselves, and what had seemed a dead end slyly opened up into a stretch of river between cliffs. As the boat glided along on the tide, the cliffs rose sheer on both sides, mouse-grey except where the wind had exposed buttery rock, as if the landscape itself was a dark-skinned creature with golden flesh beneath.

The rock had been laid down flat, layer after layer piled high like flitches of timber. As it had worn away, great slabs the size of a house had fallen off and tumbled all skewiff at the foot of the cliffs. Some lay half in the water, melting away. Where the cliff met the water a tangle of snake-like roots, vines and mangroves knotted around the fallen boulders.

This was a place out of a dream, a fierce landscape of chasms and glowering cliffs and a vast unpredictable sky. Everywhere was the same but everywhere was different. Thornhill felt his eyes wide open, straining to find something they could understand.

It seemed the emptiest place in the world, too wild for any man to have made it his home. Then Blackwood said, *See yonder?* and pointed with his blunt hand at a promontory to port. Beyond the fringe of mangroves Thornhill could see tussocky grass and trees, and a heap of something pale. *Oysters, the shells*, Blackwood said, and watched the promontory fall behind them. *Suck the guts out, chuck the shells away. Been doing it since the year dot.* He laughed. *And fish! My word they get the fish.*

Not putting none by? Thornhill said. *For tomorrow, like?* Blackwood gave him an amused look. *Aye*, he said. *Not putting none by.* He slapped at a mosquito on his arm. *Why would they? River ain't going nowhere.*

Thornhill glanced around. A breeze made leaves shiver and catch the light, casting shadows that shifted and speckled differently every moment. *Where are they, then*, he asked. Blackwood took his time answering. *Every-bloody-where, mate*, he said, gesturing up ahead. Thornhill saw smoke rising thin into the air, almost lost against the rocks and trees. He turned and glanced astern and there was another grey column. It might have been smoke or the light. Blackwood did not need to glance. *They seen us all right*, he said. *Now they're telling the others, up the line.* Thornhill stared into the tangle of trees and rocks on the bank. He saw something move: a man gesturing, or just a branch behaving like a man?

Blackwood gave Thornhill a short judging look. *One thing you best know, only time we see them is when they want us to.*

The river revealed itself, teasingly, never more than a bend at a time, calm between its walls of rock and bush. As the *Queen* rounded one high spur of land, another came in from the other side, so they interlocked as neatly as gear-wheels. One reach resembled all the others: cliffs, a fringe of glossy green mangroves, green water. Even the skyline gave no clues, each bulge of high land like the others, striped with shadows from clouds passing in front of the sun.

The wind was flukey, bringing with it a dry sweet clean fragrance. The boat was drawn up by the tide as if pulled by a string, slowly, calmly, curve after curve. The twists of the landscape closed in behind them. It was not possible to know where they were going, or to see where they had been.

They came to an island, a bit of floating forest. Beyond that a long bay, as still as a mirror, bent away from the main river. The woods crowded down the ridge right to the water. A smudge of smoke hung in the air as if trapped. Blackwood jerked his chin at it. *Smasher Sullivan*, he said. *Come out on the Minstrel along of me.* The soft look had gone from his face and there was a bitter edge to the words, a tightness to his mouth. He glanced up at the sail as if to trim it, but the wind had died and the canvas hung slack from the yard. *Burns the shells for the lime*, he said. *Plus does a lot of mischief besides.*

Thornhill looked again, and now he could see how the bay was dented by a creek. Where it met the river a chip of flat ground stood out among that parched and headlong wilderness. A speck of imported green stood out there, bright. Squinting, he could make out a crooked hut, tiny in this massive place, and around it a clearing like something flayed.

As he watched, a man came to the door of the hut and waved. He shouted across the water to Blackwood but the words were broken up into echoes by the cliffs. In spite of Blackwood's efforts to keep her pointed up the main river, the *Queen* was drifting closer, so that Thornhill could see a few fowls pecking miserably around the man's feet, and a shirt drying on a bush. The man got into a skiff now and splashed across towards them. He was a hundred yards away when he shouted, *Got the bugger!* His voice was clear in the still air. He bent to the oars again, digging them in deep. As he came alongside, Blackwood made no move to throw him a line, only glanced up again at the masthead where the sail still hung limp. *Learned that poxy thief*, the man was shouting. *Learned him good and proper!*

Smasher Sullivan had a face that the sun had burned piebald like a botched bit of frying. The sandy hair retreated from a red dome of forehead, the eyes were small and naked-looking in a face without eyebrows. He gripped the *Queen*'s gunwale and looked up with a strained eager grin that showed gaps where the teeth were missing. He glanced at Thornhill without interest. It was Blackwood he wanted.

But Blackwood was busying himself with shaking out the sail where it was crumpling in the lack of wind. Smasher Sullivan reached for some things in the bottom of his boat and held them up. *Look what I done*, he called. Thornhill thought for a moment it was fish he had caught and was showing them, or was it a pair of gloves? Then he saw that they were hands cut off at the wrist. The skin was black against the white of the bone.

Last time that bugger thieves from me, Smasher called, and gave a harsh high-pitched snigger. There was something horrible about the red skin of his forehead, his naked face. *Damn your eyes, Smasher*, Blackwood shouted, seizing one of the oars, his voice enormous between the cliffs. Thornhill heard the echo of it, the anger rumbling away down the mournful reach of water. *Get on that other damned oar, Thornhill*, he said. *Look sharp, man.*

A dozen strokes took them out of reach of Smasher's skiff. Blackwood shipped his oar and stood with the telescope up to his eye. Thornhill thought he must have been stung by something, the way he tore it away from his face with an angry grunt. He handed it to Thornhill who looked through it seeing only silver-green tree-tops at first, rounded as moss, sliding past his eye. At last he found the line where land met water and jerkily followed it around. There was the hut, a sad affair of bark and sticks, and a smouldering heap nearby. There was the corn patch, such a brilliant green it was sickening. Beside it, a tree stood silver in death, and from one of its branches a long sack hung heavy on the end of a rope.

In the first glimpse Thornhill thought it was a scarecrow put there for the birds, then that it was a beast hung up for butchering. A catspaw of wind sent the boat tinkling across the water towards the bank. He felt the eyepiece slimy with his sweat. The burden hanging there was not a scarecrow or a hog, but the body of a black man. Puffy flesh bulged around the rope under his armpits, the head lolled. The face was unrecognisable as a face, the only thing clear the yellow ear of corn stuck between the pink sponge that had been the lips.

A stirring of breeze puffed down at them from the cliffs.

Blackwood stood holding the tiller, watching for the wind across the water, his whole body twisted away from what he had seen. The wind met them and the *Queen* leapt forward, the sail bulging and the sheets taut. Thornhill took a breath to speak but thought better of it.

When Blackwood spoke, his voice was raspy with a press of feeling. *Ain't nothing in this world just for the taking*, he said. He spat over the side and stared away at where the water crinkled into glare towards the west. *A man got to pay a fair price for taking*, he said. *Matter of give a little, take a little.*

Thornhill watched the mangroves passing, the simple curve of the ridge against the sky. He could hear only the small sound of the boat, its foot sliding through the glassy water. It had become a still, pearly afternoon, the tide filling up nicely, bearing the *Queen* along.

Near the end of a long reach with a high unbroken wall of cliff to starboard, Blackwood pointed up ahead. *Got my place up there a ways.* The words came out in clots, as if something in him wanted to tell but something else did not. *Where that First Branch come in.* Thornhill peered forward and saw where another stream, glinting among reeds, veered off the main river. He waited out the silence. *Got myself a pardon, be two years this summer*, Blackwood said, and let out a roar of mirth. *Best pardon money could buy.* He stared forward gripping a stay. There was no sound but the rustle of the water under the keel. *Picked meself out a hundred acres*, he said at last. *Five mile up the Branch, Blackwood's Lagoon they call it.* He was speaking more to himself than Thornhill. *Away a ways up.*

The way he said it, it was a poem.

The thought of his place seemed to have allowed him to forget Smasher Sullivan. His mouth was soft, savouring the words, and there was a private pleasure on his face as he gazed ahead. *Catch a few fish, grow a bit of corn, brew a bit of rotgut, I can please meself.*

In Thornhill's world, a person might own some sticks of furniture, a few clothes, perhaps a lighter. That was wealth. But no one that Thornhill knew personally had bought so much as a yard of land. Even Mr Middleton had not owned the freehold on the narrow house in Swan Lane.

Yet here was Blackwood, a lighterman and convicted lag, no better in any particular than he was himself, owning a stretch of ground. Not simply owning it: naming it after himself!

How's that? Thornhill said, astonished. *They give you a hundred acres just for the asking?*

Blackwood glanced at him. *Not a matter of ask up here mate,* he said. *Get your backside on a bit of ground, sit tight. That's all the asking you got to do.*

Blackwood began to hum to himself, staring out into the silver glinting of the water. *Just as soon give the Camp a miss, tell the truth,* he said at last. *Too many buggers there never let a man forget he's worn the broad arrow.* He went on, almost talking to himself. *Long's he stays off the booze, a feller with a boat can do real good for himself.*

The First Branch angled off to starboard, and just after, the river swung hard to port, almost doubling back on itself, as if around a hinge. The long spit of land it swung around rose from the water, a sweet place with scattered trees and grass, as green and tender as a gentleman's park even in this summer season. Thornhill found himself looking for the manor house in among the trees with its windows winking, but there was only a kangaroo watching them pass, its forepaws held up to its chest and its ears twitching towards them. As the *Queen* swept around the point, he saw the rounded tip where sand had collected to form a curve of beach, and a bulge along the side.

He almost laughed aloud, seeing it as just the shape of his own thumb, nail and knuckle and all.

A chaos opened up inside him, a confusion of wanting. No one had ever spoken to him of how a man might fall in love with a piece of ground. No one had ever spoken of how there could be this teasing sparkle and dance of light among the trees, this calm clean space that invited feet to enter it.

He let himself imagine it: standing on the crest of that slope, looking down over his own place. Thornhill's Point. It was a piercing hunger in his guts: to own it. To say *mine*, in a way he had never been able to say *mine* of anything at all. He had not known until this minute that it was something he wanted so much.

But the picture of Thornhill's Point seemed too frail to be exposed to the air in anything as blunt as words. It was hardly to be thought of, even in the privacy of his own mind. He said nothing, turned away with no interest on his face, no surprise. Certainly no desire.

But Blackwood knew what was in his mind. *Any amount a good land*, he said, so quick that Thornhill had to think to make sense of it. Blackwood shot him one of his direct looks. *I seen you looking*, he said. He gazed out at where the bush stirred. *That back there.* He spat astern as if to get the taste of Smasher out of his mouth. *That ain't no good.* There was something he wanted to establish between them, some important thought that had to be conveyed. *Give a little, take a little, that's the only way.* He stared out across the water, then turned and spoke close in Thornhill's face, quite calm. *Otherwise you're dead as a flea.*

He was matter-of-fact.

Thornhill nodded, stared away upriver to where another headland was swinging around to reveal another reach of shining water. *Got no argument with that*, he said. He resisted the urge to glance back at the piece of land in the shape of his own thumb.

Blackwood watched him, reading his thoughts. *Well then*, he said, but with a doubt in his tone. The words hung between them like an unanswered question.

As the First Branch and the long point fell astern they felt the tide turning, and went ashore for the night on a low island, lying beside the fire on the sand with the forest at their backs. Before dawn they were up again, catching the tide upriver.

Now there were more triangles of flat land, like the one Smasher Sullivan had made his own, where creeks came down in folds between the cliffs. Shelves of grass and trees bordered the river in places, and rounded hills began to take the place of the rearing buttresses of stone. The personality of the river was beginning to change into something softer, kinder, on a more human scale. Approaching Green Hills, river flats stretched away on both sides, squared off into fenced fields of corn and wheat, and orchards of glossy orange trees. Behind the fields the forest was pushed back like a blanket.

All that day, watching the river change, Thornhill thought about the long point of land. He had heard the preachers mouthing about the Promised Land. He had taken it as being another thing in the world that was just for gentry. Nothing had ever been promised to him.

He knew that this was not what the preachers meant, but he took pleasure in remembering the phrase. That point of land was by way of being promised: not by God, but by himself, to himself.

~

Back in Sydney he told Sal about the wild cliffs and crags of the lower reaches of the river, the farmers grubbing out a living on the humid banks of its mild upper reaches. Blackwood had them over a barrel, he told her. Without his boat their crops might as well rot in the fields. There were two other traders on the river, but Bartlett was a drunk and Andrews a robber. All the farmers waited for Blackwood. He told her about the expanses of shining mangroves and the way the river was notched so privily into the land. Told her about the First Branch: drew a little plan of it on the ground to explain where it came into the river and showed her, with an X in the dust, where Blackwood had given his name to a piece of the wild.

His stick drew the shape of the river, explaining how it folded back on itself just where the Branch came in, how that corner was the point at which a salt river began to be a fresh one, and how upstream of it the land was tamer. He watched the tip of his stick deepening the groove that showed the course of that far-off river.

The thing he did not share with her was that his stick was also drawing the shape of a point of land. A kangaroo had stood chest high in the grass there and watched him, and he had discovered a hunger in himself he had never known before.

That place was a dream that might shrivel if put into words.

~

It was months later, on the night of Dick's third birthday in July of 1809, before he told her about it. Dick had celebrated with the treat of a honey-cake, and his mother and father had celebrated with a few tots. Now they sat together by the fire, hearing the wind roaring in the treetops, shooting down the bark chimney now and then and puffing white ash into their faces. It was a cosy feeling, to know that cold wind might bluster away all night but would never bring snow or ice, would never bring as much as a touch of frost. The first winter they got piles of firewood ready by the door and spent money on blankets. Now, three winters after they had first arrived, they knew that what passed for cold in Sydney was nothing to fear.

Sal sat yawning, staring into the flames. Bub, though over a year old, was still waking her during the night, whimpering and finally crying out until she got up and nursed him. *Oughter be in bed*, she murmured, but shifted her stool closer to him so that she could line up her leg along his. *Best bit of the day, but, this.*

It seemed as good a moment as any to try the idea on her. *There's a bit of land*, he said. *Up the river. Hard by the Branch there.* She did not turn her face away from the fire, but he felt her grow very still, listening. *We oughter get it, Sal, before some other bugger does.* He heard his voice catch on the thought so the last words were rough with urgency.

Farmer Will? she cried, her face alight with the fun of it. *You don't hardly know one end of a turnip from the other!*

Prime bit of land, he said, when she had had her fun. *Set ourselves up there like Blackwood done, never look back.* He heard the eagerness in his voice and made himself stop.

She saw that he was not joking. *We done all right up till now*, she said. *Got to know when to leave well alone.*

She was right in that: they knew other men who had got land and been too idle to work it, or squandered their profits on horse-flesh and fancy waistcoats. Some had picked a bit of land where nothing would grow and ended up worn to shadows, a paddock of weeds their reward for years of labour.

Will, she said, and hesitated as if not knowing where to start. She worked at the fire with a stick, then turned to look him full in the face. *Will, we had a lot of luck*, she said. *We could both be dead and them boys not even born.* She turned back to the fire and spread her hands out to the warmth. He saw how thin her fingers were against the brightness of the flames.

We're doing real good, Will, she said after a while. *Couple of years we'll have enough to go back.* She glanced quickly at him. *Get the house and them wherries. The stuffed armchairs and that.*

He wanted to convince her that the land would get them the wherries and the house quicker, how the children would thank them for it. But he made himself hold his tongue. Outside he heard a rustle and creak. Scabby Bill, that would be, settling down for the night.

We best grab this chance, Sal, he said. He heard his voice start reasonable and then rise in spite of himself. *Not muck about!*

But he had pressed her too hard. *No,* she said. *I ain't coming at it, Will, and that's flat.*

He could feel the children, woken by the raised voices, watching from the mattress. He glanced over to where Willie's face was a pale circle in the gloom. As the oldest, at eight, he got the part of the mattress closest to the fire. Dick had to make do with the draughty side by the wall. Bub, that puny child, had only just outgrown the cradle, and was still not used to sleeping with the older boys. He was making the scratchy noises in his throat that meant he was not yet awake enough to cry, but soon would be. They all went very still. After a moment Bub fell silent and the boys lay down again.

He was proud of the fact that his boys had a blanket each. They did not have to lie awake, as he had done as a lad, waiting for the others to fall asleep.

Sal tightened her shoulders into herself and leaned towards the fire, not looking at her husband. They had never disagreed on anything that mattered. He wished he could explain to her the marvel of that land, the way the sunlight fell so sweet along the grass.

But she could not imagine it, did not want to. He saw that her dreams had stayed small and cautious, being of nothing grander than the London they had left. Perhaps it was because she had not felt the rope around her neck. That changed a man forever.

~

He said no more, but the thought of that mild-mannered point of land was with him from the instant of waking, as if his dreams had been full of it. On his trips up and down the river with Blackwood he saw it in all weathers and conditions. Under the black skies of August he would see the curtain of rain advancing up what he thought of as Thornhill's Reach, turning the headland grey, making the bushes on the point twist and flail in the wind. As summer came, birds sang from the trees on sweet blue and gold mornings. He saw kangaroos, and striped lizards as long as his arm sidling up the trunks of the river-oaks. Sometimes he thought there was a haze of smoke rising up between the trees, but when he looked harder it was not there.

At low tide the point was lined with mud. This was not the same as slimy Thames mud, but a rich brown that looked good enough to eat. Beyond the mud were the rushes, higher than a man, packed as tight as the bristles of a broom, topped with feathery plumage. They were alive with little round brown birds, something of the order of a robin. He could hear them in there making their calls: ca chink pee pee pee wheep! Wheep!

Other birds, as bright as soldiers, stalked across the mud on long hinged legs. He watched, not two yards away, as one of them broke off a reed with its claws, holding it so its beak could strip off the outer sheath and eat the pale stalk within, one bite at a time, like a lady with a finger of asparagus.

The reeds protected the point on one side, dense mangroves on the other. Beyond the slope of the gentlemen's park, the land tilted and became a wall of jumbled rocks and scrubby woods. But between the river and the ridge there was plenty of good flat land. A hundred acres? Two hundred?

Whatever it was, it was enough.

Each time they passed the place he looked for the thing he was dreading: the dug-over patch of ground where some other man's corn was growing, the square of some other man's hut. Each time there was a moment's relief, but then the dread returned.

The thought of that point of land became a private thing, a bead of warmth in his heart.

~

Blackwood was more jovial these days than Thornhill had ever seen him. He was planning to sell the *Queen*, retire to his farm *away a ways up*, and make do on what his moonshine brought in. *Plenty of wood, plenty of water, plenty of tucker*. Blackwood shrugged when Thornhill was surprised. *I got all I need up there, and none of the aggravation I can do without*.

But he seemed to want to see Thornhill right before he disappeared into the valley of the First Branch, and seeing him right meant making sure he got his pardon.

The ticket of leave was a way to make men work, but a full pardon worked even better. Those who were already free and who had the benefits of servants assigned to them did not agree, but for the moment the Governor was handing out pardons as if they were two a penny.

Which in a manner of speaking they were. Blackwood knew a man of the cloth, a Reverend Cowper, who was prepared to vouch for the good character of anyone with a few quarts of Jamaican about him. Blackwood boasted that the term of his own natural life had turned out to be five years. It could have been less, he said, except that the blooming keg had tipped off the barrow and busted and he had to go back for another.

Blackwood told Thornhill how to get the petition written out by a fellow named Nightingale, a broken-down gentleman far gone in rum, who had a way with a fine phrase and wrote a good hand. He sat at one of the rum-stalls down by the stream with a quill and an empty inkbottle before him. A man who needed a petition for a pardon supplied his own paper and a jar full of ink, and a quantity of rum. The precise quantity was a matter of judgment. Sober, Nightingale was no good to a man, his hand shaking like a fiddler's and his eyes small with shock. But if he was given too much, rum oozed out of his pores and the pen fell from his fingers. There was a short time between the first pannikin and the promise of the second, that had him waxed just right to do the job.

At the bottom of the fine curly letters, red ink as well as black and flourishes top and bottom, Nightingale left a gap and pointed to it with his trembling finger, saying *William Thornhill his mark, there if you please*, and Thornhill took the quill. But instead of scratching a cross, he scraped his way along the letters Sal had taught him. He crushed the nib too hard against the paper, so there was a blob and a spatter, and he had forgotten how to make the small letters, so they were nothing more than a crooked line like a worm on a fishing hook. But the W and the T stood out clear. William Thornhill.

~

In December of 1810, four years after he had arrived, Thornhill and a dozen other hopefuls took a place on the *Rose Hill Packet* and sailed up the Port until it narrowed into a river they called the Parramatta. At the head of that river, on Rose Hill itself, was the Governor's house. It was a square stone box that sat above the ramshackle convict huts like a gentleman comfortable on a chair. The petitioners were taken into a large-windowed drawing room, its walls covered with portraits of whiskery gentlemen and rows of books gleaming with gilt. His Excellency stood in a fall of sunlight from one of the tall windows, blinding in scarlet and gold braid, the cockaded hat shading his face, his feet on a small square of red carpet.

At the other end of the room the lags stood with their caps in their hands. The Governor's Scotch accent was so strong that Thornhill only understood his weighty words in part, and occupied his mind inspecting the nearest portrait, a man sitting sideways at a little table with a book in his hand against a dark background. He wondered what he himself would look like sitting at a little table with a book in his hand and rich brown gravy all around. Would he appear as substantial as this gentleman, or did a man have to be born to it?

When his name was called, *William Thornhill, Alexander transport, life*, he stepped forward smartly. He shook His Excellency's white-gloved hand and heard himself pronounced *Absolutely Pardoned*.

Counting from the moment in the Old Bailey when the judge had snatched at the cap falling off his wig and delivered the sentence, the term of William Thornhill's natural life had turned out to be four years, five months and six days.

Back at the Pickle Herring, he and Sal toasted each other. It seemed only right to celebrate the Governor's pardon with the Governor's own brandy. He could feel its warm fingers inside his chest and saw the flush rise to Sal's cheeks. *My word but His Excellency does himself proud*, she said, and took another mouthful. *And may he live long to enjoy it, having freed my man.*

Her face was brown from the hard sun, and there was a toughness to her now that came from humouring drunkards while trying to watch the children: Willie and Dick running wild around the settlement and Bub staggering after them on his skinny little legs, crying to them to wait.

She leaned towards him across the table, so close he could see how the skin was white along the lines raying out from the corners of her eyes. The lines—from so many days of squinting into the sun—gave her a look of laughter that made him want to take her right there, against the wall, and hear her panting into his ear. As if she could read the thought in his eyes, Sal brought her face even closer and squirted her brandy straight from her mouth into his, so he felt the spray of it on his face.

~

With Blackwood getting out of the packet trade, Thornhill had to look for something else. He had in mind to get a skiff of his own. There was a man in Cockle Bay made one-man craft along the lines of a Thames wherry, and something like that would let him go back to working around the ships in Sydney Cove. With such a small boat he would have to work in a small way, but if he owned it himself he would do well enough not to have to thieve. He would make a good steady living, nothing grand, but reliable, and no risk of Van Diemen's Land.

By and by he would have another conversation with Sal. He had frightened her, talking about the land too sudden, not working out how it might all be done. He had to go slower, that was all.

He and Sal got out the box from under the bungwall and by the light of the slush lamp they counted the money. Thirty-five pounds. It was more money than they had ever owned. If he could make do with secondhand oars, it was enough for one of Walsh's skiffs.

Sal weighed the coins in her palm, let them pour from one

hand to the other. Held one close to the lamp, tilting it to see the gleam where a thousand hands had made it their own.

Will, she said, and he looked at her. There was something new in her tone. He saw how, in the lamplight, the centre of one brown eye was smaller than the other. *That Blackwood*, she said. *I seen in the Gazette where he's selling off the Queen.* He nearly asked her what that had to do with Walsh's skiffs, but waited. *A hundred and sixty he's asking but he'd take less.* She was thinking her thoughts out loud. *We oughter buy it off of him*, she said. *Make our pile like he done, quick-smart.*

Thornhill's eyes went to the heap of coins on the table, but she was ahead of him. *Borrow the rest*, she said almost in a whisper, *off of Mr King.*

He could not believe he had understood her right, but when he looked into her face she was ready for him, smiling. *Couple of years of the packet trade, we'll pay the lot back*, she said. He felt his mouth open in astonishment and she rushed on, thinking he needed reassurance. *I done the sums, Will, it will work out.* She was leaning across the table, urging him, coaxing him along. *Then we'll be right to go back. Home.*

He could have laughed aloud. All this time he had been nursing his secret dream, and it turned out she had been coddling a dream too. Hers had an altogether different end, but the miracle was that it had the same beginning.

She did not guess his thought, was going along the track of her own. She glanced at him, her eyes gleaming. *Couple of years is all, Will, then we'll be right. Home, Will, imagine that!*

He nodded as if he was thinking about Home, and when she leaned across the table to take his face in her hands and kiss him, he kissed her back hard enough to surprise her. *Yes*, he said. *I'll see King tomorrow.* But he was not thinking about how soon they could go Home. The calculation in his mind was how soon he could get set up in the Hawkesbury trade, so that it would be the most logical thing in the world to need a base on the river: in short, when he would be able to stand on that point of land and know it was his.

~

It was a hundred and fifteen pounds they needed, as well as what was in the box. It was a huge sum, almost so big as to be unreal, not actual money but just sounds in the mouth. Back Home he would never have taken such a step. Not even thought of it. But in this place, if a debt could keep a man awake at night, it could turn him into a man of property. Mr King agreed to the loan, and shook hands with Thornhill as if he had in that moment become an equal.

He knew the *Queen* well: an open sloop of nineteen feet, half-deck fore and aft and plenty of room in the hold. She was as clunky as a bathtub, all blunt bow and broad in the beam. She was a cranky sailor short-hauled, and had an awkward way of broaching in a following wind. But she was built strong, and was brave in a blow.

Thornhill had to down a tot before he could nerve himself. Even then, he watched his hand trembling as he signed the paper.

~

Sal came down to Sydney Cove to admire the boat. She was in the family way again, and was so far along she had to straddle the coil of rope he gave her to sit on, her legs apart to ease her growing belly. *Queen is a funny kind of name*, she said. *Da's boat, remember, he called it the Hope.* She smiled up at Thornhill, squinting into the brightness of the sky behind him. *Which is pretty much what we got to do, ain't it, not to mention pray?* He loved to see her face light up with that old smile, remembering. *It had a red stripe, Da were real particular about that stripe.*

The next time she came down to the Cove, the new baby in her arms, he and Willie had painted out the old name and put the new one in its place, the letters copied from a piece of paper provided by Nightingale. The red stripe, just below the gunwale, looked well. He could see why Mr Middleton had been particular about it. To make the thing perfect, they even painted the same line around the skiff that Blackwood had thrown in as part of the deal.

The *Hope* was made for a father and his son. Willie was going on eleven and as handy as most men. He took after his father, a big boy with a tangle of hair squashed under his cap. He was a tough one. When one day his finger got itself wedged in the thole-pins, and the oar pushed back against it, his face went the colour of dirty clay but he did not make a sound. Thornhill saw the muscles in his jaw straining to keep the pain in, so the lad seemed almost to bulge.

Thornhill recognised himself in the pain, and in the force that kept it silent.

Willie had gone with his father to Mr King's to sign. He was old enough to know what the promise to pay a hundred and fifteen pounds could mean. He loved the *Hope*, having the salt wind in his face. He never minded a bit of hard work, and the father and son came to know each other as they stowed cargo or baled water together.

For the whole of the year 1811, Thornhill and Willie and the *Hope* went wherever men needed the services of a boat, but especially worked the packet trade to the Hawkesbury and back. At Green Hills, that steamy collection of farms, the hold filled with corn, wheat, turnips, melons. At Sydney it emptied and refilled with anything the farmers might want: rope and nails, hoop-iron and hoes. The *Hope* was never empty, and at each exchange a little money stuck to William Thornhill's fingers.

Others had bigger boats, better boats, but no one in the colony could come near William Thornhill and the *Hope*. In all weathers he was out on the water, sometimes with Willie but often alone. Night or day, it was all the same. While others slept, he would get the boat loaded in the dark, row through the night against the tide and be on the way back while they were just getting the sail up. On the return journey from Green Hills to Sydney, other boats dilly-dallied in Broken Bay for gentle seas before they made the run down the coast to Port Jackson. Not Thornhill. He would set out in seas that hid the *Hope* to its mast-top.

Two things drove him. One was the piece of paper on which he had promised to pay Alexander King a hundred and fifteen pounds, plus interest. It sat in the drawer of Mr King's desk like a snake that could turn on a man and strike him dead.

The other was the thought of a future that would not be like the past. In London he had seen the hands of worn-out watermen, who at two score years were old men. On Mr Middleton's hands the knuckles were bulbous, the fingers fused like a sea-eagle's claw so he could not pick the change for half a crown out of a palmful of coins. Thornhill could not forget the poor broken-down lightermen in the almshouse at the Borough either, the way they crouched and shuffled, pitifully pleased at their bowl of thin soup.

Already on a cold morning his hands ached. He thought he could see the knuckles beginning to bulge, and the fingers to crimp sideways. He could force his body, the only thing he had ever had power over, to submit to his will, but it would weaken in the end. A man's life seemed a cruel race: to get himself and his family above the high water mark, safe from the tides and contrary winds, before his body gave out.

He lay in the nights with Sal, the four boys sleeping quietly beside them. Willie lay where he had fallen on the mattress, sleeping as hard as he worked. Beside him Dick rustled and shifted. Going on five, that child born at sea between one world and another was a solemn creature with a dreamy face in which Thornhill could not see any echo of his own. He could sit for hours crooning to himself and fiddling about with a few stones. Bub had his place between them in the bed. He was nearly three, but he still woke in the night, and the bodies on either side seemed to comfort him. He was no baby any longer, but his name had stuck.

The new one, Johnny as they called him, was a sturdy child and from the time he could sit up by himself he loved to tinker with anything that moved. For him, the whole world could come down to the way a pulley-wheel ran around its axle, first one way, then the other.

Thornhill had never seen Sal happier, even in her giddy girlhood. He looked on with wonder. He loved his sons, but could see Sal felt something for them beyond mere love. They were her attachment to life in some way that he would never know.

He held all their destinies in his hands, and during his long days on the water he knew it was his shoulders, and his feet pushing against the ribs of the boat as he rowed, that would protect them. If those muscles failed, they would all come to grief.

~

A little over a year later, in early 1812, he had managed to pay a quarter of the money back to King. He knew that if he did not make his move soon it would be too late.

Sailing the *Hope* up and down the Hawkesbury, he had worked out the details of his ambition: fantastical, but as real to him as the tiller in his hand. On that piece of land, he would keep the packet trade going, but he would grow corn as well, and raise hogs for salting. Give it a few years—things happened quick in this place—and the Thornhills would be in a position to sell up and go back to London, to that easy life he could see so plain in the eye of his mind.

It seemed that Blackwood had said right, that getting land was a simple matter. There were rules that said a man needed a piece of paper signed by the Governor. But whispered between the lines of those rules, floating behind the pieces of paper, was the truth: the Governor would turn a blind eye. King George owned this whole place of New South Wales, the extent of which nobody yet knew, but what was the point of King George owning it, if it was still wild, trodden only by black men? The more civilised folk set themselves up on their pieces of land, the more those other ones could be squeezed out. In exchange for the risk such men were willing to take, and the labour they were prepared to expend, a hundred acres of land seemed a fair thing.

All a person need do was find a place no one had already taken. Plant a crop, build a hut, call the place Smith's or Flanagan's, and out-stare anyone who said otherwise.

For all this time he had kept the thought of that thumb of land close to himself, a secret comfort he carried under his coat. Had spoken of it to no one since that night with Sal, as if that might keep it safe from other men's eyes. He could not forget the quiet ground beyond the screen of reeds and mangroves and the gentle swelling of that point, as sweet as a woman's body.

~

Sal was expecting again already, two months along. They were arriving too fast, these babies, another starting the minute she had weaned the last. In London there were plenty of old women who could look after such matters. There was one such here in Church Street in The Rocks, but her hut and her person were so filthy he would not let Sal near her.

Each child was another link in the chain that bound him to their steady life in Sydney. Each one made it harder to leap out into another place and another life. Just the same, he had to take that step. He might wait his whole lifetime for the moment to be right.

The night of New Year, 1813, they all feasted on a stringy rooster one of Sal's customers had brought in lieu of coin, and in the glow of a good feed went through a bottle of the best. Being in the family way always made Sal bolder when the lamp was out, and what with the rum and the sultry heat of the night making them slippery against each other, she and Thornhill well and truly welcomed in the new year.

Afterwards they could not sleep. Outside others were ushering in the year in various raucous ways, and the steamy heat seemed greater even than during the day.

Thornhill felt Sal awake beside him, her hand lying loosely in his. It was as if she knew he had something he wanted to tell her. But he could not compose quite the right words in his mind, and for a time each pretended to be asleep.

Sal, he said at last, the word coming out a croak so he tried it again. *Sal.*

Her voice was wide awake. *Yes, Will?*

That bit of land, he said. *Remember I told you. We'll miss out if we don't grab it.*

A bit of land! She let out a whoop. *And all this time I thought you must have your eye on some saucy moll or other, the way you gone all dreamy!*

They laughed together over the idea of some saucy moll or other, but when they stopped there was still the unfinished thought of the land that could be theirs. She got up and went over to the fireplace where a few embers still glowed, blew at them until she had a twig alight, and lit the lamp. She put it on the floor and got back into the bed, propping herself up on her elbow to watch his face.

Her hair hung down in its night-time braids. He saw in a

kind of remote startlement that there were grey threads in among the brown. How short a time a person had to be alive, he thought. How long to be dead.

You been thinking this a long time, she said at last.

He thought of Thornhill's Point, the way the water streamed past the tip at the change of tide, the way the breeze caught the tops of the trees. The thought soothed him, and it surprised him how mild his voice came out. *Give it five years, Sal*, he said. *Then we get on the first boat Home.*

He put his hand on his heart, the way he had not done since he was a boy. *Cross my heart and hope to die*, he said, forcing a smile. *Five years, as God is my witness.* He went on, even though she knew it already, the story they had told each other so often: *Remember? That little house waiting for us. Freehold. Cash on the knocker.* She still said nothing, but he could feel her picturing it. *A stuffed chair by the fire, and a girl to carry in the coals.* He felt himself warming to the story. *All the good white bread you can eat, and the Bow Bells telling us the time of day.*

He heard her say *Yes*, on a sigh, of loss or longing, and wondered if the Bow Bells had done the trick. *Think of it, Sal*, he said. *Our place.* He was surprised to hear his voice: the tenderness in it.

She heard it too. He felt her attention quicken. *You got your mind made up*, she said. *Ain't you?* And turned to him, searching his face. *Yes*, she answered herself after a moment. *You got your heart set on it.*

Her voice had changed when she spoke again. *Five years then, Will, but not till I got this baby out safe and sound.* She looked him right in the face. *Five years*, she repeated, binding him to the promise. *Long as it ain't for the term of my natural life.* Then she smiled. *Remember but, Will, you don't pick turnips off of a tree.*

PART THREE

A CLEARING IN THE FOREST

There was no one at the wharf to see the *Hope* on its way to Thornhill's Point, only a dirty white dog with a hind leg that seemed to have been put on backwards. It watched from the edge of the wharf and when Thornhill flipped the bowline off the bollard it let out one hoarse bark.

It was the month of September in the year 1813. Winter was not over yet. A milky sun shone through a glaze of clouds, and threads of cold breeze ran across the water. Soon, though, milder airs would blow in from the sea and the sun would harden in the sky. A man who wanted to put a crop in the ground could not delay.

All the way down Port Jackson towards the ocean, Sal strained backwards, staring at the cluster of buildings, pale cubes in the dawn light, that they were leaving. The *Hope* slid through the water, the sail flapping lazily.

The sound of a rooster carried over the water from the township: *cock a doodle doo*, with a long melancholy fall. When the first point of land came between the boat and the settlement, the rooster could no longer be heard, only a laughing jackass hidden in the trees, its mockery coming clear over the water to the family in the boat. Even then, Sal did not face forward, but sat with the new baby pressed against her. They had called her Mary, after Sal's mother. She was tiny, and as quiet as if she thought herself still in the womb. She slept against Sal, her blue-veined eyelids flickering while her mother stared back at the headlands of forest, waiting for one last familiar sound, one final glimpse.

Thornhill had seen the way she looked around the hut before stepping out and pushing closed the flap of bark. Scabby Bill was near the chimney, watching from under his heavy brows. *It's all yours, Bill*, she called, and he glanced at her. *Not sorry to be leaving him behind, anyroad*, she said, trying to laugh, but it caught in her throat. The children picked up something tight and anxious in their mother's voice. *There be any blacks where we're going, Da?* Dick asked. *No, son, I ain't never seen a single one.* Strictly speaking, this was true, he reminded himself, but in Sal's silence he heard her knowledge that the blacks did not have to be seen to be present.

As they rounded the great slice of North Head and the *Hope* met the ocean swell, Thornhill leaned his weight against the tiller, seeing the sail bulge with the wind, feeling the boat surge forward under him. There was a kind of thrill he felt every time, as the tiny pip of the *Hope* was caught in the hand of the wind and the water.

Such a small boat, such a vast sea.

The *Hope* dipped and strained its way northwards past the beaches, one yellow crescent after another, and the headlands between. He could give them names now, learned from Blackwood: Manly, Freshwater, the grey of Whale Point and, blue in the distance ahead, the hammer-shaped headland that marked the place where the Hawkesbury entered the sea.

Sal, a poor sailor, coming over queasy even on the tame waters of Port Jackson, sat pressed in under the half-deck, as far out of the cold wind as she could get, holding Mary against her and staring between her feet where some dirty water slopped up and down over the planks. He watched her sideways, secretly. Under this dull sky, with the wind thrumming in the rigging, she had gone grey.

Thornhill knew she was trying not to be sick, willing herself to survive this passage and whatever it was that lay ahead. He remembered the girl in the creaking bed in Mermaid Row who had fed pieces of tangerine into his mouth. He had loved her then for all that he was not. Now, watching her head bowed over the baby, in the bonnet that she had thriftily patched, he loved her all over again for the steel in her.

He looked out at where a catspaw of wind made a patch of rough water. The *Hope* was spanking along up the coast before the southerly. It would get them up as far as the mouth of the river, then the tide would do the rest, swelling up into the Hawkesbury and taking the Thornhills with it. By late afternoon they would be there.

At the entrance to the river, the *Hope* yawed in the crosswise swell, the waves at her back threatening to swallow her altogether, and he heard someone cry out in fear. There was a sudden slackening as the hammer-shaped headland cut off the wind and then they were through, safe in the quiet waters beyond.

The *Hope* travelled up the river through one set of spurs after another, each headland moving aside at the last moment so they could wind their way into the very body of the land. It was so quiet here, after the roar of the ocean, that they could hear the busy crisping of the water under the foot of the boat.

The afternoon was turning fine, though the breeze was still cool. They were sailing straight towards the sun as it began its descent, so the water ahead was a sheet of silver. Up in the bow, Willie stood watching where it was ruffled by breezes that set points of light winking. Dick leaned over the gunwale, entranced by the way the water broke and gathered itself back around his finger.

Sal was finally looking out at the cliffs, the forest as dense as moss, the sombre water that only reflected more cliffs and more forest.

Seeing the place through her eyes, Thornhill realised how far he had travelled. He was a different man now from the one who had been silenced, on that first day with Blackwood, by the colossal bulk of land, the power of this living body of water. It was a place of promise to him now, the blank page on which a man might write a new life. But he could see that to his wife it seemed harsh and unlovely, nothing but a sentence to be endured.

He tried to put his thought into words. *You'll get used to it, pet*, he said. *Be surprised, the way it grows on you.* It was just to cheer her along, but as he heard the words come out of his mouth he realised that he meant them. She made an effort, glancing at him with a smile that looked yellow, and said, *You and your gammon, Will Thornhill!*

I'll make you that snug you will think you was at home in Swan Lane! he cried, and Willie guffawed at the idea. But Sal could not find it funny. From where Thornhill stood in the stern he could only see the top of her head in the mended bonnet, and her legs gathered up tight under her.

Dick looked around at the forest and piped up. *Will the savages try and eat us, Da?* Bub looked around, fear on his little white face, and cried out, *Don't let them eat me, Ma*, but Thornhill was having none of that. *Tell you what, lad,* he said. *You would make a tough dinner, you are that stringy a little bugger!*

All the same he could not stop himself glancing towards the bow where the gun was wrapped in a bit of canvas, out of the wet and out of sight.

The day he bought it from Mr Mallory down at the Cow-pastures was the first time Thornhill had even so much as touched a gun. It was greasy in his hands, an uncompromising piece of machinery, heavy and single-minded.

Mallory had taken him out into his paddock to show him how to work it. The loading and priming of the thing was such a palaver he nearly changed his mind. From firing one ball to being ready to fire the next was a full two minutes, even when Mallory did it. When Thornhill did it, fumbling with the shot, getting the wadding jammed too far down the barrel, spilling the powder, it seemed to take forever.

He got it up to his shoulder, pulled on the trigger, felt the flint fall on the steel and make a spark. The powder exploded with a great flash in his face, and then the butt recoiled against his shoulder as if someone had struck him. He staggered and nearly fell.

Mallory got a superior kind of smile on his face then, and started on some long-winded story about shooting pheasants at Bottomly-on-the-Marsh. It was one more thing the gentry knew about, the way a gun could do almost as much damage to the man shooting it as to the man being shot at.

Thornhill could not believe he would be able to send a ball of red-hot metal into another body. But being allowed a gun was one of the privileges of a pardon. It was something he had earned, whether he wanted it or not.

Just in case, he had said, taking the gun from Mallory. He could not think now why he had been so casual.

The family had become very silent, everyone thinking their own thoughts about what was in store, when at last in the late afternoon, the shadows lying purple in the clefts between the ridges, Thornhill saw it ahead: the high ridge, square like a sperm whale's head, and the river below, which swung around the low point of land that was about to become his. Thornhill's Point.

He called along the boat to her, to make her look. *Just along here, Sal!*

But as they came around the last point he felt the tide

changing. The wash still foamed away from under the keel, the sails still strained in the puffs of breeze that came at them down the cliffs, but the water holding the body of the boat was turning against it. Pinned to the spot by the contrary forces of wind and water, the *Hope* was making no headway, and with every moment that passed the balance was tipping in favour of the tide pushing them back.

But Thornhill's Point was so close he could see the breeze flipping the leaves of the mangroves standing in the water, and a bird there on a branch.

He had to fight the feeling that the place was mocking him.

Of course they could anchor and sit out the tide, spend the night on the boat as he and Willie had done often enough. But Thornhill had waited too long and dreamed too sweetly for that. *On the sweep, Willie, look sharp, lad*, he shouted. *We done just as good to stop here, Da*, the boy called back. *Till the tide come in again.*

He was right, but Thornhill was in a frenzy of longing. It was burning him up, to set foot on that promised land. He leaped into the bow, grabbed the sweep and leaned his weight against it, feeling the strength in his own shoulders warm through his flesh, forcing himself against the river. The boat stirred sluggishly in response. Through a mouth gone stiff with passion he hissed, *By God Willie, get on that aft sweep lad or the sharks can have you*, but heard his voice disappear, nothing more than a wisp of steam in so much space.

Whatever it was that Willie saw in his face made him bend to the oar, until the bow brushed in through the mangroves and came to rest with a jolt. The tide was ebbing away almost visibly. Within a moment the keel had settled deep into the mud. They had arrived.

When Thornhill jumped out over the bow the mud gripped

his feet. He tried to take a step and it sucked them in deeper. With a huge effort he dragged one foot out and looked for a place to set it down between the spiky mangrove roots. Lurched forward into even deeper mud, pulled his other leg up with a squelch, feeling the foot stretch against the ankle, and floundered towards the bank. He put his head down and butted blindly through a screen of bushes, bursting out at last onto dry land. Beyond the river-oaks the ground opened into a flat place covered with tender green growth and studded with yellow daisies.

His own. His own, by virtue of his foot standing on it.

There was nothing he would have called a path, just a thready easing that led through the daisy lawn and up the slope, between the tussocks of grass and the mottled rocks that pushed themselves out from the ground.

There was a lightness in his step as he trod, his feet seeming to choose their own way. He was barely breathing, in a kind of awe.

Mine.

His feet led him up the slope, past a place where a trickle of water glittered over rocks, and through a grove of saplings. He came out into a clearing where trees held an open space in a play of shifting light and shade: a room made of leaves and air. It was quite still, as if every creature in the place had stopped its business to watch him. When one of the whirring pigeons flew up at his feet and perched on a branch, head cocked at him, his skin flushed with the fright of it. He felt the way the trees stood around him in a quiet crowd, their limbs stopped in the middle of a gesture, their pale bark splitting in long cracks to show the bright pink skin beneath.

He took off his hat with an impulse to feel the air around his head. His own air! That tree, its powdery bark flaking around the trunk: his! That tussock of grass, each coarse strand haloed by the sunlight: his own! Even the mosquitoes, humming around his ears, belonged to him, and so did that big black bird perching on a branch and staring at him without a blink.

There was no wind, but clumps of leaves stirred, now here, now there, in a narrow shaft of air. The shadow of the high ridge to the west was a line moving down the hillside towards the clearing, but the trees still lay in syrupy sunset light.

He could have been the only man on earth: William Thornhill, Adam in Paradise, breathing deep of the air of his own new-coined world.

The black bird watched him from its branch. He met its eye across the air that separated them. *Caaaaar*, it went, and waited as if he might answer. *Caaaaar*. He saw how cruel its curved beak was, with a hook at the end that could tear flesh. He threw up his arms and it flapped its wings, but did not leave the branch. He picked up a stone and shied at the bird. It seemed to watch the stone coming and lifted off the branch at the last moment, swooping low overhead and away down towards the river.

In the centre of the clearing he dragged his heel across the dirt four times, line to line. The straight lines and the square they made were like nothing else there and changed everything. Now there was a place where a man had laid his mark over the face of the land.

It was astonishing how little it took to own a piece of the earth.

~

It was a bigger thing to get the piece of canvas up over the rope to provide immediate shelter. He and Willie, with Dick's skinny arms quivering with the strain, wrestled with the heavy sheet. They could not make pegs go into the rocky ground to hold the sides out so they had to heave rocks to pin them in place. Finally the tent stood, lopsided and sadly creased.

By the time they had finished, the sun had dropped behind the ridge. The shadow had moved across the clearing and swallowed them into its chill, although the cliffs over the river caught the last rays, blazing brilliant orange where the flesh of the rock had been bared.

Down on the *Hope*, Sal was still pressed in under the half-deck with the baby and the two young ones. A little colour had come back into her face, but she had a convalescent look. She seemed in no hurry to examine her new home. While she went on sitting in the boat she was, in a manner of speaking, attached to the place she had come from.

Thornhill saw that although this voyage, from Sydney to Thornhill's Point, had taken only a day, and the other voyage, from London to Sydney, had taken the best part of the year, this was the greater distance. From the perspective of this unpeopled riverbank, with its whistling leaves and crying birds, Sydney seemed a metropolis, different only in degree from London.

Willie went over and squatted beside her. *We got the tent up, Ma, it's real good*, he said. *And a nice fire, get you warm.* Sal's mouth tweaked itself into a smile, and she gathered herself to stand. Willie seemed to feel she still needed coaxing. *We got the billy boiling for a drink of tea*, he said. *And a damper going.* Bub swallowed at the thought of tea and damper and glanced at his mother. Little Johnny dropped the end of rope he had been fiddling with and held up his arms to be carried. *Damper, Ma*, he cried.

Sal levered herself up, pulling the shawl around herself and the baby. She was willing enough, Thornhill saw, but could not find any words just yet. Bub spoke louder to rouse her. *I'm real hungry, Ma!* Dick took her hand to help her between the bags and bundles in the hold, and over the sticks they had laid on the mud, onto dry land.

The tent, the fire leaping between its stones, the clearing among the trees so calm, had seemed welcoming enough. But seeing it through her eyes, Thornhill knew what a flimsy home it was. By contrast, the hut housing the Sign of the Pickle Herring had been as solid as St Paul's.

It was only just coming to him how big a thing this was. Life would be hard here for Sal. She would be on her own for a week at a time while he took the *Hope* up and down, with only the children for company. If a snake got one of them there was no surgeon, not even a parson to say a prayer over a corpse. His blind passion for a piece of land had let him leapfrog over this in his mind: Sal here, making a life where only the flicker of their own fire was human.

Snug as a flea in a dog's ear, he announced. In the sceptical silence that followed, the rueful bird let out its cry of regret.

The children watched their father, their thin faces wary. Sal glanced around as if for something she could recognise. He could see that it all looked unfinished to her: the thick tufts of grass, the crooked trees, the unsettling hiss of the breeze in the river-oaks. Through her eyes this place was merely the material from which the world was made, not the world itself. There was not a stone here that had been shaped by a human hand, not a tree that had been planted.

He had camped with Blackwood often enough when the tide caught them. He knew that a person could survive such a place. But Sal had never gone beyond the Governor's garden.

Is this it then, Will, she said. *Is this the place.* It was not really a question. She pushed back the hair that was slithering out of her bonnet.

Little Johnny, usually running about everywhere on his baby

140

legs, stood pressed in against his mother holding a fold of her skirt up to the side of his face. Bub began to whimper. At five he was too old for such snivelling. There were times when Thornhill wanted to knock the child's head off.

For an instant he saw that it was impossible. How could such a flicker of humanity—this pale-faced woman, these children hardly old enough to walk and talk—make any impression on the vastness of this place?

He looked down the hill at the river, dimpling with the change of tide. Something about the tender light on it and the glow of the cliffs beyond made him forget the cold forest, the difficulty, the despair that Sal was failing to hide. The sky was full of radiance: expansive, depthless. The eye never exhausted it. A fingernail of moon was as crisp as if cut out of paper and stuck on: the very same moon that he had seen a thousand times in the evening sky over the Thames. It was, after all, the same earth, the same air, the same sky. And they themselves were the same two people who had already been through death and come out the other side.

He took a deep breath. *It ain't that different than the Thames, pet*, he said. *When all's said and done.* It was a matter of making her see it the way he did: as a promise. *Just like the old Thames before them Romans come along.* She stood sagging with the baby on her hip, that sweet mouth of hers holding itself bravely against the tears that he thought were not far away.

He should stop talking, he knew, get some hot tea and damper into her and put her to bed in the tent. In the morning, in the sunlight, it would look more welcoming. But he could not stop himself, hearing his voice carve across the clearing. *Down there by the boat—that's where Christ Church would be, and our little track the Borough High Street, see it there?*

What had begun as a fancy was taking form as he looked,

and one by one the children were turning to see Christ Church and the High Street. He pointed at the wall of the cliffs on the other side of the river. There was a place where part of the scarp had fallen away and left a pale gash like porridge down an old man's front. *Remember how steep it was like that, going up St Mary-at-Hill?* he said. *Past Watermen's Hall and that? Ain't it just the same?* He could hear his coaxing tone.

Still is, Sal said, with a break in her voice that was half a cry, half a laugh. *Still there where it always was.* She sat down on the log he had dragged up to the fire. She shook her head, as if in wonder at herself. *Only trouble is, we ain't.*

It was the closest she had come to a reproach.

Five years won't seem no time at all, he said. It sounded a weak kind of thing coming out of his mouth. But it was all he had to offer, and after a moment she accepted it. *Yes, Will*, she said, as if it was she who had to reassure him. *It won't seem no time at all, and now where is this famous drink of tea?*

~

The shadow slid up the golden cliffs opposite and turned them to lead. As darkness fell, the distorted trees went on holding the fraction of light in the air.

The Thornhills squatted around the fire listening to the night, feeling its weight at their backs. Beyond the circle of light, the darkness was full of secretive noises, ticks and creaks, sudden rustlings and snappings, an insistent tweeting. Shafts of cold air like the draught from a window stirred the trees. From the river the frogs popped and ponked.

As the night deepened they hunched closer around the fire, feeding it so that as soon as it began to die it flamed up again and filled the clearing with jerky light. Willie and Dick heaped on armful after armful until the light danced against the under-

142

side of the trees. Bub squatted close up to one side, pushing in twigs that flared brilliantly.

They were warm, at least on one side, and the fire made them the centre of a small warm world. But it made them helpless creatures too. The blackness beyond the reach of the flames was as absolute as blindness.

The trees grew huge, hanging over them as if they had pulled up their roots and crept closer. Their shaggy silhouettes leaned down over the firelit clearing.

The gun lay close to Thornhill's hand. By the last of the daylight, out of sight of Sal, he had loaded it. He had checked the flint, had the powder-horn in his coat pocket.

He had thought that having a gun would make him feel safe. Why did it not?

The damper was burned from being cooked too fast, but the steamy fragrance under the charred crust was a comfort. The small noises they made with their food seemed loud in the night. Thornhill could hear his tea travel down his gullet, and the exclamations of his belly as it came to grips with the damper.

He looked up at where even the light of the fire could not dim the stars. He looked for the Southern Cross, which he had learned to steer by, but as it often did it was playing hide-and-seek.

Might be they watching us, Willie said. *Waiting, like.* There was the start of panic in his voice. *Shut your trap, Willie, we ain't got nothing to worry about*, Thornhill said.

In the tent he felt Sal squeezed up against him under the blanket. He had heated a stone in the fire and wrapped it up in his coat to warm her feet, but she was shivering. She was panting as quick as an animal. He held her tight, feeling the cold at his back, until at last her breathing slowed in sleep.

A wind had arisen out of the night. He could hear it up on the ridges, although down in the valley everything was still. It was like the sound of surf breaking on the shore, the way it swelled and then travelled around the ridges, its whisper growing and then fading away. The valley was dwarfed by the ocean of leaves and wind.

To be stretched out to sleep on his own earth, feeling his body lie along ground that was his—he felt he had been hurrying all his life, and had at last come to a place where he could stop. He could smell the rich damp air coming in the tent-flap. He could feel the shape of the ground through his back. *My own*, he kept saying to himself. *My place. Thornhill's place.*

But the wind in the leaves up on the ridge was saying something else entirely.

~

A tent was all very well, but what marked a man's claim was a rectangle of cleared and dug-over dirt and something growing that had not been there before. He had corn seeds, a pick, an axe, a spade. It was a matter of choosing a patch of ground and opening it up to the sky.

Beside the river in a long strip the ground was flat and clear of trees, already halfway to being a field. All that was needed was to clear off the daisies and scratch the surface enough for it to take a bagful of seeds.

Thornhill walked down with Willie at first light the next morning, Dick dawdling along behind, with a hoe over his shoulder. The flat part went off to left and right. One place was as good as another to heave the pick and let it bite into the ground.

But Willie was shading his eyes with his hand, looking further along. *Look Da*, he said. *Some other bugger already digged it up.* It was true, there was a patch of freshly turned soil, laced with dew, sucking up the light. He squinted at the plants in the tumbled dirt. The brightness of the early sunlight made things hard to see. A few daisies lay loose, their thick roots broken. He scuffed at one with his heel and it came out easily.

He had dreamed of this place, had allowed himself to love it too soon. All the time he had dreamed, forced himself against wind and tide and fatigue, driven by longing, all that time it had been too late. Some other man had set his foot here, worked it with his pick. Like every other hope, this one had been snatched away from him.

He took a deep breath that felt as if it could turn into tears. Turned his face up to the sky, waiting for them to subside. He stared up, could almost see the particles of air dancing against each other.

A dankness came up into his face from the patch of raw dirt. The black bird with the cold yellow eye turned its back and flapped away.

He looked again. The dirt was not dug in a square, the way a man with a pick would do. A man with a corn patch on his mind would not have left the daisies lying loose in the dirt where they could grow again, but would have pulled them out and thrown them to one side.

He was surprised at how calm his voice came out. *Just wild hogs or such. Moles. Something like that.* He was airy about it, a man not bothered in the slightest by a bit of dug-up dirt.

Willie knew better than to go against his father. *Moles, you reckon moles*, he said. Thornhill could hear his voice thin and disbelieving.

Dick was calling out from where he had got the hoe stuck in a tangle of bushes, his voice smothered by the breeze. He stumbled out, dragging the hoe, and stood staring at the disturbed ground.

Been dug up, he said at last. Willie came back at him straight away: *No, Dick, Da says it were moles*. But Dick did not catch the warning in his brother's voice, and piped up, *It's them savages. Planting them things like you would taters*.

Thornhill stared at the patch of dirt, drying grey now the sun was on it. Dick would be right, he thought, except that everyone knew the blacks did not plant things. They wandered about, taking food as it came under their hand. They might grub things out of the dirt if they happened on them, or pick something off a bush as they passed. But, like children, they did not plant today so that they could eat tomorrow.

It was why they were called savages.

He reached down and tweaked up the stalk, with the little swelling of the root attached. *Shut your gob, Dick*, he said. *Them poxy blacks don't plant nothing*. He threw the stalk away. It flew briefly, weighted by its root, and fell back into the dirt.

~

This ground was not like the dense Bermondsey earth that stuck to the feet in great clots after rain. This was thin, sandy dirt that trickled through the fingers. The little clumps of daisies came out easily, the swollen roots glassy under the layer of dirt, and could be piled by the side of the dug-over square.

All the same, it was backbreaking work. Thornhill could pull on an oar, but ten minutes creeping and bending with the hoe made him stream with sweat. As the sun rose higher through the morning it became as hot as midsummer in England. The flies danced around his nose, into his eyes. He felt about to burst out of his skin with the steamy heat, cooked in his own juices.

Willie went at the digging madly, wanting to be done with it so he could go back down to the *Hope* and sit there whipping a rope's end or pushing a bit of caulking into a leak. Dick was willing enough but useless, dreamily scratching away at the same bit of dirt for half an hour, smiling his slight secret smile.

But they finished what the moles, or hogs, had started, and by the afternoon they had a tidy square dug over, ready for the seeds: no bigger than the tent, but enough to start with. It was not so much a crop he was aiming for, as a message. Like hoisting a flag on a pole.

He sent the boys up to the tent for the seeds and sat admiring what they had done. He could hear the *pik-pik-pik-pik* of some insect close by in the grass, and a thin high hum. A bird nearby was telling a story, going up note by note, and further away another one was making a noise like a creaky door opening and closing, opening and closing.

In this notched land, where the unbroken forest covered the hills and dales like crumpled cloth, there was nothing a man could recognise as human, other than the small square of dirt they had dug. He could hear the blood pound in his ears, his breath coming in and out of his chest.

Then he saw that he was being watched by two black men. It was not so much that they appeared, as that they had chosen to become visible. They had made themselves comfortable. One had a foot wedged up against the side of a knee, balancing on his spear, so he was the echo of the angled branches around him. The other squatted as still as a boulder.

Thornhill got to his feet. As if waiting for this, the standing one stepped forward: a grey-grizzled man with stringy shanks and an old man's boxy chest and high round belly. His parts were shameless under a bit of string round his waist which held various sticks but performed no function of modesty. The other one stood up, as big as Thornhill now that he was at his full height, a younger man in the prime of his strength with a shock of hair held off his high forehead with a band of fur. The chests and shoulders of both men were ribbed with rows of scars that gleamed pale.

They held their spears as if absent-mindedly. He could not read their faces. Their eyes were hidden in the shadows cast by their heavy brows, their mouths large and unsmiling. They stood square on to him, fearlessly. The moment was theirs.

Thornhill wiped his hands down the side of his britches. He could feel his palms rub over the seam where the fabric was lumpy. It was a comfort. He did it again, then slid his hands into his pockets. It made him feel less helpless to have them tucked away where no one could see them. In some sideways part of his brain there was an image of getting into the pocket himself, in the warm and the dark, and curling up safe.

Up in a river-oak, a bird made a twittering as if amused, and a quick breeze sang through the leaves. At last he felt that there was nothing to be done but walk towards the men, speaking as to a couple of wary dogs. *Don't spear me, there's a good lad*, he said, addressing the younger one. *I'd give you a drink of tea only we ain't got none.*

But the old man cut across his words as if they were of no more importance than the rattle of wind in a tree. He spoke at some length. It was not loud, just a flow of words like his skin, without clear edges. As he spoke he gestured with a fluid hand down the river, up and over the hills, did a flattening thing with his palm like smoothing a bedcover. Thornhill was reminded of Mr Middleton explaining the set of the tides at Battersea Reach.

But the meaningless words poured over him, and in the end they became maddening. He began to feel like an imbecile. To make up for that feeling he spoke loud and jovial across the man's words. *Old boy*, he started. He fancied the sound of that. He had never called anyone *old boy* the way toffs did. *Bugger me, you are making no sense whatever!* It was the way gentry had

148

spoken to him, wanting him to row faster and cost them less, but pretending to make a joke of it.

When he stopped, the men watched him, waiting for more. He licked his lips and made himself speak again. *You ain't making no sense to me, mate*, he said. *Not a blinking word.* A thought made him laugh, and that made him bold. *You might as well bloody bark, mate*, he said, feeling his cheeks bunch up with the fun of it.

The old man's face did not show any appreciation of the joke. Buckles of flesh creased down from his nose, and his long upper lip gave him a fastidious look. When he spoke again it cut across Thornhill's humour like water on a flame. He made a chopping action with the side of his hand, pointing to the square of dug-up dirt and the daisies wilting in a heap. This time his voice was not so much a running stream. It was more like stones rolling down a hill.

Thornhill gestured at the cliffs, the river glinting between the trees. *My place now*, he said. *You got all the rest.* He drew a square on the air with his arms, demonstrating where his hundred acres began and ended.

In the scheme of things, his was surely an insignificant splinter of this whole immense place of New South Wales.

The man was not impressed. He did not look around to follow the sweep of Thornhill's arm. He knew what was there.

There was a crashing and shouting as Willie and Dick ran down the slope with the bag of seed. When they saw the blacks the fun drained out of their faces. Sal appeared at the flap of the tent with the baby in the crook of her arm. Thornhill saw the fright blossom on her face. She grabbed at Bub who was making to rush out, swivelling him around so hard that his skinny arm was nearly yanked out of its socket, and only let go of him to take hold of Johnny as he tried to follow his brother.

149

The blacks seemed to be waiting for something. Thornhill wondered what he might offer them. The pick, the hatchet, the spade: all were too precious. He wished he had thought to bring something from Sydney for this moment. Beads. He had heard of beads being given to the blacks. Mirrors.

It would have been so easy to get a handful of beads, a couple of mirrors.

But Sal was shouting down from the tent, *Give them a bit of that pork! Look sharp, Will, here it is*, and she was on her way with the baby over her shoulder and the pork in her hand. It was the way she had dealt with Scabby Bill. Something told him that these two men were different from Scabby Bill, but at least the pork—not in its first youth, but still edible—was something to give them. With luck they would take it and be gone. *Run up quick, Willie, and fetch it here*, he said. He could hear the urgency in his voice, and something he recognised as fear.

The offering of the bits of pork and the hard heel of damper seemed a way forward: the black men at least accepted them. Then they waited with the victuals in their hands. It seemed they did not recognise the pork as food. Thornhill demonstrated by swallowing some himself, feeling his throat dry around the strings of meat. But no amount of miming would make them eat.

After a while, the younger man put his piece of pork down on the dirt. Smelled his fingers, wrinkled his nose, wiped his hand on a tussock of grass. It was true, the pork had gone a grey colour that in some lights was green. They had got in the habit of holding their breath as they ate, so as not to have to smell it.

It seemed that this was not what they were waiting for.

Thornhill thought of the coins in his pocket. There was a penny and a silver sixpence, not as good as beads, but they might do the trick. He was sliding his fingers into his pocket for them when Willie gave a hoarse shout: *Oy you thieving cunny, give us that back!* and there was the old greybeard, caught in the act, the spade in his hand. Willie was grabbing him by the elbow and trying to yank it away from him, wrestling with all his boy's sinewy strength. The old man wrenched himself free, keeping hold of the spade.

He was shouting angrily, the same word again and again, and Willie was shouting back, right into his white-whiskered face: *Give it here, give it!* The two streams of words rushed together like a sea meeting a river, pouring over each other hard and muddled.

The morning was spiralling away into panic. There were too many people here, and too little language to go around. He heard himself shout one word: *No!* What he meant was, no to this moment, in which things had got away from him. *Leave him be, Willie*, he called, and went over to the old man. He had no plan, but found that he had pushed at the man's shoulder. It was warm and muscular. He slapped it lightly, and when he had slapped once, it seemed easy to go on doing it. He pointed to the spade and with each slap shouted *No! No! No!* right into his face.

The slaps on the man's skin were like slow ironic applause.

The riverbank seemed to undergo a change of air. The old man's face closed down into its creases of shadow. His hand reached around and got the curved wooden club from the string round his waist. The younger man took a step forward, the spear up in his hand, poised on the balls of his feet, his face grim. From the trees Thornhill heard the scrape of wood on wood and knew it to be the sound of spears being fitted by invisible hands along spear-throwers. He heard Sal give a squashed cry as she heard it too, and a wail from Johnny cut short with her hand over his mouth.

There was a tight-wound moment. Then the old man gave a grunt as of disgust and turned away, dropping the spade on the ground. In a single step he seemed to recede into the flickering light and shade of the forest. It closed behind him as smoothly as a curtain.

The younger man did not leave. The powerful muscle of his arm was still taut, ready to throw. He came up so close that Thornhill could smell his thick animal scent and see the sharp chips gummed into the tip of the spear: some were stone but he saw with dream-like amazement that some were chips of glass. He reached out and pushed Thornhill hard in the chest, then slapped him three times, hard, on the shoulder. It was like watching in a mirror what Thornhill himself had just done.

The man spoke loud and hard, and gestured with the hand that had slapped Thornhill. In any language, anywhere, that movement of the hand said, *Go away*. Even a dog understood *Go away* when he saw it.

They stared at each other, the black man's face a powerful thing, the anger alive on it. Then he turned and followed the old man into the forest. There was no crashing through undergrowth, no crunching of feet along leaf-litter. One moment he was there with fury on his face and a spear in his hand. The next there was only the forest, and a bird trilling as if nothing had happened.

Young Bub's wan face peeked out from behind Sal. *Why didn't they spear us, Da,* he whispered, *while they got the chance?* Johnny had his mouth squared up to cry, but Sal ruffled his hair so hard that his head wobbled under her hand. *They got no call to spear us,* she cried. Thornhill could hear the gladness in her voice, and the relief. *We give them the victuals and that, they leave us alone.* She glanced at him. *Ain't that right, Will?*

He did not know how much she believed that, and how much was for the benefit of the children, but he was happy to agree. *We'll be right as rain,* he said. *They noses was out of joint on account of wanting the spade, is all.* He picked it up, drove it into the ground, making a deep cut in its surface. *They gone and buggered off now.*

His words came out robust enough, but the silence swallowed them up.

~

Next morning Thornhill woke at first light and crawled out of the tent. In the night it had leaned even further over. Dew lay thick and pale on the grass. Every leaf of every tree gleamed. A glowing mist hung over the river, but around the tent stripes of sunlight slanted through hanging crescents of leaves and made a tender green light. A pelican, serene with its broad wings and great beak, planed through the sky over the river.

There seemed to be saplings all around the tent, sprung up overnight. It was a sick clench of the belly to see they were spears, sent into the earth hard enough to bury their barbs.

He went quickly from one to the other pulling them out of the ground. In his hand each one was a business-like thing. He was not going to think about them flying through the air. If he got rid of them it would be as if they were never there. He was on the last when Willie spoke from the front of the tent. *Be us next time*, he said. *Won't it, Da?*

He glanced at the cliffs across the river, the dull grey forest that lay thick over the ridges. *They wanted to do us harm, we wouldn't be standing here now, lad*, he said calmly, and wrenched the last spear out. *They don't mean nothing by it.* He flung the spears onto the fire, just a handful of kindling. But there was a hollow feeling in his middle where a spear might slice.

Willie said nothing. Thornhill thought of Sal, coming out so quick with the pork in her hand for the blacks, her sureness about it. *No need to frighten your mother with what ain't never going to happen*, he said. The boy looked at him in surprise, and

153

Thornhill wondered at his own words. It was the moment of fear on Sal's face, when she heard the scrape of the spear-throwers: that was the look he did not want to see. *She's a soft-hearted little thing*, he said, man-to-man with the boy. *Don't want her worrying over nothing. Do we?* Willie nodded and scuffed his foot over the hole one of the spears had made until it looked like the rest of the dirt. *Yes, Da*, he said. *She won't never guess.*

They could both see the thread of smoke, coming from somewhere up along the First Branch, but they turned their backs on it. The spears blazed up merrily. *We get those seeds in today, lad*, Thornhill said, and Willie nodded, but did not meet his father's eye.

~

Thornhill had no faith in the shrivelled seeds he had bought in Sydney. It was hard to believe that such a lifeless knot of stuff could turn into a cob of corn that a person could get his teeth into. Willie gave voice to his thought. *We been cheated, Da*, he said. *Them things won't never grow.*

Willie was half a man, but without a man's sense of when to keep his trap shut.

Thornhill bent down and pushed a seed into the dirt with his thumb. *Ain't nothing to me if it's dead or alive*, he said breezily. *Long's it says William Thornhill got here first.*

~

Sal made a place she called *the yard*, a patch of earth that she scraped and swept until it was smooth. Within its boundary she made something domestic: the fireplace, ringed with stones, where the kettle and the pot sat on the coals, the water barrel filled from the rivulet, a slab of log laid on a couple of stones that did duty as a table. She cooked and washed and swept, and sat on a log to mend the children's clothes or grind up the hominy, like any other housewife.

Beyond the yard she went only for a call of nature, and did not dally. Thornhill would see her come back, her glance sliding over the forest, the rocks, the cliffs, the sky, until it came to the table, or the tent, or a child. Those things she could see. What was beyond was invisible to her. He watched her, the way she kept her face turned away from where the trees soughed in the wind.

Like any other prisoner, she had a place—the smooth bark of a tree near the tent—where she marked off each day. Every evening she went over to it with the knife and took her time making a neat line. The evening of the first Sunday, she sliced across the six lines already there. She seemed to enjoy the way the blade bit into the parchment-pale bark.

Five years is two hundred and sixty weeks, he heard her telling Willie. *We done a week already, near enough.* As the days passed Thornhill found himself hoping she would forget to make a new mark. Sometimes the day would go by and he would think that, at last, she had forgotten, but then he would see her take the old knife with the broken-off tip and go over to the tree.

If she met his eye on the way back she might smile at him in a bright way, saying nothing. He would smile back, and that was something else not said. They had never kept secrets from each other before, or had thoughts they did not share. It was, he thought, a part of the price they had to pay—just for the time being—for what they would get in the end.

The unspoken between them was that she was a prisoner here, marking off the days in her little round of beaten earth, and it was unspoken because she did not want him to feel a jailer. She was, in a manner of speaking, protecting him from herself.

And if she did not speak of it, how could he? How could he

say, *I am sorry that what I want more than anything is your prison?* If he said that, then he would also have to say, *So we had better go back to Sydney.*

Thornhill's private thoughts were in the shadow behind his smile, the dread of failure: of the corn dying in the ground, or the *Hope* being wrecked. He had brought them here, but could he make a life for them?

But within a fortnight of him poking those wrinkled seeds into the ground, a bright-green tube of leaf had forced its way up out of each one, strong enough to pierce the dirt. He had picked his time well: the weather was warmer from day to day, the leaves growing almost visibly in the steamy heat. He put the boys to watering the plants: the river water was too brackish, so every drop had to be got from the rivulet. When the plants got up a bit, he hoped they would not still need watering. There would be rain, he promised the boys, there was always plenty of rain in the spring. But for the time being, they had to trail up and down every afternoon with the bucket.

At his urging, Sal came down to admire it too, but he could see that the tender tubes of green did not stir her the way they did him. He watched her go back up the hill to the tent as soon as she could, keeping her face turned away from where the trees crowded around the edge of the yard.

She was afraid of the children wandering and being lost in the forest, and in the absence of anything to function as a fence she tethered Bub and Johnny to the tally-tree on long ropes. Nor would she eat anything except what they had brought with them: the salt pork, the flour, the dried peas. He tried one day to offer her a bunch of some green stuff that grew down by the river, that he had found not unlike coarse parsley, but she would not try it. *I'll wait for them corn plants*, she said, and smiled up at him. *I'm right with what we got, Will.* He was glad to see her smile, but knew she was telling him she could wait, not just for their own corn, but for the five years of her sentence.

Her dreams were all of the place they had left: long intricate dreams she told him of as they lay coiled together putting off the moment of rising to another day. *I were in the alley outside of our place at home*, she would start, or *I was walking along past Vickery's, around the corner from the old place*, and he would hear the softness in her voice.

Now that they had the first few seeds in the ground, the next task was to clear a bigger patch and put more seeds in, not just as an emblem of ownership but as a real crop. As soon as that was done, Thornhill could see that he would have to turn his hand to a dwelling more significant than a tent. Otherwise, he knew that Sal's forced cheerfulness would become threadbare.

Neither of them ever mentioned the blacks. They had not been seen since the first day. He felt sometimes that they might not exist if no one said the words: *the blacks.*

But they all felt watched. Each one of them would stop in the middle of putting a stick on the fire, or chewing a mouthful of damper, and glance into the trees. It was a thing about this place: the harder the eye searched, the more the shadows confused. Now and again Thornhill glimpsed a person watching them. But, even in the moment that he started to get up, the figure became nothing more than a couple of angled branches.

~

The hundred acres Thornhill had decided to call his own encompassed all the fertile soil near the river and ended where the ridge began. It tilted up from the gentle slope of the point as sudden as the side of a roof, bristling with canted shards of rock and thick with trees that twisted into the sky.

The first few weeks of their residence were taken up with

backbreaking labour: digging, grubbing out bushes, hacking at saplings. Under the daily ministrations of the boys, the corn was coming on apace. Thornhill thought this farming was turning out to be a simple business. Food grown from his own hand! He laughed aloud at the idea, bent to feel the leaves, smooth and cool between his fingers.

It was not until he had Willie at work on the new corn patch and had cut the twenty saplings that he calculated were the minimum to start the hut, that he allowed himself to climb the ridge. He was looking forward to it: Thornhill's spread out under him, the corn patch stamping a square on the wildness. It would be another way to possess the place, to look down and think *everything I see, I own.*

But the way up was blocked at every turn by a great bulge or overhang of mouse-grey stone. A man set against that was nothing more than an ant toiling up and down until he was swallowed. He began to feel too small for the place but forced himself on, climbing over rocks and through bushes and sprays of tough grass. He could hear himself wheezing. His hand was wet with blood where he had taken a hold of that grass to pull himself up a steep pinch. Its leathery blade had cut him as clean and private as a knife.

In the end he had to turn back and settle for the platform of flat rock that ran around the base of the ridge like a step. Above him the page of the sky opened out, scrawled with cloud. The cliffs glowed orange in the late sun. Below him the thumb was laid out plain, the river to right and left of it. He could see Sal, made small by distance, bending over the washtub on her makeshift table, and Willie leaning on his pick when he should have been digging another yard of corn patch.

I see you, Willie, Thornhill said out loud. *By God, lad, I see you there.*

His voice had no resonance in this air. He cleared his throat to cover the puny sound.

An enormous honey-coloured ant ran out of a crack in the rock near his feet and zigzagged over it as if stitching it together, running fast and high on its thready black legs, carrying along the shiny bulb of its body. It was the ant that made him notice that there was a line freshly scratched into the surface of the rock. At first he thought it a flaw formed by some natural action of water or wind. But the line joined another a little further along, and then another. Even when he saw that the lines formed the outline of a fish, his first thought was to admire the way nature could mimic a picture. It was only when he saw the spine on the fish's back, the exact fan of spikes of a bream, that he had to recognise a human hand at work.

He walked the length of the fish, four or five yards. The lines were more than scratches: they had been grooved to a depth and width of an inch, standing out as bright against the grey skin of the rock as if carved that same morning. A bulge in the rock surface made the fish seem to be bending itself against a current, and its long frowning mouth could have been just about to open on its row of teeth.

Towards the tail another cluster of straight lines and triangles half-overlapped the fish, a pattern that made no sense until he came around to look at it from the other side. Then he saw it was a picture of the *Hope*. There was the curve of the bow, the mast, the sail bulging in a good breeze. There was even a line that was the tiller, bending in over the stern. All that was lacking was William Thornhill holding that tiller, listening to the creak of the ropes and staring out into the forest on his way up the river.

He heard himself exclaim, a high blurt of indignation. It was the same tone he had heard from a gentleman in Fish Street Hill when William Warner had lifted the watch out of his pocket.

The sound was swallowed up by the watching forest as if it had never been. With his foot he scraped over the lines, but they were part of the fabric of the rock.

He looked around, but no one was there watching him, nothing but the eternal trees, and the air under them where the light was full of shadows.

It came to him that this might look an empty place, but a man who had walked the length of that fish, seen the tiller and sail of the *Hope* laid down in stone, had to recognise otherwise. This place was no more empty than a parlour in London, from which the master of the house had just stepped into the bedroom. He might not be seen, but he was there.

Far below him Sal straightened up from the dish and went over to the rope she had strung up by way of drying-line. He could not see the line itself, only the way the squares of the baby's napkins danced as she put them up one by one, and then hung still after she went back into the tent.

He would tell her about the fish, even bring her up to see it. But not yet. She was content enough in her little round of flattened earth: what was the good of showing her the other world beyond it?

The thing about having things unspoken between two people, he was beginning to see, was that when you had set your foot along that path it was easier to go on than to go back.

~

The hut was not yet finished when, in their fourth week on the Hawkesbury, they had their first visitor. Smasher Sullivan came up one day with a housewarming present: a few of the last oranges off his tree, a packet of green powder against the rats, and a keg of lime. He had guessed, as Thornhill had failed to, what a difference it might make to a woman to have some white-wash and a weapon against the vermin.

He arrived on the tide and walked up from the river with the keg on his shoulder, his dog trailing behind. Out of his skiff he was a runty fellow with the body of a boy but the narrow face of a man. In his own crude way he seemed to be something of a dandy: he had put on his best for the visit, a blue coat with gilt buttons, so tight under the arms he was like a soldier on parade, and a dirty red shirt done up to the neck.

Smasher was not a man to whom Sal would have warmed in the normal way. But she welcomed him like an old friend. *Take the blessed coat off, Smasher*, she cried, seeing him sweating in it. *No need to stand on ceremony among friends.*

She gave the baby to Dick to hold and bustled around making Smasher welcome: gave him the best spot on the logs that were for the time being the extent of their furniture, put the kettle on for a drink of tea, mixed up a batch of johnny-cakes with some of their precious wheaten flour.

Smasher made himself comfortable on the log and accepted all her offers. Yes, he would have a drink of tea, and yes, he loved a johnny-cake like nobody's business, and a sup of rum by and by would be very welcome too. He peered into the baby's face and showed Dick how he could take his thumb off and put it back on again. Thornhill sat down with him to be sociable, but he would just as soon have been off lopping another sapling.

Smasher was a man starved for company, that was easy to see. He could not stop talking. He told them his story, how he had been caught in the Mile End Road with a box that had fallen off the back of a wagon. He had been about to return it to its owner, as innocent as that babe there. *But no one believes a poor man, do they, Mrs Thornhill?* he said, and dropped a wink at Sal. *My word you make a good johnny-cake, Mrs Thornhill.*

Thornhill watched him sourly, thinking his praise only angling for the plate to be passed to him again, but after a time he saw that praising the food was Smasher's way of giving thanks for human company. *My word it does a man's heart good to have a yarn*, he said. His smile was a sudden sweet thing, opening on his pinched face like a flower. In that smile was a guileless boy on whom life had now laid its mark.

Smasher's dog was a big brindle thing called Missy. She was the softness in a hard man. She sat on his feet and as Smasher talked, on and on, until white spittle gathered at the corners of his mouth, he fed her bits of food from his fingers and bent over her, fondling her ears. *Best dog a man ever had*, he said. *Keeps a man from going dilly in this godforsaken place*. The dog's eyes narrowed in bliss.

Sal told Smasher everything: Swan Lane and Butler's Buildings, how Dick had considerately waited until they put into Cape Town to be born, why the inn in Sydney had been called the Sign of the Pickle Herring. She showed him the trunk of the tree he was sitting under, with the tally-marks, and made the day's mark then and there to show him how she did it, although it was only afternoon.

Thornhill saw for the first time how much she missed having people around her. It was a little death, not being able to make a tale out of the small moments of life and share them with someone for whom they were new. Thornhill surprised a pang, hearing her voice warm, and watching how her face came to life as it had not since they had been on the river.

She had never spoken of her loneliness. And he had not thought to ask. It was part of that area of silence between them.

After a time Dick grew restless with the baby and Sal took her so he could go and play knucklebones with his brothers. With the children out of earshot, Smasher got onto the subject of the blacks. It seemed that no story about them was too terrible for him to repeat.

They had scalped two men alive up at South Creek, he said, and taken a child from its cradle, slit its little throat and sucked it dry. Thornhill found himself picturing it: the black mouths on the white flesh. When pressed, Smasher admitted that he had not seen the event personally, but he had spoken to a man who had, and swore it was no word of a lie. They had cut open a white woman, he said, down at the Cowpastures. Had got the baby out from her womb and eaten it. He had not seen that for himself either, but swore with a hand on his red flannel heart that it was in the *Gazette*, so it must be true.

Smasher, flushed with the pleasure of an audience, did not notice that Sal had gone thoughtful. She sat on the log, holding Mary so tight that even that uncomplaining child cried out. Thornhill finally caught his eye as he embarked on another tale. *That'll do, Smasher,* he said, harsher than he intended. He tried to make his voice lighter: *You'll have us scared out of our blooming wits!*

Smasher stopped. *Oh,* he cried, full of reassurance. *You ain't got to worry, Mrs Thornhill, just so long as Mr Thornhill keeps his gun by his hand.* It was not the reassurance that Thornhill might have wished, and he stared away without answering, but Smasher did not get the hint. *I got three guns,* he said. *Loaded ready to shoot any black arse comes near the place.*

Thornhill was starting to feel he would be pleased to throttle Smasher. *That's enough,* he said, but Smasher was drunk on company. *A whip, now,* he said, addressing Sal. *A whip is a mighty handy thing to have round your average black savage.* He nodded and smiled at her. *And the dogs. Missy here, I trained her up special to go for black skin.*

Neither of his hosts responded. Thornhill put the cork in the rum bottle, making a business of doing it, but Smasher only tipped his drink down his throat and held the empty cup waiting for more. *Soon be slack water, Smasher*, Thornhill said. *Don't want to miss that tide.* At last, with many last shouted farewells, Smasher got into his boat and pushed out into the dusk.

There was nothing to say. Smasher had filled the place with noise, but he had left behind its mirror-image, a silence in which his violent stories echoed.

When the children were asleep later, rustling against each other on their mattress of dried grass, husband and wife stretched out too. It was the time of day Thornhill liked best. The whole measureless world shrank to the flame of the wick in the saucer. The shadows hid the drooping canvas of the tent around them, the muddled heaps of their belongings on the ground, the meanness their life had come down to. Sal was again that young girl, smiling her serene smile with that irresistible mouth. He cut up one of Smasher's oranges and gave her the pieces one after the other as they came off his knife. It gave him pleasure to see her lying on an elbow eating them, and to have the pungent smell all around them, hot and thick, the smell of sunlight.

But when the orange was gone she was sombre, gazing into the flame of the lamp. *That Smasher*, he said, and forced a laugh. *My word he can spin a yarn!* She glanced towards him, her face halved by the lamplight. *Just skiting, you reckon?*

He could hear the doubt in her voice, and the hope. He made his own rumble with conviction: *Gammon if ever I heard any, take it from me, pet.* But he could not forget the hands that Smasher had twitched at him, or the black bag that had once been a human, hanging from the tree.

She turned back to the lamp, staring at where the bit of twisted rag flamed away. In profile she looked as stern as the face on a coin. When she spoke again, her voice was so low he could barely hear her. *The way he were talking about that whip*, she said, and rubbed her hand across her lips as if wiping away the words that brought back the story. *I didn't like the look on his face.* She looked at him very direct. *You think I'm a foolish woman*, she said. *But Will, promise me you will never do such a thing?*

He thought of the morning Collarbone had been hanged, that long horror. And Sal, asking about it. *Clean as a whistle*, he had said, because what was the point of breaking her heart with the truth?

Cosy by lamplight, with the night kept outside and Blackwood's liquor warm in his belly, it was an easy enough promise to make. *I would never*, he said. *Not never ever*, and she relaxed against him and was asleep straight away, her weight sweet as a child's against him while he stared into the shadows.

~

A bark hut looked a simple enough thing, until you went to make one. Each stage of the building was throwing obstacles at Thornhill that he had not foreseen. The earth was too full of rocks to make a decent hole for the uprights to stand in and too sandy to hold them firm, the saplings that had looked so straight in the forest turned out to be kinked, the bark sheets split as he levered them off the trees.

Chopping, clearing, building, he was discovering a new William Thornhill, though: a man who could labour against wilderness until it yielded up a dwelling. Their round of scraped and beaten earth grew with every day that passed. The place was full of the sound of themselves—the chopping down of the trees, the crackling as they burnt the heaps they cut, the thud of the pick into the earth. The larger corn patch had taken them days to clear, and then they had discovered that something had eaten through the bag the seeds were kept in and got the lot, so the planting would have to be delayed until Thornhill went to Sydney.

By the time Sal had marked the fifth week, a hut stood in the yard. It had none of the conveniences he had hoped to give it: flaps of bark that could be folded back on leather hinges to let the light in, a fireplace, a chimney. All that would have to wait.

But the hut stood up on its patch of trampled dirt, crisp against the tangle of the forest, and it was only crooked from certain angles.

At least no one could think now that the place was empty.

The air was different inside the hut. Outside, the ceaseless hummings and clickings of the place closed around a speck of human life like water around a pebble. But once there was a hut to go into, a person became again a thing separate from the place, moving through an air of their own making.

The forest took on a different aspect, too. Outside the eye was confused by so many details, every leaf and grass-stalk different but each one the same. Framed by doorway or window-hole, the forest became something that could be looked at part by part and named. Branch. Leaves. Grass.

By night, with the lamp making a smoky bead of light, a shot of rum to hand and his pipe full, it was a cheerful enough place. He was prepared to take pride in it.

By daylight, he had to admit, it was a poor rough thing. The bark was hairy, as if the hut were the coarse pelt of some slow animal, and the underside, facing in, had an ugly flayed look. Every sheet was already warping against the next, leaving gaps big enough to put an arm through. The distinction between inside and outside was not as clear as he had hoped. One morning Willie and Dick got out of their dry-grass mattress and a long black snake slithered out after them as if thinking itself another boy ready for a slab of fried bread and a drink of tea. They all watched, a family turned to marble, as the length of dull black progressed without haste across the dirt floor, flowing around a plate, and out through one of the gaps in the wall.

Sal was the first to move. *There's mud*, she said. *Around by the place there where we get the water. You, Willie, and Dick, get round there after breakfast and we'll stop up all them gaps.* She was plain about it as if keeping snakes out of the house was something a body did every day of the week.

She never stopped surprising him.

We only got to stop up to the height of a snake, but, she said. *They can't jump, can they, Will?* That was a good joke. *And that door*—she turned to look at it, the bark flap so warped there was room almost for Mary to crawl underneath—*We'll tie another piece along the bottom. Knit it on, like. It don't need to last that long, anyways*, she said casually, as if it was all a bit of a lark. *It'll do us till we go.*

Something in him veered away from that. In bed at the Sign of the Pickle Herring, five years had seemed a long time. Now, with the notches beginning to fill up the side of the tree, it no longer had such a generous feel.

~

Seeing that Sal was lonely enough to enjoy the company even of Smasher Sullivan, Thornhill encouraged him to spread the word of the hospitality he had enjoyed, and the Sunday after they moved into the hut, they were visited by a crowd of neighbours. It was astonishing how folk appeared out of this empty place, like bugs out of the woodwork, when it was a matter of liquor dispensed with a generous hand. For himself, he could take or leave the lot of them, but he made them welcome for Sal's sake.

Smasher was the first to arrive, in his tight blue coat. It

seemed a matter of pride in him to arrive and leave wearing that coat, even though as soon as she saw him Sal urged him to take it off and he needed no second telling. As their other neighbours arrived, Smasher introduced them, his scaly face red with the pleasure of society.

Birtles was a huge man with enormous intricate ears and a great deal of hair about his face. At the back of his bald head the scalp was ridged into deep furrows like a bulldog's face. Birtles had a first name, but Smasher introduced him as Sagitty. It made a little story to get the conversation going: how, when he was a lad, some man of the cloth in Stepney had declared him sagacious for something he had done, and Birtles had been offended, thinking the parson was mocking him—the word had that flavour in his ears—until the man had explained that it was praise, and then the name had stuck.

Sagitty's life did not demonstrate much sagacity. He was caught stealing four bags of soot from Mill Street in Stepney and had served three years in irons in Van Diemen's Land. Around his ankles the scars were purple where the metal had rubbed them raw. Now he was up along Dillon's Creek, on a fertile pocket behind a hill, with a patch of wheat and a couple of hogs. He had to hump every sackful of grain he grew, up the hill and down the other side, to get it into the boat that would take it to market, and now had rounded shoulders like a clerk, and a lump as big as an egg on the back of his neck where the sacks rested. There had been a wife once, and a couple of babies, but it seemed that they had died under this extreme sun. He had an unusual luxury, a neighbour, one George Twist, but Twist had drunk himself to oblivion the night before and could not be roused to visit the new arrivals.

To hear him tell it, Sagitty Birtles was constantly being robbed by the blacks. They took his axe, he said, and the tin dish from inside the hut, and his shirt that he had washed and spread over a bush. They took the last of the flaming fowls, the two left after the wild dogs had taken their fill.

Sal gave Thornhill a quick smiling glance that reminded him of Ingram's hen.

But there was nothing funny about the theft of Sagitty's wheat, the fruit of so much labour, precious sackfuls he was about to carry over the hill to the boat. The blacks were nothing but thieving black buggers, he maintained, taking advantage of a man's hard work. He learned them a lesson whenever he saw them lurking about.

On those words—*learned them a lesson*—Thornhill saw him exchange a smirk with Smasher. Then he leaned back scratching under his chin, where the beard was coarse. The rasping was loud in the pause that followed his words.

Thornhill found himself imagining the form Sagitty's lessons might take. He had opened his mouth to change the tack of the conversation, but Smasher got in first. He spoke almost dreamily. *It's like the bleeding flies, ain't it*, he said. *Kill one, ten more come to its funeral.*

That word stopped Sal, who was busying herself at the fire with more johnny-cakes. She turned with a stick in her hand and exchanged another glance with her husband. Smasher caught the glance. *Oh, I ain't talking killing, exactly*, he said, but his voice had the airy sound of a man lying, and when Sal looked away he gave Thornhill a solemn wink. *Just disperse, like*, he said, his eyes sliding away and his laugh as he spoke a harsh wheeze.

Then Webb arrived, a skinny bit of a man with hair rough as a dog's, its tufts showing where it had been hacked against the nits with a knife the way Sal did the boys'. Webb waved away the offer of a piece of log, making himself comfortable on the ground.

Thornhill hoped the conversation would turn in another

direction, but the blacks seemed all anyone could talk about. Webb—they called him Spider—was at Half Moon Bend, bounded on three sides by cliff and forest. It was easy for the blacks to creep down the hillside. They had come one day when sickly Mrs Webb was alone in the hut. They wanted her skirt, but could not work out the placket, so they got the knife and cut the whole thing off and she was left in her petticoat. They took the meal she was getting ready—chicken, pot and all—and were long gone by the time Spider got back.

Spider was born unlucky. He was caught in Smithfield Market when a man recognised the silver buttons on his coat as the ones his master had missed from his house a week before. Now, apart from the visits of the blacks, he was the settler always washed away first by the floods, eaten out first by the corn-grubs. He had lost one boy to the snakebite and another to fits.

Thornhill thought privately that he should not have called his holding Never Fail.

From his narrow head Spider's hoarse voice was a surprise. *They's vermin*, he said, *the same way rats is vermin.* He sounded the way a man might if he had been hanged and come back from the dead, Thornhill thought. Which was, of course, true of them all.

Like Smasher, Spider was making the most of an audience. *They cut us up like you would a beast*, he said. *Eat the best bits.* Smasher, his face creased with the fun of it, shouted, *What bits would they be, Spider? You would be a lean old pick!* That changed the pitch of the laughter, as if everyone was thinking of their own body sliced up neatly for a feed.

Loveday's place was across the river from Webb's, so they had come down together. Thornhill knew Loveday from having shipped his crop of pumpkins and melons to Sydney more than once. A tall awkwardly put-together fellow, he had no more idea of farming than the man on the moon, but anyone could make things grow on the river-flats.

He sat on the log with one leg crossed over the other like a man in his parlour. Although gaunt in the face from too many pumpkins and melons and not enough of anything else, Loveday was something of a gent, enamoured with the sound of his own smarmy voice. He was out of place among these men who had no more words to rub together than they had coins. Loveday—*Parson*, as Smasher called him—was the only one there with boots on, even though his had been made for a man with much bigger feet.

Loveday had a story about the blacks, too, and stood up to enjoy his moment telling it: of how a native had speared him one day while he was relieving himself in the bushes. He even undid his britches and peeled them down at the side to show the scar on his hip. Since that day, he claimed, he had not eased himself, but was waiting to return to England where a man could attend to the call of nature without getting a spear up his backside.

Even mournful Webb laughed. Loveday looked around, his bony face flushed with the pleasure of an audience, and winked at Sal. Thornhill saw that he kept his distance from her, not wanting to overwhelm her with his height: a gentleman's delicacy. He was pleased to see her laughing back. He himself made sure he laughed the longest at the tale, so Sal would know that it was only a story to entertain some newcomers, not sober fact.

This was a valley of men, apart from two women: Mrs Webb was not visiting because one of the children was sick with a fever, but the widow Mrs Herring had rowed herself down from Cat-Eye Creek. It appeared that Mrs Herring was the nearest thing this part of the river had to a surgeon. She could deliver a baby, stitch up an axe wound, had saved the littlest Webb from the chin-cough. She was no beauty, with a high square forehead, eyes that seemed to bulge out of her face and a one-sided smile that always had a stained white pipe in it.

Mrs Herring was a shrewd old soul. That lopsided mouth looked as if many thoughts were going on behind it, but she kept most of them to herself.

Sal embraced the widow Herring like a long-lost sister when she arrived. She could hardly credit that Mrs Herring lived alone on her few acres at Cat-Eye with nothing more than her fowls for company. *Mrs Herring, ain't you lonesome up there?* she asked. *With no one near?* Mrs Herring took the pipe out of her mouth and began to poke around inside its bowl. *Better my own company than many I've known*, she said. She glanced at Smasher. *As for the blacks, I give them when they ask.* She hesitated. *They help themselves now and then, I turn a blind eye.* Thornhill saw Smasher make a crooked mouth as if he had bitten a lemon. Mrs Herring stuck the pipe back in her mouth and spoke around it: *Way I see it is, I got enough. One old biddy is real cheap to run.*

Sal smiled, rocking the baby in her arms to get her to sleep, but watched Mrs Herring, waiting for more of an answer. She looked as if she might ask again, but there was a rustle of amusement around the men, and Smasher hawked up a knot of phlegm and got up to spit it out behind a bush. Turning back, his glance was caught by something down by the river. *Tom Blackwood's on his way*, he said, and Thornhill saw another glance exchanged between him and Sagitty, and a hardening of Smasher's mouth.

Better tie the dog up, Smasher, Sagitty said. He turned to Thornhill. *Missy goes for him, same as if he was one of them black buggers*, he said. *Funny ain't it?*

In the five weeks they had been on the river, Thornhill had not seen Blackwood, even though he knew that he still went up and down in the dory he had bought to replace the *Queen*, supplying the Crown and the Blue Boar at Green Hills. Blackwood's liquor was unmistakable, burning all the way down the gullet and leaving a person next morning blinking at a world gone sharp and painful. But there was plenty of it, and the price was right. There was a living to be made from it, and if he was not a rich man, Blackwood did not seem to care.

When Blackwood entered Thornhill's clearing late in the afternoon, a keg of liquor on his shoulder as a housewarming gift, he made the place seem small. There was an authority about him so that even boastful Sagitty went quiet, watching Blackwood glumly and fingering the beard around his mouth.

Thornhill knew Blackwood better than any other man on this river, and yet he did not know anything of what went on behind Blackwood's face. He had never seen Blackwood's Lagoon. More than once he had suggested he might pay him a visit, but something about Blackwood discouraged the idea. Thornhill supposed it was because of the still. It seemed a silly kind of delicacy, when everyone knew he had one, but if Blackwood wanted to be private, Thornhill was not inclined to intrude.

Blackwood made Smasher edgy. His voice took on an aggrieved tone. *Them thieving buggers come down last night*, he said. *Pinched me bloody shovel that I use for shitting, saving your presence ladies.*

Blackwood had refused the offer of a log and had taken up position squatting off to the side. His face in profile was as if carved out of stone: that imposing nose, the muscular mouth that gave nothing away. Smasher started again: *They got no right*, but Blackwood cut straight across his words, speaking direct to Thornhill. *Them daisies down there.* They all watched as he picked up a length of cord lying on the ground, that the whipping had come undone from, and coiled it in his hand. *Daisy yams, I call them*. He jerked his head sideways to show where. *There ain't hardly none left*.

That was true enough. The daisies were easy to get rid of because once they were dug up they did not grow back again, the way other weeds did.

They give me a couple when I first come, Blackwood said. No one needed to ask who *they* were. *I gone and give them a nice little mullet for them*, he said and shook his head at the memory. *They was lumpy sorts of things like a monkey's balls*. His laugh was so loud it startled the baby awake.

Thornhill could see Blackwood tasting the flavour of the thing in his mind. *Pretty good eating, taken all round, ain't they*, Mrs Herring said, and puffed away on her pipe, ignoring the surly looks from Smasher and Sagitty. *Sweet like*, Blackwood agreed. *And mealy after they been in the coals a while*. But Blackwood had not come to talk about the flavour of yams. *See, them yams grow where you putting in the corn*, he said. *You dig them up, means they go hungry*. Having said his piece he turned and looked across the river, where the sun was beginning to set.

But Sagitty burst out angrily. *They never done nothing*, he cried. *See them breaking their back to dig it up and that?* He thumped his pannikin down so hard on the ground that its contents slopped out.

Blackwood, not taking his eyes off the cliffs, rode over him as if he had not spoken. *There was a meeting*, he said. *Governor come up on the Porpoise, anchored off the point there*. His head jerked to indicate the place. *There was one of the blacks had a bit of English*. His thick fingers were carefully rewinding the whipping and he seemed to be talking to the cord rather than the people around him. *Upshot of it was, Governor said there'd be no more white fellers downstream of the Second Branch*.

You're lying, Tom Blackwood, Sagitty shouted, but Blackwood

174

calmly knotted up the whipping and snipped it off with his teeth. *Shook hands, the lot*, he said. *That's how it was.* It was clear that he did not care whether Sagitty believed him or not. *I were there on the aft deck, whipping a rope's end like I just done.* He looked at Thornhill and winked. *Nobody sees a waterman, ain't that right, Will Thornhill?*

Smasher was swelling with indignation. *They ain't nothing but thieves*, he shouted. *Don't know how to do nothing but thieve off honest men!*

Blackwood turned his face towards him, as if amused at a pup trying to bite his ankle. *Honest men*, he repeated. *You ain't never done no thieving, Smasher Sullivan. Oh, my very word no.*

Smasher was the only one not laughing. Thornhill could see the muscle in his jaw clenched tight, holding in his rage. Mrs Herring went so far as to take the pipe out of her mouth so she could enjoy the joke.

But Blackwood had not finished. He turned the great slab of his face towards Thornhill and waited for the laughing to stop. *You got to work it out your own way*, he said. *But when you take a little, bear in mind you got to give a little.* Then he got to his feet as if he had done what he came to do. Sal called a farewell as he went back down to the boat, but he only waved without looking around.

As Blackwood's arrival had changed the mood, so did his leaving. No one seemed to have any more tales they wanted to tell. Those who lived upriver reminded each other that they had better get the tide while it was still flooding, and trailed down to the boats. Only Smasher, waiting for the turn of tide to take him downstream, sat on. There was a grim look about his face as he stared down towards the river, and the Thornhills left him alone.

Give a little, take a little. Was it a warning or a threat? But

Blackwood was not a man you could ask to explain himself. And Thornhill was not interested in hearing any advice that Smasher Sullivan might give.

~

The thought of that hundred and fifteen pounds, plus interest, kept him awake at night. It had got him the *Hope*, which was the way to make money, but the *Hope* had been tied up idle for more than five weeks now while its master had become a farmer and a builder. It was well into October already, the store of food they had brought from Sydney was running low, and the seeds for the real crop not yet in the ground.

Before they left Sydney, he had applied for convict servants to be assigned to him, on the strength of the service he would be doing in bringing food to Sydney. Why not? A man had to think on a big scale to do any good for himself. Nightingale had done out the application in exchange for a couple of quarts of the best and, having had experience of other applications, advised Thornhill to ask for four men, hoping for three.

Now, just in time, Andrews from Mullet Island brought word that Thornhill had been assigned two men off the transport that had just berthed. Thornhill could hardly believe it was that easy.

Should have asked for ten, Sal said. She was as astonished as he was. *Then we'd a got five.*

All he had to do was to get to Sydney and take his pick.

~

He would be gone a week, and if the winds were contrary it could be a fortnight. Willie, a lad of twelve, would be the nearest thing to a man the household would have for all that time. Once Thornhill returned with the convicts, he could leave them on the place while he and Willie went backwards and forwards on the *Hope*. But he had to leave the family unprotected first. Whichever way he turned the thing around in his mind, it came back to the same problem.

Smoke from the blacks' fires was visible every day, sometimes from the ridge behind the hut, sometimes from downriver, at other times a short way up the First Branch. They were all around, all the time. But in the five weeks the Thornhills had been on the river, they had only seen the blacks on the first day. If they were going to cause any trouble, Thornhill told himself, surely they would have done it by now.

He had to take the risk, and pray for fair winds to speed the *Hope* to Sydney and back.

Sal put a brave face on it, knowing as well as he did how little choice they had. As the *Hope* streamed away on the tide, she stood with the children on a rise that gave her a view right down the reach, holding up Johnny's plump little hand and waving it with every appearance of good cheer.

He waved back, but as the *Hope* slid down the river, all he could see was how vulnerable Thornhill's Point was. The hut was hardly visible in its patch of beaten ground. Around it were the bulges of the forest, shadowed even in the brightest sun, a tangle of light and shade, rock and leaf.

When the first point hid the figures from view he turned away. He realised he was sweating with the knowledge of how fragile their hold was on the place. Riding the *Hope* as hard as it would go down the coast, he was haunted by what a frail figure Sal had been, standing on the rise and bravely waving.

~

Off the Government Wharf the *Scarborough* transport lay black against the bright water. Shouts carried across to Thornhill as he stood on the wharf, and the flat clank of chains as the convicts were mustered on deck. He remembered how it was to be brought up from the darkness and stench to the sunlight, like a white grub revealed in rotten wood. It was too easy to remember: some things went too deep to fade.

But the memory belonged to another life that had nothing to do with this airy spring morning, points of light sparkling off the water and the fine salt of the breeze around his face. In that other life, this teasing dance of light or that immense forest with the breeze sighing through it would have seemed nothing but a fancy. Yet here he was: William Thornhill, almost-owner of the sloop *Hope*, a man with a hundred acres he called his own.

It was a nasty surprise to find that Captain Suckling, late of the convict transport *Alexander*, was down on the wharf in his silver-buttoned waistcoat. Thornhill had heard he had been given land, the way gentry were, with a piece of paper to make it theirs rather than the sweat of their brow. But fortunes were made and lost quick in this place, and Suckling—too proud to work his land himself, and too fond of a drop—had lost his. He was now nothing more than a minor functionary of the Commissioner of Convicts.

A mass of tiny broken veins covered his cheeks and his eyes were an old man's, set in rheumy sockets. His nose had become a swollen red thing, a separate organism that had taken up residence on his face. His jacket was fraying round the cuffs and his shirt had no collar.

In his hand he had a ledger with the names—the same ledger, or one just like it, in which Thornhill's name was forever written. He glanced at Thornhill as if he were of no more account than a bollard, flicking at the flies with a long soiled handkerchief.

Then their eyes met, and Thornhill saw that Suckling was still sharp enough to remember him. He stood straight and looked Suckling in the eye, reminding himself of the pardon he had in the tin box.

Suckling spoke loud, the booming voice of a man who had shouted orders most of his life, careless of who might hear: *Thornhill is it not, Alexander transport?* and flicked about himself importantly with the handkerchief.

Thornhill did not answer, glanced away, hated himself for glancing away. Suckling smiled a neat little smile. *I never forget a felon's face,* he said. *William Thornhill, Alexander transport.* His voice was rich with satisfaction.

Thornhill made himself stony, watching as a fly landed on Suckling's jaw, where there was a gleam of soap lather, and began to climb up into a nostril. Suckling snorted and flinched. *Stand back, man,* he cried, and flapped peevishly around him. The flies lifted and settled back on his hair, his forehead, that irresistible nose. *Back man,* he cried again. *Get back.* He shooed Thornhill away with both hands as if he were a dog. *Stand back for God's sake, man,* he shouted. *You harbour the flies so!*

In an instant the glories of Port Jackson became a prison once more, the sunlight lost its colour, the closed-in township became a poisonous place where a man might choke to death. He could buy the pardon, he could get the land, he could fill his strongbox with money. But he could not buy what Suckling had. No matter how shabby Suckling became, no matter how far gone in drink, he would always be able to hold his head up high, a man who had never worn the stripes.

Suckling stared at Thornhill, daring him to answer back, but he made himself wooden, as he had learned to do in that other life, on the *Alexander*. He had thought the man who knew the knack of absenting himself from his body was dead. It was an old pain returning to find that William Thornhill, felon, was waiting under the skin of William Thornhill, landowner.

He took a step back and had a sudden sharp memory of his binding at the Watermen's Hall, shuffling backwards towards the fire until his britches were nearly alight. He had thought then that it was all part of the price a boy paid for getting up in the world. It seemed that a man had to go on paying.

~

The felons were being pushed and prodded over the plank onto the wharf and stood bowed under the ferocity of light, awkward in their irons. Their heads had been recently cropped so their necks were pale like sprouted potatoes, the scabby skin showing where the shears had bitten too deep. They stood on the wharf in a tight bunch, afraid of so much space.

Thornhill had looked forward to this moment. He had pictured how he would stride and point at the men he wanted. But he hung back now, so he would not have to face Suckling's smirk.

The Governor's man had already creamed off the prisoners with skills: the carpenters and builders, the sawyers and farmers. Now the gentleman settlers, with their braying voices and their coats that fitted as if they had been born in them, were singling out the strong ones and the ones on whose faces life had not laid too hard a stamp. Then the emancipist settlers made their choices, and there was not much left when Suckling was beside him again out of nowhere. *Take your pick, Thornhill*, he said, and made a shopkeeper's expansive gesture. His smile was yellow in the blaze of sun. *Feel free, won't you?* he said, and gave *free* a little lingering weight.

The two that Thornhill chose were the best of a bad lot. The one who called himself Ned, no other name forthcoming, was a dim thin soul with a long jaw like the heel of a foot, and a wet red mouth and eyes too far back in his head. He reminded Thornhill of poor Rob back in London, a few bricks short of a load, but he seemed willing enough. The other had been a barrow-boy at Covent Garden, he said, although he was no longer a boy. He was haggard in the bright glare of the day.

They were a miserable enough pair. But his own.

The barrow-boy was squinting at him through the painful light. *Why, Will Thornhill, is it?* he said, coming up closer so Thornhill caught the smell of the ship on him. *Will! Dan Oldfield, remember?*

Thornhill looked at him: the gaunt face, black whiskers beneath the milky skin giving him a starved look, the mouth, starting a grin, ajar on gappy teeth. He remembered Dan Oldfield now. He had seen his father laid out dead on Herring Wharf full of river-water. He remembered the hunger they had shared together, and the cold, and the way they had stood one day pissing on their own feet, just for the moment's warmth of it.

The old place sends its regards, Will, Dan cried. His voice was louder than necessary. *Wapping New Stairs ain't the same without our Will Thornhill!* In the face of Thornhill's lack of response, his smile was stiffening.

Thornhill spoke as mildly as a man might who has nothing to prove. *Forgetting your manners are you, Dan Oldfield*, he said, and saw the grin close down. He thought of the way Suckling smiled, not showing any teeth, and tried it himself. *It is Mr Thornhill, Dan*, he said. *You would do well to remember.*

Dan looked away, blankly, at the headlands across Port Jackson, the thick-packed bush, the trembling silver of the water. *Mr Thornhill, then*, he said, his voice emptied of expression. Thornhill watched him staring down at the water, where shafts of sunlight sent pale fingers into the glassy green depths, saw the way he was clenching his jaw. He kept shading his eyes with one hand, then the other, his head down. The sunlight showed how thin the wisps of hair were on his pointed head.

Thornhill remembered how he had stared down at the water in just that way, the day the man with the beard full of breadcrumbs had assigned him to Sal. It was a way of not being present at what was happening. Staring into the depths of the water, a man could become a fish, or the water itself.

He knew what it was like to be Dan. That was the trouble. He might be entitled to stand in power over him, but in the eyes of men like Suckling, he and Dan Oldfield were the same. He saw what he had never seen before: that there could be no future for the Thornhills back in London.

He remembered the way he himself had once thought about men who were transported: they had something like the pox and ought to be avoided in case it were catching. Even the barrow-boys at Covent Garden might feel they were above a man who had once had the leg-irons around his ankles. Certainly the well-fed gentlemen in the Watermen's Hall, safe behind their acre of mahogany table, would not care that a man had his pardon. No matter how much gold he might have about him, they would never trust a wherry or a prentice to a man who had been a guest of His Majesty.

What was worse, he saw in that same airless moment that the children of a man with the taint would be tainted too. So would his children's, and his children's children. Their very name—Thornhill—would carry the taint. He pictured them, a row of pink faces in white lace bonnets, the sons and daughters of his children, floating off into the distance in their cots. But blighted, a shadow over their faces.

Now he understood, as he had not before, why Blackwood's mouth had always grown soft when he pointed his boat up the river and coiled his way deep into the land. The Hawkesbury was the one place where no man could set himself up as better than his neighbour. They were all emancipists in that private valley. There, and only there, a man did not have to drag his stinking past around behind him like a dead dog.

Sal had known Dan Oldfield in London too, and like Thornhill she did not let him presume on the past. Dan and Ned had to share the hut with the Thornhills that first night, and it was close quarters with all of them in there. The newcomers had a square of dirt with a few bags spread out on it, hard up against the Thornhills' bags.

By God, Sal, Dan said, kicking at a corner of bag. *Ain't this snug.* It was as if Sal had been waiting. *You had best call me Mrs Thornhill, Dan*, she said, quite loud so there could be no mistake. Dan said nothing, but gave her a look under his brows, and she began to bluster a little. *It will work out best that way.* Thornhill, watching from the doorway, heard her remember some dandified words she must have heard somewhere. *It will work out more satisfactory*, she said, and then remembered another phrase. *I think we will find.*

He thought of the pleasure they had both taken in playing the game of master and servant, in the early days in Sydney. This business with Dan was another kind of pleasure altogether, and no game. The reality was that they had power almost of life and death over Dan Oldfield, and something in them both was enjoying it. His own pleasure in it, as he had bullied Dan on the wharf, had come as a surprise to Thornhill: he had not known that he had it in him to be a tyrant. A man never knew what kind of stuff he was made of, until the situation arose to bring it out of him. Sal's evident satisfaction in being called Mrs Thornhill by a man she had shared stolen roast chestnuts with was another surprise. He saw Dan flick a quick look between the two of them, as if wondering to himself what it was about New South Wales that could bring about such a change.

In Sydney he had got two gifts for Sal: a few hens and a

skinny rooster in a wicker cage, and an engraving of Old London Bridge glassed and framed. With a forefinger on the glass she traced the lines of the streets as if walking along them in her mind. When she turned to him her eyes were full of tears. *Will*, she said, her voice snagged on a sob, *you know me that well, there'd be no hiding nothing from you*, taking his hand and squeezing it hard. He could feel hers, rough in his, the hand of a woman who never stopped working. *It's a treasure, Will*, she said, *and you are a dear to think of it*, and he saw that she had heard what the engraving was saying: *I have not forgot my promise*.

He hung it on a wooden peg wedged into a hole in one of the hut's uprights. *Where I can see it first thing when I wake up, Will*, she said. When he came in later he saw that she had run a cord through the bit of roof-tile and hung that from the peg too, so it was suspended below the engraving.

That night, after the wick in the saucer was snuffed out, they all lay together in its smell of burned fat, packed into the hut like kippers in a box. Thornhill could feel Sal stiff beside him, with Dan not a yard away, hands behind his head.

The solitude they had enjoyed up till now, although not without its problems, was a gift they did not quite know how to do without.

Ned fell asleep straight away. After a time of deep noisy breathing he began to mutter from a dream, turning and scuffling on the bags. Then they heard him get up and stand like a horse asleep on his feet saying thickly, *Fleming get away out of it Fleming*. With an angry grunt Dan got up and pushed him back down on the ground, and he slept soundlessly at last.

At breakfast by the campfire Thornhill saw Dan looking around between mouthfuls of damper. He took in the cliffs on the other side of the river, the valley of the First Branch where it bent up between the furry ridges to the north.

Thornhill knew what was in his mind. Others had tried to walk to China through that forest. Sometimes they would stagger up to some settler's hut, wild-eyed, nearly dead from hunger and naked from where the blacks had stripped them down to the skin. From time to time a skeleton would turn up in a remote gully. Mostly they vanished forever, absorbed into the endless formless distance.

But Dan had not been in the colony long enough to know what happened to felons who were fooled by the absence of walls.

Thornhill waited until Dan's gaze at the ridges and valleys met his. *Looks real easy, don't it, only fifty mile back to Sydney.* He made sure his voice was mild. Dan looked away sullenly at the cliffs across the river, hanging in a dark wall with the sun behind them. The cliffs stared back. Thornhill felt his mouth shaping that superior Suckling smile. *You got me down here*, he said. *Or the forest and the savages out there.* Dan gave him a glance he could not read. *Up to you*, Thornhill said. *No skin off my nose.*

~

That first morning—the morning of the first day of their seventh week, as Sal remarked over breakfast—Thornhill set Dan and Ned to making a lean-to on the back of the hut where they could sleep, while he made a place for the fowls where the wild dogs could not get them at night. He had already cut the saplings for the lean-to and Willie had stripped a couple of sheets of bark off the trees. All his new servants had to do was trim the saplings for the frame and make holes in the bark to tie it on.

It became apparent, though, that Ned was inclined to fall down in fits just when he was most needed. Even when upright he had a nervy tremulous way with him. He could not be trusted with the axe, so Thornhill gave him the gimlet to make the holes in the bark. The threat of Thornhill's hand over him could make him go through the motions, but he could not make a proper job of it. By the time he had finished, what were supposed to be neat holes in the bark were long useless splits.

Ned took satisfaction in stating the obvious. Looking at the ragged edge of the bark he announced, *Don't look too good, Mr Thornhill,* and laughed a silly whinny. Thornhill looked at him, the loose grin that seemed to show too much of the inside of his lips, the eyes that were a little loose in their sockets.

Could a man be punished for the pitch of his laugh?

After so long on the transport Dan was not a fit man, and the breathless heat of these spring days made the pasty skin of his face break into blotches. As he heaved with the axe at the hard wood he panted and his nose dripped with sweat. The minute he thought himself unobserved, he would lean on the axe and stare out at the forest. His back in the striped slops flickered with a mass of flies, but what they liked best was his eyes, his mouth, that expanse of sweaty cheek. He flapped his hand and squinted and blew and tossed his head to dislodge them. They circled but always landed again. In the end he nearly sliced his leg open with the axe, trying to twitch them off his hand.

He flung it down in a temper and looked at where Thornhill stood in a patch of shade. *Give us a break,* he said, and the *Mr Thornhill* that he did not add hung in the air. *Give us some water at least.* He squinted against the sun, hitting out at the flies.

Thornhill remembered how it felt to be sweating and panting and begging from another man. He realised now how begging made a man ugly and hardly human: easy to refuse.

Regulations, Dan, felons to work during daylight hours. He heard the rich pious tone in his own voice, lying. *I ain't going against what the Governor says, being an emancipist myself.* He smiled blandly, enjoying the words. *Get on now, finish that and we'll see how things go along.*

Dan looked at him, his face wooden. He made no move to pick up the axe and get back to work. Thornhill wondered if he had gone too far, whether Dan was going to call his bluff and refuse to work. He pictured it: Dan holding out through bread and water, through beatings. He had seen it on the hulks, men who got it into their head not to give in. He had seen them rather die than yield.

In the end it was a fly that did it, getting up Dan's nose and making him flinch. Such a tiny creature, but it had the power to break a man's spirit. He took up the axe and began to chip away at the sapling. Thornhill saw the flies crawling undisturbed over his face and his eyes screwed up against them. In the white blaze of the sun he was a bowed and lowly creature. The tendons stood out along the back of his neck, white and vulnerable.

Thornhill flipped the switch of leaves that he was using as a fly-whisk—he had found that the long stringy needles of the river-oaks were the best—and walked over into the shade. He felt something swell inside him like a yawn welling up from the belly. *Strolling.* That was the word. He was strolling, and carrying nothing more backbreaking than this little spray of leaves. Strolling as a gentleman might from the Old Swan to Temple Stairs, jingling the coins in his pocket and waiting for the watermen to beg for his custom.

Perhaps Dan would get his turn, but not yet.

~

Tying a few sheets of bark onto a frame took Ned and Dan all day, and in the end the lean-to was more a kennel than a human habitation. But that night the two of them crawled in there to sleep. Through the cracks in the wall the Thornhills could still hear Ned muttering and Dan shifting in his sleep, but it seemed a different sort of sound now that there was a barrier, no matter how flimsy, between them. It was the sound of two men below them on life's ladder.

Sal turned to Thornhill, her face young in the lamplight. The brown of her eyes gleamed translucent and when she smiled there was a dimple in her cheek that he did not remember having seen for a long time. *We will get the place real good, Sal*, he whispered. A thought came to him and he spoke without thinking. *You won't never want to leave.* She took it as a good joke: *Never want to leave!* Hearing the astonishment in her voice he wondered where his words had come from, and to cover them he took the jest further. *I'll be dragging you on the boat to go back Home*, he said. *You'll be down on your knees.* He made his voice high and mincing. *Please, Will, let me stay!*

That got her laughing so hard that he could see the tears glistening on her cheek. Cautiously, not to make too great a rustling among the fern under them, the husband and wife embraced, front to back like a pair of spoons. He loved the feeling of Sal's buttocks in his lap, his thighs running along against hers, her back swelling in and out with each breath against his chest, her breasts under his hands. Her musky smell was all about him as they breathed together.

Beyond the wall of bark his servants slept. He had the feeling that some slow engine had been set in motion: wheels turning, cogs meshing greasily. New South Wales had a life of its own now, beyond any intention that any man—the Governor, even the King himself—might have. It was a machine in which some men would be crushed up and spat out, and others would rise to heights they would not have dreamed of before.

There was a companionable silence between husband and wife. The lamp was nearly out, the fat in the saucer all gone and the wick consuming itself. It was part of the difference between today and all the days before it, that neither of them got up to pinch it out and save the bit of wick for another day.

He lay listening to the night outside. Through the cracks in the walls the air streamed in, a sweet damp smell, almost medicinal. Some creature out there was making a tiny piping cry as clean-edged as a razor, and down by the river the song of the frogs thickened and faded, thickened and faded.

Five years, that was all he needed.

~

It was November, and the hot weather was starting. Even at dawn the sun was an enemy to avoid and by mid-morning the inside of the hut was unendurable. The trees gave no shade, only scattered the sunlight, and the strip of shadow that the hut made grew smaller as the day went on. By noon it had shrunk to nothing and the clearing lay flattened under the heat.

It made the new corn come along well, though, and there was enough rain—sudden fierce storms out of towering thunderheads—that watering by bucket was unnecessary. Instead, every spare moment that any of them had was put to chipping the weeds that threatened to swallow the plants.

At first Sal thought it was just the heat making Mary fretful as she nursed, so that she tugged painfully at sore breasts. *A nice cool night will put me right*, she said. But the next morning, even though it was cooler, she was burning up with fever and her breasts were hard as drums. Thornhill put off the trip he had planned upriver for the barley crop, and went to fetch Mrs Herring. Good soul that she was, she came straight away, pronouncing the problem to be milk fever.

In spite of the pain it caused Sal, Mrs Herring was firm that the only cure for milk fever was to go on suckling. She ministered to Sal with hot poultices and steaming rags, then put the babe to the breast, holding her there until she had sucked her fill.

But Sal did not get better, only lay in the hot afternoons, shivering, clammy under a rug, her face flushed and grey by turns, her eyes small and dull. Bub and Dick took it in turns to sit beside her with a little whisk to keep off the flies.

Thornhill was cold with the idea of losing her. Hated the sky for coming up day after day so blue, as if nothing was the matter. Hated the birds, calling away indifferently. Hated himself, for bringing her here. Hung on every word Mrs Herring had to say and the tone of the answers she gave to his questions: *As well as can be expected*, or *No worse than yesterday*.

Finally, at the risk of offending her, he sailed up to Green Hills and offered twenty guineas to the surgeon. It was too far, the fellow said, for any money: four or five hours in the boat, even with the tide behind it. And between the words, unspoken, Thornhill heard the real reason: Sal was only the wife of an emancipist.

In the afternoons, while Mrs Herring ground up the hominy and chivvied the children to fetch her some little sticks to make the fire hot, Thornhill sat with Sal. He watched her lying there, her eyes closed, her face wan against the pillow. That sweet worn face of hers was the only soft thing in his life. He could still see the girl in the kitchen at Swan Lane, who had laughed out of a pink mouth and helped his fingers hold the quill.

She did not seem afraid of dying, and underwent Mrs Herring's ministrations without complaint. He dared to remind her one afternoon of Susannah Wood, whose husband's delight in mathematical instruments had included measuring to the last drop the fluid his wife had been relieved of. He thought he saw a slight movement of her mouth that meant she remembered, and was amused, but she said nothing.

It seemed she was not afraid of death or pain, but was filled with terror of being buried in this thin foreign soil, under the blast of this other sun, of her bones rotting away under those hard scraping trees. She stared at nothing and sighed, lying stiff in the bed, and one day said *Bury me facing the north, Will.* It was so long since she had spoken, he had to ask her to repeat it. *North, Will. Where Home is.* Then she pressed her lips together and watched him, waiting for his promise.

At first he blustered like a fool. *There won't be no burying, Sal,* he cried, but she closed her eyes. She was not interested. He watched her, that face he knew so well. He knew what her words had been asking. But even in this moment, when the thought of life without her was a blank like death itself, he could not make himself say the words he knew she longed to hear: *we will go Home.*

~

News travelled fast along the river. Smasher rowed up with a couple of mangrove crabs in a wet sack, their claws tied shut with hairy string, and Sagitty brought a bit of hog belly down that he had killed fresh that day. Sal would touch none of it, but the rest of them feasted themselves to a standstill. Spider sent her a bottle of best madeira he had got from somewhere or other. Even Blackwood strode up from the river one afternoon with a mess of eels from his lagoon and a bag of new potatoes.

It might have been Blackwood's eels that did it, or the way he sat by the bed and told her how he had gone about jellying them, the way his mother had taught him back in Eastcheap. *Grantley Street,* he said. *There by All Hallows.* Sal smiled and found the strength to nod. *I know,* she whispered. *Stickley's draper round the corner.* She sat up at last, propped weakly on the pillows, and ate a few good mouthfuls before she pushed the plate away and slid back down under the bedclothes.

The next day when Thornhill woke up he saw Sal sitting up in the bed, Mary clamped onto her breast, and looking around her.

Will, she said, and smiled, almost her old smile. He took her hand, squeezing it too hard in his gladness. *I ain't no oar, Will, leave off*, she cried, but squeezed back, as hard as she was able. *Now tell me, Will, how long have I been lying here like a lump? Did anyone make the marks, or have you gone and lost track?*

He put a smile on his face. *We done the marks on Sunday, Sal. It's five days past the nine weeks.* But he had to work to keep the disappointment off his face, that the marks on the tree were her first thought.

PART FOUR

A HUNDRED ACRES

With his servants on the place, he was less anxious about leaving with the *Hope*. Dan and Ned were gormless sorts of men, but they were men: it was a little wrench each time to leave Sal, but at least it was not just one woman out there alone among the trees.

Things were beginning to go smoothly. He and Dan had wrestled the awkward stones into place to make Sal a fireplace in the hut with a sod-lined bark chimney and wide enough to take lengths of fallen timber. In the heat of mid-November it was hard to imagine ever needing a fire, but Webb had warned him that the winters here were sharper than in Sydney, and he looked forward to sitting in the hut with the fire blazing. He thought he would never tire of the way a fire here was not a mean creaking thing, two frugal pieces of coal balanced against each other, but an extravagant licking of clean yellow flames around a heap of wood.

The children were flourishing on the river as they had not in Sydney. Johnny, going on for two years old, was on the go all day, poking things into other things or balancing things on other things, always with some scheme in his mind that made his little face go blank with concentration. Dick was growing into a straight and sinewy seven-year-old, the baby clucked and crooned to herself, and even Bub had turned the corner. Far from suffering from the rough diet, he appeared to be thriving on it. He was still inclined to burst into tears more than a boy of five should, and there were still mauve shadows under his eyes, but he was finally putting on flesh.

Business was good. The Governor had decreed that townships with garrisons of troops be made along the upper reaches of the river. That way, even though the blacks were frequently committing their outrages and depredations, the farmers themselves would be safe and not abandon the place. So humble Green Hills became regal Windsor, and the scattering of huts upstream of it became Richmond. The redcoats patrolled the riverside farms, and went out into the wilds every other week to hunt down and bring to justice the perpetrators of the outrages.

Townships suited a man with a boat full of desirable objects. Instead of putting in to one isolated farm after another, Thornhill need only call in at the new villages and be relieved of his goods on the spot, and load for the return trip to Sydney.

He made a point of getting some little gift for Sal on every trip to Sydney: a pair of teacups, a mat for the dirt floor, a blue shawl to remind her of the one her father had given her, although this was coarse compared to that cobweb of soft threads.

For himself he bought a pair of boots, the first he had ever owned. When he put them on he understood why gentry looked different. Partly it was having money in the bank, but it was also your boots telling you how to walk.

Each time he approached his own place from the river— either on his way down from Windsor with a load of cabbages and corn, or coming up from Sydney with calico and spades— he felt himself tighten. He said nothing to Sal, and swore Willie to discretion, but in the townships there was always news of another outrage by the blacks. Each time he rounded his point and saw the smoke calmly rising up out of his chimney, the fowls pecking away around the yard and the children running down the slope to meet him, he felt a flush of relief.

On a certain day in December, the year 1813 nearly over, he sailed up the reach towards Thornhill's Point. A hot squally westerly had made it a rough trip from the Camp, and he was glad to be home. He had hardly slid the *Hope* into its place in the mangroves when there was Willie running down towards him from the hut, his hair wild, his face twisted with yelling. He had to swallow his panting breath before he could make himself plain: the blacks had come.

Thornhill felt his chest clench, like a hand, in pain. Straight away he pictured Sal on her back, the blood drained out of her face, her dead eyes staring up at the sky. Mary beside her, a little bundle of still rags, the blood sucked out of her. Bub and Johnny scalped, sliced up, roasted alive, eaten. Their *best bits*.

But when Willie found enough breath to say more, it seemed that no one was actually dead yet. He pointed, his narrow chest heaving up and down, his dirty face long with fear, but all there was to see was a line of smoke, the echo of their own, lifting in a leisurely way from some place further around the point and catching in the trees, making them blue and misty.

Thornhill felt no fear, just weariness. He wanted only to go about his business, sailing the *Hope* up and down, growing a bit of corn, enjoying the labours of his servants and climbing the ladder of prosperity. It did not seem much to ask, but here they were back again, unavoidable.

Hold your noise, lad, for God's sake, he said, and listened. The breeze brought no sounds but the languid barking of a dog, the single distant cry of a child. A woman's voice called out high and quick. He stared at the smoke, waiting for it to vanish, and the blacks with it.

Willie was watching him, a frown between his eyebrows. *Get the gun, Da*, he said. *Let them see the gun.*

There were days when Thornhill wished Willie was still that young lad for whom his father was a god, and not a boy who thought he was already a man.

Now Sal was at the door of the hut with Mary hanging off her hip. *They come yesterday*, she said. *They ain't come near us but.*

He saw with relief that she was not frightened.

Take this down to them, Will, she said, holding out a bag. *A bit of pork, some flour and that. And a bit of your baccy I thought you could spare.*

Thornhill did not reach out and take it. A bit of meat, that first day, was one thing. But this matter-of-fact handing over of their food and even his own tobacco: that was different. It had less the look of a gift. It felt more like when she gave him the coins every Monday to take to Mr Butler of Butler's Buildings.

At last he took the bag, but only to put it back on the table. *We give them something every time, we'll never see the end of it*, he said. *They'll be want want wanting, till we got nothing left.*

Dan had come up from the boat and was watching them. He was supposed to bring the oars up when he came, but was empty-handed and Thornhill wanted to hit him, the way he stood there, arms dangling, listening. He was a vile little snipe, but quick. He did not try to hide the pleasure he was taking in the fact that Mr and Mrs Thornhill were about to disagree.

But Sal, the clever thing, disappointed him. *There's sense in that*, she agreed. She looked out the door towards where the smoke smudged the sky, thinking it through. *They're like them gypsies back home*, she said. *Ain't they. Da give them his old shirts when they come to the back door, but not every time. And never let them in the house.*

198

He felt a spurt of love for her, that she was providing a way to explain the new world to herself. *We got to steer it narrow*, she went on. *Like Da done.* Her hands, pressed together, weaved to one side, then the other. *Keep them happy, but don't let them take advantage.* She looked up at his face. *And they'll be gone by and by, with their roaming ways.*

She had put into words his own sense of the thing. A line had to be drawn with the blacks. Just where you drew it was something he could not see. But he knew that it would be no good waiting for the blacks to draw it for them.

He made his voice casual. *I'll step down and have a word*, he said, as if speaking of any other neighbour. *Get things straightened out.* He saw a little furrow form between her brows at this. But she had nothing better to offer.

Come back quick, she said.

He thought to take Ned or Dan, but this was not a matter of arithmetic: so many men on one side, so many on the other. If it was, the Thornhills were beaten before they had even started. It was some other thing, although he did not know just what kind of a thing it might be. He set off towards the smoke, striding along the ground like a man measuring it up.

All the same, he felt naked.

~

The blacks had made an encampment around on the far side of the point, not far from where he had seen the fish on the rock. It was a good spot for a camp, soft grass and scattered trees making a sweet shady place that caught the breeze from the river, and there was another rivulet, although smaller than the Thornhills'. Two humpies—bark and leaves heaped in a mound on a few branches leaning together—sat in an area of cleared ground as clean-swept as the one around their own hut. There

199

were bark dishes lying together, a pile of knobbly berries, and a big saucer-shaped stone with a handful of grass-seeds in it ready to be ground up.

It took him a moment to see two old women by the fire, as still and dark as the ground they seemed to grow out of. They sat with their long bony legs stretched out straight in front of them, their spreading breasts down to their waists. One of them had paused in the act of rolling threads of stringybark on her sinewy thighs, turning it into coarse brown string. A child stood behind her and stared at Thornhill. The women glanced up at him but with as little interest as if he were a fly come to watch them.

They were all stuck in this tableau until a skinny dog got up stiffly from where it was lying in the shade and barked half-heartedly. The woman making string called out at it, only a word, and it stopped. The dog snapped at a fly, then lay down again, watching Thornhill from one eye.

The other woman stood up, a dead snake hanging limp from her hand. She flicked it onto the coals as casually as if it was a bit of old rope, then bent forward with a stick and scraped some ashes over the top of it. Then she sat again and began to pick over the berries in the dish, not looking at Thornhill.

Youse lot best bugger off, he said, mild enough but firm. The words seemed to drop out of the air. The women did not move. Their faces remained folded like fabric around their thoughts, their eyes turned away from him. Their long upper lips, and the deep buckles of skin that cut down their cheeks beside their noses, gave them a stern haughty look. *Best stay away out of it*, he said. *Out of our place.*

The words swelled and passed, leaving silence behind. He took a step closer. Without haste, the one making string put it to one side and stood up. Her long breasts swung, the nipples staring blindly down at the ground. She stood watching him, the way a tree stood on its piece of the earth.

He could not bring himself to look at her straight on. He had never seen any woman naked. Even Sal he had only ever seen in parts. She had never stood before him like this woman, with nothing covering any of her except for a string around her hips. If she had, he would have rushed to cover her up. But these women seemed not to feel ashamed. It seemed that they did not even feel naked. They were clothed in their skins, the way Sal was clothed in her shawl and skirt.

The one who had thrown the snake on the fire lifted her arm and flapped a hand at him. She began to speak, brusque and emphatic, her deep-set eyes catching the light. She had no fear of the man in his hat and britches, and whatever she was saying, she did not expect any disagreement. After she spoke she turned away as if shutting a door between them.

He hated the way she did that, as if any response he might make was of no account. *Old dame*, he said loudly, *I could fetch me gun and blow your heathen head off easy as anything*. He could hear his voice straining to fill the space around itself. The woman did not look towards him but her face was heavy with disapproval. The other one spoke now, and jerked her head sideways. He understood that she was telling him where he should go: back the way he had come.

Something made him turn. Behind him was a group of men standing together watching. They had arrived so quietly they might have risen up out of the ground. There were six of them, or perhaps eight, or ten. Something about the way their skins were shadows among the shadows of the trees made it hard to see them straight.

In London William Thornhill counted as a big man, but these men made him feel small. They were as tall as he was, their shoulders sinewy but powerful, their chests defined with pads of muscle. Each held a few spears, the lengths of wood shifting like insects' feelers.

He stood legs apart, his heavy new boots planted on the ground. He imagined the way he looked to them: his mysterious clothes, his face shadowed under his hat.

It seemed important to act the part of host. That way, they were his guests. He made himself hail them in a jovial way, looking them right in the face, as if they were dogs that would bite if they caught the scent of fear.

Good-day to you gentlemen, he called. *How are you this fine day?*

He heard his words evaporate, thin and silly, into the air, and was glad that Ned and Dan were not with him to hear. He felt something hot in his chest: anger? Or was it fear?

He wished he had the gun.

A bird began a long tweetling somewhere in the trees and the humming in the grass swelled and faded, swelled and faded. A stick fell in the fire with a soft collapsing sound.

A haze of steam was starting to come up from the place in the coals where the snake was cooking, and a good greasy smell was wafting over to him, like nothing so much as a nice fat mutton chop. He found himself wondering if a yard of serpent might not be such a bad dinner.

Cat got your tongues, he said. *You black buggers?* As if this was a signal, they came towards him, moving in that loose-kneed way they had, the spears easy in their hands. One—the same grey-beard he had slapped the first day—separated himself from the others and came right up to Thornhill, reaching out and placing a long black hand on his forearm. Authority radiated from this naked old man like heat off a fire. A stream of words began to come out of his mouth.

Thornhill forced himself to break the spell. *Very good, you old bugger*, he said, his voice harsh, cutting across the flow. *Now you listen*. He bent down and with a twig drew marks on the dust: a curving line that was the river, and a tidy square representing his own hundred acres. *This mine now. Thornhill's place.*

The man stared at him.

You got all the rest, Thornhill said. He could hear his voice getting louder. *You got the whole blessed rest of it, mate, and welcome to it*. But his words seemed to flow past the man as if they mattered as little as a current of air. He had not noticed before how white the white part of the man's eyes were. He wondered if it was that, the darkness of the skin against the whiteness of the eyes, that made his eyes seem to be lit from within.

The old man took a step towards the fire and from one of the bark dishes picked something up: a cluster of the daisy-roots, six or eight narrow tubers dangling from the stem. He pointed at the roots and spoke again. Finally he took a bite of one of them. Chewed, swallowed, nodded. Even with the words as meaningless to Thornhill as the cry of a bird, he understood. The man snapped off a finger of root and held it out to Thornhill. The flesh was translucent, glassy, crisp-looking, something in the nature of a radish.

But Thornhill did not intend to eat. *Kind of you, old boy.* That was a joke that had not lost its savour. *But you can keep your radishes.* He looked again at the thing on the man's brown-seamed pink palm. *Monkey food, I would call that, mate, but good luck to you.*

The man was vehement now. He was explaining something in detail. He turned and pointed towards the river-flats, holding up the bundle of roots. There seemed to be a question in his voice now, a phrase repeated, as if he wanted agreement.

Yes, mate, Thornhill said. *You can keep your monkey's balls that you like so much.* The old man said something, loud and sharp, and Thornhill recognised the same phrase.

He longed for words.

It seemed that the old man was ready to wait all day for an answer.

We'll stick to our victuals, mate, you stick to yours, Thornhill said. He met the man's eyes and nodded. The old man gave a curt nod back.

A conversation had taken place. There had been an inquiry and an answer. But what inquiry, which answer?

They stared at each other, their words between them like a wall.

~

Good as gold, he told them all when he got back to the hut. *Not a worry in the wide world. They'll be off again by and by.*

Through Christmas and the scorching early days of January, he looked out the door of the hut every morning, hoping that the sky would be empty of their smoke. But each morning it was there, painted on.

Sal seemed to be reassured. *They'll be off again by and by*, she said one day when she caught him frowning at the smoke. *Just like you said.* He had to agree, but he was starting to realise that there was a kind of loneliness to telling a story too well.

It took him some time to admit to himself that his hundred acres no longer felt quite his own. A small group of the blacks was always about, even if mostly unseen. Their bodies flickered among the trees, as if the darkness of the men were an extension of bark, of leaf-shade, of the play of light on a water-stained rock. The eye could peer but not know if it was a couple of branches over there, or a man with a spear, watching.

Their manner of walking was like nothing Thornhill had ever seen before. Their bodies seemed all long thin legs, the weight carried low over the hips, their feet setting down softly on the layer of brittle leaves and bark-scrolls. Somehow they could simply float over the ground.

Thornhill would have said all the blacks looked the same, so it was somewhat surprising to realise after a time how easily he could tell them apart. He began to give the men names: humble sorts of names that made their difference less potent. It made something domestic—just another kind of neighbourhood—out of this unpromising material.

The old man reminded him, in the grimness of his mouth and the whiteness of his stubble, of a certain old Harry who had sharpened knives around Swan Lane, and so was christened forthwith: Whisker Harry. Thornhill kept to himself his knowledge that this stern old man was nothing like any London knife-sharpener. The man who had slapped him on that first day was a tall man and stood straight and he became Long Bob. The other younger man was no darker than any of the others, but his heavy face had a brooding look about it that was less alarming once he was called Black Dick.

Whisker Harry would stalk around on his skinny shanks, unhurried, deliberate. Or he might stand with one foot wedged in against the other knee, his spear upright beside him, watching the distance. When he came face to face with Thornhill, he looked through him as if he were made of air.

Long Bob and Black Dick sometimes watched Thornhill chipping the weeds down on the corn patch with Ned and Dan. They stood or squatted, their spears blending with the other spindly verticals in the place.

They were never without their spears.

Thornhill and Dan had seen Black Dick use his spear one

day, aiming at something in the grass. He had bent himself tautly backwards, steadying the air in front of him with his free hand, and shot it with a movement as quick and invisible as the crack of a whip.

Sweet Lord Jesus, Dan breathed. *Did you see that.*

The men never came so close to Thornhill and his men that words had to be attempted, but the women were more forthcoming with Sal. They skirted around the hut as if it were a new boulder, and got into the habit of singing out to her as they passed.

Thornhill watched one day, coming back up to the hut for a drink of tea with Ned and Dan behind him, as a group of them filed out of the forest and across the end of the yard. Signalled to Ned and Dan to stop and be quiet as Sal came out of the hut with the quart-pot in her hand, and in the still air he heard her call to them *Oy Meg, what's that you got there?* He stood to watch, gripping the spade harder in case they turned on her, ready to shout out to Ned and Dan to rush them.

There were so many of them, and only the one Sal in the whole wide world.

But the women came up to her and showed her what was in their wooden dishes, crowding around and screeching with how funny it all was. One had a big speckled lizard hanging limp from the string around her waist, slapping against her knee at each movement. She held it up, fat and heavy, its legs splayed out from its pale belly, shouting at Sal as if she was half a mile away. *Very nice I'm sure, Polly*, he heard Sal say, *but you ain't going to eat it surely?* pointing at the lizard, miming eating, pointing at the woman, and they all shouted and laughed at her, copying the way she had gone hand-to-mouth and pretended to chew. Their teeth were the most astonishing white Thornhill had ever seen, strong and shining in their faces. Sal was enjoying the joke of being able to say what she pleased. *Ain't you the saucy one, Polly, what about rats, and how would you go about stewing a nice little pot of worms?*

Behind the older women the younger ones hung back, laughing behind their hands with each other. One, bolder than the rest, darted forward and took hold of a bit of Sal's skirt and then dropped the unfamiliar texture with a little shriek as if it had burned her. But Sal took a step towards her, holding the skirt out and offering her a handful. *Why, you're no better than a dumb animal*, she said, smiling, and the girl took it for permission, darting in and this time picking up the fabric in her hand and feeling it. Now the others crowded in around her. One touched Sal's bare arm, her hand very black against it, first quickly as if it might bite, then laying her whole hand along it and watching Sal's face, and behind her another was dabbing at her bonnet, the rest screaming encouragement.

Then one of them had Sal's bonnet off and on top of her own head, sitting white and incongruous on the black curls. It was the funniest thing any of them had ever seen: Sal was doubled over, and the girl did look a sight, stark naked but for the bonnet crooked on her head, her face under it split with mirth. The other women all wanted to try it then, so the bonnet was passed from hand to hand, head to head, until the lot of them were staggering with laughter.

A man could be blinded by the little breasts and the long thighs of the young girls. When one of them reached out for the bonnet the skin moved silkily over the round gleaming bosses of her shoulders, the buds of her breasts. Thornhill glanced around and caught Dan staring hungrily at these shameless girls, his eyes blazing in his pale face. Ned put it into words. *Look at them titties*, he whispered hoarsely, and cackled. *Get an eyeful of them titties!*

Now Sal was showing by signs that she was interested in

looking not at the contents of the wooden dishes, but the dishes themselves. The women obliged, pouring the little objects from several into one, so that Sal could turn the others up to admire the underside. Much parlaying ensued, and Sal was holding out her bonnet and making signs to them. *You give me, I give you.*

The women caught on at once. The oldest, the wrinkled one who had been making the string when Thornhill first saw her, engaged in some exchange with Sal, who went into the hut and came out with a twist of sugar. *Our sugar!* he nearly called out. *Leave it, Sal!* They went into something of a huddle then, but at last the white woman in the skirt and bodice was separating herself off from all the naked black ones, and a deal seemed to have been struck: the oldest of the black women had the twist of sugar and the bonnet in her hand, while Sal had one of the wooden dishes.

As she made to go back into the hut she caught sight of Thornhill standing there and called out, glad as a girl: *Look what I got, Will, one of them bowls, ain't it an oddity?* holding the dish out for him to admire. *We got dishes, Sal*, he said. *That ain't no good to us,* but she brushed this aside. *Will, Will,* she cried, *you blessed dingbat, it ain't to use, it's a curio.* She mouthed the unfamiliar word awkwardly. *Mrs Herring says gentry pay good money for them kind of things, back Home. I get one a month for five years, we'll make a pretty penny when we go back!*

Her fingers caressed the crude dish. *And it were only that old bonnet that's had its day,* she said. *And a mouthful of the sugar. Buck up with your long face!*

She was as proud of herself—of her cordiality with these neighbours, and of the deal she had struck—as a child. *Mrs Herring got the right idea,* she said. *There ain't no need for any of that other business.*

In the face of her triumph, how could he not smile at last,

and give her a hug around her waist, which was such a nice shape under a man's hand?

Thornhill glimpsed the women later down by the river where they dug among the bulrushes. The scrap of paper that the sugar had come in lay on the ground between them, licked clean. Sal's bonnet was being modelled by the woman who had had the lizard dangling from her waist: not on her head, but on her stuck-out arse, and they were all laughing in a way he would not have wanted Sal to see.

~

The forest had never revealed dinner to Thornhill. He had never so much as glimpsed the things the women got, which Sal showed him samples of—little hard fruits, dry-looking berry-things, knobs of roots—much less thought they could be eaten. All he had ever seen in the forest were ants and flies, and birds watching him askance from branches, and those huge speckled lizards—which he did not think he could bring himself to eat—staring at him, their long heads held high and their eyes never blinking, ready to run up the nearest tree if he tried to get close.

He wondered whether that was why the women found the newcomers so funny. The Thornhill household sweated away under the broiling sun, chopping and digging, and still had nothing to eat but salt pork and damper. By contrast, the blacks strolled into the forest and came back with dinner hanging from their belts.

He supposed that from a certain point of view it might seem funny.

Ned and Dan both scorned the blacks, as being even lower in the scheme of things than themselves. Looking at one of the men squatting in the shade with his spears upright beside him one sunny afternoon, Dan blurted, *By God see his bumcrack with the hair coming out of it, a dog has more of a modest way with him!* Ned, in whom there was madness at times, threw his head back and yowled.

Never see them do a hand's turn, Dan grumbled that night as they all sat glumly chewing. *Just sitting with their balls hanging out, saving your presence Mrs Thornhill, watching us bust a gut.* Sal said, *We could put them to work, Will, civilise them enough to use a spade and that.* They all tried to imagine Whisker Harry or Black Dick putting down his spears and bending over a spade. *Even them gypsies been known to do a day's work now and then,* Sal said, but Thornhill could hear that she had lost heart in the idea.

~

Thornhill's blind and deaf conversation with Whisker Harry replayed itself in his mind but never yielded any enlightenment. He knew the discussion was not finished.

One Sunday Sal came back thoughtful from making her mark on the tree. *They been here a good long time,* she said. *They come our fourteenth week, that was December, and now we're up to seventeen.* She busied herself by the fire, with her back turned to him. *I'd a thought they'd of been gone by this.*

It was a relief to have the thought out in the open. *Didn't want to fret you, Sal,* he said. *But I been thinking the same.* Now she turned to look at him, smiling as she squinted against a thread of smoke from the fireplace. *Not fret me,* she said. *Think I might snap like some fancy lady if I got fretted?*

A few days later they heard a sudden commotion from the camp, a couple of the dogs having a spat and then voices calling out. Sal was sitting on the log outside with the corn-mill between her knees. *Mrs Herring says they come more than they go,* she said. *They like it here by the river same as we do.*

Thornhill looked at her, startled. *You asked her?* he said. *You asked her about them?*

Mrs Herring had a way of looking at Thornhill, her shrewd eyes on him as if seeing into his thoughts, that made him awkward with her. He might have his secret thoughts hidden from Sal, but he did not think a man could have any secrets from Mrs Herring. He could imagine her ironic look if he had tried to talk to her about the blacks.

Sal was concentrating on the little mill: it had a way of slipping from between her knees when she turned the handle, the whole thing flying out across the ground, the cornmeal spraying out onto the dirt. *Course I done*, she said at last, tight-lipped with the effort of grinding. He took the contraption from her—a hopeless thing, he planned to get a better one as soon as they had some ready money—and ground away himself until the hopper was empty, and tipped it up into the bowl she had ready.

She stood with the bowl in her hands and looked him straight in the face. *Coming and going is one thing*, she said. *But coming and not going, that's something else.* She was not going to go into detail about what that something else might be, he could see. But he knew what it was, because he felt it too: not fear, not even fret. Just a shadow over the part of their world where the smoke of the strangers' fire never stopped rising into the air.

Mrs Herring got a different case from us, Thornhill said. *Just her all on her nelly up there. She ain't got no choice.*

Sal stirred the cornmeal in the bowl with her finger. He could see a few white specks in there: weevils, ground up along with the hominy. *And us*, she said. *We got any different choice?* He thought for a moment she was challenging him, but then saw that she was really asking. *Will?* she asked, searching his face. *Ask that Tom Blackwood, I would. See what he got to say.*

So in the colourless dimness before dawn the next day, he

rowed the skiff over to the mouth of the First Branch and let the flooding tide take hold of it. A line of foam travelled along with the boat on the slick surface of the water. Thornhill needed only to sit in the stern with an oar by way of rudder, and allow the skiff to be carried up the stream.

Blackwood had found a way to live here, but his wisdom had always been too much riddles. *Give a little, take a little.* What did that mean when it came right down to it—not just words, but an act in time and place? How did it apply to a moment like the one down by the blacks' fire, when a white man and a black one had tried to make sense of each other with nothing but words that were no use to them?

By the time the sun was lighting up the topmost leaves of the forest, he was away a ways up the valley. It was a still and silent place. The water, although clear, was as brown as strong tea. On either side mangroves masked the banks. Beyond was a narrow strip of level ground where river-oaks hung, and then the ridges angled up, steep and stony on either side.

The mosquitoes were ferocious. Thornhill watched a big one with striped legs land on his arm and push its needle-like biting part against the stuff of his shirt until it bent. Somewhere ahead of him in the top of a tree, a bird made a measured silvery sound, again and again, a little bell being struck. A fish launched itself out of the water and through the air in a flash of silver muscle. The place held its breath, watching.

Some five miles up the Branch, the land beyond the screen of mangroves opened out as if the river had cleared a space with its elbow, pushing the stony ridge further away and making a generous crescent of level ground between it and the river. It was there that he saw the smoke that must be Blackwood's, rising into the air.

There was no wharf, not even a clearing among the

mangroves for a boat to land. Thornhill passed it before he glimpsed a gap, had to get on the oars to back down and point the skiff into it. It seemed to be a dead end, but he pushed through the screen of branches and found a stretch of clear water again, and at the end there was a neat corduroy of logs, and Blackwood's dory drawn up in privacy on the grassy bank.

The place was as his own had been on that first day: the mangroves, the thicket of river-oaks, and then open ground with scattered trees. Over in the crook of the ridge a lagoon shone like a piece of zinc in the early light. It was lined with river-oaks, a length of the river broken off and abandoned there under the mass of rock.

He could see Blackwood's place, a neat slab hut with a bark roof, and his corn patch, luminous green in the early light and a few fowls bobbing at the ground. The hut and the cornfield sat easily among the trees. Blackwood had not cleared his place the way Thornhill and the others laboured to do. There was no bald patch defined by heaps of dead wood that marked where civilisation began and ended. This was a place where clearing and forest lived together on the same ground.

Blackwood was waiting for him, his bulk filling the doorway of the hut. *You've got yerself up here, Will Thornhill*, he said. *Stickybeaking without no one axed you.*

It was not much of a welcome.

We are real private up here, he said, and watched Thornhill while he looked for *we*.

I got a blacks' camp along of me, Thornhill started. *Come out of the blue.* He could hear how his voice was uncertain. His words made no difference to the great rock of Blackwood's face. He stopped and looked away towards the lagoon. There was a thread of smoke there rising above the trees: the still, he supposed, where another batch of Blackwood's gripe water was brewing.

Just come without so much as a by-your-leave, Thornhill tried again. He wanted to explain the airless feeling of having the blacks so close. The way they treated the place as if it was their own. The foolish feeling of trying to explain to the old fellow about his hundred acres.

He could not think of the words to share any of that. There was something intimate about it, like some pale hidden part of the body it was shameful to expose.

The blacks come and give you a fright, is that it? Blackwood said at last. Thornhill had the feeling that he was amused. Blackwood thought for a moment, then said abruptly, *Best you and me have a drink of tea then.*

They sat together with their pannikins of tea on a bench outside the hut. Blackwood had picked a sweet spot, with the grass spreading under the trees, the lagoon glinting in the sun at a distance, and the birds carolling away near the corn patch. He had made himself comfortable. He had a stumpy stone oven where a loaf was proving under a rag. Beneath a shady tree there was a bench with his wash-basin on it and the razor-strop hanging off a peg hammered into the bark, and a bit of mirror stuck in a crack.

Over by the lagoon, the smoke billowed up, faded away, strengthened again. Below the noises of the birds and the breeze in the leaves, Thornhill thought he caught other sounds. Voices, was it, and a dog barking? But just as a sound was beginning to come clear, a bird would start a long liquid warbling.

When Blackwood began to speak, it seemed to have nothing to do with anything. *Come back from Sydney one day*, he said, all in one piece. *Not a breath of wind and the tide going out fast. Up round Sandy Island, that bit of beach.* It was as if he had thought his way along a considerable conversation, but only this end-point had surfaced as words. *Blacks there waiting for me.*

Thornhill tried to imagine it: Thomas Blackwood standing on the beach at Sandy Island, the black men coming to meet him. *Did you now*, he said, then waited. He had learned not to rush Blackwood. He could be an obstinate bugger.

His patience paid off. *They come down, see*, Blackwood said. *Tell me to bugger off.*

Bugger off, eh, Thornhill said, waiting.

Had their bloody spears up ready, I was pissing myself. Blackwood showed with his thick hands how they had stood around him. *Like they was waiting.*

Blackwood glanced across at the cliffs. The sun had risen behind them so that they were blanks in the landscape. *Give them some victuals*, Blackwood said. *But they wasn't having none.*

Thornhill thought he might have heard enough stories about how dangerous it was to be a white man on the lower Hawkesbury, but Blackwood's slow way could drive a man mad, and silence was threatening to take hold around the words again.

So what was they waiting for?

Blackwood glanced at him as if in surprise that he was there. *Search me, mate, but I took me flaming hat off me head and give it one of them.* He went on, smiling to himself, seeing the scene before him. *They wasn't fooled*, he said. *You know, a man's hat!* He swirled the dregs of his tea around his pannikin, tossed them out in a sparkling arc on the ground. *Long and the short of it was, they let me stay. Made it real clear—stay on the beach. Couldn't a been clearer if they'd of spoke the King's English.*

This was not quite all. *Had a good old sing-song later on up the hill. You know, sticks and that.* Blackwood clapped, a steady rhythm, and moved his head as if to music he could hear. *Kept away like they said.* He smoothed his palms together. *Never got me bloody hat back.* He laughed. *Buggers kept me hat.*

There was another silence. Thornhill was wondering if there

was any part of the story he might apply to his own case. *Give a little, take a little.* The exact mechanics of that were still vague, unless it meant laying in a good supply of hats.

The smoke had faded to a shimmer of thicker air above the trees.

Blackwood seemed to have said everything. He took the empty pannikins and got to his feet. But as Thornhill stood up too, there was a voice calling out, definitely a human voice, coming from the lagoon where the branches of the river-oaks made a net of dark and light. Thornhill looked, seeing no one, but Blackwood called out in response, the form of his words unclear, jammed up together, and then one of the shadows moved forward and resolved itself into a black woman. She stood at the edge of the trees and Thornhill could see her mouth shaping itself around a running jumble of sounds, but he recognised the angle at which she was holding her head. When Sal held her head that way it meant she was angry.

She took a few steps and now he saw there was a child behind her, invisible except for a hand like a pale starfish on her black thigh. The woman curled a hand around the child's shoulder and with the other she gestured at Thornhill, her voice becoming louder. There was no mistaking that Thornhill was a cause of displeasure.

Blackwood answered her, and at first Thornhill thought that he was blurring the words together and swallowing them in his usual way. It took him a moment to realise that Blackwood was speaking in her own tongue. The words were slow and clumsy, but Thornhill could see the woman listening and understanding. The child edged out from behind her, staring at Thornhill with a fist up to its mouth, and he caught a glimpse of straw-pale hair and skin the colour of watery tea, shocking against the woman's black leg.

Blackwood turned to Thornhill, watching him watching. He waited for his neighbour to look at him and was ready, meeting his eyes straight on. Thornhill could not remember ever seeing Blackwood's eyes before. They were a blaze of astonishing blue in his brick-like weathered face, eyes that in a woman would have made her a beauty, that hyacinth blue, and the long lashes.

I find them quiet and peaceable folk, Blackwood said at last. *Which a man cannot say about many of his neighbours.* He made a movement with his fingers, feeling out the words he needed. *I telled her you'll keep your trap shut. About what you seen here.*

The glare out of his eyes was as hard as a raised fist. *I better have got that right, Will Thornhill, and if I ain't, by Jesus your life ain't worth a brass farthing.*

~

When Thornhill told Sal what he had seen, whispering so Ned and Dan would not hear in their lean-to, she said nothing for so long that he thought she might have fallen asleep. At last he felt her stir, heard her sigh. *That's a different case again*, she said. *No more help to us than Mrs Herring. Got to work it out for ourselves, looks like.*

~

Going on eight now, Dick was old enough to have his jobs: feeding the fowls, collecting kindling for Sal—*no bark mind*, she would call as he trailed off into the trees, Bub running behind with a sack, trying to keep up, *just them nice little sticks*—and filling the water barrel. Dick lugged the pail along the path to where the rivulet left a bright green crack down the side of the hill. Bub was not allowed to go that far. They had dug a tank and lined it with stones: sweet enough water, although they had to strain it through a bit of muslin to get the wrigglers out of it. It took six trips back and forth to fill the water barrel outside the door, and one more to fill the iron pot that sat by the fire.

But once Dick had done all this he would disappear, leaving Bub calling him to come back. *You're too little*, he would tell him. *Only five, Bub, you know Ma don't want you to wander.* He padded off through the clearing, past the heaps of laboriously cut-down trees waiting to be burned, past the paperbarks rustling together and speckling the ground with their shadows, and even beyond that, right up into the hillside, into the hot dry ticking dream of the forest. There he would spend the whole day, as if learning the place by heart.

He brought things back to the hut for them to look at: a gumleaf curled around on itself like a sleeping dog, a translucent round pebble, a piece of wood so eaten by the white ants it had become a sponge. The others glanced briefly. Bub might marvel at the sleeping leaf, Johnny might finger the pebble before Willie took it for his slingshot, but they would not have gone looking for them, and if they had they would not have picked them out of the clutter of the woods, where the eye was blinded by so much detail.

At other times Dick went down to the river. Thornhill had seen him there more than once, around on the other side of the point. *The blacks' side* was what they called it. He had seen Dick there on a spit of sand, playing with the native children, all bony legs and skinny arms shiny like insects, running in and out of the water. Dick was stripped off as they were, to nothing but skin. His was white and theirs was black, but shining in the sun and glittering with river-water it was hard to tell the difference. He ran and called and laughed with them, and he could have been their pale cousin.

As the white men bent over the plants in the hot sun, chipping away at the weeds that seemed to grow knee-high overnight, they could see the children, slippery and naked, sliding in and out of the river, and hear their high voices carrying up the slope.

Thornhill said nothing to Sal of this, but Bub was not a child to protect the brother who was always leaving him behind. He ran up to the hut one day, panting and red in the face, the words falling over themselves in his urgency to tell them that Dick was *down with the blacks ain't got no clothes on!*

Sal went very still, stopped in the middle of mixing up cornmeal dough, her hands covered with the gritty yellow stuff. *You best go down and fetch him back, Will,* she said calmly. *He got to learn when he's gone too far.*

He came across them down on the track to the camp: a dozen children crowding around Long Bob, who was squatting on the ground among them. It took Thornhill a moment to see his son there, staring so hard at what Long Bob was doing that he did not notice his father. *Dick,* he called, and the boy glanced over at him, his little face closing like a fist. *Come away from there and where are your britches, lad?*

Dick did not move. *He's showing us how you make fire, Da,* he called back. *No flint or nothing.* Thornhill had heard about this business of making fire by rubbing two sticks together. Had thought it was just one more of the stories people told about the blacks. He went over, prepared to enjoy this bit of tomfoolery.

Long Bob did not so much as glance up as Thornhill came near. He had split off a bit of dried black-boy stalk, exposing its soft inside, and had laid it flat on the ground, gripping it with his feet as if they were another pair of hands. He had fitted a second stick upright into it, which he was rolling between the palms of his hands so it twisted against the flat one after the manner of a drill. Thornhill saw the strong muscles of his back moving under the skin and his hands patiently applying themselves to the job. Beside him on the ground was a leaf off a cabbage-tree filled with tinder.

He watched, but there was no sign of fire, nothing even as much as smoke. He tried to meet Dick's eye, waiting to tip him a wink, but Dick was watching the spot where the two sticks met. His whole being was fixed on that spot, his father forgotten.

Come away there now lad, Thornhill started, but his words were lost in a shout from the children. In the spot where one stick twisted into the other, a tiny column of darkness was wisping away into the air. Quick as thought, Long Bob tipped the sticks into the leaf and wrapped the whole thing up, tinder and sticks and all, into a loose parcel. Then he stood in that way they did, without any of the cumbersome procedure of getting up, and began to whirl the package round at arm's length, and to Thornhill's amazement the thing burst into flames. He dropped it onto the ground and fed it with a few twigs, and there was the fire, neat as you please.

Then he looked straight at Thornhill. It did not take any words to understand. *Match that, white man.*

Thornhill chose to laugh. *My word but that is a good trick*, he said. He glanced at Dick and saw his tense face relax. *Ain't it, Dick lad?* But the boy did not risk agreeing. There was a pause while the black man and the white man took the measure of each other. The children watched, but when nothing happened they crowded down around the fire.

Thornhill put a hand against his chest. *Me, Thornhill*, he announced. His voice sounded loud, the syllables bold, cutting across the children's light voices. Long Bob glanced at him, then away as if he had not spoken.

Me, Thornhill, he said again. *It's me name, get it? Me, Thornhill.*

From the corner of his eye he felt Dick watching. Long Bob looked at him at last and his face broke up into a smile that showed his teeth, strong white tools carried in his mouth.

In all the mouths of London there had never been such teeth.

Me, Thornhill, Long Bob said, as clear as could be, and Thornhill laughed aloud in his relief that the moment had turned the corner. He took a step towards him to clap him on the shoulder, but there was something about that shoulder, striped with pink scars and hard with muscle, that discouraged a casual touch.

Yes! he shouted. *Only it ain't you, mate, it's me that's Thornhill!* He was almost dancing, poking himself in the chest.

Long Bob flicked a hand towards him. *Thornhill,* he said. Then he laid his hand against his own chest and his mouth moved quickly around a string of sounds.

Thornhill caught the first sound but the rest evaporated into the air like steam out of a kettle. But a man who could write his own name, William Thornhill, along a piece of paper, could not be made to look a fool by a naked savage. *Jack,* he said confidently. *Good-day to you, Jack.*

The black man spoke the sounds again, his forefinger bending against his breastbone. There was the first sound, made with the mouth pushed forward. That was clear enough, but the rest was not. It was as if a word that had no meaning could not be heard.

Yes, mate, Thornhill said. *But Jack for short, you got such a bleeding mouthful of a monicker.*

In the late afternoon sun the man's eyes were deep-set points of light. His face was creased around his thoughts, shadowed and secretive.

With no one but blacks around him, other than his own son, Thornhill saw that their skins were not black, no more than his own was white. They were simply skins, with the same pores and hairs, the same shadings of colour as his own. If black skin was all there was to see, it was amazing how quickly it became the colour that skin was.

You're a fine fellow, Jack, Thornhill said. *Even though your arse is as black as the bottom of a kettle.* He heard a noise from Dick, a blurted laugh smothered as soon as it was born. *But we'll get you all in the end.* The words came out of his mouth before he had thought. *There's such a bleeding lot of us.*

He had a quick piercing memory of Butler's Buildings, the coughing and cursing of dozens of men and women pushed in together. He could hear the great machinery of London, the wheel of justice chewing up felons and spitting them out here, boat-load after boatload, spreading out from the Government Wharf in Sydney, acre by acre, slowed but not stopped by rivers, mountains, swamps.

The thought made him gentle. *There won't be no stopping us,* he said. *Pretty soon there won't be nowhere left for you black buggers.*

Long Jack answered, a few words that got the children going again. Thornhill saw the pink tongues as they laughed, their powerful white teeth. Dick was laughing too, but uncertainly, his eyes going from Jack to his father.

Thornhill made himself join in, as if it were the funniest thing in the world. He found that he was rubbing his hands together the way the parson at Christ Church used to when ill at ease, and made himself stop. The children, still squatting around the fire, looked up at him, hiding their grinning mouths behind their hands.

He was reminded of the way Mary beamed up at him with her single tooth, crowing and chuckling, as if at some fine joke. The difference was, he never had the suspicion that Mary was mocking him.

~

Sal sat Dick down that night and tried to explain. *They's savages, Dick. We're civilised folk, we don't go round naked.* Thornhill watched the boy's face go blank and tight, although her tone was mild enough. Among his own family he was a watchful and wary boy. She saw it too, and tried to make light of it. *Think I best take off me bodice, Dick, and go about like them? Your father strip off his britches?* This made the children laugh. Even Dick gave a pale smile.

Thornhill was weary of the way Dick was inclined to vanish when there was work to be done. *You're too old for them tricks, lad,* he said, and heard his voice harsher than he had intended, so Sal glanced up. *Time you pulled your weight, not play about with savages.*

But Dick, for all his dreaminess, was a stubborn little thing. *They don't need no flint or nothing, like you do,* he sulked. *And no damned weeding the corn all day.* Thornhill felt the rage burst in him. He grabbed the boy by the arm and pulled him outside, and in the last of the sunset, in a din of laughing jackass birds, he pulled off his heavy leather belt and beat Dick with it. Felt his arm heavy, reluctant, but would not stop. Heard the boy cry out as if surprised at each blow.

He had never beaten any of his children before. Cuffed them around the ear, the way his own father had done to him, or given their backsides a slap to make them remember. But something in him had burst. During the long three months that they had been in this wild place, the anxiety and the fear had been curdling within him and turned into fury.

Sal was quiet when he came back inside, and would not meet his eye. She put the children to bed quickly and they sat together, staring into the embers. It was always hard to leave them, they glowed so richly in the night.

You think I shouldn't have, he said at last. The silence between them had become unbearable. *You think he ought to go about with them* . . . he tried to remember a word he had heard someone use . . . *them primitives?*

Sal's voice was careful, neutral. *It ain't that, Will,* she said. *But if he goes about a bit, it's the way you and me did.* She held out her hands to the coals, although the night was not cold. *That place down Rotherhithe way, remember? Only he ain't got no Rotherhithe to go to. He never even heard of the place.*

In the corner he could hear Dick making smothered gasps and noises. He saw that Sal was right: these children of his had no notion of any place that was not Thornhill's Point. They knew nothing of streets and cobblestones, of houses jammed in cheek-by-jowl, the bricks sweating in the fogs from the river. They knew nothing of feet numb with cold, dead hands gripping an oar as cold as a piece of iron, knew nothing of drizzling rain that seeped out of the sky day after damp day, the dread of the bone-chilling cold. In their mouths the very names of that other place had a peculiar sound.

This, for better or worse, was the only world they knew.

Thornhill could still feel the heat on the palm where he had gripped the belt and brought it down, as if it were he who had been beaten. *Just the same he'll come along of me and Willie on the boat from now on,* he said. *Do a fair day's work for his dinner.* He saw her nod absently and touched her on the shoulder. *We call it a day, eh?* he said, and felt her hand on his cheek so he heard the bristles scrape.

We can call it whatever you please, Will, she said, her smile pushing up the corners of her eyes so the skin there crinkled in the way he loved. They went to lie down together, but just before they did so she hesitated. *About Dick,* she whispered. *Not to fret, Will, it will come good.* The smart on his palm, and the other smart, the one somewhere in his heart, was soon soothed by the feel of his wife's body in his arms, her breath in his ear.

~

In spite of the beating, it was the very next day that Thornhill found Dick over in a hidden place near the soak, twirling one bit of stick on another, his face red with the effort, his little mouth set rigid.

When he caught sight of his father he dropped the sticks and sat staring up at him. Thornhill looked at the sad mess of twigs and tinder. The boy's thin face stared up at him, frightened, but ready to defy too.

Thornhill felt a moment's rage. *Do I got to get the belt out again lad?* he said, but even as he said it the anger left him. He saw the boy's face close down against him and remembered the way the belt had felt, hot in his hand. If beating him once did not do the trick, beating him twice would not do any better. He had learned that much on board the *Alexander*.

Squatting down beside Dick, Thornhill shook him gently by the shoulder. *Just joking, lad*, he said. *I beat you once, that were enough.*

The boy looked up at him, his eyes still distrustful. *Let's try this savage's trick*, Thornhill said, and picked up the sticks that Dick had been rubbing away at. The first difficulty was to hold the bottom stick securely. Long Bob, or Long Jack as he was now, had sat cross-legged and held it with his feet, but Thornhill did not think his legs would bend like that, or his feet be much good as hands.

Here lad, hold this one tight, he said, and Dick held the bottom stick with both small hands while Thornhill rolled the other one between his palms. It was harder than he could have imagined, keeping the point of the stick pressing on the same place, keeping the thing rolling smoothly between his palms, and all the time crouched over so the blood began to pound in his head. *Me bloody hands are burning*, he panted. *Not the bloody stick.*

Dick sat hugging his knees as he watched. *Let me, Da*, he whispered at last. *Give it here.*

Trying to keep the stick moving while he gave it to Dick, Thornhill felt the boy's small rough fingers. He glanced at him, at his face lit up with the pleasure of trying this new thing, at how intent he was. He was an odd concentrated creature.

But Dick soon flagged and Thornhill took over again, rolling the stick in one last frenzy, and there it was: the tiny vapour of dark air. Quickly he tipped the whole lot into the tinder he had waiting on a leaf. It was all just as he had seen Jack do. He got clumsily to his feet, feeling his knees creak, and began to whirl it around his head.

Perhaps too fast. The package flew open and the sticks and tinder fell out, stone-cold. Dick looked away, making himself small, for fear he might be blamed.

Thornhill hated to see that. *Must be some trick to it, lad*, he said, still panting, and suddenly saw the funny side of it. A grown man, trying a savage's trick!

Better get him to show you again, he said. Dick glanced up at him, uncertain. Thornhill laid a finger to the side of his nose. *Only not a word to your mother.*

The boy's anxious face split into a smile. But he was still a stranger to his father.

~

Even at twelve years old, Willie still had a few shreds of London left in his memory from his first five years there. He could describe the turn of the stairway at Butler's Buildings and the way a twisted rope of shadow fell from the balustrade. He had a memory, too, of a fearful emptiness in which voices echoed and columns rose up on either side. Thornhill thought that was the Old Bailey. He remembered it too. It was a fresh scald every time.

As far as the other children were concerned, though, the place their mother and father called Home was nothing more than a word, something they needed to be taught.

Thornhill stood outside the hut where a convenient crack brought Sal's voice to him and listened to her putting them to bed with the same stories she had told him in the days of their new-wed happiness. *Get the grape-scissors, the old thing says.* He remembered how the bed had shaken, the two of them laughing so much. *Get the grape-scissors and cut yourself a sprig.* The children did not laugh. They had never seen scissors of any kind, much less grapes, and were wary, guessing that this story carried a meaning for their mother that they could not know.

She sang them the old London songs, her voice a wavering thread in the attentive air of the twilight forest. He realised he had not heard her singing since they had been together in the room in Mermaid Row, in the days when they were happy, the first baby on its way, the wherry at the wharf, the future waiting for them. Her singing was as tuneless now as it had been then, but hearing it filled him with sudden gladness.

Oranges and lemons say the bells of St Clements, she sang. *Ha'pennys and farthings say the bells of St Martins.* Dan came trudging up the track from the cornfield, and Thornhill signalled him to be quiet. *St Clements, that's in Eastcheap*, Sal was explaining. *Dick, you remember what I told you yesterday about Eastcheap?* Dan made a noise that was not quite a snort, but was near to it, and turned it into a sniff.

The gladness in Thornhill closed down. The song was not for pleasure, then. It did not show that happiness might be possible under this different sky. It was instruction, pure and simple, and preparation for a return.

When the song was done, she walked them through the streets of Bermondsey. *Now, to go from Butler's Buildings to Sufferance*

Dock, she started, and he could hear the delight she took, seeing it in her mind's eye. The children were silent, listening to a prayer. *Down Bermondsey Street, left at White's Grounds, across Crucifix Lane and then cut down through Gibbon's Rents.*

But that was wrong, and Thornhill spoke through the crack in the wall. *It ain't left at White's Grounds but right, left took you into the almshouses, remember?* She called back, *Left, Will, the almshouses was the next street over.*

Then Dan said that it was not right or left, because the almshouses were at the end of Marrow Street, on the other side altogether from White's Grounds.

London, that place of hard stone and cobbles, was becoming just another story, its exact shape gone fluid.

~

Towards the end of January there was a few days' respite from the heat. Fine shreds of high cloud muted the force of the sun and the air had a weight of coolness. One pearly morning they woke to the smell of smoke. Thornhill went out and saw a long grey plume drifting up from near the blacks' camp.

They gone and lit a fire, Mr Thornhill, Ned said. At close quarters like this, day after day, Ned's love of the obvious was becoming wearying. Sal came out of the hut and stood with them, looking down at the smoke, and then the children came out one by one. Bub said what they were all thinking: *They coming to get us?* No one answered.

They could see the fire moving slowly up the slope, but this was not the wild animal of flame, pale and furious, that they created when they set alight to their heaps of cleared timber. This was a different species altogether, a small tame thing that slid from tussock to tussock, pausing to crackle and flare up for a moment and then licking tidily on.

Around the edges of the fire the blacks were standing like part of the landscape, holding leafy green branches in their hands. When a flame began to swell, whoever was closest took a leisurely step and flapped with the leaves until it subsided. Black Dick was moving around with a firestick in his hand, dabbing it at any unburnt tussocks until they began to let off clouds of white smoke. Long Jack was behind him with a whisk of leaves in his hand.

Whisker Harry stood closest to the Thornhill household. His body was very straight, the smoke swirling around his head. Now and then he called out brusquely to one of the others. Thornhill watched his profile, waiting to meet his eye and smile or gesture, but the part of New South Wales that included the Thornhill hut seemed to have become invisible to the old man.

This had the look of a routine that had happened countless times, and had nothing to do with the newcomers. As they watched, they saw the one they called Meg take a step forward towards the rim of flame and strike with a stick at something on the ground. She bent and picked up a lizard that struggled in her hand. With an unhurried movement she shook it and it hung limp. As she tucked it into the string around her hips, she called out high and shrill to Saucy Polly, and Thornhill could see Polly's white laughing mouth as she called back and flicked her hand towards the lizard. Even the way they gestured was different. Their hands were so fluid it seemed that they had extra joints in their fingers, and a wrist that was constructed in some other way altogether, along the lines of rope rather than bone and sinew.

Thornhill waited for them to turn towards him, hold the thing up, call out so that he could smile and call something back. Beside him, Sal seemed to have the same thought. *Polly!* she called. *Oy Polly, what are youse all up to?* And took a few steps towards them, her arm ready to wave. *Poll!* But none of the women so much as glanced at her, although it was evident from some slight alteration in the way they held themselves that they had heard.

Sal dropped her arm back to her side, came to stand by Thornhill. *She don't know her name's Polly*, she said, more to herself than him. He could hear an uncertainty in her tone. *I give her that name but she don't know that.* She was starting to believe as she explained it to herself. *She ain't learned it yet.*

But she went on watching the women, waiting to catch their eye.

Lizard! Ned blurted on a spray of spittle. *They's going to eat that lizard!*

Lizard is real good! Dick cried, but then his face closed down to take back the words. Sal glanced at him but said nothing.

The fire, having travelled up the side of the slope, was petering out along a buckle where the bones of the rocks showed through the ground. On those slabs of canted rock it faded away to smoke. The blacks had finished what they had come to do, and the shape of the place would put the fire out. They called backwards and forwards to each other and trailed back down to their camp.

The fire had left behind a blackened area a couple of hundred paces across, tussocks of coarse grass burned down to stubble, small bushes crisped up to nothing, the scattered trees singed around the base of their trunks.

Dan hawked elaborately and spat. *Burn the whole place for a couple a lizards*, he said. *Got less sense than that babe there.*

At least the small slow fire had not been a threat. But it left an uneasiness in the Thornhills as they went about their morning. It had not been a threat, but it might have been the threat of a threat.

~

A few days after the fire, those high clouds combined and sent down rain: not the usual kind, bucketfuls hurled down out of clouds so black they were almost green, but a comfortable drizzle. Thornhill felt the dampness on his head, and for a moment was back at the steps at St-Katherine-by-the-Tower, watching the grey water roughened and Butler's Wharf softened in the veil of rain. Sal came outside and stood bareheaded, holding her palms up to the sky as if for a blessing.

Then the heat returned, and overnight the burned patch was transformed. From the heart of each stubbled tussock long strands of green grew almost fast enough to watch and the bare dirt erupted into tiny bright leaves, like violets hugging the ground. With the tender green came the kangaroos, families bounding down from the ridge to feed late in the afternoons, springing lightly over fallen logs and rocks and becoming, as soon as they stood still, another grey rock in the dusk.

One afternoon Thornhill saw Black Dick stalking along with a small kangaroo dead over his shoulder. He felt the tongue shift in his mouth. He could not remember when he had last eaten fresh meat. They would have a chicken in the pot one day, but not until the few fowls had multiplied. He caught Sal's eye as she came to the door of the hut. She went back inside and had the gun down as he came in. *Fresh meat, Will*, she said, her face alight with the prospect. *Think of it!*

Thornhill hid himself behind a fallen tree with the gun. The last of the sun slanted sideways, sending fingers of shadow across the grass. Six or seven kangaroos were grazing, a big buck and some females. One had a joey in her pouch that was invisible but for a single long foot sticking out.

Seen up close, a kangaroo was a creature out of a dream, put together from different parts: the ears of a dog, the muzzle of a deer, that thick tail like a furred python. Something was wrong with the proportions, so the back feet were nearly as long as the tail, while the forepaws were stolen from a child. Grazing along the grass they swung themselves forward between forepaws and tail, the tail curving, taking the weight as the animal shifted forward to another tuft.

A kangaroo was a freak of nature. But Thornhill was discovering that if a man looked at a kangaroo for long enough, it was the idea of a sheep that became peculiar.

He had his eye on the buck. Just that tail, as thick as his own forearm, would fill the pot. He felt the spit gush into his mouth at the thought of it: a savoury brown stew that would fill a man up the way the salt pork he brought back from Sydney never did.

The buck seemed to be moving closer to where Thornhill crouched behind the tree. He was getting pins and needles in his foot where it was bent under him and had been bitten on the tender flesh between his first two fingers by sharp ants. A mosquito whined at his ear but he would not wave it away. His finger on the trigger became like wood and his eye squinting along the barrel began to swim with tears. He felt invisible and soundless and hardly breathed. He had become part of the log, part of the air, part of the evening itself.

The buck was so close now that he could hear the little cropping sound as it pulled at the grass with its mouth. He could see a fly dancing around its ears and its delicate whiskers, lit up in the last of the sun. He could even see its long eyelashes. He was close, but did not trust himself or the gun to be close enough. The animal was moving up the slope towards him. If he could remain nothing but wood and air for long enough, it would come so close he could not miss.

Finally he knew that he had to tell that wooden finger of his to pull back on the trigger, or something in him would break. He made no sound, there was no movement, only the small muscle in his finger, and yet the animal knew. Its head lifted from the grass and its ears swivelled around towards him. With one powerful thrust of its tail it sprang away, sailing over the grass, over the rocks, into the forest, and all the others bounded away after it.

In flight, the way they were constructed made the most perfect sense.

He stood up behind the fallen tree, listening to the crashes and thumps as they leaped up the ridge through the forest and the rocks. The gun hung useless from his hand.

Sal was standing at the door of the hut when he came down the hill. She watched while he hung the gun back on its pegs and put the bag of powder on the shelf. He could not trust himself to speak, disappointment a stone in his chest.

There was no conversation around the fire that night as they held their bits of pork on sticks over the coals, catching the drips with the dry cornbread that crumbled into pieces as soon as it was handled. His throat closed against the food, the smell of it in his nostrils made him gag. Sal ate, doggedly, beside him, but he could not. She glanced at him, at the food in his hand, but said nothing.

Dan was the first to smell it, his head turning like an animal's to where the scent came up on the evening air all the way from the blacks' camp: the smell of fresh meat, roasting. Thornhill could hear his guts rumble with longing.

~

A few days later, seeing Long Jack and Black Dick sauntering back to their camp with another kangaroo slung on a stick between them, Thornhill slipped into the hut and took one of the small calico bags of flour and made his way down to their camp.

The old women were sitting by the fire the way they always

seemed to, with their legs stuck out straight in front of them. They did not glance at Thornhill as he arrived. The one they called Saucy Polly was poking around with a stick at something in the ashes. Meg had a baby on her lap, a chubby thing squealing at some game she was playing with her fingers. She glanced at Thornhill and the bag in his hand. The baby took hold of her finger and laughed into her face.

A little way off, the men had dug a pit and lit another fire in it. As Thornhill came up they threw more sticks on, heaping them up high. Long Jack was there, and Black Dick, but they seemed intent on the fire. If he had not known better, Thornhill might have thought they had not seen him.

He could see the kangaroo stretched out stiff beside the pit, most of its hair singed off. The spear-hole gaped in its side. The spear had gone right through, in one side and out the other. Nearby was the spear itself, slick with blood. Nothing more than a length of wood thrown by a human arm, and it could pass through fur and skin, muscle and sinew.

He had never seen what a musket ball did to a body, whether it also would pass through it from one side to the other.

Whisker Harry stood by the pit. Like everyone else, he did not seem ready to acknowledge the visitor. His face was turned in the general direction of Thornhill, but the space occupied by him was nothing more than a piece of air the shape of a man.

Thornhill took a step towards him, holding out the bag. Among so much that was dark—skin, earth, wood, stones—the calico bag had a grubby look on the end of his arm. *Fair exchange, old boy*, he said. His arm was beginning to feel foolish, stretched out towards the unmoving old man. Was it absurd to suggest the idea of purchase to him? Or was it that the bag of flour was not enough?

Thornhill did not see the old man's mouth move, but he heard a few words and Long Jack moved to take the bag. He undid the knot at the neck—Thornhill's hands went out to show him how, but it did not seem to be necessary—and took the bag over to Whisker Harry, who reached in and got a handful of the flour, held it up to his nose to smell it, inspected it on his palm, tasted some with the tip of his tongue. For all the world he was like a fussy customer at Covent Garden.

He turned and called to the other men, the words blunt and choppy, and flicked his hand towards the kangaroo. The forefinger with its long pale nail was as expressive as a dance. Black Dick bent over the kangaroo with his little stone-bladed hatchet, working away at it, and straightened up with part of the animal's leg in his hand. He gave it to the old man, who handed it to Thornhill. Some words came out of his mouth, unsmiling and peremptory. It seemed that the notion of a transaction had been understood.

The bit of kangaroo that Thornhill now held in his hand instead of the bag of flour was not the part he would have chosen, being mostly the foot, with a claw of brown horn, and the sinewy first joint with a small amount of meat on it, the whole still covered with a considerable amount of hair that had missed being singed off. If he had had the words, he would have haggled. But the old man had turned away. It did not seem that the idea of haggling was part of the idea of purchase.

There was no further interest in the white man standing with the kangaroo leg in his hand. Whisker Harry spoke sharply and the men began to scrape some of the glowing embers out of the pit with sticks and heap them at the side. Black Dick picked up the kangaroo and threw it down into the pit and they all got to work covering it with the scraped-out embers. They did nothing quickly, and yet the carcass was covered over, first with a smoking layer of coals, then with dirt and sand, until the pit was filled up to the top.

Good luck to you, boys, Thornhill said. It was hard to keep the scorn out of his voice, that these savages had no better way of dealing with meat than bury it with a few hot embers. Long Jack glanced at him and his mouth moved around a thought, but he said nothing and a moment later Thornhill realised he was alone by the faintly smoking dirt of the pit with no company other than one of the skinny dogs, its yellow eyes watching him.

~

Sal looked askance at the kangaroo shin, but Willie went to it with the knife, trying to slit the skin to peel it off. The knife would not go through the skin, only sawed away uselessly at the fur: the boy might as well have taken to a tree for all the progress he made. His father took the knife from him and by sheer brute effort managed to make a cut. If it had been a sheep, the skin would then have peeled off like a sock. But with this lump of wood-like meat the skin was glued to the sinews beneath. Thornhill could feel the blood pounding in his ears with the frenzy to get at the meat, the rage swelling up to choke him. The thought of the way the blacks did it, flinging the carcass onto the coals, enraged him all the more.

Finally he cut the thing up with the axe, out on the ground, right on the dirt. The lumps he dropped into Sal's pot were all fur and bone and gristle.

The exchange he had made was looking less satisfactory by the moment.

They ended up with a kind of soup with a scum of hair that had to be strained through muslin. In the liquid were lumps of bone and strings of sinew gone like bootstraps. Even Willie could not get his teeth around those shreds of meat. All they could eat in the end was the juice, a rich dark soup like an oxtail. It was something to flavour up the mealy old cornbread and as they ate they remarked, until they were weary of saying it, how excellent the broth was. But a piece of good meat was what they longed for.

They won't never believe it back in Bermondsey, Sal said, wiping her chin of the juice. *That we eaten kangaroo!* The meal had made her cheerful in spite of its shortcomings, and he tried to join in her mood. *Not so much eat, Sal*, he said, *more like we drunk kangaroo.*

Later she heaved over on the mattress to lie against him, sighing with the pleasure of a bellyful of something warm, and fell asleep at once, breathing serenely. He lay awake, hearing her scratching at a flea, and thought about their neighbours, thanks to whom the Thornhill family had eaten better than usual.

It was true the blacks made no fields or fences, and built no houses worth the name, roaming around with no thought for the morrow. It was true that they did not even know enough to cover their nakedness, but sat with their bare arses on the dirt like dogs. In all these ways they were nothing but savages.

On the other hand, they did not seem to have to work to come by the little they needed. They spent time every day filling their dishes and catching the creatures that hung from their belts. But afterwards they seemed to have plenty of time left for sitting by their fires talking and laughing and stroking the chubby limbs of their babies.

By contrast, the Thornhill household was up with the sun, hacking at the weeds around the corn, lugging water, chopping away at the forest that hemmed them in. Only when the sun slipped down behind the ridge did they take their ease, and by then no one seemed to feel much like fun and games. Certainly no one seemed to have energy to spare for making a baby laugh.

On the point of sleep the thought came to him: the blacks were farmers no less than the white men were. But they did not bother to build a fence to keep animals from getting out. Instead they created a tasty patch to lure them in. Either way, it meant fresh meat for dinner.

Even more than that, they were like gentry. They spent a little time each day on their business, but the rest was their own to enjoy. The difference was that in their universe there was no call for another class of folk who stood waiting up to their thighs in river-water for them to finish their chat so they could be taken to their play or their ladyfriend.

In the world of these naked savages, it seemed everyone was gentry.

~

Thornhill was less anxious now each time he sailed away from the point. The bit of practical commerce—kangaroo for flour—had reassured him that the blacks could be absorbed into some version of a normal society. Trade was picking up too. Nearly six months after they had come to the river, the *Hope* was never empty and he had his regular round now, of farmers who waited for the *Hope* rather than some other, less trustworthy boat.

Smasher Sullivan was one of those regulars. Lime was at a premium in Sydney, where stone and brick buildings were going up apace, limited only by the lack of ingredients for mortar. Carrying the lime to Sydney was a good trade, five shillings the keg.

But Smasher's Arm had never sat right with Thornhill. It was a crooked length of water between high wooded ridges that bent away into the wild plateau beyond. In there the sun seemed to shine coldly and the water was a black mirror. Even when a nor'-easter was ruffling the main river, not a breath of wind stirred the glassy surface or blew away the stain of smoke that hung between the ridges.

Smasher had his place on a triangle of flat ground wedged between two hillsides that rose up uncompromisingly. He had cleared it, after a fashion. Now it was a lumpy patch of land thick with the stumps of trees, a ragged stand of corn struggling in the sandy soil. Beside the corn he had built his hut, but too far up the slope so the whole thing tilted downhill all skewed and ramshackle. Beyond the clearing and the crooked hut the forest pressed down.

The third side of his triangle was bounded by the water, the shoreline a strip of bare dirt. He had hacked down the mangroves for fuel, and bald scraped places on the shore showed where he had scratched at the shell-heaps left by the blacks, gathering them for lime until he had got down to the original dirt. The fires that reduced the shells to lime burned day and night. So much burning had left the place stripped of every tree and bush.

Thornhill was always in a hurry to get away from Smasher's. Load up quick, get away under the hour with the tide ebbing out to speed him on his way. That was the way he liked to do it.

The forest beyond the clearing seemed to be holding its breath as the *Hope* glided in on the last of the flood tide. Smasher's dogs, those biters he was so proud of, were chained up outside the hut, all except Missy who never left his side. When they picked up Thornhill's scent they started to snarl and bark and hurl themselves against the end of their chains.

Thornhill stood in the stern, coming up to the jetty. He glanced towards where the black sack-thing had hung and twirled. There was nothing there now: no tree, no body.

Smasher was down by the water moving around a mound of sticks. He hallooed and waved, shouting across the water to Thornhill, who waved back but said nothing. Something about the brooding watchfulness of the place made him reluctant to break it with his voice.

Close up, Smasher stank of dead oysters and his own rotting

teeth. He had a firestick in his hand and was lighting the dry leaves heaped around the pile and thrusting the stick into gaps he had left. Wedged in among the sticks were the shells: not dead ones but whole fat fresh oysters shining pale among the twigs. A dangerous crackling was beginning deep inside the heap and bulges of smoke floated away.

His voice always took Thornhill by surprise, high like a boy's. *Thornhill*, he called, *have you got any baccy about you, I would kill for a plug*. Reluctantly, Thornhill handed him his pouch and watched him cut off a plug and put it in his mouth.

He saw an oyster in the top of the heap feel the first lick of flame. It tightened itself down hard, straining to stay shut. Then a bead of juice ran out and sizzled and in the same moment the shell sprang open.

Smasher was watching him. *None a them other ones now*, he said. *Finished all them piles the blacks left.* All through the heap there was a tinny crackling as the oysters opened and urgent plumes of steam shot up out of the vents in the mound, followed by streams of black smoke that smelled of burning meat.

Thornhill had eaten his share of Thames oysters as a boy. They were tough, no bigger than a walnut, prised off the rocks before they had a chance to get big and juicy. These Hawkesbury oysters were the size of a man's hand, great generous flat things. At the start he had made himself sick, gobbling them down as if it were his last chance. But there was no need to gorge himself: nobody's hunger would ever make a dent in so many.

Looking now at the rocks around Smasher's place, stripped of every last shell, he wondered.

Only good thing is, they gone and buggered off now. Nothing to eat here. Smasher laughed, coughed, spat. *One way to get rid of them.* His laugh rang out hard across the water.

~

As they were rolling the last of the kegs of lime from the hut down to the boat, the barking of the dogs took on a different pitch, high and hysterical, and Thornhill glanced around. Every time one of the blacks appeared out of nowhere it gave him the same cold shock. This one must have come up in the canoe that sat tilting on the shore like a big brown leaf. Now he was standing, waiting for them to see him. He held no spears, only a couple of plump oysters with the water still running from them.

When he had their attention he opened one, just like that, with a twist of his thumbnail. He made it look as easy as squashing a louse. Then he tilted his head back and sucked down the contents. They could see the powerful muscles in his neck as he swallowed. He opened a second oyster the same way, with nothing but his bare thumb, and held it out, offering it to Smasher and Thornhill. He spoke at length, gesturing with the oyster, talking loud and clear, as to someone stupid, pantomiming how good it was to eat.

Smasher was not a man to take a lesson from a black. *Want a free feed do you,* he shouted. *See you in hell first.* The man ignored him, going over to the mound, from which oily clouds of smoke were now pouring. A blackened oyster rolled out and lay steaming on the dirt. He pointed at it, gesturing insistently, and then down to the rocks where the ebbing tide was exposing the white scars where the burning oysters had once grown.

He was shouting, an angry man.

But Smasher would not let a black have all the running. He went for the whip in his belt and cracked it beside the man with a sound like a gunshot. *Be off,* he shouted. *Damn your eyes, be off.* The black flinched but stood his ground. The next flourish of the whip caught him full on the chest and the black skin blossomed a long red stripe. He took a step back and stood glaring at Smasher, his deep-set eyes catching the light, his mouth a hard line. Smasher lifted his arm to strike again but with a movement too fast to see, the man caught hold of the end of the lash. There was a long moment in which he and Smasher stared at each other, joined by the whip.

Then without a word the black man let go and turned his back. He went down to his canoe and slid it into the water. Smasher ran to his hut and snatched up the flintlock leaning against the wall, but by the time he had run back down, fumbling with the bag of shot, the black man had poled his canoe out into the current and was being carried out of sight around the rocks. Smasher's shout echoed around the inlet with the angry blur of the dogs' barking, the strangled noises of them gagging as the chains jerked at their necks.

He whirled around to Thornhill over the din of the dogs. *You,* he shouted. *We know about you, cosying up to them bastards.* There were grey specks of foam in the corners of his lips. His eyes were small with dislike. *You and that Tom bloody Blackwood. I seen the two of youse.*

His face was too close, his voice too loud. Thornhill took a step back. *Shut your gob,* he shouted. *You ain't seen nothing.* But he felt a kind of panic. He had stepped on a great wheel that was spinning him away somewhere he had never planned to go. He had thought Blackwood's arrangement was a private thing, his own knowledge of it private too. Now he saw it was not private at all. But he did not want to look at what that might mean, or where it might lead.

Smoke continued to pour over the water. Smasher turned his head away to spit a long brown stream onto the dirt. *They'll get you one fine day,* he said. The thought soothed his rage. *You think they won't, you're a bigger fool than I took you for.*

Now Thornhill could not bear to stay a moment longer. *Look sharp, Smasher,* he said. *I miss this tide, you're a dead man.* In silence they rolled the last keg along the jetty and into the belly of the *Hope*. As Thornhill cast off, his face turned away towards the open river, he heard Smasher call out after him. *Don't come crying to me, Will Thornhill,* he called. *When you get a spear in your guts.*

PART FIVE

DRAWING A LINE

It was on Thornhill's return from that trip to Sydney that things began to change.

It took them some time to realise that a crowd of blacks was gathering on the point. They came down from the ridges in twos and threes, the men walking in that deliberate way they had, burdened only with a few spears. The women came after, each with a baby on her hip and a long bag hanging from her forehead down her back. Others came in canoes, drifting up or down the river with the tide, the little slips of bark holding a man and a woman, with a child between, and the water by some miracle not coming in over the gunwale.

They came, and they did not seem to go again. Where one feather of smoke had lifted into the sky around the point, now there were many smudged together. Where the Thornhills had occasionally heard a shout or the cry of a child, now they could hear voices all the time, things being chopped with a dull thudding, and the sounds of women calling that came to them on the breeze. There were more kangaroos than there had ever been, and every day groups of blacks could be seen coming back with an animal swinging between them slung on a stick.

The mood at the hut became a little thoughtful. No one liked to meet anyone else's eye. Even the children became silent and careful. Sal kept them close under her hand. Thornhill went about his business, cutting down another tree near the hut and standing over Ned and Dan while they broke it up to burn. But he found himself stopping as he worked, listening for sounds beyond the clearing.

Sal had made the mark that meant they were into the month of February of the year 1814. It was the steamy height of summer, the cobs of corn growing almost visibly. Every morning the sun came up already in its full heat and filled the valley so there seemed no air left to breathe. Night brought no relief. The valley began to feel like a funnel in which the Thornhills were trapped with their black neighbours. Thornhill knew that Swift and O'Gorman were waiting up at Ebenezer for the *Hope* to come and collect their potatoes, but from day to day he postponed the trip.

One afternoon he set the men to widening the track down to the river and slipped away. No one saw him as he made his way up behind the hut and onto the rock platform, following it around the point, past the fish and the boat in the rock, until he was directly above the blacks' camp.

It was a shock when he looked down through the trees. Where there had been half-a-dozen adults and a handful of children around one little fire, now there were more blacks than he had ever seen together at one time. There was a settlement of humpies crowded close to each other, and campfires everywhere. The people themselves were as hard to count as ants, moving around, disappearing into the shadows and reappearing again.

On one count he got to forty. That was enough.

He went back to the yard where the family was trying to make themselves cool in the shade. *Just having a bit of a get-together*, he said airily. *Same as we might ourselves.*

Sal, knowing him so well, heard something in his tone but

248

said nothing. She went about her business, wiping Mary's face clean with the flannel, concentrating on getting every speck of dirt off. *I got a few jobs for you up here this afternoon, Will, if you would*, she said, looking up at him. *Don't go back down the corn patch.* Her voice was light, but he saw Mary's eyes turn to her sideways, her chin still held firm in Sal's fingers while she worked away with the flannel.

Are the savages coming for us, mumma? Bub asked, quite matter-of-fact. *Silly thing*, Sal cried, *they ain't coming nowhere for nobody*, and started on his face with the flannel so he said no more.

Thornhill went into the hut, feeling the heat radiating down from the bark roof, and got the gun down from its pegs. He looked along its length and checked that the powder was still dry, the shot handy in its bag. Peered down into the circle of darkness that death could come out of. When he heard Sal approaching the door, he quickly put it back on the wall. But she knew. She looked at him standing with his hands empty and her eyes went to the gun on its pegs. He saw her start to say something, and cut across it. *Nest of damn spiders in the barrel*, he said.

They had their meal early that night. There was a feeling of needing to be ready.

Thornhill did not ask himself, ready for what?

It was only just dusk when Sal got the children into bed and sang to them. *When I grow rich, say the bells of Shoreditch. When will that be, say the bells of Stepney. I do not know, says the great bell at Bow.* Her voice sounded parched. He heard in it a quaver of tenderness.

Or perhaps of fear.

The two of them sat up late over the last of the fire, watching in silence as the draughts flickered over the coals. In their corner the children snuffled and sighed. Dick flung himself over and called out something in a blurred voice. From the lean-to Ned was snoring with a noise like a shuddering saw. They heard him cough, could imagine Dan turning him over, and in the silence that fell they could hear the sounds coming from the camp.

At first it was a sharp clapping, insistent as a heartbeat. Sal turned her face to Thornhill's. In the firelight her eyes were pools of shadow but he saw how her mouth was tight. Before he could think of reassurance, the singing started: a high strong wailing of a man's voice, and other voices in a kind of drone underneath. It was not a tune, nothing cheerful that you might listen to like Oranges and Lemons, more a kind of chant as you might hear in a church. It was a sound that worked its way under the skin.

Thornhill tried to speak up loud. *Having a bit of a sing-song*, he said, but his mouth had gone dry. He tried again: *Like that Scabby Bill. Remember Scabby Bill?* Of course she remembered him. But she knew, as well as he did, that this authoritative chorus of noise was very different from the thin song that Scabby Bill had managed in return for a mouthful of liquor.

He had to force himself not to whisper. *They'll get sick of it by and by.*

Out there, between the cracks in the walls, the night was as black as the inside of an ear. The huge air stirred, full of hostile life. He imagined it: the blacks creeping up to the hut, silent as lizards on their wide quiet feet. They might at this very moment be peering in at them. The noises were getting louder, the sort of sound it would take an army to make.

The words not said were like a creature pacing up and down between them.

Now Ned and Dan, woken out of their sleep, came in. Ned went over to the lamp and stood beside it as if the glow would keep him safe. *They coming to get us, Mr Thornhill*, he said.

Hear them laughing, Dan added. *They can't hardly wait.*

It was true, they could hear distant laughter. Thornhill felt fear cold on his skin at the picture in his mind of them preparing their spears with a butcher's glee, how sharp they were, how quick they would kill a white man.

Ned's voice was on the edge of panic. *They coming to spear us in the guts, ain't they*, and Bub's voice came quavery, *Don't let them spear me Da!* He could hear Johnny catch the fear and set up a snivelling that set Mary off too. Sal went over to where they lay and wrapped her arms around them.

If they'd a wanted to spear us they'd a done it ten times over by now, Thornhill said. Then he thought that might not be the best argument to follow. *We got no call to worry*, he announced, but no one seemed convinced.

Now Willie was speaking up. *They get away with it, we'll never see the end of it, Da*, he said. *We best show them good and proper.* To Thornhill's ears, the words had a secondhand feel about them, borrowed from someone else. Smasher perhaps, or Sagitty Birtles.

He saw the boy anew: a mulish skinny lad who had outgrown his strength, all bony neck and bat-ears and a mouth that was trying to be strong. Willie stood squinting at him, scratching the back of one leg with a long bare foot. *Get the gun, Da, whyn't you get the gun?*

But Dick had got up from the stool and faced up to his brother. *Ain't no call for the gun, Willie*, he said. *They just having a get-together, like Da says.* Willie grabbed his shoulder and shook it. *Bulldust*, he cried. *Bloody bulldust that is, we got to get the bloody gun.*

Shut it the both of youse! Thornhill heard his voice filling the hut, and the boys said nothing more. Then Dan spoke out of the shadows near the fire. *I got the knife here in my hand*, he said, his voice rasping on his fear. *Them buggers come close, they get it in their black guts.*

After he had spoken, the high indignant voices and the rattle of the sticks seemed louder. The hut had become a compressed cube of fear.

Standing by the half-open shutter, Thornhill remembered the nights in Newgate, listening to the beating of his own heart, not able to stop himself waiting for the next beat, the next, and the next, and trying not to wonder how many heartbeats he had left. He was stifling in the hut, could not bear the closed-in feeling. It was too much like being in a coffin deep in the earth.

He started to speak, fell over the words, coughed, tried again: *I'll just take a look.* His voice was thin in his own ears. *Make sure they're not up to no mischief.*

~

It was a relief to be outside in the fragrant night. A full moon rode in the sky, dimming the stars and lighting the forest in shades of grey. Under the noise from the point, the place was going about its business, ticking and whirring secretively. Something rattled in the dry bark near the woodpile and the black shape of a bird swooped over the clearing.

Glad of the moonlight, Thornhill made his way up to the shelf of flat rock and around towards the camp. He wanted to be unseen, but he knew how his shirt, dingy though it was, must stand out bright against the trees. His skin, that inescapable envelope, glowed white and dangerous. He tried to move without making a sound, but by moonlight his familiar place had become somewhere else. Rocks came at him unexpectedly, trees were not where they were by day. He stumbled along against the grain of the place until, from behind the powdery flank of a paperbark, he could see the camp. No one turned or pointed. If the blacks

252

knew the white man was there, they were not concerned.

They had a huge blaze going at the centre of their camp. He could see the firelight illuminating the trees from beneath, flickering on the skin of the trunks, making a cave of light. Figures passed in front of the fire so it winked on and off.

A circle of men stamped and jumped around the fire, and one sat at the side with his legs crossed and his face tilted up, singing in that way that made everything urgent. They were striped with white, their faces masks in which their eyes moved. The firelight made them insubstantial, webs of light dancing.

Women and children sat around them clapping sticks together to make that brittle pulse underlying the song. The women's long breasts were outlined with white, with a collar effect around the upper chest that was absurdly like the neck of Sal's bodice. Their faces, like those of the men, were barred with white. The children were painted too, even the smallest of their faces. It was only a bit of pipeclay, but it gave them the look of the very earth made human.

War paint, he thought. They're doing a bleeding war dance. He was surprised by the calmness he felt at the idea, and realised he had been expecting this moment for a long time.

The dancing was recognisable as being from the same world as Scabby Bill's, but it was as little like his as Thornhill's warped hat was like the Governor's plumed tricorn. Scabby Bill had danced with his eyes nearly closed, his face blank, absenting himself from the moment. These men danced with their eyes full of light from the fire, the lines of white on their bodies twisting with life.

After a moment Thornhill recognised Long Jack. He crouched with the others, his spears in his hand, then leaped with a powerful spring and came down again stamping his feet and scuffing the dust up into the air. Jack was no longer a man, but a kangaroo made human.

To the man listening behind the tree, there was no more sense to the sound than there was to an insect's drone, no sense of it having a beginning or an end. But then the sticks all stopped on the same instant, the voice of the singer gave a final flick and was silent. He realised it was the same as the way everyone in church stopped singing at once, because they knew that they had got to the end of the hymn. Watching from behind the paperbark, Thornhill was the only one who did not.

They started up again, with a different beat this time. Now there was one old man dancing alone, his feet stamping into the ground, so that the dust flew up around him, glowing with light: Whisker Harry. His body was sinewy with muscle, turning into the dance like a fish in a current. The pounding of his feet seemed the pulse of the earth itself. When he began to sing, he threw the song up into the air, its long crooked line the sound of the blood in the veins of the place.

Thornhill saw that this person was not Whisker Harry, who existed only in the minds of those who had given him that name. This man, dancing in his white paint, wrapped in a mystery of song, was another person entirely.

The others watched, clapping one stick against another. He saw that they were not simply watching a man dance, as people might sit at the Cherry Gardens and watch folk do a jig. There was a drama alive on their faces. There was a tale that they all knew being told in the language of this dance. It was like Christmas at St Mary Magdalene: everyone in the church took pleasure in the telling of the nativity, the same from year to year.

This old fellow is a book, Thornhill thought, and they are reading him. He remembered the Governor's library, the stern portraits, and the rows of gleaming books with their gold lettering. They could reveal their secrets, but only to a person who knew how to read them.

Watching the power in this man's thighs as he thudded his feet into the dust, Thornhill remembered that he had slapped him and scolded him like a child. It had been a mistake, and it frightened him now. Whisker Harry was not just a stubbly fellow with an old man's spindly shanks, as unimportant as the almsmen at the Watermen's Hall, doddering along for their bowl of gruel. This man was old in the same way the Governor was old. A man should no more push and slap him than he would the Governor with his shiny sword hanging by his side.

The steady clapping of the sticks and the rise and fall of the wailing voice beat back from the cliffs, muddled and multiplied, a river of sound bending over its stones. Thornhill stood behind the tree, feeling drawn deep into the sound, the beat of the sticks like the pumping of his own heart.

~

When he got back to the hut, Dan pulled him in. *Get the bleeding door closed for pity's sake*, he cried. *And the bar up quick.*

It was stuffy inside. The lamplight flickered on their faces as they turned to him. *How many of the buggers is there?* Dan said. *A hundred, two hundred?* His voice had gone thin, frightened of the answer it might get. *No more'n a dozen*, Thornhill announced. *Maybe not so many.* But this lie sounded as hollow as a quart-pot.

Sal had got the children up and dressed. They were all crowded around the table on which the slush lamp gave off its smoky light: Ned and Dan, and the children wan in its light. Only Dick was not around the lamp with the rest of them. He lay on the mattress, staring up into the rafters.

On the table Sal had set out everything they owned: the pannikins, the teacups, the knife with the broken tip, her other skirt neatly folded. There was Willie's pocketknife and a bonnet she had just finished sewing. There was the bag of flour, the smaller one of sugar, and the hand-mill for the hominy. They were laid out on the table as if on a shop counter.

They'll leave us alone, Will, if we give them what we got, she said. *Just let them help themselves. Mrs Herring done it one time.* Her voice was very matter-of-fact, as if she had often dealt with savages. *They got no call to do us no harm.*

In the shadows, someone went *huh* in disbelief. Thornhill thought it might be Willie and turned on him, but the boy stared back expressionlessly.

Ned spoke up: *We kin shoot the buggers, cain't we?* His voice was uncertain. But Dan cut across him, his voice gone high as a woman's. *They'll burn the place*, he cried. *Flush us out like possums.*

It was a relief to channel fear into movement. Thornhill took a step across the room to Dan and belted him on the side of his head. *Shut your gob, Dan!* he shouted. He forced himself to speak calmly: *Let them know what we got, that's all we need to do.* He took the gun down, and Willie was beside him straight away handing him the bag of shot, the pouch of powder, the ramming-rod.

He felt everyone's eyes on him as he loaded the gun. He knew, as perhaps they did not, how pointless a thing it was. He could go through the rigmarole of loading it up and squinting along its barrel and firing. But after that, what? He could imagine the fumbling panic to reload: to ram home the shot and the wadding, pour the powder into the pan, cock the flint and fire.

In the time it took to do all that, they would be pincushions, if that was the way the blacks wanted it.

He felt a bubble of laughter press upwards, and forced it back down. He saw with surprise that his hands were steady as he poured the powder.

Then he went to the shutter, pushed it open and stuck the barrel out blindly into the night. *Put this in yer pipe and smoke it*, he shouted. The recoil was a blow into his shoulder that made him stagger and he was blinded for a moment by the flash. The explosion blasted his eardrums.

He lowered the muzzle and listened to the endless echoes of the shot bound and rebound, rumbling away down the river between the cliffs that hemmed them in. *That'll keep them off*, he said, and closed the shutter like a man with a good job done.

But down on the point, the clapping and the singing did not miss a beat. Thornhill imagined the blacks down there, hearing the shot, turning back to the dance with their faces stern. He imagined Long Jack, his face a landscape in itself, gazing up towards the hut, listening.

~

For every night of that week, the blacks danced and sang. All those nights, the cliffs echoed with the sharp chips of sound from the sticks, while the people in the hut lay listening, their possessions outside the door, covered with dew in the morning but untouched. After that first dawn, when they awoke amazed to be unspeared and unscalped, the fear was less. Whatever was happening, it did not seem to have anything to do with the family in the hut, but was some imperative of the blacks themselves.

Then they disappeared, as quietly as a tide going out, leaving only the usual handful of people coming and going in their unhurried way.

The Thornhills tried to go about their business, but nothing was the same. In the hut, so few: two men, a halfwit and a stripling. A woman and four infants. And the gun hanging on the wall, nothing but a machine for noise and hot air. Thornhill had known all this before, but now he could not forget it, even for a moment.

Sal knew it too. Something in her had shifted. He did not hear her humming any more, and came across her sometimes staring at nothing, a crease between her eyebrows. When the women trailed past the hut on their way into the forest, she waved and smiled, but kept her distance. She did not go over among them anymore, and no more bowls and digging-sticks were added to her collection.

~

It began to seem a dangerous innocence to have only one gun, and only one man who knew how to fire it. Thornhill bought three more guns from John Horne up at Richmond and made pegs for them to rest on, one on top of the other up the wall. Then he spent a day showing Dan, Ned and Willie how to fire the things.

To his amazement, Ned proved a natural with the gun. Clumsy with everything else, he was deft at pouring the shot into the barrel and tamping it down. He hardly seemed to take aim, and there was the block of wood they used as a target tumbling off the fence-post again. Ned had at last found something he was good at.

Dan was awkward, dropping the ramming-rod, spilling powder everywhere, could not seem to get the hang of pressing his cheek against the butt and fitting it into his shoulder. The block of wood was never as much as scorched by any of his shots. He preferred the idea of a club he could swing in his hand. He spent a morning in the forest, coming back with a stick that had a hard bulge in one end, and spent his evenings whittling away until it was weighted and shaped to suit him.

When it came his turn to try the gun, Willie was pale. He wiped his hands down his britches. Thornhill saw that his hands were shaking as he poured the powder onto the pan. *You're only a lad, Willie*, he said. *No call for you to do nothing.* But the boy was determined. The first time he did not push the butt firmly enough into his shoulder and when he pulled the trigger the gun gave him a blow that sent him tumbling backwards. But he was up in a moment, grim-faced, to try again.

Thornhill knew that four guns, and three men who could use them, would not be enough if the blacks came for them. But that outline, man plus gun, was something they knew to fear. The hope was that their fear would do the trick, rather than the gun itself.

He could not forget the way it had felt in the nights of the war dances, to know how close the wall of forest crowded down. A spear could sail out of the trees and strike a man down without him even seeing the hand that threw it.

He determined to clear a space around the hut. But how wide would such a moat have to be? He cut down a stalk from one of the grass-trees and felt something of a fool, standing with his spear in his hand and everyone watching. Sal had a look on her face he could not read as she stood in the door of the hut.

Do I make a good savage, lads? he asked, trying to make a joke of it, and even Ned had the wit to laugh. Thornhill turned himself side-on, the way he had seen the blacks do, to gather together the muscles of his chest and shoulders. He felt the spear leave his hand and pictured it curving smoothly through the air, the way theirs did, and landing tip first in the ground. But his stick only wobbled, and skidded along the dirt a few yards off.

He turned to the watching men and laughed. *See what I mean*, he called. Up at the hut Sal watched. *No call to get ourselves fussed.* He did not share with them the way his shoulder hurt.

Now Dick was picking up the spear, hefting it in his small hand. He seemed hardly to be trying, but there the thing was, singing along the air and skewering the ground a good fifty yards away, far in among the trees.

It was easy to see it was not the first time Dick had thrown a spear, or even the twenty-first or the hundred-and-first. Thornhill saw on his face that the boy realised what he had told them, but this was not the moment to take him to task. This was the moment to realise how far a spear could travel, even when thrown by a skinny boy not yet eight years old. That could wipe the smile right off a man's face.

He paced out the distance the spear had gone, added another few yards, and got them to work. Every tree—apart from the one on which Sal marked the weeks—was hacked at with the axe until it fell. Every bush was grubbed out, every loose rock was rolled away and the whole lot fenced. As far as this bumpy land could be, a protective circle around the hut was flattened. Nothing remained that any man could hide behind.

They won't try nothing on us now, he told them. He could see Sal watching his mouth make the authoritative words, and could not meet her eye.

He had made something of this place. He had cut down trees, got rid of bushes, chopped out the tussocks that were big enough for snakes to make a home in. With each day that passed, a little more progress could be measured: one more tree cut down, one more yard of bushes cleared, another length of fence.

He loved the thing a fence did to a place. The tidy square of ground inside a fence had a different look from the ground outside it. A fence told a man how far he had travelled, and beyond the last length of fence he could see where he might go next.

There was this about it, though: no matter how much a man did in this place, the everlasting forest could not be got rid of, only pushed back. Beyond the patch of bare earth he was so proud of, the river-oaks hissed and the gumtrees rattled and scraped the way they always had. Up above the cliffs a flock of birds, black against the heat-bleached afternoon sky, heeled and veered together like a scarf flying in the wind.

~

The idea of Smasher's biters had become more interesting to Thornhill. He was not looking forward to Smasher gloating, but swallowed his pride one calm Sunday at the beginning of March and took the skiff downriver.

He could hear the dogs long before he could see the hut. Their barking echoed raggedly around the valley. As he walked up to the hut they lunged at him on the ends of their chains. He gave them a wide berth, skirting round to where Smasher was clearing bushes off another few yards of land.

Smasher straightened up, watching Thornhill. His face was sour and pale under his hat like a man not eating any greens.

Thornhill did not waste time on pleasantries. *Want to buy a couple of dogs off you*, he said, straight off. But Smasher wanted to spin it out. *Savages come visiting I hear*, he said, his smile full of gaps. *Won't leave you be after all, that it?* but Thornhill did not wait to hear him out. *Couple a bitches and a dog, five pound, take it or leave it.* Smasher pretended to consider, scratching his jaw so the stubble rasped. *Thing is, lot of call for my dogs just now*, he said. His narrow face was rubbery with triumph. *I could say not less than ten pound, Will, and cheap at the price.*

But Thornhill would not be sneered at. *Guineas, Smasher*, he said. *Five guineas my last word*, and turned, was walking back towards the boat when Smasher gave way, as he knew he would. *Got to stick together*, he called, and Thornhill looked back.

Smasher was a sad skinny figure, standing crooked on his crooked bit of land, his trousers flapping ragged around his ankles, his bare feet caked with dirt, sweat streaked down his face. *Give us the five guineas then*, he called. *One white man to another.*

~

On their way back to the hut for Thornhill to pick out his dogs, Smasher shouted over their barking: *Got something to show you.* Some sly excitement in his voice made Thornhill hesitate but Smasher edged him into the doorway.

After the brilliance of the sun it was hard to see much inside, just a shadow split with bands of brightness where the light came in between the sheets of bark. But there was some sense of movement in a corner, and a powerful smell, part animal, part something gone rotten. As his eyes adjusted Thornhill could make out something, a mattress was it, with a thin hot ribbon of sunlight, and beside it a dark shape. There was the clink of a chain, and another breathing, not Smasher's and not his own. He thought it must be a dog, but in the moment of the thought he saw that it was a person crouching with a stripe of sunlight zigzagging down its body: a black woman, cringing against the wall, panting so he could see the teeth gleaming in her pained mouth, and the sores where the chain had chafed, red jewels against her black skin.

Smasher pushed past Thornhill and shouted, *Get your idle black arse out of there.* Thornhill saw the whip catch her around the small of the back as she stumbled outside. In the sunlight her skin was flaky and grey. She stood holding up the chain that joined her ankles.

Under that sun, so white-hot it seemed to make things dark, Smasher was a puny man with a whip at the ready in his hand. He was smiling a small wet smile. *Black velvet,* he said, his tongue flickering out around his lips. *Only kind of velvet a man's got round here, unless that old Herring piece takes your fancy, which she don't mine.* When he had enough of laughing at the idea of Mrs Herring, he came up close to Thornhill. *She done it with me and Sagitty*, he whispered. *Back and front like a couple a spoons.*

For a terrible vivid instant, a scene lit by lightning, Thornhill imagined himself taking the woman. Could feel her skin under his fingers, her long legs straining against him. It was no more than a single hot instant, the animal in him. *You game, Thornhill?* Smasher was asking. *Only watch out, she got claws like a poxy cat.* Thornhill could not find any words, managed only to shake his head and turn away.

Smasher took flame as if he had been waiting. *Too good for a bit of free fanny, are you?* he shouted, and spat out of the side of his mouth. The spit glittered as it arced through the air and fell on the dirt. *When even your precious Thomas Blackwood has a black bitch.*

Thornhill was seized with a desperation to get away from this airless place. If he did not he would stifle to death there and then. *Damn your eyes, Smasher, forget them dogs,* he shouted harshly. Smasher's tight smile faded. *Give us just the five then,* he said, but Thornhill did not want the dogs now, not at any price. They were maddening him, snarling and barking, their teeth shining with spit, their muscular tongues working in and out of their long throats.

It was a relief to shout. *I said forget the dogs!* Shouting let something out, burned it off. He heard his voice echo from the ridges. Felt that the whole place, every tree, every rock leaning down the slope, was listening.

But Smasher was not impressed. *Takes a certain kind of a man, don't it,* he said after a while. *To handle them dogs.* His tone was conversational. *Maybe you ain't that man, Will Thornhill.*

As Thornhill got into the skiff and heaved at the oars, forcing the boat along, he turned his face away from Smasher. The greasy smoke hung low over the water.

~

Imagining the moment of telling Sal about what he had seen—even thinking the words in his own mind—filled him with shame. It was bad enough to carry the picture in his memory. Thinking the thought, saying the words, would make him the same as Smasher, as if Smasher's mind had got into his when he saw the woman in the hut and felt that instant of temptation. He had done nothing to help her. Now the evil of it was part of him.

~

If he picked his time right, when every man on the river was getting in his harvest, a trader with a boat full of reaping hooks could do well on the Hawkesbury. Thornhill had bought ten dozen at the beginning of February and had sold the lot by the steamy first week of March, even the one with the split handle. Now he was gliding down on the tide by moonlight, the *Hope* riding high and skittish on the water.

For the sake of a quiet life he always agreed with Sal when she reminisced about the way things were back Home. He agreed that the light was too harsh here, the days too hot, the nights too cold. There were too many snakes and things that stung. It was the end of the earth, with the nearest neighbour an hour away in the boat. He never tried to explain to her that, in spite of the mosquitoes and the brassy sun, the Lower Hawkesbury had its consolations.

The river was all silver and black in the moonlight. Above the cliffs a waxy moon floated over the frayed horizon of trees, making the stars pale in its light.

Night on the river could be sweet, and part of the sweetness was how well it was known to him. He could see the rounded hump of his point along the metallic water, the way the ridges dipped and rose over the valley of the First Branch. They were as familiar to him now as Wapping Stairs and Swan Wharf had been.

He was calmed, full of pleasure as he sat in the stern of the *Hope*, feeling the river push back against the tiller like another person. He had thought to die a kind of death in coming here, but was beginning to see that a man did not have to be Jesus Christ to rise from that particular death.

He took his time making the *Hope* fast, reluctant to leave the night. On the way up the slope he paused beside the corn, listening to its little secretive creaking sounds in the moonlight. Like everyone else's, his was ready to harvest. The cobs with their soft gold tassles had flourished in the heat of these summer days, growing five and six on a plant, wealth on a stalk, crowding around him with their papery rustle.

They would harvest in a few days and, at ten shillings the bushel, they would make a good few pounds. Easy money, when all he had done was stick a peck of seeds into the earth and wait.

~

By night the hut was no longer a box sitting hard on the dirt but a loose container of yellow light streaming out between each sheet of bark. Where it poured from the doorway onto the ground outside, it made the bloodless moonlight seem another kind of darkness.

He knew how it felt to be in there with the fire leaping up the chimney and the lamp on the table: safe, enclosed. But from out here it was obvious what a frail and porous thing the hut was. The bulge of the ridge dwarfed it and the breeze smothered the sounds of the people sitting in their hot yellow bubble.

He knew that Sal had callers: he'd seen the boats drawn up at the landing-place. As he came closer he could hear the rumble of men's voices from inside.

He had not spoken to Smasher since the day, two weeks ago, when he had seen the woman in the hut. Turned away when he sailed past Smasher's Arm. He let Andrews from Mullet Island do the trade in Smasher's lime now. He had tried to put the picture of the woman and the red jewels of blood on her skin away in some part of his memory where he did not have to see it.

A person coming in from the leafy smell of the night was like to suffocate in the hot stink of men and rum, and be blinded by the dirty light of the lamp. Smasher was there with Missy at his feet. Sagitty had brought his neighbour George Twist, an angry stumping man with legs bowed from rickets and his hat jammed down tight over his eyes night and day. Loveday's gawky length was slumped over the table and Mrs Herring sat up prim on the other side. In the corner beside the chimney Blackwood sat cupping an elbow, his face half-hidden by his hand.

At the sound of the door opening Sal turned, fright on her face. Loveday turned too, in an exaggerated way, drunk enough to have become a clumsy machine. *Here is your breadwinner, Mrs T*, he said, and Smasher did not miss a beat, coming in on top of him. *Crumb-winner, more like*, he shouted, and that got them started. Sagitty thumped on the table with his hand, he thought it was so funny, and laughed with a strange high noise that could have been sobs. Thornhill saw what he had not seen before, that Sagitty was something of a lickspittle to Smasher. *Like a couple a spoons.*

Sal poured her husband a tot and gave it to him. *They got Spider, Will!* she said. *Smasher, tell him about Spider.* Smasher did not need any encouraging to tell the story again. Mrs Webb had been alone with the children on that sad chip of civilisation called Never Fail. Webb was away down the river borrowing a reaping-hook, his own having been stolen by the natives the week before.

When Webb was on the place, he did not let the blacks come within his fences, ran out with the gun if he had to, to make them leave. But with Spider away, Sophia Webb had let them come right up to the hut, and they charmed the silly woman, too softhearted for her own good. One of them got her talking at the door, capering about and playing the fool, so that she gave him a dish of tea and a doughboy to go with it. Meanwhile half-a-dozen of the others were busy out of sight down in the field, and while Sophia Webb was pressing another doughboy on her new friend they had stripped every last cob.

Telling the story again, Smasher was blotchy in the face with anger. *Whyn't she ask them in to have a little kip in the bed while she were at it?* he said. *And a puff of her man's pipe and a sup of his rum?* He was so entertained by his own wit that the few teeth in his mouth could have been counted. But Thornhill could see he did not find it funny. His laughter was just another way of being eaten up with rage.

The widow Herring was speaking up from over by the fire, chuckling around her pipe as she spoke. *Poor booby, she were taken in just like old Mr Barnes in Hatter's Lane*, she said. *My brother Tobias kept him gabbing at the door and I slipped in behind. Fingered a card of ribbon off of his counter, got a half-crown for it later.* She puffed away, smiling. *They do got a charming way about them when they please.*

I ain't got no cards of ribbon, Mrs Herring, Sagitty said. He could not hide a shake of anger in his voice. *I had four bags of wheat, just into the bags and that, buggers come and robbed me.* George Twist had caught alight at Mrs Herring's mildness, too. *Asking for trouble, ain't they*, he said, his chin sticking out as he looked around waiting for anyone to disagree.

Twist was never a happy drunk. He had hogs up on his place and was a good customer, buying as much salt and as many kegs as Thornhill cared to bring him, and shipping the pork out on the *Hope*. Just the same, Thornhill could not warm to him. He had never told Sal, but Twist was famous for the fact that one of his hogs had killed his youngest infant, and rumour on the river had it that he refused a burial on the grounds that the hog might as well finish what he had started.

There was more to the story about Spider. He had come back with the reaping-hook while the blacks were still there. He had the gun with him and got off a shot, but the blacks overpowered him while he was trying to reload. One stood over him, daring him with his spear, while they made Sophia cook them every egg the hens had laid, scoffed all the pork, and ate their precious store of sugar out of the bag in handfuls.

They did not molest her, poor toothless skinny woman that she was. Even Smasher did not suggest that. But they put on the few clothes the Webbs had: Sophia's good bonnet with the pink ribbon, the shawl that had been her mother's, Spider's spare shirt. Shiny with pork-fat, they capered around in these, jabbering away as if a bonnet with a pink ribbon were the best joke in the world. Finally they carried away everything that could be carried away: the axe, the spade, the box of tea, the pannikins, even the little girl's rag doll that one of them fancied.

Webb's oldest, a surly freckled boy, kept saying, *Stop them, Dad, stop them*, but his father could only stand there watching everything go. The boy burst into angry tears.

The last one turned and called something over his shoulder that made the others laugh. Wiggled his black arse at them as they stood in the door of the denuded hut, wiggled it and slapped it mockingly. It was a detail that Smasher enjoyed telling, demonstrating with his own arse and his own hand. Ned watched with his mouth open.

The message was clear, and Spider had decided not to wait

for another. He would turn his back on Never Fail. He was going to try his luck at Windsor, where the blacks could not get into the township. Set up a public house there and sell Blackwood's liquor. He would let other men grow the corn and deal with the blacks.

Loveday was so drunk he had gone rigid, not blinking, one hand holding his pannikin, the other clenched on the table like a man having his portrait painted. But suddenly he thundered across the room so that everyone looked around: *No set of people in the known world were ever so totally destitute as these are of industry and ingenuity!* Ned nodded, looking solemn as befitted the grand phrases. *Their innate indolence renders them inattentive to the very means of subsistence.*

But the story was Smasher's and he was not going to be bested by any ragged gentleman with a mouthful of words. *Meaning they are lazy thieving savages*, he interrupted, but Loveday for once stood his ground. He belched, slapped his hand on the table for attention and went on, unstoppable as a tide. *Our sable brethren, lazy savages as you so rightly call them, reap by stealth and open violence the produce of a tract they are themselves too indolent to cultivate.* His eyes were unsteady in his head but the phrases rolled splendidly out of his mouth.

Thornhill looked into his rum, silenced by so many words. Smasher whirled around, miming a gun to his shoulder. *They understand this lingo all right, Parson*, he shouted. Sagitty held up his pannikin in a toast, but stopped it on the way to his lips, struck by a thought. *Keep back a couple of them gins eh?*

Mrs Herring sniffed. *Mind how you speak, Smasher Sullivan*, she said sharply. *There's those of us don't fancy it one bit.*

At this a silence fell around the table. Smasher smirked at Thornhill. Thornhill licked his lips and looked away. He wondered if all of them had been invited to share that woman who crept along the wall in chains. Sagitty was smoothing the beard around his mouth smiling.

Ain't no one listens to an old woman, Mrs Herring said. *But I tell you straight, you are heading for your come-uppance, Smasher, carrying on like you do, and you too Sagitty Birtles, don't think I don't know what goes on.* And stuck the pipe back in her mouth hard, as if putting a cork in other words she would like to say.

Across the room, Thornhill felt Blackwood watching him. There was something insistent about it, a challenge. He made his face show nothing at all, looked away, rubbed at his eyes. There was so much smoke in the room a man could hardly see.

Loveday held up a finger for attention and declaimed *It is a well-attested fact that the blacks have no word for property.* He was going to go on, but Smasher rode over his light dandified voice, and he subsided back into his pannikin. *Got two of the buggers on their way to Darkey Creek last week*, Smasher said, then took a bite of one of Sal's baps and spoke through it. *Picked 'em off like a squire with a brace of grouse.* He looked around but no one spoke, and went on through a mouthful of crumbs. *Only thing them savages is good for is manuring the ground.* The flour on his lips gave them a scaly diseased look. He said it again. *Make real good manure. Bring the corn on a treat.*

Thornhill saw him glance at Blackwood and if provoking him was what Smasher wanted, he had succeeded. Blackwood was on his feet, a big man in a small room, enlarged with rage. *You, Smasher*, he shouted, then stopped, his massive arms folded across his chest and his face like a stone.

Thornhill was afraid that Blackwood had gone wordless, the way he did. If that happened, Smasher would be on him in a second. But Blackwood went on in a voice that shook with feeling. *By Christ Jesus*, he said. *One of them blacks is worth ten of a little brainless maggot like you.* The room was silent, everyone sobering on the spot, the laughter dying in their throats. No one had ever heard Blackwood profane before, or heard that steel in his voice.

He came right up to Smasher, his face grim. He seemed about to hit him but turned with a grunt of disgust and was out the door, into the night, before anyone realised what had happened.

That bastard going to be real sorry he said that. The rage in Smasher's voice was tamped down like one of his fires.

Thornhill stared out at the black rectangle of the doorway. Followed Blackwood in his mind, down the track, onto his little dory and along the First Branch. He imagined Blackwood sitting in the stern, winding his way into that closed moonlit landscape of ridges and cliffs. Up there, the blacks would be expecting him. He would go into his hut, blow the fire back to life and sit watching the flames blazing under the kettle.

Perhaps the woman would sit there with him, even the child as well. It was a girl, he thought, but he had only caught a glimpse.

~

The attack on the Webbs was one of many *outrages and depredations* that March of 1814. They erupted up and down the river, always in a different place. It seemed that every man with a crop waiting to be harvested had an encounter. Fields were set on fire, huts were burned down, spears were flung at men out with their reaping-hooks. Farmers had to start again with another lot of seed, hoping to get a new crop before winter, or they abandoned the whole thing, walked off their places, and went back to Sydney.

As a result, business was bad for William Thornhill. No one needed the *Hope* when there was nothing to take to Sydney. No one had the money to buy calico or boots. Thornhill tied up the boat and waited for better times. He was glad of the excuse. It was a time when a man needed to sit tight on his holding and keep a sharp eye out for trouble. He acted untroubled, a man who could rise above any setback. He made a big thing of picking the corn from that first patch, enough for a couple of meals, letting Dick and Bub eat their fill as payment for all those buckets of water. But underneath his good cheer there was a hard knot of worry.

~

His Majesty in London, embodied in the person of His Excellency in Sydney, did not especially care about the emancipists who grubbed in the dirt on the banks of the faraway Hawkesbury. But to make a fool of one white man was to make a fool of them all. In its own stately time, the mighty instrument of the law swung against the blacks. His Excellency issued a warrant. His Majesty had shown patience and forbearing but was, reluctantly, obliged now to take action against the native raiders.

His Majesty's instrument in this case was a certain Captain McCallum, late of Shrewsbury. He came down from the garrison at Windsor with his men in one of the Government longboats and tied up next to the *Hope*. Thornhill's Point was a convenient starting point for the campaign he planned.

Waiting for him in the hut, Thornhill could hear the flat sour sound of the little drum marking his approach. It was clear that the captain was a man careful of his dignity.

He swept into the hut, unfurled his map on the table and began to explain his plan to the soldiers with him. They were like insects in their red coats with the black bands crossing their chests, their plumed caps. Their sweating faces held in by their chinstraps did not reveal what they thought about the captain.

Thornhill stood by the doorway with Sal beside him, the children squatting on the floor. His private thought was that the answer to *the native problem* did not lie in anything the Governor might do. That man, in his red coat and his gold braid, was as irrelevant to what was happening on the Hawkesbury as was the King, or even God Himself.

But Captain McCallum had worked out an ingenious strategem that he was sure would trap the natives down on Darkey Creek. He had a way of saying the name of the place as if it were ridiculous or amusing. There was nothing amusing about Darkey Creek. It was a little place along from Sagitty's, no good to a white man, being a gloomy cleft where a narrow arm of the river ran between ridges so steep that the sun only shone in at noon. Word was that natives who were driven away from the farms were taking refuge there. Thornhill had seen the canoes, slipping in and out where the creek joined the river, had seen the smoke from their campfires drifting up between the spurs. As far as Thornhill was concerned, Darkey Creek was a useful kind of cupboard, where the blacks could be forgotten about behind a closed door.

For Captain McCallum, though, the narrow cleft of the place suggested other possibilities. He was planning a pincer-movement that involved what he liked to call a human chain. The idea was that the troops would link arms and proceed along the cleft for its full length, driving the natives ahead of them.

As one might drive sheep, the captain explained.

Captain McCallum was a gentleman and had a gentleman's strangled way of speaking, as if someone had him round the neck. Thornhill found him hard to understand, but this was not turning out to be a problem as Captain McCallum did not even glance at the Thornhills. They were, after all, emancipists. He had refused a drink of tea from Sal, would not take even so much as a drink of water in spite of the heat.

He demonstrated on the map how the natives would be penned in against the end of the gully, where cliffs rose up sheer. There, His Majesty would dispense justice.

He reached under the table and with a conjurer's flourish brought out a canvas bag. *The Governor has personally issued me with six of these bags*, he said, and cleared his throat modestly. *He told me, that he has every confidence that we will bring them back filled*. If he had expected a roar, or even a murmur, of approval, he was disappointed. The men in their red coats shuffled, shifted, breathed, but said nothing. He glanced around at their expressionless faces. Thornhill could see him decide that he needed to be more explicit. *Six bags, do you see, six bags for six heads*.

The room was silent as everyone watched him hold up a bag to demonstrate how the drawstring could be pulled tight. Thornhill saw Dick craning to see, his mouth open in disbelief.

On the map, Captain McCallum's plan looked childishly simple, and on the map it was easy to imagine it: the human chain, the proceeding, the justice being dispensed. The map was correct enough. There was the river, hooking around the point at Thornhill's, and Dillon's Creek another mile along, with Sagitty's place drawn on as a square, and just before that, the crooked line of Darkey Creek. The cliffs at its end were indicated by hen-peckings on the paper. The map was correct, and there was no arguing with the captain's logic, the elegance of the pincer-movement and the human chain.

But Thornhill had been there and knew that the map was correct only in its generalities. He knew that, in the real world, the ground that McCallum indicated as being where the human chain would proceed along the creek, was an exhausting jumble of trees, bushes and boulders. The hillsides bristled with fins and plates of rock, the gullies were full of mangroves and reeds in mud thick enough to swallow a man. Every tangled vine, sprawling root and whip-like bush would resist a single human, let alone a detachment, passing through. Mosquitoes would eat them alive, leeches slide down into their boots no matter how tight-laced, ticks would drop into their hair and burrow into their skin, and they would be forced into a series of exhausting detours that would increase the journey along the cleft by ten or twenty times its distance on the map.

Captain McCallum, not long from Home, his rosy cheeks already blistering in the colonial sun, could not be expected to know any of that. He had been taught to think in terms of an army taking up a position and confronting another army. The problem was, there was never any army here, only those ambiguous figures that vanished when a man looked at the movement they made. They were too cunning to have anything as vulnerable as an army, for they knew what the Governor and Captain McCallum did not: that an army clumping along was as exposed and vulnerable as a beetle trundling over a tabletop. It was those invisible bodies that would win battles here, hurling a sudden rain of spears from nowhere, and disappearing so there was nothing to shoot at.

From his spot over by the door, and against his better judgment, Thornhill decided to speak. *If I was to put my oar in sir*, he said, *it is pretty rough going thereabouts.* He felt Sal straighten her shoulders and stand tall against him in support.

McCallum stared at him glassily for a moment, glanced at Sal, looked away from them both. *Thank you for the warning, Thornhill*, he said, addressing a portion of the wall above their heads. He was very brisk about it. *I would not expect you to have had experience of a fully-trained corps of soldiers.* His look hinted—except in your capacity as felon. *We are a disciplined fighting machine, Thornhill, and are used to rough going, as you call it.*

Thornhill felt Sal go tense with indignation and hoped she would not speak. Quickly squeezed her hand to warn her. He heard her give a breath through her nose that was a close cousin to a snort, but she said nothing, and they listened while McCallum recited a speech he had clearly planned well ahead of time. *This colony rests on a knife-edge, men,* he announced. *It is up to us to hold the line against our treacherous foe.*

At this point it seemed that Captain McCallum might have forgotten the rest of the phrases he had prepared. There was a long pause before he added, *I trust that every one of you will do his duty to his King and his country.* It looked as though he expected someone to call out *Hear, Hear,* but the roomful of people simply stared at him. As for Thornhill, King and country had never done too many favours for him. He coughed, and McCallum shot him a sharp look.

~

When McCallum returned a week later he had deflated like a bladder. The collar of his red jacket was half torn away so it flapped loose at the side of his neck and one sleeve was ripped as far as the shoulder. Both knees were wet circles of mud, his cap was gone, his hair was falling into his bloodshot eyes and his face was livid with mosquito bites.

He said nothing to the Thornhills, keeping his chin up and his eyes elsewhere. Later his underlings, enjoying Sal's johnny-cakes after their time in the wilderness, spoke freely. It appeared that they had made the human chain, had proceeded, had done the pincer-movement and so on up the valley of Darkey Creek. After tremendous obstacles involving mud up to their waists, ridges and gullies in a series of walls, after every difficulty of snakes, spiders, leeches and mosquitoes, they had arrived at the cliffs, expecting to see the natives they had driven before them trapped there, cowering. There was not a single native, not so much as a dog. But dozens of spears had sailed out of the forest and trapped them, just the way they had hoped to trap the blacks.

They fired blindly into the bushes, but three redcoats lay dead, and four others wounded, before they were able to drive the blacks away.

~

The failure of Captain McCallum's expedition did not stop His Excellency, it only made him turn to another instrument. Redcoats with pincer-movements having failed, he prepared to unleash the settlers themselves. A Proclamation was printed in the *Gazette* which Loveday read out to a gathering at Thornhill's.

The hut was full. Smasher, George Twist, Sagitty, Mrs Herring. Even Blackwood had come to hear what the Governor had in mind. Dan and Ned squatted by the door and the children, big-eyed with the moment, were crowded onto the mattress out of the way.

The page had been handled so often that the paper was fluid as fabric, the words fading off the page. Loveday's voice took on extra depth, being the Governor. *March the twenty-second, eighteen hundred and fourteen,* he started. *The black natives of the colony have manifested a strong and sanguinary spirit of animosity and hostility towards the British inhabitants.*

Sagitty had already had a skinful before he arrived at the Thornhills' and called out bitterly, *Meaning, they stick a spear in you any time they get the chance,* but Blackwood took no notice. *Just get on and read the poxy thing, will you?* He stood near the door, had refused a tot of rum or a stool to sit on. It was clear that he was only here because he could not read the Governor's proclamation for himself.

Loveday read on in a fluty voice: *On occasion of any native coming armed, or in a hostile manner without arms, or in unarmed*

277

parties exceeding six in number, to any farm belonging to British subjects, such natives are first to be desired in a civil manner to depart from the said farm.

Loveday was enjoying himself, mellowed by liquor and a hut full of people listening to him, but Smasher could not let him have the floor. *Civil manner on the end of my gun*, he interrupted, his eyes glittering small and dangerous in his flushed face. But Loveday was in full flood now and would not be stopped. He held up a hand and raised his voice: *And if they persist in remaining thereon, they are then to be driven away by force of arms by the settlers themselves.* He stopped and looked around at his audience. *Put plain, you may shoot the buggers any time you get the chance*, he said, and in one draught drained the pannikin by his elbow.

Give it here, Mrs Herring called out. *Give it along here to me*, and Thornhill saw she did not believe that Loveday had read the thing right. Loveday passed her the paper and she signalled Sal to help her. The two of them bent close over the words, spelling them out to each other in whispers, their fingers running along the lines of print. Thornhill saw them reach the end of the piece and look at each other. Mrs Herring had laid aside her pipe for once and her mouth was dour.

Sagitty, flushed with liquor, called out, *Devil take that one-at-a-time shit. Give 'em a dose of the green powder.* But now Smasher was on his feet, his voice filling the hut. *Think I need any bit of paper from the damned Governor?* He pulled something out of his britches pocket and laid it on the table beside the lamp, something like a couple of leaves tied together with a strip of leather. *What's mine is mine and I ain't never waited for no by-your-leave.*

Sal, near him at the table, reached out to touch one. From across the room, Thornhill saw her eager face in the lamplight and knew that whatever the things were, they would not be anything as innocent as leaves, but could not get across the room in time. He saw her face contort and her hand flick the thing away as if it had bitten her, heard her cry out in disgust. *Get them out!* she cried. *Out! Smasher! Before them kids see!*

They were a pair of human ears, dark brown, hacked off rough. Where the blood had dried it had crusted almost purple, like any other meat left out too long.

Smasher laughed and picked them up from the floor. *All right, missus,* he said, *no need to get yourself fussed.* The children were craning to see, but Sal got over to them and tried to block their view.

Smasher watched Thornhill, taunting him. *Got a bob for the head off a feller in Sydney,* he said. *To measure and that.* He picked up the pair of ears and shook them together. *Got to boil it up real good first. Get it nice and clean.*

They all contemplated the boiling-up of a human head. Thornhill forced his face to be a stone. The thing about Smasher was, it was hard to know when he was boasting and when he was in earnest. In either case, Thornhill wanted him gone.

He could see Sal's face in three-quarter, her mouth rigid. He had kept so much from her. Now, in one moment, all that was undone.

Sagitty released a long expressive belch. It seemed to activate Loveday who called out, *Pickling.* The word was unclear and he said it again, very loud: *Pickling.* He looked around at everyone watching him and went on. *Better than boiling, Smasher, my good man,* he said. *For the scientific*—he missed the word, tried again—*for the scientific gentlemen.* His hand resting on a cushion of air to steady himself, he turned his whole body to Smasher as if he did not trust his head alone to swivel. *Pickling retains a greater degree of data,* he said with elaborate clarity, and abruptly arrived at the next stage in the stations of his drunkenness, a stupor from which he would not be roused.

Smasher reclaimed everyone's attention by showing how he hung the ears from his belt with the leather strip. *For good luck.* There were times when Thornhill could almost find it in his heart to feel sorry for Smasher, his greed for the admiration of other men was so naked.

~

Smasher was still fiddling around with the ears on his belt when Blackwood burst across the room at him. At any time Tom Blackwood would have been more than a match for Smasher. He grabbed him around the neck and forced his head down onto the table, squeezing words out from a tight-clenched jaw. *You damn little maggot!* Still holding him around the neck, he jerked him upright and ran him backwards into the cornerpost so the whole hut trembled. Smasher jolted with the shock of it and scrabbled with his feet, but Blackwood's arm kept him up off the ground as he said, *You had this coming a real long time Smasher*, and punched him, the weight of his whole body against Smasher's face.

Smasher's head snapped sideways but his eyes were still open, fixed on Blackwood, and he was trying to speak. Blackwood sent his fist into his face again. Everyone in the room heard the crunch. Blackwood let go and stepped away from him. Smasher stood swaying, his hands up to his face, blood pouring from his nose and mouth, crying out wordlessly like a baby.

Now Sagitty and Twist were on Blackwood, and Thornhill too, taking hold of his arms, feeling the muscle hard under his shirt. Blackwood shrugged them off and in a few strides was out of the hut. They all listened to his heavy footfalls going back down the path.

When he had gone, Smasher whispered through the blood in his mouth, *Give us a tot, will you, after a man been damn near killed.* Sagitty slopped out a pannikin and Smasher drank it down like water. His lip was split in several places and he had lost his few remaining front teeth. His voice came hoarse and reedy and at every word Thornhill could see the blood on his lips stick together and pull apart again. *That bugger'll be sorry he done that*, he said. With the back of a shaking hand he wiped at his mouth and took another drink. *They all going to be real sorry.*

~

When everyone had gone the Thornhills lay down to sleep, but it did not come. At last Sal spoke, as he knew she would. *We maybe better go, Will*, she said quietly.

He whispered back, *Go where, where have we got to go?* He heard her snort in disbelief. *Home, Will, where else would we go. Sell up and go.*

It ain't five years yet, only half a year! That was his first response, but even as he spoke he knew this was not a matter of keeping to the letter of a promise. *We ain't got enough, Sal*, he went on quickly. *Nowhere near!* She propped herself up against the wall to see his face. *How much then, Will?* she said. *How much is enough?*

But he would not put a number on it. *I ain't going back to a lighterman's life*, he said. He felt indignation rise up in him, pressed it back, made himself speak with no more passion than if they were discussing the weather. *Remember Butler's Buildings*, he said, and he could feel her remembering: the heaps of musty rags where they had slept and the fleas that rose from them in clouds, the bugs that nipped all night. Butler's Buildings was a place she could still smell.

Yes, Will, she said, and he saw she was ahead of him, had known what he would say. *What about this then, we go to Wilberforce or one of them other towns where the blacks don't come. Business can go along just as good from there.*

He was silenced by surprise, that she had thought the thing out so carefully. Like any good haggler she had been cunning enough to start with the highest price, so as to make a show of coming down to what she had meant to pay all along. She turned to him, her face indistinct in the near-dark. *Get the Pickle Herring going again like we had back in Sydney. Be making money hand over fist.*

It startled him: she had been thinking over their choices, and seemed to have arrived at something of a certainty. *Look Sal,* he started. He heard his blustering tone and quietened himself. He was talking about the most unimportant thing in the world. *If they was going to do anything, they'd of done it by now.* He touched her ear, where the firelight caught its softness. *We said five years, remember. We got the worst part behind us.* She stretched a leg out against his and said nothing, so he went on. *They got their place, we got ours,* he said. *We don't give them no grief. Plus they know we got the gun.*

She lay back down under the blanket and after a moment he heard a long sigh from her. *I don't want that Smasher showing his face here no more,* she said. *That man's going to bring down trouble on the whole lot of us.* He heard a darkness in her voice. It was the sound of someone who was prepared to yield, but against the grain of what she believed.

He felt a misgiving that he had convinced her. Another sort of woman would have cried, shouted, forced him in the end to go to Wilberforce. He loved her for not being that woman, but he knew she was right: trouble was coming.

He could not turn his back on this place. How could he bear

to go on passing in the boat and see some other man there? It would feel like giving up a child.

He listened for Sal to fall asleep, but she did not, only lay on her side facing him. But not touching him, thinking her own thoughts.

PART SIX

THE SECRET RIVER

One blue and silver morning a week after the attack on Webb, the *Hope* glided past Darkey Creek. It was an absence that Thornhill noticed. For once there was no smoke rising out of the gully where Captain McCallum's men had been routed. Only birds, rising, circling, dropping down below the trees.

He might have sailed by, but an impulse made him push the tiller over. The tide was rising and floated the boat up the creek easily. The wind died to nothing as the mangroves closed around him, brushing the gunwales on either side. The boat slipped along the water to where the bank opened out on to level ground.

As he stepped out to wade ashore, Thornhill felt the silence deepen. He wanted to get back into the boat and push it down the creek, away from this dense silence. He called out *Oy!* to hear a human sound, and the silence flowed back over the noise. Even the mosquitoes seemed to have abandoned the place. It was a relief to step onto the land. The quicker he could see what there was to see, the quicker he could be gone again. The blacks had a few humpies around the coals of a dead campfire. They had burned around them, the way they did, so the ground was clear. A couple of empty flourbags lay about, bright against the dirt, and a bark dish where a damper had been mixed, the scraps dry and yellow.

He waited, but nothing moved. Above him the birds flapped and shifted in the branches. He stooped to look into the nearest humpy. He saw nothing at first, just shadows. Then he saw that the shadows were a man and a woman, and they were dead. A mass of shiny flies crawled and buzzed around them. The man lay on his back, arched even in death, his mouth ajar, his chin crusted where he had vomited. His eyes were open but dull with death. The woman had one hand flung out grasping at the air. He could see the lines on her yellow palm. The smell of shit was overpowering.

He backed away into the light. Beyond the humpy were more bodies: another man, and a woman with a dead child still in the crook of her dead arm. Even the child had the pale stickiness around the mouth where the flies seethed.

There was an unnatural clarity to everything, each twig on the ground more real than itself, the way the sunlight made a sharp copy of it out of shadow.

When he heard a sound he thought it was himself, groaning. When it came again he told himself it was a bird, or a branch rubbing on another. But when it came a third time it was unmistakable: another human, alive, here with him in the clearing. His feet took him towards the sound against his will, feet in a nightmare.

It was a boy, still spindly in the arms and thin in the chest, a lad no more than Dick's age, on the ground, his knees drawn up to his belly. From his mouth hung tendrils of the vomit that was all around his head and the lower part of his body was shiny where it had emptied itself.

The boy arched his body in a spasm and groaned again. His head jerked, trying to vomit. Flies were crawling on his face and his chest where the vomit was slick.

Thornhill could not think what to do, only felt the humid

sun boring into his back and shoulders. He looked away from the boy, at the comfortless forest all around. Above the gully, way up, there was the sky, that eternal hard blue, and two ducks crossing it, wing to wing.

He made himself speak, to break the evil spell: *Ain't nothing I can do for you, lad.* He wanted to turn his back, leave all this, let someone else come across it later.

But somehow he could not. He would give the boy some water. He could at least offer that gesture. Then he could leave.

The familiar details of the *Hope* were a comfort. The place in the bow where he kept the keg. The tap on the side that came off unless it was turned the right way. The sound of the water hitting the bottom of the pannikin. This was the world he knew.

By the time he walked back up to the humpies he had convinced himself there would be nothing there. No one frozen with a fatal gripe in their guts. No lad coiled over himself, dying by inches.

But the bodies were there and the boy still lay blinking at him. He had turned on his back, his knees pulled up. As Thornhill approached, his face twisted and he turned his head from side to side. Seeing the dipper of water, he licked his lips, whispered, reached towards it.

Thornhill knelt beside him. Was surprised at the softness of that black hair. Under it he felt the shape of his skull, the same as his own.

Gingerly he put the pannikin to the boy's lips and he drank, but even as he was drinking his body jerked, the water vomited straight back up along with strings of greenish slime.

For God's sake, Thornhill shouted in fright. He had not intended it, but heard it as a kind of prayer.

The boy did not move. The water did not seem to have done him any good, and he had still not closed his eyes. He made a weak movement to draw his knees up to his chest and stared at Thornhill. His eyes were glassy. Thornhill thought perhaps he was dead, but then he groaned again and a thread of mucus slid down his chin. Thornhill felt as if everything in his own body had stopped. If he moved or took a breath he would feel the poison burning away at his own guts.

There seemed nothing to be done except walk back to the boat. He pushed it away from the bank and poled back down the creek between the cushions of mangroves. When he came out into the open river, it felt as if a lid had been lifted. He could not get enough of the river air, stood in the bow taking lungfuls of it, clean and cool. He did not look back, to see the place where the birds circled over Darkey Creek.

He knew that he would not tell anyone what he had seen. Some of them would know already: Sagitty for one. He was the man who had talked of the green powder.

He knew he would never share with Sal the picture of this boy. That was another thing he was going to lock away in the closed room in his memory, where he could pretend it did not exist.

~

Next morning Dick came running up to the hut, his feet flicking up the dust as he ran, to tell his father that the blacks were in the corn. *Not just in it*, he panted. *Picking it! Filling their dilly-bags with it and taking it away!*

Even before the boy had said his piece, Thornhill realised he had been waiting for this, that the calm he had been living in was a blank sheet ready to have this moment written across it. His rage swelled, sweet and simple. It was a clean feeling, like a length of the sea massing into a wave.

He got the gun down off its pegs. Noted that his hands were

trembling as he went through the business of wadding the charge into the barrel and priming the pan. He walked down the track with the gun along his arm. The sun was already hot.

He could see the blacks among the corn. They made no effort to hide or run. They glanced at him and then away again. They were everywhere, hands reaching out for his fat cobs and wrenching them off the stalks. He could see Long Jack and Black Dick near him. On the edge of the field the women were calling in their raucous way to each other. Their long breasts shook with each wrench of the cobs.

As he came close they fell silent. They went on ripping the cobs off the stalks, lifting their arms high, deliberately, showily. They knew the owner of the corn was there, and they were going to ignore him.

He grabbed one of the women by the hair. *Get off you bugger, get away*, he shouted. She was strong, but he was stronger, and was not going to let go. Another woman was on him now, clawing at his arm. He smelled her, spicy and pungent, as she dragged and scratched at him. He saw her lift the stick she had in her hand and felt it come down square on the top of his head, heard himself grunt with the shock of it, felt the gun drop out of his hand. For a moment everything went grey.

Get out of it, you thieving black whores! he shouted. The pain in his head made things clear and he took his chance to boot the first one as she turned. Her body arched with the force of it and she would have fallen but he was still holding her up by the hair.

Now an old woman, with terrible shrill cries, was on him, and a girl had him round the throat from behind. But he had not for nothing grown up in the streets of Bermondsey. He elbowed her savagely and felt himself connect with something soft that could have been her bud-breast. She gasped and the

291

hands round his neck fell away. He managed a good kick at the old woman's knee, so she retreated too, hopping on one leg, and now he grabbed the arm of the first one. He held her while giving the second one a wild back-hander, but she flew at him again so he made a fist and got her right in the face. Her hands went up and blood of a glossy redness was everywhere, pouring between her fingers.

It is like mine, he surprised himself thinking. Just the same colour as my own.

Dan was running down now with his club in his hand and Ned was close behind him with a gun, crashing through the corn.

He might have broken the woman's arm. When he let her go it hung limp by her side. He picked up the gun and saw her flinch away from it.

Long Jack and Black Dick were coming at him, and he turned the gun towards them. He had never pointed the gun at a human before. There was something of an intimacy to it. The gun was between them, but it joined them, too, along the line the shot would travel.

No take our tucker, he shouted. Behind the gun, his voice sounded very sure of itself. He stamped on the earth to make his point and a cob rolled away from under his boot. *This belong Mr Thornhill, youse bugger off*, he said and took a threatening step towards them.

They ran, Jack half-carrying the limping old one, the woman with the dangling arm holding it tight against her ribs. Willie was bellowing into the quiet morning in his boy's cracking voice, *Shoot 'em quick, Da*. Sal was beside him, Mary crying in her arms. She shaded her eyes to look at the broken stalks everywhere. *They nicking our corn, Ma*, Willie shouted as if she could not see for herself.

The blacks had got to the edge of the forest now, and they

all disappeared into it except Long Jack, who turned and looked straight at Thornhill.

Be off! he heard himself bellowing. *Be off!* But Jack did not go. It was as if he was memorising the way Thornhill looked with the gun in his hand. Or daring him to use it.

Thornhill got the gun up to his shoulder and pointed it. At the last instant, as his finger pulled back on the trigger, he shut his eyes. The sound engulfed him, the gun threw him backwards. There was that sharp blast of bitter smoke.

When he opened his eyes there was no one over by the trees. No Jack watching him, no Jack dead on the ground. The forest gave nothing, only the shadow of one tree moving against the shadow of another. The puff of blue smoke floated away on the air. When the rumbling echoes had faded away, a silence settled.

It had been a good noise. The heat of the barrel was a comfort in his hand. But it left an emptiness, too. There was the impulse to do it again.

His head swam and his mouth was not completely under his control. His neck hurt where the girl had gripped it and there was a smarting place on his face where fingernails had dug in hard.

He leaned the gun on the ground, holding it to steady the shaking of his hands. *That'll learn them good and proper*, he said in a reedy voice.

Put that in yer pipe and smoke it, Blackie, Willie called into the forest, but not too loud.

Sal rounded on him. *You shut your lip, Willie*, she said, and there was something in her voice that made Willie obey.

~

They heard Dan yelling from the far side of the field. He had got hold of a boy not above twelve years old, as spindly as a grasshopper, all gangly legs and knobby knees, one eye lost in swollen flesh. Dan had the club in his hand, matt with blood. He had the boy's wrist up behind his back so he was trying to bend forward away from the pain, and the further he bent over the higher Dan pushed the wrist up his back so the two of them were locked together like dancers. On the boy's fleshless leg, a flap of skin hung down bright red.

Ned was eager. *Did you get one with the gun, Mr Thornhill?* His pink mouth worked away at the idea. *I never seen a dead person, you know that?*

Dick stared at the boy. He stood rigid, his arms by his sides, every muscle tensed. His face was stricken. His mouth opened, but no words came out.

Dan jerked the boy's head around and pushed his chin up so he could shout right into it. *Mind your manners, this is Mr and Mrs Thornhill come to see you.* His voice was rich with the pleasure of being able to shout at another person. The boy trembled and tried to keep his face down. Dan took hold of the boy's head and turned it, so he was forced to look at Thornhill. His chest was going in and out quick as a dog's, the ribs moving up and down under the skin. His tongue came out and licked his lip, where there was a lumpy wound.

Dan started to say, *Now that we got one*, but the boy wrenched himself to twist free and Dan jammed his arm further up his back. Dick shot out a hand to ward something off.

Tie this one up like bait, shoot the others when they come to fetch him, Dan panted. He nodded to Thornhill for approval, but Thornhill looked at the boy, the way his feet were tensed against the dirt as if hoping to spring up like a bird and be free. *Smasher done the same*, Dan said. *Told us it worked real good*, Ned laughed his blurt of a laugh. *Learn 'em real good*, he shouted, shooting an imaginary gun, recoiling from the imaginary force of the imaginary shot, his face shiny with excitement.

But Thornhill could only see that the boy might be the brother of the one in Darkey Creek. This boy had the same narrow shoulders where the bones could be seen moving under the skin, the same black hair.

That's enough of your lip, Ned, he said, and saw Dan and Ned exchange a glance. Dan's face went wooden. Thornhill bent down so he could speak right into the boy's face. Tears gleamed on the black cheeks. *Why don't you just bugger off the lot of youse.* He was almost pleading. He felt Dan and Ned watching him. *Just get away out of here.*

The boy had gone slack now, sagging against Dan's arm.

Let him go, Will, Sal shouted, her voice stringy with feeling. *Can't be no good come out of this.* She took a step towards the boy to release him herself and he cringed away from her in fear. *Dan, for God's sake let him go!*

But Dan only looked at Thornhill. *Let him go*, Thornhill said, and Dan started to say something, but Thornhill took a step forward. *Or you get a flogging the both of youse*, and Dan let the boy go then, but not without first hawking up a gob and spitting it on the ground. Not on Thornhill's boots exactly, but near.

Released, the boy could barely stand. The spongy wound around his eye had begun to weep down his face. His skin had a chalkiness to it. He seemed not to understand that he was free. They almost had to push him away. *Go*, Dick said in a small tight voice. *Go.*

The boy stumbled through the corn, lost his balance and staggered, nearly fell. He had hardly reached the trees before the forest absorbed him, and only the patch of trampled corn showed that he had ever been there.

The corn rustled around them. A sudden wind was blowing in off the river, shaking the trees. Thornhill looked up at the forest, tufts of leaves from everywhere waving at him. A cockatoo screeched, was answered by another. A cicada started up a long high vibration.

Bub, hanging onto Sal's skirt, said, *They gone, Da, ain't they?* and Thornhill looked down, startled to see him there. His little face was pinched with worry. Thornhill said, *Yes lad, they've buggered off.* Bub fingered the barrel of the gun, still warm from the shot. *Where but?* he asked. *With us stopping here now?* and Thornhill pointed up at where the forest covered the ridges. *They got all that,* he said. *They ain't fussed.*

His legs were trembling, the muscles in his knees quivering. No instruction from his brain seemed able to stop them. It was amazing how a man could say one thing while his knees were saying another.

Bub was still not sure, but Dick pushed him aside. *We can give them bread and that,* he said urgently. *Can't we, Da?* But Willie went glum at that, for he was a lad always hungry, there was no filling him up. And now his brother was talking about giving away someone's dinner.

We ain't got no call to worry, Thornhill said. *They buggered off for good and all this time.* He heard the false authority in his voice, whipped away by the breeze.

That afternoon they brought in what corn they could. Even Bub was put to work, piling the cobs in the baskets, and Johnny sat with him entranced by the way the tassles shone and swung. Sal hardly ever lay the baby down on the ground but she did so now, the little thing kicking at the sky and crowing away.

It was slow work. The cobs grew out of the stalks with a strong stem that resisted being snapped off, and the plants grew so close together there was no room to move. Sal worked mechanically and kept her eyes on the cob in her hand, or the one she was reaching out for. Thornhill tried to work beside her, but she seemed to be making sure there were always a few plants between them.

He watched her face in profile as she reached and pulled: not so much angry as removed, as if busy listening to a conversation.

They'd a taken the lot, he said. *Six months' work.* She gave no sign that she had heard. He took a breath to say it again, but she cut him short: *I heard you the first time, Will*, she said, and went on wrenching the cobs off their stalks so hard her cheeks shook.

While the sun hung high in the sky, they could pretend. Thornhill even heard Dan whistling as he worked. But when the sun started to sink he fell silent, and by unspoken agreement they began to pick up the few baskets of corn they had gathered so far. The line of shadow from the ridge swallowed the hut, travelled over the river and up the cliff-face on the other side. Behind it, everything held its breath, waiting. The smoke from the chimney went straight up into the pale twilight sky and the river was as still as a cup of water.

In the light that remained when the sun slipped behind the ridge, Sal pushed the children inside. Clipped Johnny on the ear when he tried to come back out, so hard that he stumbled against the doorframe and set up a wailing that filled the whole valley before she grabbed him and shoved him inside.

Thornhill watched her heaping wood on the fire with a crash. The children stood watching warily. He knew what had happened to her, because it had happened to him too: fear could slip unnoticed into anger, as if they were one and the same.

~

In the moment of waking he smelled the smoke. From the door of the hut he could see how the valley was full of it, a haze hanging low over the river, and every breath smelling of ash. A bird balanced on a fence-rail and cocked its head at him. From the river came the chorus of birdsong, every kind of sound joined together, as if nothing was the matter.

Down at the corn patch, the haze was thick above a tangle of blackened stalks. In the air was a bitter smell that got into his chest and brought tears to his eyes: the stink of corn turned to ash.

That corn patch was the first thing they had made, half a year before. He had dug that dirt, he had poked in those seeds, had watched them send out their tender tubes of leaf. He had chipped out the weeds, feeling the weight of the sun. Had done it again and again. He had come down at dusk to stand among his crop and see the way each plant built its buttress of roots. He had caressed the leaves, so smooth and cool, and the plumpness of the cobs under their sheaths.

He might as well have done none of it.

He had thought himself secure at last on his hundred acres, with his boat and his servants. Had begun to take for granted his tin of tea, his strongbox filling with coins. What a blind hope that had been. His corn was gone, not just the cobs themselves, but the promissory note for a future. Life had been lying in wait for him all this time, waiting for him to trust it again. Now it had pounced, in the form of those black men who with nothing better than a burning stick could destroy all that he had sweated for.

The birds had come down and were watching from a branch, those big black birds with unblinking yellow eyes, but there was nothing left there to interest even a bird. The ground was still hot. The heat beat back from the bare blackened earth.

There was no smoke rising from the blacks' camp, none of the sounds they were used to. No child shrieked, no dog barked, no stone chopper knocked against wood. He caught himself wishing he could hear those familiar sounds.

Sal was looking down from the door of the hut, Mary held under her arm like a piglet. She stared at the ruined corn, a woman turned to wood. He went back up the slope and stood with her. He tried out various words in his mind but none seemed right to offer to her silence.

Even in the worst days in London, when they had both thought him as good as dead and her only future on the streets: even then she had not gone into herself like this. Without looking at him she set off along the track the women had worn, coming up past the hut. Just beyond the yard she stopped and glanced back. He realised that this was further than she had ever gone before. She had probably never seen the hut from this distance. She had certainly never seen the blacks' camp.

He was close behind her, but her gaze slipped past and she turned away and went on down the track. *Sal*, he said to her back. *Listen, pet, we best leave them be.* But she flung back over her shoulder at him, *They ain't there, Will.* He grabbed her hand and brought her up short. *Then where are you bleeding well going?* he shouted, and she came back sharp as a slap. *They come on our place*, she shouted back. *Now I'm coming on theirs.* And was away down the track before he could stop her.

At the camp, the domestic arrangements of the blacks were as they had always been. There were the two humpies, the large one and the smaller one. He had never noticed before how neatly the leafy boughs were tucked in together to make a roof. Inside the roomier one there were a couple of wooden dishes and a digging-stick, and a tidy coil of bark string. There was the fire-place with its ring of stones and its deep bed of fine grey ash. A shiver of heat still rose from the ashes. To the side was the grinding stone and its grinder sitting in the groove it had made. All around, the ground was as clear and clean as Sal's own yard, the dusty bough that served as broom leaning against the main humpy.

It was quiet as a trap. *Come away*, he whispered. *Quick Sal, we best come away.* But she ignored him, moving around the camp, looking at the things that made it a home: the way the stones were arranged around the fire so there was a flat place to put the food, the pile where the bones and shells had been neatly collected at the edge of the clearing. When she got to the broom she picked it up and brushed once at the ground before dropping it.

They gone all right, Mrs Thornhill! There was Ned with his silly words, Willie and Dick behind him, and all the other children trailing down the path into the camp. *Not to worry!* Dick picked up the broom and propped it up against the side of the humpy.

They was here, Sal said. Seeing the place had made it real to her in a way it had not been before. She turned to Thornhill. *Like you and me was in London. Just the exact same way.*

She shifted Mary from one hip to the other but the child kicked to be let down, and she bent to sit her on the ground, but absently, as if the child were nothing more than a parcel. *You never told me,* she whispered. *You never said.*

He flared up at the accusation not voiced. *They got all the rest,* he said. *For their roaming gypsy ways. Look round you, Sal, they got all that.*

They was here, she said again. *Their grannies and their great grannies. All along.* She turned to him at last and stared into his face very direct. *Even got a broom to keep it clean, Will. Just like I got myself.*

There was something in her voice that he had never heard before. *Why ain't they here then,* he said flatly. *If they reckon it's their place.* She looked away down the river, where the mangroves packed in: dense, green, secretive. Tilted her head to take in the wild ridges on every side. He had never before seen her look at the whole place.

They are, she said, *out there now this very minute. Watching*

300

us, biding their time. Her voice was light, as though she were discussing the weather. *They ain't going nowhere*, she said. *They ain't never going. And mark my words, Will, they'll get us in the end if we stop here.*

No call to give up on account of a few savages, he said. He forced himself to speak as calmly as she did. *Anyroad, I got something in mind for if they come back.*

But this whipped her into feeling. *It ain't if they come back*, she cried. *You're a fool if you think that, Will Thornhill. It ain't if but when.*

He put out his hand to touch her, but she ignored it. *We got to go, Will*, she said. She was gentle with him, like someone breaking bad news. *Don't matter where, but we got to get them children on the boat and go.* She glanced over at where Willie and Dick stood watching. Dick shook his head, but he might have been getting rid of a fly. *While we still got the chance, Will. Today.*

For a moment Thornhill tried to imagine it: turning his back on that clearing carved out of the wilderness by months of sweat. Letting some other man have it in exchange for nothing more than a few numbers on a piece of paper, some other man who would walk over it, smiling to himself at all its possibilities.

He knew his place now, by day and by night, knew how it behaved in rain and wind, under sun and under moon. He thought his way along all those green reaches of the river, those gold and grey cliffs, the whistle of the river-oaks, that sky.

He remembered how it had been that first night, the fearsome strangeness of the place. Those cold stars had become old friends: the Cross, nearly as good as the Pole to steer a course by, the Pointers, and the Frying-pan, which was nothing more than Orion, only upside down. He could tell over the bends of the Hawkesbury the way he had once been able to tell over the bends of the Thames.

He tried to show himself the picture he had so often thought of, the neat little house in Covent Garden, himself strolling out of a morning to make sure his apprentices were sweating for him and that no man was stealing from him. But he could not really remember what that air had been like, or the touch of that English rain, could no longer quite believe in those streets. White's Grounds, Crucifix Lane. The picture he and Sal had carried around with them and handed backwards and forwards to each other was clear enough, but it had nothing to do with him.

He was no longer the person who thought that a little house in Swan Lane and a wherry of his own was all a man might desire. It seemed that he had become another man altogether. Eating the food of this country, drinking its water, breathing its air, had remade him, particle by particle. This sky, those cliffs, that river were no longer the means by which he might return to some other place. This was where he was: not just in body, but in soul as well.

A man's heart was a deep pocket he might turn out and be amazed at what he found there.

The sun had risen now, high enough to brush the crests of the trees on the cliff, puff-balls of brilliant green glowing against the shadows. The white parrots all rose at once out of the tree they roosted in and spread like a scatter of sand into the sky, the sun catching the brightness of their wings.

Beyond the cluster of people waiting for him to speak, the cliffs hung over the river, mysterious, colourless in the early morning shadows. At this hour the cliffs were a coarse cloth, the weft of the layers of rock, the warp of the trees straggling upwards. Beyond the ragged line of tree-tops, the sky was a sweet blue. A sudden gust of wind on the river ruffled it into points of light and the forest heaved under the morning breeze.

I can have us packed in an hour, Sal said. *Be miles away by dinner-time.* She was holding out her hand for Johnny to come with her, but the calm knowing angle of her mouth as she spoke lit a flame of rage inside Thornhill. *They ain't never done a hand's turn,* he said. He could feel himself swelling into his own indignation. *They got no rights to any of this place. No more than a sparrow.* He heard the echo of Smasher's phrases in his own words. They sat there smiling and plausible.

That's as may be, Will, she said in her matter-of-fact way. *All I know is, better even Butler's bloody Buildings than creep around the rest of our lives waiting for a spear in the back.* Little Johnny was picking his nose with one hand and scratching at a mosquito bite with the other. Bub and Dick and Willie stood together with their bare feet broad on the dust. None of the children was looking at their father.

He jerked at Sal, at the arm still reaching out for Johnny. *We ain't going,* he shouted. *It's them or us and by Jesus Sal it won't be us!* He saw her stagger as he grabbed her, but she would not look at him. He took her by the shoulders, and the puniness of them filled him with despair. She stood there, frail as a bubble, but stone-hard too. *Them blacks ain't going to stand in my way!* He came at her hard, yanking her around, her face next to his. *Nor you neither, Sal!*

We ain't staying here and that's flat, she cried back. She sounded like someone shouting into a gale. He found himself taking a step and standing over her, tall so she had to tilt her face to look at him. *Damn your eyes,* he shouted. *We ain't going nowhere.* His arm moved up and his hand opened itself out, almost of its own accord, to strike her.

She looked up at him, at his raised hand, with something like astonishment. He saw that she did not recognise him. Some violent man was pulling at her, shouting at her, the stranger within the heart of her husband.

But the stranger was not going to cow her. *Hit me if you please, Will,* she cried. *But it won't change nothing.*

He saw her as she had been in that other life, with her saucy look. The picture as clear as a glimpse through a door. Then it went. This moment, with his hand raised against her, was all there was.

He dropped his arm. The heat of his anger was gone as quickly as it had come. What curse had come down on his life, that he was full of rage at his own Sal? He had a piercing wish to go back, do everything different from the start. It was too late, it was all gone too far. His life was a skiff with no oar, caught on the tide. He had got them into this place, and it had pushed them into a corner from which there was no way out.

Look Sal, he started, but now Dan was there with them, panting and red in the face, trying to tell them something. They had to wait while he bent over, heaving, to catch his breath. *They're burning Sagitty out,* he gasped. *I seen the smoke from down on the point.*

Thornhill waited for Sal to look at him, but she would not. *Willie,* she called, *bundle up all our things, there's a lad, and get them down to the river. And you, Dick, gather up all them tools.*

She set off for the hut, getting a fresh grip on Mary and snatching Johnny's hand. Thornhill had to take hold of her arm to make her stop. *Look Sal,* he said again, but she spoke over him. *You go and help Sagitty out,* she said. *The minute you get back but, we're on our way.* At last she looked at him, full in the face. *With you or without you, Will, take your pick.*

~

As soon as they got the *Hope* out into the stream they could see the smoke rising into the sky from Sagitty's place. As the boat edged up into the mouth of Dillon's Creek, Thornhill leaned over the bow, squinting ahead. He could not see the hut, and there was no skiff drawn up on the riverbank. He had an impulse to turn the other way, watch the cliffs on the other beam and the sprays of breeze on the water.

But Ned was craning over the bow, saying *Something's up for sure, Mr Thornhill*. He put the oar over reluctantly.

No living thing could be seen: no Sagitty, no dog, no fowls pecking about.

Then they saw the skiff. It was hard to smash in the bottom of a boat, but it had been done, a ragged hole in the planks either side of the keel, and the oars broken into splinters. Beyond a field of burned corn like Thornhill's, where Sagitty's hut had been, there was only a smouldering heap from which one or two charred timbers protruded.

Dan's voice was scratchy with fear: *The blacks got him!*

Nothing moved in the valley, only the smoke slowly rising. Thornhill got the guns out from their place in the bow and took his time loading them. He had left the fourth with Willie and let himself imagine the boy's pride in walking about with it. Prayed he did nothing silly. Dan got out his knife and strapped it onto the boat-hook.

But no matter how slowly they went about their preparations nothing changed in the place that had been Sagitty's.

At last Thornhill, gun in hand, led the way. His hand was slick with sweat on the stock of the gun. He heard a crunching under his boots and looked down to see Sagitty's smashed plates. The rags of a shirt flapped from a bush. A tin cup had been crushed with such force it had been driven into the ground.

Near the ruins of the hut, Sagitty's dog was still on her chain, but her throat had been cut.

305

The only thing not burned was the water barrel. Behind it they found Sagitty. He was lying on his back like a man admiring the sky, except that the full length of a spear was sticking up out of his belly.

In the instant Thornhill saw him, he longed for him to be dead. You are dead, he thought. But he was not dead, although it was clear that he would be soon. His face was a dirty grey, his eyes were sunk back into his head. Blood so dark that it was almost black had welled up thick out of the wound, through his shirt. Thornhill could see where the cloth had been pushed into the flesh by the spear. Flies swarmed over the place. His mouth was ajar but no words came out. Only his eyes spoke, never leaving Thornhill's.

The end of the spear quivered with each shallow breath he took.

Thornhill longed, like a physical need, for it to be yesterday, or even an hour ago, a time in which this thing did not have to be dealt with.

He heard Ned make a noise part surprise, part disgust. *The buggers have gone and speared him*, he blurted. He took a step forward and made to touch the spear, but Sagitty gave a terrible urgent cry. Dan spoke from behind his hand, as if Sagitty would not hear him. *He ain't got a hope, do he, Mr Thornhill?* Sagitty blinked and one of his hands closed slowly, as if around an oar.

Die, Thornhill willed him. For God's sake die.

But Sagitty did not die, only went on staring at them. Blinked and stared again. Around them the clearing was steamy, airless. Beyond Sagitty's field the forest was like a wall. Thornhill felt caught up in events that he was not prepared for. It felt as if someone else was speaking. *Get him on the boat, up to Windsor,* he said. *The hospital.*

They went back to the boat and cobbled together a stretcher

out of a sail and a couple of oars. It was a comfort to be dealing with objects. Sail, rope, oars: all behaved in the usual ways. The making of a stretcher could seem a normal enough thing to do, as long as they did not remember that it was because a man lay with a spear through his vitals not fifty steps away.

When they got back to the place where Sagitty lay, he had still not died. He cried out, one single strangled sound, when they lifted him onto the stretcher. It took the three of them to carry his weight, so they had no free hand to hold the spear steady. Sagitty gripped it with both hands to keep it still and made a high urgent sound with every step they took. His knuckles were white with holding the thing so hard. Thornhill felt himself running with sweat. But at last they were in the boat and could lay him down. *Here matey*, he said. *You'll be right now.*

Dan put the rum bottle to Sagitty's lips and tilted. The liquor ran down his chin, blood and rum mixed. Why do you not die, Thornhill thought, looking down at him. He hated him for not dying. Got out his handkerchief and covered his neighbour's face with it to keep the flies out of his eyes and nose.

And to stop him looking.

~

The tide was with them, Windsor no more than a couple of hours away. Throughout the journey, Thornhill could not look at where Sagitty lay in the dirty water that slopped backwards and forwards over the planks. He could not go on watching that length of dark wood sticking out of his middle, swaying with every movement of the boat.

There would be no keeping this from Sal. She would not, thank God, see what a spear did in its precise details. She would not have to hear the small noises made by a man with a spear through his entrails. But she would not need to. If he had hoped to persuade her to stay, that hope had died in the moment of finding Sagitty behind the rain barrel.

He knew her well enough to take her at her word. When he got back from Windsor the hut would be nearly empty, the bags of food and their few clothes packed and ready, the rope that she hung the washing on taken down and coiled away. There was not much to take: the things she had carefully laid out every night for the blacks would fit into a couple of bundles. She would take the kettle and the pot from the fire, the engraving of Old London Bridge, her blue shawl. What else? The wooden dishes, the digging-stick, the string made of bark. And the roof-tile from Pickle Herring Stairs.

She would leave the place without a backward glance.

After they had gone, it would not take long for Thornhill's Point to melt back into the forest. Weeds would spring up on the yard, the bark blow off the hut. The door would be the first to go, and then the creeping things would move back in: the snakes, the lizards, the rats. The corn patch would sprout fresh grass that the kangaroos would come down and nibble at, knocking the rails of the fences apart. In no time at all, it would be as if the Thornhills had never called it theirs.

They would set up house, in Windsor or Sydney. Perhaps one day they would go back to London, that place as remote now as the moon. He would go on making money. They would be happy enough.

But nothing would console him for the loss of that point of land the shape of his thumb. For the light in the mornings, slanting in through the trees. For the radiant cliffs in the sunset and the simple blue of the sky. For the feeling of striding out over ground that was his own. For knowing he was a king, as he would only ever be king in that place.

~

At the township, other men got Sagitty out of the boat and carried him up to the hospital there. He was out of sight, but Windsor consisted of two dusty streets and a wharf. There was nowhere out of earshot of the scream when someone pulled the spear out. Even from the bar of the Maid of the River, Thornhill could hear it, a scream that was like no sound a human made.

He did not need to see, to know that Sagitty was dead. He had been dead from the instant the spear had entered his flesh. The hours in the bottom of the boat had not been part of any cure, only an extension of his death.

A silence hung over the township when the scream stopped. Inside the Maid of the River, Spider poured out a generous tot all round, on the house. No one was able to look anyone in the eye. Each man was thinking of the way a spear would feel, deep in his own guts.

Word travelled fast. As the afternoon wore on, the Maid of the River filled with men who had heard. Thornhill told the story to Loveday and Twist who already knew. *Copped a gutful of one of them spears*, Thornhill said. Men he hardly knew began to drift in, men from Sackville and South Creek, their faces avid for details.

When Smasher arrived he took the story over. Anyone would have thought he had been there himself. Every time some man came in who had not heard it, he told it again, adding another detail. There were fifty of them. They forced him to cut his own dog's throat. They scalped him.

Nothing Smasher could invent was as bad as what had really happened.

Men were buying Smasher round after round. His face was aflame and he had whipped himself up almost to tears. His outrage was genuine, his voice cracking with it. Thornhill drank and said nothing. He was reminded of what he had not thought of for years, the yard at Newgate, the men rehearsing their stories so often that they took on the substance of fact.

He wondered if there was something the matter with Spider's rum, that it was not making him drunk. He could not get out of his mind the picture of Sagitty lying behind the barrel. The way the spear had quivered, delicate as a flower on a stalk. His eyes, begging. That length of wood locked into the private darkness inside a man.

Behind his own counter, with his name above the door and his sign swinging outside, Spider had become a bigger man. He stood leaning on the bar, his palms flat on the wood like a preacher starting his sermon. *We got to deal with them,* he said. His voice had not changed, was still reedy with effort. *Get them before they get us.*

It was a picture Thornhill could see as clear as his hand in front of him: all their tomorrows stretching out, and every one of them with a spear waiting in the forest. It would come sailing out fast enough to enter his body just above his thick leather belt. He would end up like Sagitty, staring out at a world gone grey and irrelevant. Worse—impossible even to imagine—would be to see Sal lying out on the ground with her eyes imploring him.

It was only a matter of enough tomorrows.

Smasher was speaking so low, the men had to lean in to hear him. *Ain't none of them at Darkey Creek no more,* he said. *Sagitty saw to that. But there's a whole bleeding camp of them up at Blackwood's.* He spat the name out as if it tasted bad.

Thornhill felt something inside him slow down.

We can get there tonight, Smasher said. *Settle the lot of them by breakfast.* The men were turned in to Smasher, watching his mouth as it made the words. Something in his tone made them want to listen, want to follow. Ned laughed his high whinnying laugh. *Get meself one of them's fingers,* he shouted. *Use it for a pipe-stopper*, and Smasher nodded, but only as a way of going on with what he was saying. *We got to finish the job*, he said and drank off the rest of his glass, thumping it on the counter for Spider to fill again.

The men closed in around him and there was a sound of agreement from many throats. It was not the voice of any one man but the voice of the group, faceless and powerful.

Thornhill said nothing. Looked into the liquor in his glass, watching it run greasily around as he swirled it.

Sterminate them, Smasher said. *No one going to come straight out and say it but ain't it the only way?*

When Thornhill glanced up he found that Smasher was watching him, and the others were looking where Smasher was looking. Smasher enjoyed the moment. Then he said, as if it were the least important thing in the world, *Only thing is we got to have the Hope to get us up there.*

Thornhill heard Ned breathing loudly through his mouth. He could feel them watching him, those familiar faces: Ned, Dan, Loveday, George Twist with the eternal hat down low over his eyes, Spider with his now-prosperous cheeks. They seemed the faces of strangers, dark-grained and seamed in the smoky lamplight.

The mood in the room was becoming wicked. He felt it tugging at him the way a pannikin of liquor might, to get his mouth around it and feel it warm in his chest. There was a dull ache across his forehead and he wanted to be gone, but the thought of getting Dan and Ned into the boat was too difficult.

Loveday was waxed enough for eloquence. He held up a hand and intoned, *We must grasp the nettle, painful though it may be, or else abandon the place to the treacherous savages and return to our former lives.*

There was a silence in which they all thought of their former lives.

Dan was beside Thornhill, his cheeks shining with the heat of the rum. He leaned in so close Thornhill could hear the air through the gaps in his teeth. *Get rid of the blacks and she'll stay, Will*, he whispered, and leaned back to watch him slyly. *Ain't no other way to hold her.*

It was what Thornhill knew, and he hated Dan for putting it into words. Unless the blacks were settled, Sal would leave Thornhill's Point. It was as stark as that.

How could he choose, between his wife and his place? Making things so that she would stay was worth any price.

Smasher was watching them with a knowing smile. *Nobody won't never know, I swear*, he said. *Not our wives even. Not anyone other than us. And we ain't telling.*

Thornhill drank off the rest of his glass and spoke quickly, without letting himself think: *Tonight then, and be home by breakfast.* His voice sounded like another man's, more sure of itself than his own could be.

But not a word, any of youse, he said. *Word gets out we done it, I come and slice out the tongue that blabbed.*

~

Half crazy with liquor and high feeling though he was, Smasher had thought the thing out better than Captain McCallum. There was a daintiness of thinking to Smasher, Thornhill realised, that would have been better employed if his life had been different.

Smasher knew that the tide was running out that night, and it could get a boatful of men down as far as Thornhill's Point, where the First Branch angled off the river. They could drop anchor there and wait until midnight when the tide would turn. About then the moon would rise, so that a boat could be worked silently up the First Branch on the flooding tide. They would tie

312

up just short of Blackwood's so his dogs would not smell them. Then all they had to do was wait for the first light of day.

No one put into words what would happen then.

At the Windsor wharf, Dan and Ned pushed the *Hope* out into the river. Under the weight of a dozen men it rode low but they made quick time with the ebbing tide. On Smasher's instructions they put in at various settlements to tell the story of Sagitty again and pick up another man or two: bony old Matthew Ryan from Wheelbarrow Flat, John Lavender and his brother from Portland Head, Devine from Freeman's Reach.

They swept down past Half Moon Bend, past Cat-Eye Creek, past Milkmaid Reach, and by the time he could see the ridge above his own place, distinctive even in silhouette, there were seventeen men aboard. Just there, at the entrance to the Branch, they dropped the anchor-stone to wait for the turn of the tide.

Thornhill sat up on the stern deck looking down the length of the boat, where his passengers were sprawled against each other, dozing. He knew all of these men, had laughed with them over a drink, haggled with them for their wheat and pumpkins. By and large he had never considered them to be bad men.

And yet their lives, like his, had somehow brought them to this: waiting for the tide to turn, so they could go and do what only the worst of men would do.

Over there, not half a mile away across the water, Sal would have put the little ones to bed. *London Bridge is falling down, falling down, falling down.* She would have cooked up enough damper for the next day and put the bundles by the door so there would be no delay when Thornhill returned. He strained to see the light from the hut, but it was hidden by the rise of the point. Willie would have banked the fire with clods to keep it alive all night, so she could make them a last dish of tea before they left in the morning. He would have put the bar up in its brackets on the door and got the gun ready primed. Sal would have lain down at last with Mary wrapped up beside her. She would not have slept.

She would have guessed more or less what had happened at Sagitty's, and that Thornhill had gone upriver. But she would not guess that her husband was so close at that moment that, if he had stood up and hullooed across the water, she would have heard him.

How had his life funnelled down to this corner, in which he had so little choice? His life had funnelled down once before, in Newgate, into the dead-end of the condemned cell. But the thing that lay ahead of him there had been out of his hands. There was a kind of innocence in waiting for Mr Executioner.

The difference with this was that he was choosing it, of his own free will.

The noose would have ended his life, but what he was about to do would end it too. Whichever choice he made, his life would not go on as it had before. The William Thornhill who had woken up that morning would not be the same William Thornhill who went to bed tomorrow night.

He could not stop gnawing away at the thing.

He and Sal could argue the toss for the rest of their lives. She would not stay, he would not go.

It was like a knot in old rope, he thought, hard as a fist. There was no point trying to tease it out: it was just a matter of getting hold of a good sharp knife. He glanced at the cliffs, a dense wall against the sky. There were times he felt those cliffs were going to fall on him and blot him out. Above them, the moon had risen and was sailing between shreds of cloud, a pale plate in the sky, dimming the stars.

The boat shifted under him, swinging around with a shudder as the tide turned under the keel.

They would need to have their story ready. Yes, they had gone to have a parley-voo with the blacks. Yes, they had shown them their guns. They had even fired over their heads. The blacks were not stupid. They had got the hint. They had dispersed.

If there was any doubt cast on the story, the very absence of the blacks could be brought forward as evidence of its truth.

It always hurt to cut good rope, but once the thing was done no one would complain.

He hauled up the anchor-stone, dripping silver in the moonlight. The water seethed with the mingling currents of the tide coming in and the river flowing out. He leaned his weight on the tiller and slowly the tide grew stronger than the river, pushing the *Hope* up into the opening of the Branch.

At the first bend, when the main river was shut out behind them, the air seemed to become closer, more watchful. The moonlight was so bright that he could see every leaf of every mangrove on either side. The water glinted blackly.

Thornhill tried to put from him the picture he carried in his mind: the blue water of the lagoon, ruffled in the breeze. Blackwood standing at the door of his hut. The thread of smoke from the cooking fires. The woman coming towards them, cocking her head in the same way Sal did. The child, pale beside her, who had never seen the world beyond the lagoon.

It was easier to think of Sagitty. He could still smell the blood on his coat and hear the cry that had echoed through Windsor while the men in the Maid of the River stood with their glasses halfway to their lips.

He made himself go over it again. The sound that came out of Sagitty's mouth when they moved him. His white knuckles around the spear. His imploring eyes before Thornhill covered them with his handkerchief.

They made a line fast around a mangrove just short of

Blackwood's before settling again for another few hours' sleep. Loveday's old double hunter said it was two o'clock in the morning. By a miracle the dogs had not heard them.

As the dawn began to make shapes, Thornhill could see Ned crouched against the half-deck, his chin sunk on his chest, and hear his familiar snores. Smasher was alert, moving from man to man and whispering. He came to Thornhill last. *Get the men first*, he hissed. *Then we clean up the breeders.*

In the first dim light, the men slid over the side of the *Hope* and waded to the shore. Beyond the shifting mass of the river-oaks Thornhill could see the lagoon, where the blacks had their camp.

He stood on the bank, holding his gun. It was possible—more than possible—that the blacks had heard them long ago on the river, in spite of all their efforts to be quiet. The skin on his back crawled, imagining the spear.

Nothing moved as they approached the camp.

On every side there was only the tangle of forest, the stiff lacework of bushes, the shadows swaying, where a hundred warriors could be lifting their spears to their shoulders. He would never know till he felt one in his body.

Once he had imagined a man in those tangles he could not get the idea out of his head. He spun around, but then his back was facing another piece of forest. Whichever way he turned, it would make no difference. It would be the same whether the spear entered his body between the shoulderblades or between the ribs.

At that moment a gun went off with a colossal report. His heart constricted and he whirled around. There was a black! In among the bushes! He fired, the gun jerked him backwards, he staggered, recovered, looked. The figure stood as it had stood before, its arm raised, a fire-blackened tree still gesturing with its branch.

316

Everyone was shooting now, not at the bushes but at the humpies. He saw Smasher run over to one and stoop to glance in before firing through the opening and jumping back. A man came out of the humpy so fast he tore it open like a leaf: ran out, took a step or two, then fell to the ground with the side of his head a mass of bright blood. Behind him a woman and a child flung aside a possum-skin rug, the woman grabbing the child round the middle. But she had taken no more than a step towards the forest before George Twist was on her with his sword and, as Thornhill watched, her back and shoulder opened up in a long red stripe. She dropped the child and whirled about to pick it up again but John Lavender was there first with his sword and with one mighty swipe took off its head. It fell near his boot and he kicked it away.

A dog snarled and snapped at Devine who shot right into its threatening jaws. It convulsed, its back legs collapsed, and lay tossing its head, its mouth smashed.

Lavender's brother and Spider and Matthew Ryan had surrounded a humpy, were breaking it apart with the butts of their guns. Black Dick burst out of it with his curved club, lifted his arm and brought it down on Ryan who twisted into a heap on the ground. Black Dick turned to Spider with his arm raised again, but Dan ran up and hit him on the back with his club so hard he seemed to bend under it, and the next moment Lavender was standing over him with his pistol held in both hands firing straight into his chest.

Another black was running with a spear up at his shoulder towards Smasher, who had his powder-horn out to reload, but from across the clearing Loveday took an uncertain step towards him, stumbling in his over-large boots, and fired with his head turned away from the report and his face squeezed up, and the man fell with his knee a flower of blood.

Twist ran in front of Thornhill to a broken-in humpy where a woman was trying to shelter under a fallen sheet of bark. Thornhill could see her pushing the limbs of a baby under the possum-skin rug but Twist got her by the hair, yanked back her head, and sliced across her neck as if she were one of his hogs. She got to her feet with the baby pressed against her, shielding it with her arm, a hand to her throat where the blood was pumping out, calmly walked a few steps, then folded down into the ground and toppled over sideways.

Ned was squinting, legs wide apart and his mouth open too, along the barrel of his gun. He fired at a woman running awkwardly with a child in her arms. Thornhill saw how she was pushed forward by the force of the ball, as if by a blow in the spine. Her feet could not keep up with her body hurtling forward, her head snapped back. She tripped, almost danced for a moment to stay upright, the child still tight in her arms, across her chest. She half turned to see what had happened to her—he saw her face, her eyes wide, astonished, her mouth open as if to ask a question—and as she turned, her knees going out from under her.

A black stood in front of one of the humpies with a spear up at his shoulder and was beginning the coil of his body to launch it, but there was a shot and he gasped like a man about to sneeze. He threw the spear but was collapsing as he did and it dropped to the ground.

All over the clearing men fired and reloaded and swords rose and fell and came up all over blood in a din of screaming and roaring and the high panicked cries of children. After that first shot, things had moved too fast around Thornhill. He pointed his gun at blacks as they ran but the muzzle was always too late. He stood turning in the clearing, the thing up against his shoulder, watching.

There was a shout, and Tom Blackwood in his undershirt and socks, gun up to his shoulder, was aiming straight at Smasher and roaring, *Get back away, Smasher,* and running at him, but Smasher had his whip and without raising his arm he flicked it at Blackwood underhand, one flick and then another. Blackwood reeled back, dropped the gun on the ground, his hands to his eyes. He tripped, flailing at the air with his arms, toppled backwards over a log and went down so heavily the ground seemed to jolt.

Thornhill opened his mouth to call out, but Blackwood was on his feet again, his hands still up at his eyes as he stumbled on one of the bodies, fell heavily, struggled to get up. Thornhill could hear now that he was roaring just one word. *No, no, no, no, no.*

Then Thornhill felt a blow on his hand where it held the gun so that he dropped the thing, and heard a great bellow from Dan, pointing at the bushes. As Thornhill turned, a blow to the side of his head made everything go dark behind his eyes. He bent for the gun and was knocked over by another rock in the small of the back. For a moment he was sprawled with his face in the dust, helpless as a beetle. He heard Ned screaming, high like a girl, that they had got him in the damn nuts, he would kill them buggers as God was his witness.

Thornhill got to his feet and put the gun up to his shoulder again, seeing more rocks coming out of the forest. The place was spitting parts of itself out at them. He could feel something slick running into his eye and his hand came away crimson with blood when he touched his face. Ned was shouting, his face twisted, furiously tamping down another shot. Thornhill could not hear the words, only saw the frantic movements of his arms. Loveday was scrabbling to reload too, the hair flopping into his eyes and his hands shaking as he tried to pour the shot into the gun and look around at the same time.

The clearing, squeezed between the lagoon on one side and the ridge on the other, was a trap.

There was a breathy whistle and he saw a shadow cutting through the light and piercing the ground beside his boot, becoming a spear still quivering from its collision with the dirt. He turned to it, stilled with surprise. There was a moment in which he might have been waiting for it to speak.

Another spear flew from the trees and struck Devine on the shoulder. He screamed like a woman, grabbed it with both hands and wrenched it out in a frenzy. Thornhill looked and where the thing had come from was a boy at the edge of the clearing, a heavy spear in both hands. His small face was broken open on a cry of fear and rage as he launched it with his whole body. It seemed to move too slowly to do any damage, but there was Twist down on his knees with it dangling from the side of his head, the brim of his hat impaled along with the ear.

Thornhill got the gun up at his shoulder but he was too slow again. The place where the boy had been was empty, only the trees looking back at him.

Then Whisker Harry, wiry and fragile, calmly stepped out from them. Thornhill could see his arm trembling as he fitted the spear into the thrower and got it up to his shoulder. His face contorted with effort as he leaned his body back to launch the spear.

The gun was still up at Thornhill's shoulder, his finger was against the trigger, but he could not move, a man in a dream. He was aware of issuing orders to his finger to pull back on the trigger, but nothing happened.

He watched as the spear left the black man's hand. Across the clearing Smasher took a step forward as if to catch it. When he stopped short, the spear was vibrating out of his chest. His hands went to it and he stood in the chaos, the spear coming out of his chest like some terrible mistake.

Thornhill could see his mouth making words although he could hear nothing. Smasher was walking towards him, holding the spear off the ground with both hands. He came so close to Thornhill that the end of the spear brushed against his arm, and stood staring at him without seeming to know who he was. *Lord Jesus and Holy Mother of God*, Smasher said. A small amount of bright blood was beginning to ooze into the shirt around the spear.

There was an impulse to wrench it out, make everything the way it had been before. But Thornhill knew what happened when a spear was pulled out of a man. He went on standing, the gun to his shoulder and a great emptiness in his being.

Smasher was rasping as if the wood in his chest had got into his voice: *Jesus Christ Almighty, Jesus Christ Almighty.*

And there was the old man looking at his spear in Smasher's chest. He made no move to throw another or to take cover. He simply stood watching, his face stern.

The gun went off with a puff of blue smoke and a pop that sounded puny in all this air. He thought he must have missed, for Whisker Harry was still standing there with that look on his face, as if nothing could touch him.

The old man bent slowly forward until he was on his knees, holding his belly. It seemed the longest time that he stayed like that, as if by becoming a rock or tree he could eject the thing that had entered him.

A fly was around Thornhill's face and he brushed it away. He closed his eyes. Like the old man on his knees he felt he might become something other than a human, something that did not do things in this sticky clearing that could never be undone.

Now the old man was bending in on himself, holding his middle in that polite way. He lay on the dust. Blood came from his mouth, just a trickle like spit, but so red. He knelt in the dust and kissed it with the blood from his mouth.

When he straightened his body so he was lying on his back, Thornhill could see the wound. There was something in there moving like a lip. It pulsated, a small evil animal inside him.

It seemed impossible that anyone with such a thing in his flesh could go on living.

Thornhill could only hear his own ragged breathing. At last he lowered the gun and laid it carefully on the ground. He heard a fly buzz past his ear. The first rays of the sun were slanting in through the trees, laying stripes of colour along the grass. He listened for the blacks running through the forest, but even the humming things in the grass had fallen silent.

Every tree, every leaf, every rock seemed to be watching.

Black bodies lay among the ruins of their humpies. He saw the big body of Black Dick, laid out full length with the flesh of his chest torn open by a ball. Near him, with half his head shot away, was Long Jack, who had once been Long Bob. A woman lay in a pool of sunlight, sleeping with her sleeping baby beside her, except for the way her head was twisted, attached to her body by only a strip of ragged flesh. The back of the baby's head was crushed purple.

Whisker Harry lay where he had fallen so neatly.

From under a body the wail of a baby filled the clearing. Dan went over with the club in his hand. Thornhill saw his face, absent, like a man mending a piece of harness by lamplight. He struck once, twice, and the cry stopped.

Blackwood lay spreadeagled in the remains of one of the humpies. His hands still covered his eyes. Under them his face was streaked with blood, his mouth an inhuman square.

Someone had taken Smasher by the elbow and was leading him over to the shade. He would not let go of the spear. The end of it flexed with each step he took, like some grotesque ornament. The spear had gone right through. When they ripped the shirt off, they could see its barbed tip sticking out of his back. He was too shocked even to cry out. Once in the shade he stood swaying. Refused to sit. Pushed away Spider who was coaxing him to lie down.

George Twist moved to help him hold up the spear but Smasher waved him away. He stared at nothing, concentrating on holding the spear steady, a man whose world had shrunk to the feel of his hands around a length of wood. At one corner of his mouth a small line of bright blood ran out and in the same moment his knees appeared to hinge under him so that he sat awkwardly on the ground. Blood was coming out of his nose, and when he coughed with a wet sound, more poured out of his mouth. The flies drank at the place where the inside of a man had been opened up. One hand made a gesture as if he wanted to say something, but he dropped forward as far as the spear would let him and hung there, dead.

The sun hardened around them. The clearing had a broken look, the bodies lying like so much fallen timber, the dirt trampled and marked with dark stains.

And a great shocked silence hanging over everything.

THORNHILL'S PLACE

Rains fell, season after season, and the sun slid up over the ridges as it had done since the beginning. The river filled and shrank with tides and floods, trees grew and died and melted back into the dirt that had given them life. Ten years made no impression on the shape of the river, of the convoluted ridges that hid it. Only down on the flats was there change, and that was mostly a matter of names.

A man called Millikin lived on Smasher's piece of ground, now Millikin's Inlet. Where Mrs Webb had stood laughing while the natives made off with an acre of corn, Benjamin Jameson had harnessed the creek and called the place Jameson's Mill. Mrs Herring was one of the few left of the old neighbourhood, still on her place along at Cat-Eye Creek, but she had become something of a recluse. William Thornhill had bought Sagitty's old place, plus another hundred acres that went from the headwaters of Darkey Creek all the way down to the river. It was not called Darkey Creek now, but Thornhill's Creek.

With no more trouble from the blacks, new settlers had taken up land on every bend. Unmolested, their crops and families flourished, and trade on the river was good. Thornhill had repaid King his hundred and fifteen pounds, with interest, and borrowed more: nearly three hundred pounds, to have a vessel purpose-built for trade. The old *Hope* and the new *Sarah* never stopped. In winter, when trade was slack on the river, the *Hope* went for coal from the new penal station at Port Stephens, and the *Sarah*, captained by Willie, went further afield getting the cedar wood that the settlers called red gold. From the place at Thornhill's Point—expanded to three hundred acres, and carrying hogs and beef as well as grain—the Thornhills victualled the Government chain-gangs making roads in the area. They had plans for a third boat in which to make the crossing to New Zealand for the fur-seal trade, twenty pounds a pelt.

For the newcomers, William Thornhill was something of a king. When he was not on the river, he sat on his verandah, watching with his telescope everything that went by on the river. His wife had become something of a queen, celebrated for her Christmas entertainments, complete with Chinese lanterns and string bands.

~

The Irishman Devine had built a fine stone house for Mr Thornhill, although it seemed that the proper thing was to call it a villa. The word had a tone about it that Thornhill liked, even though it came awkwardly to his tongue. They had named it Cobham Hall. It was Sal's idea, but they both enjoyed the private joke.

He had stood up on the rock with the fish carved in it and pointed at where the house would go. Devine, a man who knew which side his bread was buttered, was full of admiration. *I would of picked this spot myself, Mr Thornhill*, he said. *Just this very eminence.*

Thornhill had never grown tired of being called Mr Thornhill. Never heard it without a pulse of pleasure. He did not so much enjoy the way Devine threw *eminence* about when what he meant was plain *hill*.

Devine was full of ways to make the place a fortress. The eminence itself was the start of it: *A hundred of the buggers could not cut you off here, Mr Thornhill,* he had assured. The walls were to be of stone, half a yard thick. At the back and the sides they rose up to the roof unbroken except by one low and deep-set door. *Put a man at that door,* Devine said. *He'd pick them off like flies.* He had contrived an ingenious mechanism within the stair-case so that it could be hinged up after the manner of a draw-bridge, with convenient slits the size of a gun-barrel. Behind the house, the hillside had been stripped of every bush. There was nothing that a man might hide behind.

The finished place was not quite what Thornhill had pictured. Something was wrong with the way the pieces fitted together: some were too big, others too small. The front door was a quality piece of joinery, but too wide for its height, and the arched fanlight over it had a slipped keystone like a crooked front tooth. The semi-circular stone steps going up to the verandah were exactly what he had drawn—the ones he remembered from St Mary Magdalene in long-ago Bermondsey—but translated from paper to stone they had become dwarfish and awkward. A cricket had taken up resi-dence somewhere behind them and chirruped all night.

He had pictured lions on the gateposts, rearing up with their teeth showing as had the ones at Christ Church. It was some other, hardly recognisable William Thornhill who had once hurled a handful of mud at them. He had ordered them from London, a hundred guineas the pair. When they arrived, they turned out to be a more domestic type of creature. Rather than snarling at inter-lopers, they lay on their haunches, paws spread, like tabbies in front of the fire. But he would not show his disappointment in front of Ned, still with him after so long and still stickybeaking when he should have been chipping the corn. *Just what I ordered*, he announced. *Just the thing*. Sal caught his eye and saw it all in that glance: his disappointment, his pride. Gave him the smallest of smiles, gone before anyone else had a chance to see it.

He had the lions put high on the gateposts so they could not be seen well. They were not what he had planned, but there was no mistaking their message: *Watch your step, you are on my place now*.

Cobham Hall was a gentleman's residence. Did that mean he was a gentleman? There were moments when he felt this must all be an elaborate dream. He would not have thought that William Thornhill could ever have any relationship with a house like this except that of trespasser. But if a man had enough by way of money, he could make the world whatever way he wanted. No wonder those men in his wherry, all those years ago, had had such an air of serenity. They took their ease, gazed about them, while the boatman bent to his oars. He knew that feeling now: the feeling that whatever a man wanted, he could have.

Under the house, covered by the weight of Mr Thornhill's villa, the fish still swam in the rock. It was dark under the floorboards: the fish would never feel the sun again. It would not fade, as the others out in the forest were fading, with no black hands to re-draw them. It would remain as bright as the day the boards had been nailed down, but no longer alive, cut off from the trees and light that it had swum in.

Sometimes, sitting in the parlour in the red velvet armchair, Thornhill thought of it underneath him, clear and sharp on the rock. He knew it was there, and his children might remember, but his children's children would walk about on the floorboards, and never know what was beneath their feet.

~

Sal had long since stopped making marks on the tally-tree, and the lines she had already drawn had grown over, swallowed into the fabric of the trunk. Sometimes she still said, *When we go Home*, and she still kept the old bit of roof-tile in her workbox. But there was never a time put on that *when*, and *Home* remained a comfortable but distant idea. He let the phrase go when she used it, turning the conversation elsewhere: a fine pony he had his eye on for Mary, or the grant of land he had got for Willie up on the Second Branch.

He did not spell out to her what they both knew: that they were never going to return to that Home. Too many of the important parts of their lives had happened here. Their children, for a start. For them, Home was nothing but a story. If they were to go to London they would be outsiders, with their sunburnt skin and their colonial ways. They might see London Bridge and hear the great bell of Bow, that Sal had told them about. They might even see Cobham Hall and its grape arbour. But they would be places with a shrunken look about them, places from a story that belonged to someone else.

As every twist of Crucifix Lane had once been known in his own body, this place was known in theirs. In sleepless nights it would not be that foreign river called the Thames that they would follow down through the bends into sleep, but their own Hawkesbury. They would hanker for these astringent smells and this hard-edged sky. For them, the strangeness would be to spend their lives in the crush and crowds of the Borough, and terror would be to be buried in the sour wet soil of the churchyard of St Mary Magdalene.

Sal had never said it in so many words, but she would not leave them, those native-born children.

So, rather than taking them Home, she had made Home here, and Thornhill had gone along with it in every way he could think of. He made sure she had all that Home had promised: a couple of sprung armchairs in the parlour and a sofa to go with them, a girl to cook and clean and another to do her washing for her, a paisley shawl from India with a peacock on it that had cost what he would have worked for a year to make on the Thames.

And a pair of green silk slippers. The slippers were a private thing between himself and his memory. She laughed when he gave them to her. *What am I going to do with silk slippers, Will?* But she had not complained when he put them on her feet that night, and took her in them for the pleasure of feeling them up around his ears. The complicated satisfaction it gave him was something he did not try to share with her.

As it had been her idea to call the place Cobham Hall, it was also her idea to have a high stone wall around the entire garden. He did not ask her whether Cobham Hall also had such a wall, but gave his instructions to Devine. It was his suspicion that it had not, and that her desire for one here was something else. But it was one of the things that remained unasked between them, and unanswered.

That wall—higher than a man, and with only one gate in its perimeter—kept out everything except what was invited in. It pleased Sal, and he did not begrudge the money, because it pleased him too. He had so often been on the wrong side of such a wall.

Within the wall the ground had been cleared and levelled for Sal's garden. On that bleak rectangle a garden along English lines was planned. Daffodils and roses were planted. Paths were marked out with string and laid with crushed white sandstone in lieu of gravel. It glittered harshly in the light, but it divided the garden up into squares in the way she wanted. Between the garden and the house there was to be a lawn and, on Devine's advice, expensive turf was imported from Ireland. She would be

332

safe behind it, he promised, because it was a well-known fact that no snake would ever cross Irish turf. He placed a long-fingered pale hand on his chest, where his Irish heart could be assumed to beat, and the deal was done.

Most of all, she had longed for trees: real trees, she insisted, with proper leaves that fell off in the autumn. She showed him where she wanted them, in a double row up from the river all the way to the house. He guessed what she saw as she looked down the slope: the carriageway at Cobham Hall, a whispering green tunnel that cast dappled shadows on the ground. He did not mock her for it. A person was entitled to draw any picture they fancied on the blank slate of this new place.

Jerome Griffin in Sydney was an enterprising fellow who was making a good thing for himself out of poplars for homesick ladies, his being the only poplars on this continent, and Thornhill bought up his entire stock. The delight of laying about him with his money was one he did not think would ever grow stale.

Twice a day, morning and evening, Thornhill saw Sal urging Ned and the other men—they had seven servants now, as well as three girls in the house—to refill the water cart and give the new plants yet another bucket of water. Her day became a battle against the sun that would draw the moisture out of the ground, the hot wind that would dry the leaves.

In spite of her care the garden did not thrive. The roses never put their roots down. They clung to life, but were little more than stalk. The daffodils were planted but no trace of them was ever seen again. The turf yellowed and shrivelled and finally blew away in wisps of dry straw.

The only plant that flourished was a bush of blood-red geraniums that she had got as a cutting from Mrs Herring. They gave off a musty sort of smell, but at least they provided a splash of colour.

Of the two dozen poplars they had planted, most became nothing more than twigs after a few weeks. Sal could not bear to pull them out of the ground. When the wind blew, the corpses swivelled loose in the ground in a parody of life.

She loved the survivors all the more for the deaths of the others. At dusk she would go down and stand in the triangle made by the three remaining saplings. Their glossy green leaves twittered and shivered together on their long stems. He watched her sometimes, standing among them. Watched her pick a leaf to feel its cool familiar silkiness, hold it up to the sun to look at its secret veins. She would touch the tender new growth as she touched the cheeks of the children and sometimes Thornhill thought she talked to them as she stood in the dusk fingering their heart- shaped leaves. *Bury me here when I go*, she told him. *So I can feel the leaves fall on me.*

She moved more slowly these days, but was at peace. She had had one more baby, another girl that they christened Sarah but always called Dolly for her pretty face and fair ringlets. After Dolly, Sal had grown stout on the good living they could afford. He watched her walking along one of the gravel paths. He had not thought his cheeky young wife would come to be this placid matron, fat with smiles.

He was slower, too. The pads of muscle around his shoulders were growing soft and the calluses on his hands, that he had always thought he would take to his grave, were nothing more than a thickening of the skin.

~

A portrait, *William Thornhill of Thornhill's Point*, hung in the parlour, where it could remind him of the person he had become. There was another, too, but it was hidden away under the stairs.

That first portrait had been an unhappy experience. The

334

painter was fresh off the boat, with a nice houndstooth jacket only a little threadbare as to cuffs, a distinguished head of silky hair and a tripos from Cambridge. Thornhill did not ask further, having no idea what a tripos from Cambridge might be, but the man seemed a gentleman. He would have the best, whatever that was, pay top price, so everyone would know that his money was as good as the next man's.

The fellow had got him to stand with the little table from the parlour beside him, took pains to get him to a look *a little off to the side, a little more, just look at the corner of the mantle, if you please, sir.* There was pleasure in being called *sir* by a gentleman with a tripos from Cambridge, even if he knew that William Thornhill was what they called here an old colonialist, which everyone knew was polite for *old lag*.

While the gent in his houndstooth peered and dabbed, he made delicate inquiries about the history of his client, and Thornhill obliged.

This story had William Thornhill not born in dirty Bermondsey but in clean Kent, by the chalk cliffs. Had not been caught greasy with fear at Three Cranes Wharf, sweating over pieces of timber belonging to Matthias Prime Lucas, but by the excise men on some pebbly beach with a boatload of French brandy. Had not swung for it, because on the outward trip he had worked for the King, carrying English spies into France.

It was a well-made story, every corner of its construction neatly finished, as it had come to him from Loveday, whose story it had been. No one was the poorer for the theft. In this place, where everyone had started fresh-born on the day of their arrival, stories were like those shells down on the beach. A crab might live in one for a while, until he grew too big for it, and then he would scuttle around to another, the next size up. Loveday had found a new story, too, involving a young girl, a cruel father and a false accusation. He was not going to ask for his old one back.

Sal looked at her husband sideways as he spoke to the gentleman from Cambridge, out of the side of his mouth so as not to spoil the pose. Under her gaze he added a moonlight elopement with the daughter of a well-to-do shipowner, and she said nothing.

But the gentleman from Cambridge painted a poor picture. In wishing to ingratiate himself with his employer—perhaps hoping for more commissions, of the six children perhaps, and the wife too—he modelled the image on the best specimen of manhood with whom he was familiar, to wit himself. So Thornhill, built on a big scale, was portrayed as a delicate fellow with one bony knee propped forward in an unlikely way, a pretty head with hair curling around the ears and a watery look on his face.

One hand held a book half-open. Thornhill had wanted the book, but there had been a look of distaste on the Cambridge man's face as he arranged his customer's fingers into the pages. The scoundrel had tried to make a monkey of him, for it turned out that the book was upside down. Everyone pretended it was an oversight, but Thornhill could not bear to see the thing in front of him. He paid up without a murmur, the way a gentleman would have done, but no portraits of the children and the wife were suggested.

Loveday recommended a man who could do another, an *old colonialist* like himself.

Upton's portrait had taken him by surprise.

He was sitting by the table in his cutaway coat. Upton had got him to hold the telescope but in a way no human had ever held a spy-glass before, prissily, along his wrist. He regretted not having insisted on some better arrangement. Tell the truth, he was not sure about the whole business of having a glass in a portrait. He wondered whether it revealed something about him that would expose him to ridicule, the way the upside-down book had.

It was an odd uncertain look that Upton had caught. The picture was the sum of all the things that had ever happened to him. He could see there was a hardness there, but there was some other thing too, a bafflement. It was the picture of a man puzzled by what life could turn up.

~

The *Gazette* had run a piece about the day up at Blackwood's. In her slow reading-aloud voice, that distanced itself from the words it was saying, Sal told Thornhill what it said. The natives had been guilty of depredations and outrages. There had been an affray and the settlers had dispersed them.

It was not exactly false. Nor was it quite the way Thornhill remembered.

The *Gazette* did not mention the woman Thornhill could not forget, baring her teeth at him in the gloom, the blood so bright on her skin. Or the boy, arching like a fish against the hook in Sagitty's damper.

When he arrived home after the great bonfire—they had had to pile wood on it all day and into the night to get the job done— she was waiting for him, holding the lamp up so it cast a long black band across the wall behind her. She had got the things ready, put everything into bundles, made a stew out of all the salt pork that was left.

He told her the story: the parley-voo, the showing of the guns, the dispersing. She listened in silence. *There won't be no more trouble, Sal*, he said at last. *As God is my witness.* Her eyes searched his face so that he had to look away, pretending to be busy taking off his jacket. *They gone for good and all this time,* he said, as casual as could be. *No need for us to go anywhere just yet awhile.*

She put the lamp on the table and stood for a long time with her back to him, staring into its flame. *I hope you ain't done nothing*, she said at last. *On account of me pushing at you.* He could hear her recoiling from the words even as she spoke. He rushed in full of cheer: *What are you on about, Sal?* But she was clanking away now at the fire, getting the kettle out of the coals. Whatever words he threw at her, and whatever cheerfulness he summoned, she was not going to hear. She turned from the fire with the kettle and filled the basin. *Here, Will, give your hands a wash*, she said. Her voice was ordinary enough, but she would not look into his face.

He had washed his hands and face clean in the river before he had walked up to the hut, and up at the First Branch before that. Had made sure to get all the blood out of his clothes. Had even torn the tail off his shirt, where the blood would not come out. But now he wound his hands over and over against each other, slippery with soap, and plunged them into the water. He felt her watching them as if they were her own. She still did not look at his face, even when he took the towel from her, even when she dished him out a plate of stew.

He wished that she would speak, but she said nothing. Not then and not later. He would even have welcomed an accusation. If she had accused, he could have replied. He had his answers ready. But she never did. She unpacked the bundles and put the curios back in the rafters. She hung the engraving of Old London Bridge back on its peg and spread the blankets out again on the ground. She put up the drying-line again, and sang all the London songs to the children. She went about her life as she always had.

She continued to make the marks on the tree, but the idea

of going Home gradually became vaguer. When Dolly got a fever and had to be nursed day and night, Sal was too busy to make the marks, and when the child was up and running about again, she did not go back to the tree. A season passed, the tree shed its bark, and the lines showed up less sharp than before.

Thornhill noticed, but said nothing. It was part of the new thing that had taken up residence with them on the night he had come back from the First Branch: a space of silence between husband and wife. It made a little shadow, the thing not spoken of.

He was not sure what she knew. Mrs Herring might have known the truth: there was not much that happened on the river that she did not know. But Mrs Herring stopped visiting, and Sal rarely spoke of her.

But whatever Sal knew, or guessed, was with them and could not be shifted. He had not thought that words unsaid could come between two people like a body of water.

They were loving to each other still. She smiled at him from that sweet mouth. He took her hand to feel its narrowness in his own and she did not resist. Whatever the shadow was that lived with them, it did not belong just to him, but to her as well: it was a space they both inhabited. But it seemed there was no way to speak into that silent place. Their lives had slowly grown around it, the way the roots of a river-fig grew around a rock.

~

The *Gazette*'s piece made no mention of Thomas Blackwood, who was still in his hut up on the First Branch. He was silent now, a big man slumped into himself, his shoulders hunched, his step fearful. One eye was a sunken closed-over thing, the other squinted painfully at shapes of light and dark.

Mr Thornhill, that good citizen and generous neighbour,

made the trip along the Branch from time to time, tied up at Blackwood's old jetty and went to the house with a sack of flour, some oranges off his tree, a pound of baccy. He would get the sack up onto his shoulder, his muscles straining, more used to watching other men hump and sweat now than doing it himself, and feel the attentive stillness of this place.

He would glance over at where river-oaks circled a patch of bare yellow earth beside the lagoon, marking where the bonfire had burned into the night. Something had happened to the dirt in that spot so that not as much as a blade of grass had grown there ever since. Nothing was written on the ground. Nor was it written on any page. But the blankness itself might tell the story to anyone who had eyes to see.

Blackwood would not speak to Thornhill, only sat with his head down. Thornhill's words poured over him, a fall of rain that he was waiting to end. The hut was quiet with the sun beating down on the shingles. Each time Thornhill was there he listened for another person, a person who wore her nakedness like a gown, and the child with hair the colour of straw. He heard nothing, and could not ask.

With Blackwood in the hut was Dick. Others spoke piously of how good William Thornhill was, and his wife too, sending their son along to help poor Tom Blackwood. Toadying, he recognised. They wanted to stay on the good side of William Thornhill, who was too rich a man to make an enemy of.

He did not put them right on the matter of Dick. In fact, the boy had not told either of them that he was leaving. He had gone by himself one day some time after the affray. Still a young lad, he had paddled across the river on a log and then walked all the way along the Branch till he got to Blackwood's. When Thornhill went up to find him, the boy only said that he would stop here along of Mr Blackwood for the time being.

And, while Blackwood could not meet his eye, Dick would not.

Dick scratched around in Blackwood's fields, growing enough to keep the still going. He was eighteen now, and could manage Blackwood's old dory to deliver the rum up and down the river. Now and then he pulled in at Thornhill's Point and went up to see his mother, but never when his father was at home. Thornhill saw him on the river from time to time, standing up in the stern pulling on the steering-oar while the tide pushed him along. He had made a good waterman, after all. Thornhill stared and waited, but the boy never even glanced towards his father. Thornhill saw only the back of his head, in an old cap, and his shoulders, broadening with muscle. He was becoming a man, but had chosen to do so without assistance from his father. There was a tightness in Thornhill's chest as he watched the dory glide up the river and out of sight. He had lost something that he had never known to value it until it was gone.

Newcomers did not know that he was William Thornhill's son. Once he even heard them talk of him as Dick Blackwood. It gave him a shocked feeling, like the cut from a razor. There was the moment of cold nothing where the open flesh could be seen, and then the ache came on.

~

Of the blacks, Long Jack was the only one left on that part of the river. Such others as there might have been had retreated to the reserve that the Governor had set aside at Sackville, and lived on what the Governor was pleased to provide. It was thought they would die out. They did not seem to have the constitution needed to succeed. Those who did not die would marry among the lesser kind of whites. Learned gentlemen had announced that the blackness would be bred out in a few generations.

341

The learned gentlemen did not go to the Sackville Reserve to look, but if they had they would have seen that they were wrong. The place was full of children running and calling everywhere, and even if some of them had lighter skins than others, there was no mistaking that they were part of the tribe. In spite of everything, it seemed that the blacks were not going to disappear.

Smasher's shot had not quite killed Jack. The place on the side of his head where bone as well as skin had been blasted away could still be seen. It had bound itself together lumpily. The shot had done other damage too, that had left one leg dragging and his whole body crooked and effortful, warping sideways as he moved along. There was something wooden about his face now. The shot had broken him in some central way so that his face showed nothing: no pleasure, not even pain.

He sat by a little fire around the point, where he had once, in another life, exchanged names with Thornhill. Sal had taken him on as something of a project. A penance, it had occurred to Thornhill. She gave him clothes: an old pair of britches that had once been her husband's, and a jacket that had plenty of warmth left in it. She even knitted him a pair of stockings and a woollen cap. At her urging, Thornhill set aside a patch of ground for him, fenced it nicely, and gave him some tools and a bag of seed. Even had his men build him a snug hut, and Sal had come down to give him a pot and a kettle, and shown him how to boil up a dish of tea and how to do a damper just right.

But he never put on the britches or the jacket. In cold weather he wrapped himself in his old possum-skin cloak. The clothes lay out in all weathers, decaying into the dirt. One of Sal's stockings had blown into a bush where it flapped in the wind. He never picked up the tools or even stepped through the doorway of the hut. The damper Sal had made, showing him how, had remained on the ground until the rats and possums finished it off. He sat by his fire, on the dirt, with a humpy nearby. He came and went, sometimes arriving at the back door to beg victuals, although never when Thornhill was about. At other times he would disappear for weeks on end, until the Thornhills would agree that he must have gone to join the others at Sackville.

One morning when the weather was turning cold Thornhill went down with a blanket for him, and a few sacks he might sleep on. When Jack glanced up at him Thornhill saw how dull his eyes were, almost with the look of a blind man, as if trying to see beyond what was in front of him, to some other place. He was so thin now he was like a bundle of sticks gathered up on the ground. Thornhill did not remember him so skinny, his ribs standing out in the barrel of his chest, the shoulderblades prominent, the flesh between fallen away.

Thornhill remembered hunger well enough. He thought a man who had once known hunger would never forget it. He dropped the blanket and the sacks beside Jack and said, *Here Jack, keep your black arse warm*, but Jack did not so much as blink at the hearty tone.

Thornhill said, *Get yourself some tucker, up the house*. He was finding it hard not to shout. He made signals of hand-to-mouth, but could not catch Jack's eye, said it again louder. *I give you tucker, round the back*, making a circular gesture to show how Jack should go around the house to the kitchen. But, after that first glance, Jack did not look at him again. The smoke of his fire swirled around their heads in a flurry and cleared.

Thornhill was exasperated at the way Jack sat like a stone. When he had been hungry, no one had ever offered him the good things he knew waited for this bundle of bones in his kitchen: the fresh bread, made with his own wheat, the freshly salted pork from his own hogs, the eggs, the crisp green cabbage, the tea with plenty of sugar. *I would, mate, honest to God*, he said, his voice reasonable, the voice of a kindly man. *Plenty tucker, good bloody tucker, mate.* He leaned down to take his arm and make him stand. *Along you come then.*

At his touch Jack came to life. *No*, he said.

It was the first time Thornhill had ever heard him use an English word.

Jack slapped his hand on the ground so hard a puff of dust flew up and wafted away. *This me*, he said. *My place.* He smoothed the dirt with his palm so it left a patch like the scar on his head. *Sit down hereabouts.* His face closed down then and he stared into the fire. A breath of wind shivered the leaves in a tree overhead, then stopped. In the fire, a damp stick was singing a tiny high-pitched song.

Thornhill felt a pang. No man had worked harder than he had done, and he had been rewarded for his labour. He had about him near a thousand pounds in cash, he had three hundred acres and a piece of paper to prove it was all his, and that fine house with stone lions on the gateposts. His children wore boots and he was never without a chest of best Darjeeling in the house. He would have said he had everything a man could want.

But there was an emptiness as he watched Jack's hand caressing the dirt. This was something he did not have: a place that was part of his flesh and spirit. There was no part of the world he would keep coming back to, the way Jack did, just to feel it under him.

It was as if the very dirt was a consolation.

Anger kindled in him and he shouted, *Bugger you then, Jack, you can bleeding well starve and good luck to you!* He tramped away up the track without looking back. He had done more than a man was obliged to. Could have shot him, the way other

344

men would have, or had him whipped, or set the dogs on him. It was out of his hands. If that blackfeller was hungry, well, it was no fault of William Thornhill's.

He still saw smoke from the point now and then, but he did not go down there anymore.

~

As each day ended he sat in his favourite spot on the verandah, spy-glass in his hand, watching the sunset glow red and gold on the cliffs. He had had a bench made, not too comfortable, a plain wooden bench, that was what suited him. He would have Devlin bring him a madeira on a silver tray, and a cigar. Watched the poplars in the afternoon breeze, the roses and lilacs which in the late light looked greener than during the day. There was his wall. There was his wife, in a silk gown from Armitage that had cost twenty-two guineas, taking the air along the path. He could hear the lowing of his cattle, waiting to be milked, and the shouts of his servants getting them in. Could smell the quality horseflesh in the stables behind the house. He had never ridden himself, but he had made sure his children were taught to sit a horse the way the gentry did.

Looking down at his estate it was possible to imagine it a version of England. The wall shone bright with its mortar and whitewash in the sunlight, so bright it was painful to the eyes. Foursquare, immovable, it was like a stately chord of music in this rumpled land. This was what he had worked for. He had lain awake planning, had burst his heart rowing and carrying, and here it was, given to him like the madeira: the good life.

But beyond the wall and the silver tray was another world, where the cliffs waited and watched. Above the roses and the rest of it was the forest. The harsh whistle of the breeze in the river-oaks, the rigid stalks of the bulrushes and the reeds, that hard blue sky: they were unchanged by the speck of New South Wales enclosed by William Thornhill's wall.

He watched Sal coming up from the garden, having paid her daily visit to the poplars, now tall enough to meet over her head. She turned to admire the drama of light and shadow playing out on the cliffs. When she caught sight of him her face softened. Her fine skin was worn and crepey now in the harsh light outside, but her smile was the same as it had been by the Thames.

Still watching? she asked and sat beside him on the bench. He could feel her leg, warm, solid, a comfort against his, and they sat in silence. Sometimes it felt as if their bodies could speak to each other, even if they themselves could not. Then she said, *You'll wear out the glass, Will, the way you go on.* He did not answer. He thought she knew what it was he was watching for, and wanted to hear him say it.

She spoke a sudden thought. *You know, Will, I thought you was wonderful, when I was a little thing.*

He could feel the air of each word separately against his face. He watched her, the smile on her face as she remembered. *Why, pet?* he asked. *Why was I wonderful?*

She laughed. *Because you spit such a long way!* she cried. *I told Da, I says, Will Thornhill can spit such a long way!*

Only Sal, in the whole world, would remember such a thing. He heard his startled laugh, the sound going around the verandah. *I ain't lost the art, Sal,* he said. *Only in this dry place a man needs all his spit for himself.*

After a time she got up, laid a hand on his shoulder for a moment, and went inside. He could hear the fire being lit in the parlour. In a while he would go in and sit in his armchair, enjoying the way the light gleamed around the room and shut out the night.

~

Watching the light on the cliffs was like watching the sea. Even after so long of living with them, their face was as unknowable as ever, new-formed each moment. Through the glass he would study a spot where gold and grey made a particular sort of pattern. While he looked at it, he knew that combination of rock and shadow as well as he knew the face of his wife. But if he glanced away and then tried to find it again, the light fell in a different way and it was gone. Like the ocean, it was never the same twice.

It was hard to judge of distance or size over there; the ramparts of rock could be just a little step, or a hundred feet high: the trees seemed mere saplings, crooked scrawls against the grey and gold of the cliffs. Without the advantage of a human figure over there, it was as slippery as a mirage.

Through the glass, the trees were flaked and cracked. The rocks were what seemed alive, something old and solemn out of the sea, their grey skins speckled with white lichen, creased and furrowed and ridged. Through the eye of the glass, he became acquainted with each one. He could see how those tumbled at the base of the cliff must have once been part of its lip, where the forest ended as abruptly as the edge of a table. One by one each had snapped and racketed down.

He had never seen part of the cliff fall away, although he sometimes held his breath, staring through the glass, to be watching at the moment it happened. Was it slow, the way a tree creaked away from the vertical? Or was it a clean break that sent the birds squawking up from the trees? He sat with the glass to his eye, resting his elbow on the back of a chair, until the landscape began to swim in his vision. But he had never caught a rock in the private act of falling.

There was a drama, every time, in watching the black shadow of the hill behind him—his own hill—move down across the garden, leaving everything behind in grey dusk. At the river the shadow seemed to pause in its progress. At last he would see a line at the base of the cliffs. Then it seemed only to take a few minutes to move up and engulf the fluid shifts of light.

Sometimes the top of the cliffs, where the forest stopped as if sliced off, seemed an empty stage. And if the cliff was a stage, he was the audience. He scanned the line of forest, back and forth, up there where the stage dropped away. There could still be a few of them living up there. It was possible. Scratching a living, the way they knew, out of bark and roots, possum and lizard. Lighting their fires only at night. They could still be up there, in that intricate landscape that defeated any white man— still there, prepared to wait.

If they had wanted to be seen, he knew that he would have seen them.

Sometimes he thought he saw a man there, looking down from the clifftop. He would get to his feet and go eagerly to the edge of the verandah, would lean out squinting to see the man among so many confusing verticals. Never took his eye off the one he was sure was a human, staring down at him in his house.

He knew they had that capacity for standing in the landscape and simply being. He stared back, and reminded himself how patient they were, how much they were part of the forest. Told himself that was a man, a man as dark as the scorched trunk of a stringybark, standing on the lip of the stage, looking through the air to where he sat looking back. He strained, squinted through the glass until his eyeballs were dry.

Finally he had to recognise that it was no human, just another tree, the size and posture of a man.

Each time, it was a new emptiness.

For all it was what he had chosen, the bench he sat on here felt at times like a punishment. He had never forgotten the narrow bench in the passage at the Watermen's Hall, where William

Thornhill had sat with dread in his heart to see whether he could become an apprentice. That bench had been part of the penance a boy paid for the chance at survival. This bench, here, where he could overlook all his wealth and take his ease, should have been the reward.

He could not understand why it did not feel like triumph.

At that late hour the wind had dropped so the river was as still as a pane of glass. The cliff rose up from the water and its reflection dropped away into it. Far over against the bank, a breeze roughened the water and made a narrow band of light between the cliff and its reflection. It separated them, or perhaps it joined them. The two cliffs completed each other into something peaceful and perfect.

He put the telescope down with a hollow feeling. *Too late, too late.* Every day he sat here, watching, waiting, while dusk gathered in the valley, scanning the trees and the silent rocks. Until it was fully dark he could not make himself put the glass down and turn away.

He could not say why he had to go on sitting here. Only knew that the one thing that brought him a measure of peace was to peer through the telescope. Even after the cliffs had reached the moment at sunset where they blazed gold, even after the dusk left them glowing secretively with an after-light that seemed to come from inside the rocks themselves: even then he sat on, watching, into the dark.

ACKNOWLEDGMENTS

Many people provided me with help beyond all expectation during the research for this novel, giving unstintingly of their time and knowledge. Others took time from busy lives to read the book in draft form. I am indebted to you all. The book would not have been possible without your generosity.

One of my ancestors gave me the basis for certain details in the early life of William Thornhill, and other characters share some qualities with historical figures. All the people within these pages, however, are works of fiction.

In the course of research I consulted countless documents, published and unpublished, and adapted them for my imaginative purposes. Readers of, for example, the Old Bailey transcripts for 1806, or the Governor's dispatches from early Sydney, may recognise a few lines. I acknowledge with gratitude the work of others in making such resources available to a writer of fiction.

My great thanks go to the School of English, Art History, Film and Media at the University of Sydney for its support during the writing of *The Secret River*.

The book could not have been written without assistance from the Literature Board of the Australia Council. I am extremely grateful for this support.